The huge beast came tearing over the lip of my pit in a sudden avalanche of stones, twisting to lie flat, watching back toward a new enemy that shouted its way downriver.

The hunter was simply awesome, a quadruped the size of a shortlegged polar bear with the big flat head of an outsized badger. Around its middle, crossing over the piledriving shoulders, ran broad belts that could have been woven metal. The beast's weight was so tremendous that the stones beneath it shifted like sand when it moved suddenly; so powerful that it had plowed a furrow through the tailings crest in its haste to find shelter . . .

I had a clear field of fire as the searchlights swept the horizon again, but the hunter was fifty yards away; too far to risk wasting a single round. It was intent on the 'copter and hadn't seen me yet. I gunned the Porsche directly across the water, intending to make one irrevocable pass before angling upslope on my damaged fans toward the river. There should be time for me to empty the Smith & Wesson.

There should have been. But there wasn't.

HIGH TENSION

HIGH TENSION

DEAN ING

SF
ace books
A Division of Charter Communications, Inc.
A GROSSET & DUNLAP COMPANY
51 Madison Avenue
New York, New York 10010

HIGH TENSION

Copyright © 1982 by Dean Ing.

An ACE Book
First Ace printing: March 1982
Published Simultaneously in Canada

2 4 6 8 0 9 7 5 3 1
Manufactured in the United States of America

Acknowledgements

"Domino Domine" first appeared in *Destinies*, copyright © 1979 by Charter Communications, Inc.

"Malf" first appeared in *Analog Annual*, copyright © 1976 by The Condé Nast Publications, Inc.

"Vehicles for Future Wars" first appeared in *Destinies*, copyright © 1979 by Dean Ing.

"Vital Signs" first appeared in *Destinies*, copyright © 1980 by Dean Ing.

"Liquid Assets" first appeared in *Destinies*, copyright © 1979 by Dean Ing.

"Gimme Shelter" first appeared in *Destinies*, copyright © 1980 by Dean Ing.

"Why Must They All Have My Face?" first appeared in *Destinies*, copyright © 1980 by Dean Ing.

"Down and Out on Ellfive Prime" first appeared in *Omni*, copyright © 1979 by *Omni*.

"Living Under Pressure" first appeared in *Destinies*, copyright © 1981 by Dean Ing.

"Banzai" first appeared in *Analog*, copyright © 1978 by The Condé Nast Publications, Inc.

"Fleas" first appeared in *Destinies*, copyright © 1979 by Dean Ing.

TABLE OF CONTENTS

For Valerie and Dana

Instead of mumbling and kicking a rock, I'll just flat-out admit it: other writers still motivate me. My first story (1955) aped the no-nonsense engineering stories of Harry Stine, alias 'Lee Correy'. And I didn't even realize it until I saw my story lined up with one of Harry's in Astounding. *I wasn't nearly as good a Correy as Harry was; maybe, I surmised, I was really Eric Frank Russell! Capering in my Russell suit for that second story (1957), I began to see why young painters copy old masters. Even during the next eighteen years when I wasn't writing sf, I enjoyed studying masters like Blish, Knight, and Sturgeon, who could sculpt styles as Olivier sculpted his putty noses—and to equally devastating effect.*

Then a few years ago Damon Knight wrote "I See You", and herniated my ego with his comment that it was a five-thousand-word novel. I hadn't noticed that on my first reading but in its sweep, character development, and juxtaposing of viewpoints, Damon's short piece was a sort of dehydrated novel. All the calories were there; he'd just magicked the water out of it. Damn the man!

By that time friends were kidding me about my style, claiming it was never necessary for me to have a byline. The evidence was mounting that after my tatty little masquerades in the fifties I had become inevitably, hopelessly, myself. It was time, I thought, to jounce out of my rut occasionally. What better challenge than an exercise a la Damon?

Still, I didn't want to copy a master outright—even if I could. It'd be enough if I managed to condense a range of connected themes in a short piece that also used settings and phrasing alien to me. I selected several god-themes, holy wars, blood-of-the-lamb sacrifice, religion as opiate and as cultural spearhead, a final permutation of my own,—I forget

1

them all. What I remember is how I sweated to polish away the marks of the crowbar I used to wedge them all into such a small space. It might be more apt to say that while Damon carefully dehydrated his story, I abraded mine into submission.

And of course, you mustn't blame a Knight for a vassal's roughness. You must hide my vassaline.

Domino
Domine

Long before he saw signal fires through the great spyglass, Pontifex knew the taste of victory, and of fear. The new landbridge—conceived in love from heaven, born in the fury of undersea tectonics—was a sword with two edges.

The Presence was no godlet of vague or paltry predictions: He had promised the landbridge, miraculously formed before the Infidel could garrison their coastal city. The steam carts of Pontifical legions had dashed across baking mudflats to capture the Infidel city in a single day. Soon that city would furnish youths for the Sacrifice of Innocents in accord with the pact between Pontifex and The Presence in the holy flame. Still, it was one thing to capture a city, quite another to hold it against the aroused Infidel.

If the invasion failed, soon the landbridge would be choked in ignominious retreat. The half-trained savages of Pontifical legions would be followed by sturdy yeoman Infidel farmers; one beachhead would go, then another; and soon, like game tiles toppling one against the next, the very redoubts of The Presence might fall. For most of the priesthood, failure of the holy war was unthinkable. For the high priest it was all too thinkable. For, if Pontifex was first among the devout, he was also prone to question. It was a burden he shared with none but The Presence.

Pontifex blinked as he turned away from the eyepiece, caught the eye of his aide. "Flash the message, Delain," he said; "the Infidel city is ours."

Delain, militarily correct, let relief show in his tanned features as he bowed himself out of the observatory. Pontifex often wondered at the wisdom of using a brigade colonel as he used Delain. Yet Delain knew his place, and that of every man in the Pontifical forces. If a signal mirror or a guard or a weapon failed, Delain saw to the replacement without asking instructions. It was a virtue uncommon on this side of the narrow sea, Pontifex thought with chagrin. Unquestioning fidelity to The Presence caused a dependence in men's minds. *It embrittles the soul,* he thought, and quickly diverted himself from this heresy.

The heliograph was already flashing the news to his own city, far below the mountain heights. Before Pontifex could descend his funicular railway to the temple, the message would be shouted to every hovel, would be filtering toward the hill tribesmen and the laboring peasants. And the clattering sulphurous funicular would give Pontifex time to compose himself for audience with The Presence.

The old priest found Delain staring across mudflats toward a twinkling on the horizon. "Some genius with our assault battalions already has his flasher in use, your grace," said Delain, surprised as always at efficiency in the ranks. "Shall I stay here and decode?"

"I shall need you to make ready for the solemn rite," Pontifex replied. "Surely the innocents will be rushed back immediately."

"Even before our wounded, sire," said Delain, his tone making no secret of his disapproval. "Need you rush? We can hardly spare the oil for a mass sacrifice now, of all times." The priest said nothing as he settled his slender old body in a funicular seat; his stare was reproof enough. Delain gnawed his lip. "And I am not a priest, but a fool to meddle in priestly matters," he said, bowing low. The faintest suggestion of a smile tugged at the mouth of Pontifex. Delain saw forgiveness and took a calculated risk. "Or has The Presence revealed how to double our reserves of oil?"

Pontifex engaged the lever that would begin their descent. Always alert, Delain had pinpointed the problem. If they were to proceed with transport of vital troops, it must be within days. The steam carts would need all of their available processed oil and much of the wood. Yet the mass sacrifice would use half of the hoarded fuel.

"Be tranquil, Delain," said the old priest over the railway's clacking; "I can only say that the bargain has been struck. The Presence will provide."

Delain sighed unhappily. "I must accept what I fail to understand. It takes many precious barrels of oil to incinerate a thousand children."

Pontifex frowned. He was thinking the same thing.

The innermost temple portal dilated at the voice of Pontifex, who had long ago ceased to wonder at such minor miracles in the sanctum. Soon, replenishing aromatic oil in the crystal flameholder, he had rekindled the holy flame and, in time, was rewarded.

"Rise, Pontifex," said the familiar voice, its gentle thunder thrilling with vibrato. Filling the flame was, literally, the Godhead; and the face of The Presence was beautiful. Wise brown eyes gazed below tight black ringlets. The full beard surrounded a mouth that some might call faintly sensuous, and the mouth was smiling. The face of The Presence could be as cold as ocean depths but on this day it was warm and loving. The flame danced and shuddered as the voice issued from it. "You may speak."

"Victory, Lord," replied the priest. "Our steam carts will return within a day's time, laden with captives. The day after, we will perform the rite."

"Then smile, Pontifex. I am pleased." Yet something in the voice was less than pleased.

Pontifex tried to smile. "I—my aides are troubled, Lord. The problem may be trivial, but the sacrifice will consume most of our oil reserves. Am I presumptuous?"

"Yes; but you tremble in your presumption. I am not threatened, Pontifex." Then, more sternly: "Not by mortal impudence, in any event. I shall provide."

"Thank you, Lord. Where will we find the oil?"

"You will continue to extract it as always."

"Lord, we proceed at full capacity. Without more oil, we would allow the Infidel time to mobilize and overrun our positions. If our troops lose heart they will panic. And presently, Infidel farmers might sweep into this very sanctum with my blood on their boots."

"Unless diverted by a locust plague in their fields," said The Presence.

Pontifex considered this. "And if they elect to abandon their fields to the insects?"

The face hardened. "The sea bottom shook once to raise your landbridge," it reminded. "Am I impotent to sink it again?"

Pontifex dropped his eyes. "Infinitely potent, Lord. You would do all this?" He did not dare—or need—to ask the fate of the assault battalions in such an event.

"I shall do what I shall do. Two days hence, the mouth of the infinite will attend your mass sacrifice."

Pontifex let his delight show. "May I call the faithful to the temple as witnesses?"

After the briefest pause: "Even the heavens grow uncertain—but by all means, call the faithful if you like. And now make haste, Pontifex; do not tarry with your women."

The priest sensed, as he had a few times before, a wry amusement in The Presence. He smiled back as the flame dimmed, its Godhead fading. "My Lord is jealous with my time," he said amiably.

And from the dying flame: "All gods are jealous, Pontifex."

The suggestion of many gods was a heresy so profound that Pontifex took it for a divine jest. The priest hurried to the portal, his confidence rekindled. Perhaps Delain could oversee a massive stockpiling of wood for the steam carts. With piles of wood at waystations along the mudflats? Perhaps. Such questions were below the notice of a god. *All gods*, his mind whispered.

Old Pontifex stood in bright sunlight before the temple facing the vast stone bowl between himself and the faithful throng of the city. He did not permit himself the luxury of a frown as he saw a guard hurl one of the captive children into the depression. Even though the children had been drugged during meals, they would feel some pain.

And Pontifex was not a cruel man. Far better, he felt, if the children went peacefully into the shallow lake of oil. From his vantage point he saw the piles of wood that already began to dot the horizon. Delain had insisted that only by a miracle would the waystations be sufficient—and Pontifex had agreed with a secret smile.

By now, more than half of the children had slid into the huge oil-filled depression. Most of the city's people were gathered below to witness the ancient holy rite. Or more correctly, they had gathered to behold the mouth of the infinite, the enormous cyclonic void that would form above the blazing pool to swallow the sacrificial smoke.

Once, the people across the shallow sea had made similiar sacrifices until some herbalist fool had found means to control the birthrate. It was only a matter of time before this technology became a religious issue, then an enmity; and now the Infidel refused to sacrifice their surplus youth since, they claimed, there was no surplus. This final refusal had provoked the eternal, all-wise Presence. For as far back as records existed, sacrificial rites had always been demanded by The Presence. What right-minded person could deny a deity who so willingly demonstrated His existence?

Pontifex regretted the need to give youthful lives but, in his regret, stepped forward with his torch. The last of the captives stumbled forward into the pool.

And then, incredibly, a group of half-grown children scrambled from the pool, oil glistening on their naked bodies. They had waited for the approach of the high priest and now flew into an organized pattern of action that suggested careful training. Twoscore of the youngsters fell on the guards, while a similar number sprinted toward Pontifex.

Obviously, the group had refused their drugged food. They had been taught what to expect, could plan independently, were fired with a desperate valor unknown to the ignorant legions they defied. Pontifex stood his ground on

leaden feet, unwilling to show his fear. A detached segment
of his mind marveled at the display and wondered if Delain
were napping behind him.

Delain's response was a barked command. The heavy
whistle of thrown spears passed over Pontifex into the on-
rushing children. Delain led the countercharge, hacking with
his shortsword, fending off the pummeling empty hands.
Only a lad and a girl, both near puberty, escaped. Oblivious
to the screams behind them they drew nearer, until a flung
shortsword pierced the boy's side. He fell, sliding in blood
and oil, yet the girl did not falter.

Pontifex hurled the torch. The girl staggered, fell to one
knee, and in that instant her body was sheathed in flame as the
oil on her body ignited. She stood again, faced the priest as he
folded his arms in a crucial show of disdain. Through the
flames she stared at Pontifex; and in her face he saw a terrible
resolve. She managed to reach him, clasped him in fiery
embrace.

Pontifex held his breath, slid from his crimson robe as the
girl reeled gasping. When she fell, she did not rise again, and
Pontifex paused only to recover the torch before striding to
the lip of the sacrificial pool. Though unharmed he was too
shaken to pronounce the invocation, but all the city's mul-
titudes applauded as he let the torch roll into the oil below.

The roar of the pyre found its match from a hundred
thousand throats; invoking The Presence, drowning bleated
cries from inside the smoky inferno. Delain took his position
behind the priest, the guards scrambling back from the heat
while Pontifex, ritually proper though half unclothed, backed
away pace by stately pace.

From Delain, behind him: "The fault was mine, sire."

"Nonsense. Who could expect such resolution from captive children?"

"I could, sire."

"Yes, perhaps you could. A great pity."

"A great waste."

High above them, the mouth of the infinite swirled into

being. Roiling greasy smoke arose slowly at first, then thrust itself curling into the vortex that wailed overhead, an enormous invisible maw sucking the sacrificial smoke into nowhere. There were no more cries from the victims, no more hails from the crowd; only the steady cyclonic howl from above. It could not happen, yet it always happened. Therefore it was miraculous, an awesome demonstration of the power of The Presence. Through many tomorrows, thought Pontifex, the devout might fight more faithfully now.

They would need to. As individuals, the Infidel made the superior fighter. Was The Presence, then, a lord of inferiors? This thought would not subside, and Pontifex knew that its open expression would destroy him.

Gazing aloft, the old priest feared that The Presence had read his thoughts, for the huge mouth flickered from existence, reappeared, wafted from view again. The charnel stench of human sacrific spread as the smoke continued to rise from the pool of fire. Presently it drifted, a horrifying omen, over the city and its frightened people. Never before had The Presence rejected such a sacrifice.

Pontifex tended the holy flame with trembling fingers, trying to ignore the sensation of ice that lay in his vitals. For a time the flame danced by itself over the carven crystal, uninhabited. At last, when fear overhung Pontifex as the smoke pall overhung his city, there was a swirling in the flame. It bade him speak.

"Lord," he croaked, and faltered. "Lord," he tried again, failed again. Ignoring arthritic pain, the priest abased himself on the cold flagstones. Muffled: "I failed you, Lord."

"No, Pontifex. You have served well."

"But—you refused the Sacrifice of Innocents?" The priest rested on his knees, tears streaking the lined old face.

Something in the hallowed features seemed awry. If a god could register perplexity, it might be registered thus. "The failure was not yours, Pontifex." A wisp of smile. "I was—distracted." It seemed that more was to be said, and then it seemed that The Presence had thought better of it.

"The people call it the worst of omens, Lord. Their fear spreads to the provinces. My aide reports flasher messages from across the landbridge. Our gains are imperiled, though there is hope." He attempted a summation; could only add, "All is not well here."

"Nor in the heavens. Has it occurred to you that your aide fears to tell you the worst?"

"It has, Lord. Delain fears me too much. In some ways it might be better if I did not pretend to godlike knowledge."

There was a long silence, as the face in the flame studied the troubled priest. Then: "Sufficient knowledge equals divinity?"

"I did not suggest that, Lord."

"No; I did. Pontifex, if you took Delain into your confidence, explained your miraculous wisdom, would he be the better for it?"

Pontifex wondered how he should reply and decided upon total candor. "For himself, probably yes. For my purpose—which is to serve you, Lord—certainly no. Did I answer wisely?"

Something between a chuckle and a sigh. "I hope so. You have served me as your Delain has served you. Even while hating the bloody work I gave you."

"You saw my thoughts, Lord."

"I saw your face, Pontifex."

"The Presence is all-seeing," the priest murmured.

Quickly: "And what if I were not? Is it possible to forgive a god that fails?"

Pontifex felt the tears drying cold on his cheeks, overwhelmed by the deeper cold in his belly. "Lord: a god cannot be a god, and fail."

"True." Softly, with a note almost of pleading: "And I foresee that I must fail you."

Pontifex, misunderstanding, cried out. "What have we done to deserve your forsaking us?"

"Nothing. The universe takes little note of the deserving poor. Let me reward your devotion with truth: I can no longer maintain the energy source that permits me to interfere with your natural events. I might be an observer; nothing more. Seismic disturbance, plague, even the mass transfer locus you call the mouth of the infinite. All will be lost to me, therefore to you."

Pontifex cast his mind ahead to guess at a future without divine guidance. "The people believe in me, Lord."

"As you believed in me, Pontifex. *As we believed in our gods,*" the voice thundered in savage irony. *"As our gods did in theirs!"*

Pontifex clasped his head between his palms to keep it from bursting. "It is painful to hold such thoughts," he muttered. "Why must you abandon us?"

"Our gods tell us that *their* gods are losing a great war," was the reply. "When we lose assistance from above, those below us must suffer the same fate. Perhaps the universe grows tired of gods."

"Or of wars in their names," the priest said bitterly. "What use did you make of the ghastly sacrifices we perpetuated in your honor?"

The flame steadied as the voice fell silent. When it spoke again, it spoke with reluctance. "A flavoring, Pontifex. A condiment highly regarded by my civilization."

The priest stood erect. "Spice," he whispered. "Can you have been victimized as badly by your own gods?"

"Considering the holy war we seem fated to lose on several worlds? Oh, yes. Yes, we think so. There may be a spark of the savage in all beings, Pontifex. We defaced our temples. Are you civilized enough to forgive?"

"Were you?" With agility that surprised him, Pontifex smashed the crystal flameholder. Small pools of oil spread across the altar and over the stones, feeding blazes that flickered toward ancient draperies.

As the sanctum began to burn, the old priest shed his robes. The portal dilated for the last time, and staring back, Pontifex saw in each flame the same once-beloved face. In unison, the images called to him. "Absolution, Pontifex," they pleaded.

To no avail. Many generations would pass, the burned temple a long-forgotten ruin, before hearthfires on the peaceful world of Pontifex were entirely free of the voice that begged from the flames.

It's a short chronological step back from "Domino Domine" and divine error, to the human errors in the next story. "Malf" was endless fun for me, in part because it was the first sf I'd written in nearly twenty years and I'd collected a few new tricks in the interim. Some of those tricks show up in the detailed preliminary design of hardware in the story. I'd been a senior research engineer, built and raced small-bore prototype cars, then moved to Oregon where the timber people drive the damnedest vehicles you ever saw.

I'd learned different tricks during postgrad work in Oregon, while they steeped me in communication theory. One rarity, Dr. Robert Mertz, even denied that speculation had to be 'mere' and flashed a streak of whimsy when handling ideas that were distinctly science-fictional. Mertz saw no reason why you couldn't put media theory to work in the craft of fiction. Why must an academic stay retarded at the analysis level through fear of criticism? Go thou, and synthesize!

Then I became an assistant prof in a midwest university where my sandals and ideas were future shock. Most of the free-swinging speculation I heard there was from students. A few of my colleagues also kept me from total brain death— but I shall protect them here with anonymity and a stage-whispered 'thank you'.

It was during a glorious, psyche-boosting session with one of these closet speculators that I focused on the problem of malfunctions in man/machine systems. Given complementary malfunctions in a duel between such systems, which might win? Why?

I went home and snuck into my closet and synthesized. There was a tree-harvesting machine to be designed for the *precipitous Cascades range; extrapolation on Oregon's future; and even a cop who needed a sex change between drafts because given equal opportunity, she could do his job. God, but it was fun!*

Before final-type I could see that some sly pundits had been covertly adding to my little bag of tricks. From that time onward, I had a forum for ideas too speculative for quarterly journals.

"Malf" was speculation, Oregon, synthesis, upbeat, and media theory at play. Why not just dedicate it to the evergreen memory of Bob Mertz? Consider it done.

Malf

Infante nudged his Magnum's front axle against the big tree with that little extra *whump* that said, "grandstander." Old Tom Kelley and I knew that, but Howard Scortia was duly impressed. The lumberman had come to see a hundred and fifty feet of Oregon fir harvested in sixty seconds and Kelley knew, between Infante and me, who was more fun to watch.

"Clear?" George Infante's voice rang from his polycarbonate bubble amplified and more resonant than his usual soft delivery.

"Clear," I sang back, louder than necessary for Infante, whose audio pickups could strain a voice out of the screech of machinery. I was grandstanding a little, too, for Kelley's sake.

Everyone jumped when Infante triggered the spike driver. Ten thousand pounds of air pressure will slap your ears when it's shooting a ribbed spike ten inches into a living fir trunk.

All I did was position a quartz fiber strap around the tree just above the paint mark; but it was a crucial operation if the hinge was to sit tight. I dodged out between the tree and one of the eight-foot Magnum tires. Then I ran.

When I replied to Infante's "Clear?" again, I was still sprinting. I knew he wouldn't wait for me to get entirely clear before querying, and he knew I wouldn't make him wait. Machismo, maybe; stupidity for sure. Though Infante had been with us only six months, since November '85, he and I could judge each other pretty well.

Infante's reflexes were honed like microscalpels, or else he started the stripping a nanosec before I cleared him. I scuffed

forest humus on Mr. Scortia's boots as I slowed to a stop. He
didn't notice; with everybody else, he was watching those
gangsaws strip the fir.

Imagine a gang of curve-bar chainsaws arranged in a
circle, mounted pincer-fashion on an extendable beam.
They're staggered so they won't chew each other up as they
pivot toward the center, and God help what's in the center.
The saws are run by airmotors, making whoopee noises but
with low fire danger.

Infante's eye was good. Correction: it was perfect. He ran
his gang of banshees whooping up that fir trunk like a squirrel
up a sapling, and branches rained all over the Magnum
Seven. Infante had his steel cage flipped over the bubble and
stared straight up through the falling junk, hands in his
console waldoes, judging how close to strip the larger limbs.

Then he pulled what heavy equipment operators call a Mr.
Fumducker, a piece of mechanically amplified horseplay that
looks cute if it works, and kills somebody if it doesn't work.
He topped the tree.

The Magnum could bring the tree down top and all, gentle
as praying. But George Infante, without a line or any other
control, topped her so fast she didn't know which way to
fall—and that's what makes it horseplay. With six saws
chewing at once, any one may bite through first and it's
possible the thing will flip. Or it could drop vertically, a great
fletched pile-driver on the operator below. And that would
ruin Mr. George Infante's whole day, cage or no cage. For an
instant, Kelley lost his smile. He muttered, "Barmy little
bastard," not loud, but not joking.

Infante hauled the beam back so fast the pneumatics
barked, made an elbow of the beam, and sideswiped the top
as it fell. My eyes are good, too; I knew Infante could hear
admiring feedback from Mr. Scortia's men because he was
grinning. I liked the Magnum system; it did a heavy dude's
job with precision. Infante—well, I think Infante liked what
he could do *with* it. The distinction didn't seem large until
you had to repair an overtaxed Magnum.

Mr. Scortia rumbled, "Thirty seconds," and I saw him

holding a big antique timepiece; railroadman's watch, if I was any judge. I craved it instantly. He stood watching the gangsaws, now stilled, form a ring near the fresh stump a hundred feet up the fir.

But Infante could do that without looking; he was that good. Meanwhile he had his other waldo working the big left front extensor with its single huge chainsaw. Infante flicked the extensor back toward him, the saw snarling as it engaged. He was cutting the tree in one long swipe like a man sawing his own leg off from in front.

He stopped the cut at precisely the right instant. Mr. Scortia obviously expected the tree, all fifty tons of it, to come thundering down on poor little hapless George Infante. Kelley and I knew that poor little hapless George was nearly home free.

As Infante lowered the tree, our simple brawny hinge kept it from kicking off its stump. The entire trunk came down lamb-quiet and Infante placed its upper end in a yoke amid the rearmost of the Magnum's three axles. Time: fifty-seven seconds. I knew we had sold our first Magnum.

I also knew Infante had goddamn-near dented his. In haste to make a record stripping he had left a stub branch long enough that, as he lowered the tree, the stub slammed his cage with shivering impact. *Well,* I thought: *if I can't teach you caution, maybe that will. I'd hate to see you graunched.*

If Kelley noticed he wasn't letting on. Infante magicked the hingepin out with his little extensor. With feet and his other hand, he maneuvered the Magnum several ways at once.

The Magnum's third axle is remoted by a telescoping spiral stainless tube. The idea is to provide mass, leverage, and steerability with the remoting axle and yoke. When Infante had the remote axle tucked closer, he quickly swung the Magnum's legs down. Then, carrying a hundred thousand pounds of cellulose on the hoof, Infante's Magnum stood up and walked the hell out of there. No cheering this time; just unhinged jaws.

The ambulatory feature of the Magnum is mechanically

simple, with pneumatics. But feedback circuitry is fiendishly tricky, and nobody made it really work until Kelley learned to calibrate it for a given operator. It's a mite humbling the first time you see it work on heavy equipment. Infante didn't need to walk her out, but a demo is a demo; with one eye on his rear video, he chuffed over a rise and out of sight.

Kelley listened to the turbine doppler down in the distance. "Instant toothpick," he said, chuckling. "Oh: Keith?"

I glanced around. "Sir?"

"Run down with the Six and help George pull a postops check"—he eyed me significantly—"and then grab a beer at the shack."

I grinned to myself at the word. Howard Scortia's geodesic dome was hardly a shack: more a statement of life-style according to the Prophet Fuller. If Mr. Scortia liked making statements of that sort, he was probably an ideal customer for Kelley. With ecology an enshrined word, the big lumber interests were helpless when government annexed "their" private rights to forest, range and watershed. The Department of the Interior might single out a lone prime tree for harvest, and threaten your license if you clipped a twig from the tree next to it. The hallowed jargon was shifting. It was *harvesting*, not *logging*—and very selectively. Snaking was only for pulp cellulose, since it damaged prime logs to drag them with a chain. You didn't snake, you toted. And the Kelley Magnum was just the rig to do it all.

I headed for my rig, the Magnum Six, which I herded around when I could get her to walk straight. The Seven had more flexible programs and better stability in walk mode. The Six had developed an intermittent malf— malfunction—we couldn't fathom. Kelley wanted it checked out before the Six put a foot wrong and leaned on somebody a little. Eight tons of alloy with the blind staggers isn't much of a selling point. I started the turbine, which was down near the pressure pumps. It was the pumps that did everything; tried-and-true airmotors powered the wheels, gangsaws, and most other subsystems. Like Lear and Curran, Kelley knew when to bluesky and when to opt for standard hardware. That's why he had a working Magnum while AMF was still doping out system interfaces.

I found Infante playing with the damned tree as he tried to balance it upright at the loading ramp. Given time, I think he could've made the big fir stand alone. For a few minutes, anyway—or until somebody nudged it.

He saw me smile and interpreted it correctly: funny, but only as an idea. Impassive, he rolled back and let the huge log fall. Its butt kicked up nearly against the Seven. I silently cursed Infante for gashing the prime wood he had harvested, and risking his vehicle. But his pneumatics coughed, the nearside legs literally bouncing him safely away. That little lunatic could *move*.

"Kelley sending in the second team?" Infante's deceptively mild voice came through my com set.

"Wants us to check out the Six and—I'll tell you while we do it," I said. Ordinarily Infante was happy to drive while I inspected mechanical bits; George at his console, all's right with the world.

But now Infante flatly refused to handle the Six further. "If you ask me, that thing belongs in a straitjacket," he snarled. "You drive; I'll check the leg rams for binding."

As we went through the checkout, I wondered if it were only my imagination that made the Six seem more tractable for me than for Infante. Or maybe his low boiling point interfered with his fine touch. But even granting some difference, the Six had problems. Why *did* the bloody thing stagger? The malf was systemic, I decided: not traceable to any one leg. I hardly blamed Infante.

If Infante was an operator at heart, I was basically a troubleshooter. I'd had most of a five-year B.E. in systems engineering before I learned, during summer work, to make fast money highballing an earthmover. Dumb stunt, but I dropped out and chased the bucks. I wanted to design and build and race against the best Formula cars, and I did—with just enough success to keep me broke and hoping. I was exactly right for Kelley's operation after I sold the race car: just enough experience in vehicle systems, and just sick enough of myself to want somebody to believe in.

It was easy to believe in Tom Kelley. He did his own things, but they were useful things like the Magnums. Having helped him through some bitchin' chassis development problems, I had more time in our two prototypes than Kelley did himself. He was lean and mean for a sixty-year-old, but had the sense to trust younger synapses. They weren't helping me find the malf in the system, though.

Finally I gave up on the checkout and signaled my frustration to Infante. "I could use a ride in something that works," I added, nodding toward the Seven. "Let's see if Scortia really has that beer."

Infante scrambled down from his handholds on the Six. "But why doesn't my Seven act up the same way? They both have the same parts."

"Mechanicals, yes," I hedged. "The differences are mainly in that solid-state stuff Kelley dreamed up."

Pausing before swinging into the Seven's bubble, Infante gave me a wink full of fatherly wisdom. "That's where your malf is," he husked.

I gave a damifino shrug and followed. Those wise nonverbals seemed funny on Infante, but I didn't laugh. When he suspected you were laughing at him, George Infante was not likable. I preferred him likable. He wasn't quite my bulk, two years my senior, with big brooding eyes bordered by the longest lashes I have seen on a man. Women didn't seem to mind his macho ways. I liked him too, when he wasn't overcompensating for looking like a small latin angel.

We rolled back to the Scortia dome and Infante put the Seven into a run as we neared the place. Kelley and I had discussed the theoretical top speeds of the Magnum in walk and wheel modes, and it was Kelley's dictum that we would not try to find out until he'd sold a few. Infante must've been secretly practicing high-speed runs, though: we were not merely trotting, we were running hard and crabwise as we neared the dome. Infante tooted, in case anyone failed to see us approach. The toot was redundant. Kelley and Mr. Scortia stood in the doorway, Kelley's face a study in feigned satisfaction. Infante went in for his beer. I sat in his harness a few moments, figuring how he had obtained that angled gait. Infante was given to unpredictable moods and furies, an abrasive man for teamwork. But as a solo operator he was brilliant.

As I entered the dome, Mr. Scortia handed me a beer, holding it like a fragile toy in his great paw. "I hear good things about your ways with machines," he said.

Infante started to respond, realized the lumberman was addressing me, and quickly turned away. I said, "It may be a case of their having a way with me, Mr. Scortia."

I perched on a stool near Kelley, who mused, "Keith and my machines are easy to figure: they think alike."

Scortia chuckled from somewhere deep in the earth. "That's why I need him, Tom." I glanced up; so did Infante. Kelley missed neither look. There was a moment's utter silence.

"As I said, Howard, it's really up to Keith," Kelley said. He looked alternately at me and Infante. "Howard Scortia wants to chop costs by having his operator trainees learn here on the job. And only from our best man. That's you, George—or you, Keith. As an operator—and I'm being up front with you both—George, you're so good it scares me." I caught the gut-level truth of that, though Kelley's glance at me was bland. "Another month in a Magnum and you could enter the effin' thing in the Winter Olympics!"

We all laughed to relieve tension. Scortia lifted his beer in silent toast to Infante, who seemed less edgy now. The big man put in, "But I asked who trained *you*, George. And who's the best on-site consultant for maintenance gangs." He turned to me. "And Tom says they're both Keith Ames."

Kelley said wryly, "Keith, I explained we need you on assembly interfaces at Ashland and he could forget about borrowing you. And this Neanderthal says we can forget about the five Magnums while we're at it . . ." Kelley went on banking his rhetorical fires. Five Magnums! Too attrac-

tive an offer by far. Scortia was not a bigger name in the
Oregon Cascades only because he liked to manage all his
operations. If he sprang for a handful of Magnums, everybody from Weyerhaeuser on down would follow suit.

I half-listened to Kelley drip drollery instead of excitement. Like Scortia, Kelley was self-developed and knew his
best operational modes. Kelley had started as a cards-lucky
kid in the Seabees and never lost his fascination with heavy
equipment that functioned with precision. But he also had an
eye for what the equipment was all about, the massaging of
man's world. When he realized the future of glass fibers
around 1950, he sank a month's poker winnings into Corning
and didn't regret it. By the time I was born he was building
military runway extensions and saw what was about to happen in air travel. He got fatter on Boeing, then on fluorocar-
bons. Finally he saw he was still gambling with paper when
he wanted to do it with hardware and his goofy solid-states.
And he took his twenty million right in the middle of the
recession and sank it into man-amplifier systems. The Magnum was his heavy bet.

"I know what your contract says, Keith, but I also know
what I told you. And if Howard Scortia doesn't take Magnums, his competitors will," Kelley finished, whistling in
the dark.

I swirled my beer, thinking. "Well, it's nearly June. By the
time we have enough Magnums, there'll barely be time to get
'em in full operation before the rains." Scortia nodded; in
Western Oregon you aren't a native until your gill slits begin
to function. "Fifty days of familiarization. I can lift down to
Ashland in an hour if you need me," I said to Kelley.

"And what if you have to start training with only one
Magnum," Kelley asked softly. Infante was perfectly still,
listening to something in his head.

"Add thirty days," I hazarded. "I don't see how we can
spook up a new Magnum before July, though. Unless somebody slips a cog and we sell a proto."

Now Scortia laughed openly. Kelley made a rueful face:

"Guilty as charged, I guess. Keith, I promised him the Seven."

"When?" Infante's question was soft but his corneas were pinpricks in his eyes.

"Is she a hundred percent now?"

Infante hesitated. Kelley glanced to me, and I nodded. Kelley spread his hands. "Then she stays here. Anything wrong with that?"

"I hear rumors you're the boss," I grinned. What bothered me was George Infante. I wished I could read behind those eyes.

"One thing," Scortia said. "Could I hitch a, uh, walk to my Cottage Grove office? I want to enjoy my Magnum before she gets all scruffy. A walk through town is more than I can resist."

"*I* can resist it," I said, counting off on my fingers. "No street license, too wide for state code, and a risk of equipment, for starters."

He winked, "I'll take care of any problems. I want my new rig under my office window for a few days."

Somehow I had never thought of the Magnum as a status symbol. But there it was: the kid in Howard Scortia was loose in our toyshop. "I believe this man has it worse than we do," I said to Infante. "Promise you won't kick any Buicks?"

"It's your show," Infante replied easily. "Why don't you tote Mr. Scortia downtown?"

I was glad to; we had no experience in real-world traffic yet, and this was underwritten. But as we sauntered out to a chill afternoon breeze, I filed a question away. What made Infante so ready to divorce his amplified self, the Magnum Seven? Whatever had been behind his unreadable expression, it had changed when Scortia asked me to park the Seven in town.

I highballed down from Scortia's site to the interstate freeway in an hour, keeping to the verges with all subsystems fully retracted. That way we made a package twelve feet wide,

thirty-two long, and scarcely ten high. It was only a bit
cramped in the bubble, though I'm average size and Mr.
Scortia is a fee-fie-foe-fum type. Naturally we picked up a
patrol cruiser as the Seven walked chuffing into town. When
he heard the beeper, Mr. Scortia waved joyfully. The cruiser
was almost as massive as Caddies of the old days, and
dwarfed normal traffic. Yet from the Magnum it seemed a
bantam, challenging the cock of the—ah—walk. Whoever
said, "Power corrupts . . ." maybe I should give him his
due. Sacrifice a goat to him or something. I was uncomfort-
able with the thought that, momentarily, the police seemed
insignificant. Walking a Magnum is walking very, very tall.

The police beeper and beacon went off; the cruiser drew
alongside and the big man made sign talk to the effect that this
was *his* rig and Gawd, Nell, ain't it grand? They didn't stop
us, but they didn't leave us either. My rear video was full of
cop cruiser from there to the Scortia offices.

Once in his parking lot: "Waltz us around, this is private
property," he said. I did, while he watched me. I knew my
first trainee would be Howard Scortia and smiled, wondering
how many miles he would perambulate his Magnum around
that space in the next few days. Then we set the operator
harness for the Scortia bulk and got a half-assed calibration
for his particular combination of synapses and rhythms. Once
an operator is thoroughly calibrated you can insert a program
card for him into the console. But for a new operator, the
calibration is rough. Under the lumberman's control, the
Seven lurched a few times just as the Six did, until I set the
verniers again.

By nightfall my trainee could amble around with reasonable safety. I keyed all extensor subsystems for access only
by primary operators, so I wouldn't worry about Scortia
accidentally shoving his remoting axle through a brick wall
while I was in Ashland. Then he hauled us all into Eugene
where we feasted at some place called Excelsior. Then we
met a copter at the river and lifted down to the Ashland plant.

Infante, Kelley and I stayed at the plant awhile, burping
Quiche Lorraine and debriefing. Kelley made notes. Infante

shuffled call-ins before deciding to answer a miz and arrang-
ing to be picked up. To my surprise, he asked if I would make
it a foursome. To my further surprise I said OK. I wanted to
say good-bye to a miz, expecting to be gone awhile, and
thought it would be less a problem if I did it in company.
Besides, it did not seem the right time to make George Infante
feel rejected. So much for Keith Ames, boy psychoanalyst
. . .

I don't know how long the phone buzzed before I lurched
up from a maelstrom dream and slapped the ''accept'' plate
by my bed. I said something nonaccepting.

"Always the last place you look," Kelley grated, not
amused. I lay back, glad I had no video on my phone, and
tried not to breathe hard. It hurt. The light hurt too. I kept my
eyes shut. "How long've you been there?"

I thought for an eternity, and even *that* hurt. "What's the
time?"

Kelley delivered a word he keeps for special occasions,
then, "Eight-fifteen, and time you answered my question!"

"I—honest to God, I don't know," I moaned. "Mr.
Kelley, I need time to think. I feel rotted away."

"You may get fifty years to think while you sure 'nough
rot away," he said, and my eyes snapped open. Whatthehell
now? "Keith, if you're not at the plant in ten minutes you can
handle this mother alone! Uh, you're not hurt?"

"I'm mummified. But I don't think I'm—"

"Move your ass, then! And walk. Up the alley. All the
way." He slapped off.

Once on my feet I felt better, but nauseated. I struggled
into a turtleneck and coverall, nearly passed out while putting
my boots on, and shouldered past my back door wishing I had
something to barf up. Whatever was wrong, it was screwed
up tight and twisted off. I had gone three of the six blocks
down my friendly informal alleys when I heard police beep-
ers heading down Siskiyou, and so fuzzy-minded I didn't
connect them with Kelley's call.

Tom Kelley opened the alley gate himself and hauled me in

with desperate strength, as though the plant meant safety.
Maybe it did. Hurrying to his office, he held my sleeve as a
truant officer had, once. He kept gnawing his lip and muttering. I began to feel well enough to hit somebody. Infante,
maybe; what had I been swilling?

Halfway through a skull-ripping question-and-answer session with Kelley, I was still trying to get his drift when the
phone buzzed. The close-cropped curls of a lady cop flicked
onto Kelley's video. Kelley made the right decision: yes, I
was with him and no, I wasn't their man, and since I was in no
condition to visit the station, could they come to the plant?

When police lieutenant Meta Satterlee arrived, I was trying not to spill mocha on the table every time I shuddered.
Satterlee reminded me of a loose-jointed math prof I knew.
She asked for a blood sample and took it herself, expertly, but
I fainted anyway. They both eased up then. The police
already knew where I'd been until midnight, from a talk with
my miz. Some of it came back to me. I hadn't been drinking
heroically, but somehow I got a gutful of something so
potent, Infante took me to my apartment. That's all I knew.
"Maybe Infante can shed some light on this," I said.

Kelley and the cop exchanged a wry look. "A meeting
devoutly to be wished," Satterlee replied, savoring her line.
"Mr. Kelley has been less than completely open with us up to
now, but I think we can all benefit if I can see some personnel
files." She raised a questioning brow toward Kelley, who
mooched off through the deserted offices to hunt up our files.

Satterlee sat on the table edge, swinging one trousered leg.
It was quiet for a moment, except for the ball bearings
someone was grinding in my head. "I'll accept as probable
that you didn't know about the APB out on you," she said at
last.

"Who told you that?"

"Did you?"

I realized Tom Kelley had known even if I hadn't. "No."
The leg began to swing again. "I woke up with—uh—
buzzing in my head, and something seemed all wrong, and I
got up and walked down to the plant like I usually do."

"Uh-huh. You usually run down alleys every Saturday morning?"

I raised my head, not wanting to shift my eyeballs, and almost managed a smile. "If I had tried to run, lady, my body would've simply disintegrated. You have no idea how I feel."

She caressed the blood sample. "Not at the moment," she admitted. She added something under her breath and left quickly, returning without the sample. I wondered how many cops were milling around in front of the plant. Hell of a public image.

Kelley spread a pair of folders on the table. Satterlee took them, evidently speed-reading, then tapped one with a finger while looking off into the office gloom. Then she said, "I have to take some risks in this business, Mr. Kelley. I'm taking one on you now: are you certain Ames is not involved?"

Tom Kelley stared his best two-pair bluff straight into her face. "One—hundred—percent."

She registered faint amusement. "I'll settle for ninety-five," she replied, "if I can place him in your custody."

A nod. I looked from one to the other. "Will you goddamn kindly tell me *what has happened,*" I asked. "A hit and run?"

"Altogether too good a guess. Using that vehicle of yours."

I was slow. "My Porsche?"

"Your tree harvester," she said tiredly.

I put my hands over my face. "Oh dear goddy," I said. Infante!

Satterlee went on. "I'm from Eugene; we have a copter waiting . . ."

"Hold it," I said and looked up, alert. "Where's the Seven?" Satterlee was slow this time. "The Seven. The Magnum. My bloody tree harvester," I cried, exasperated.

"Mr. Infante seems to have it at the moment," Satterlee said, "and we have nothing that can catch him." She saw my alarm and went on quickly, "Oh, we'll take him eventually;

and I understand your concern over your new machine. But right now I wish there were somebody else with a similar vehicle.''

"There is," Kelley said. He jerked a thumb at me.

Satterlee taped my statement as we lifted North to the Eugene-Cottage Grove strip city. She began to leak the story as she had pieced it together and Kelley glumly watched wet green-black forest and fogwisp slip below the copter. Editing out my questions and some inevitable back-tracking, Satterlee put it roughly this way: "Sometime around three a.m., a poker crowd in Cottage Grove heard chainsaws ripping through a third-floor wall nearby. All they knew was, it was one awful racket for a few seconds. This was near the city limit where the cities are snarling over jurisdiction.

"Turned out someone was after a payroll in the Daniel mill. Don't ask *me* what it was doing there on a Friday night, some of these old outfits keep a bushel of raw cash around with only a steel-faced door between themselves and bankruptcy. About eighty-five thousand in cash was taken, minus the change.

"Then a Eugene prowl car spotted something proceeding East at high speed. The officer gave chase. Very excited. Said the thing ran *on legs* across a suburban mall but that he was catching it.

"And then it caught *him*. It evidently grabbed his cruiser near the front window and picked it up, judging from the debris, and threw two tons of prowl car into the Safeway front window, setting off the alarm. And incidentally," her jaw twitched once, "killing the officer.

"We were fit to be untied after that hot-pursuit crash. A bright cadet found oval depressions big as coffee tables in the mall and surmised it truly was a hellacious big machine on legs. Road blocks all negative. Then Pacific Tel reported vandalism on some old phone lines over a street in the East outskirts of Cottage Grove. Something tall as a telephone pole took the lines down like a grizzly through a spiderweb.

But no oval tracks. Then a drunk convinced us there was a gaping hole up on the Daniel Building.

"From then until now, it's been our biggest Chinese fire drill since the Bowles escape in the Seventies. A Mr. Howard Scortia reported the theft of his Magnum from his very own personal parking lot in the night, and you can imagine the confusion then." Kelley and I swapped miserable chuckles. She continued, "When we realized he was talking about a big vehicle instead of a handgun, we first hypothesized Scortia was involved. But he had some things going for him: an alibi, a local rep any politician might envy, and the nearest thing to a genuine speechless rage I ever expect to hear. He put us in touch with Mr. Kelley. I was already airborne so I lifted for Ashland.

"We got some fingerprint ID's then, but prints can be planted. Mr. Kelley couldn't believe either of his top operators had done anything offbase, but he gave us a pair of names. The Ashland force is very sharp. I suppose it helps when they know everyone in town."

She gave a little snort. "Oh, yes: there's a traffic control officer in Cottage Grove who verified that Scortia could've driven your monster machine. Said officer is in deep yogurt for failure to report your attractive nuisance meandering through congested traffic yesterday. If he'd logged a description in, we'd've been hours ahead."

I explained the traffic incident, adding, "There are lots of odd agriculture rigs. Since we *didn't* by-God disturb traffic, maybe he dismissed us as just another new plow or something."

"He may shortly face another kind of dismissal. I can't even guess all the ways your new plowshare can be used as a sword."

I was in a better position to guess. Even in darkness, Infante could use infrared video to guide an extensor through a hole in a wall, using his gangsaws. I didn't see how an extensor could scoop up cash, but since Infante's prints were in the cash room, that one was simple enough. He had shinnied up the duralloy beam and personally ransacked the place. "If he filled his plenums first," I offered, "he could do it all on air pressure for several minutes without using his turbine. Quieter, except for going into the wall. You could park nearly a half-block away and run the gangsaws out to a wall, so long as there was room to extend the remote axle as a balancing moment."

Meta Satterlee broke out a sheaf of faxed maps, confirming that Infante could have done it that way. "Your inferences are awfully good," she said, "for someone who hasn't seen an aerial map of the scene."

"Maps," I yelped. "You have charts of the terrain east of here?"

She did. Kelley came alive then, and we began tracing the likely paths Infante might take. Satterlee was optimistic about the Six and called to get its fuel tanks topped off by Scortia's crew. As we swung up a valley I could see Cottage Grove to the northwest. Copter lights blinked in and out of a low voluptuous cloudbank advancing on us from the Cascade range. Patrol copters were running search patterns with IR, radar, and gas analyzers, but had turned up nothing promising. That wasn't surprising, our pilot announced. The Cascades are so steep, with so many sources of heat and emissions to check, it might take days to find a Kelley Magnum. Especially if Infante was smart enough to minimize the use of his turbine. The heavy weather front made it worse. It doesn't rain all the time there in May; only half the time.

It was an hour to lunch when the copter whirred down in the clearing next to the Magnum Six. Satterlee shook her head in dismay, perhaps beginning to realize the full destructive potential of the beast we hunted. With lifting heart, I saw Scortia in the Six's bubble, manfully trying to hotwire her ignition. Standing alert in the drizzle were a dozen of his gang. Not one lacked a shotgun.

While I checked out the Six and filled her plenums, the others lifted to Scortia's dome to confer with remote units by com set. My head was clear by then and, best sign of all, I was hungry. I highballed back to the dome and was met outside by an oddly different Meta Satterlee.

"Whether your friend Infante is working alone or not," she said, "I'm happy to report he is not your friend."

"Where were you yesterday," I grumped.

"It's where the Ashland lab people have been that'll interest you," she said, matching strides with me toward the dome that shed rivulets of Oregon rain down its faceted flanks. "You, sire, were drugged like a horse. Ah—it's safe to say you didn't brush your teeth or gargle this morning."

"Jeez, is it that bad?" I tried to smell my own breath.

"Could be worse, dear. Somebody hypoed more alkaloids into your toothpaste, and made an interesting addition to your mouthwash."

"For Christ's sake! What for?"

"To zonk you out the minute you became functional again. A cute little notion favored by the Families back east, I'm told. Which ties in nicely with George Infante—if you call that nice."

"Mafia?"

"Splinter groups of it. The man with George Infante's fingertips was believed to be wheelman on a major crime last year in Gary, Indiana. Not arraigned; lack of evidence. They gave him a long, long rope and it led here. Nice of 'em to warn us. Oh, hell, too much of that and I suppose we'd have a police state."

Infante a getaway driver: it figured. The sonofabitch was a natural. I began to shake with anger as well as low blood sugar. In the dome I calmed down with sweet coffee and eggs served up by Scortia himself. My only cheering thought was that Satterlee seemed to be accepting my innocence as very likely.

A burly captain of the Oregon Highway Patrol mumbled with Satterlee over the high-relief area charts. He had some trouble with her gender; not because she was all that attractive a miz, but because she insisted on doing her job like any other cop.

Reluctantly he offered her a heavy parcel, which she pocketed. "Pretend you're using a carbine," he said. "Forget about long leads or aiming high. And watch that recoil," he sighed, with a glance at her narrow shoulders.

"I've qualified with boosted ammo," she said a bit crossly. "I only wish we had some of the new API stuff."

"It's coming from Salem," he said helplessly. "Can you wait?"

I interrupted her negative headshake as I approached their work table. "I still don't see why Infante tried to poison me when he could've just as easily cut my throat," I said.

"He wanted you alive but on ice," Satterlee explained. "My guess is, he didn't expect to be seen, and thought he'd have until Monday before we connected the payroll job with a missing Magnum. Since you could've done it as easily as he did, he wanted you as a live decoy. By the time you were on your feet, he could be back in Ashland, maybe having switched your mouthwash. Then he could wallop himself with his own drugs and have a story at least as good as yours. He just didn't plan on his murder spree."

The OHP man rasped, "Sure as hell didn't shrink from it."

"Lieutenant, you really think George Infante planned to stick around after the job, with his known background, and put his word against mine? Does that make sense?" I asked.

Satterlee tapped a finger against the projection of the Three Sisters wilderness area in impatient thought. "Not really. From the profile we're developing on him it's hard to say. I could give you a long academy phrase for Infante, but let me give it to you without the bullshit: I think we're dealing with a crazy man."

"Foxy crazy," the captain reminded her. "We may never find out how he got from Ashland to Cottage Grove so fast; and you don't know how he got a fix on that payroll. But he damn well *did it*. And unless the forestry people are crazy too, he tried to get up here to your other unit—the Six?—early this morning."

This brought Howard Scortia onto his feet, his stool over

backward. It suddenly occurred to me that this old gent had started in his business when it was a brawler's job. "You didn't tell me that," he roared.

"Betcherass I didn't." The OHP man grinned. "You'd be chasin' around up there with a willow switch—"

"And my eight-gauge!"

Kelley spoke up from his well of gloom. For the first time since I'd known him, he was sounding his age. "Barring luck, Howard, you might as well have one as the other. They're right, it's plain stupid to go after the Seven without special weapons. But what's this about it being around here?"

Infante was no longer roaming the heights above us, but there were fresh prints skirting a nearby ridge, and they hadn't been there the day before: prints only a Magnum's feet could make. I calculated this would've been about dawn if Infante went cross-country. And he would not have kept to the roads. Infante wasn't *that* crazy. "One thing sure," I said. "Infante didn't intend to switch to the Six. Hell, he won't even operate it, he thinks it's hexed. Maybe he wanted to destroy it."

"Probably something scared him off," the captain said.

"Beats me what it would've been," Scortia mused. "I called and put a crew on guard only after I realized my Magnum was gone, around eight a.m. or so."

"Damn, that's right." Satterlee was tapping like mad. "This is rough country; knowing it halfway is infinitely better than not knowing it at all." Scortia nodded. "What if he wasn't interested in the other vehicle?"

"Then why come up this way?" This from Kelley.

"I don't know. He could buy time by evasion in these wilds. He probably has the money with him. All he needed to do was ditch the vehicle and catch the valley monorail to Portland. *Unless he had further plans for the Magnum!*"

Kelley and I burst out talking, convinced she had doped it right. The OHP man was vehicle-oriented, sending us back to the relief charts with: "If that thing can do only seventy on wheels, how does he expect to escape in it?"

One answer was, he could select a mountain lake and ditch
the Magnum in it. But he might not get it back. A second was,
he had a rendezvous with an equipment carrier within fuel
range of the Magnum. The third answer was that Infante was
nuts.

If it were number one, the Magnum was already underwater. I didn't think Infante would drown his alter ego. If
number two, we might try searching every road that could
accommodate a semi-rig or transporter. And if number three,
logic could gather dust on the shelf. Infante might be reasonable all the way, or some of the time, or not at all. Or he might
change modes every time a bell rang in his noggin. The OHP
and Eugene forces were patched into the captain's neat com
set and, given time, would have all the people needed to
comb the area. But Satterlee decided against waiting and
prepared to lift up to some nearby lakes in her copter, to
check on the "drowned Magnum" hypothesis.

She had already lifted off when the OHP announced
paydirt. A hint from copter radar was followed in dense fog
by a highway cruiser. An old diesel transporter was stashed
away not far off Highway 58 near Willamette Pass. It was on
firm ground, fitted with wheel ramps, and had jacks under
one set of duals but nothing evidently wrong to justify the
jacks. It could have been there a week or more.

We heard Satterlee's cool contralto ask for a stakeout at the
transporter, and she was trotting back to the dome a few
minutes later. "This looks likely," she said, "but could
Infante have parked it himself during the past ten days? It's
crucial: he may have help in this, and there are"—her gaze
flickered past me—"complications if a second equipment
operator is in on this."

I knew, but let Kelley think it through for himself. Satterlee would value it at zip, coming from me. "Yes," Kelley
said slowly, "last weekend. We all knew we'd have both
Magnums up here for the Scortia demo."

"So did fifty people in my organization," Scortia rumbled. "It wasn't exactly a state secret."

Satterlee smiled, a brief sunburst of good teeth. "Which

gives us fifty more suspects—but no matter. The patrol officer took microscan prints from the transporter, and we can get positive print ID by video." She was standing as if relaxed, but if I had said boo she would have ventilated me by reflex action. I realized Satterlee had returned with the idea that somehow I was, after all, tied in with Infante. I liked her, and I didn't like her. Perhaps it was just that I couldn't blame her, but I wanted to.

I walked to the coffee pot, a huge old veteran that had seen campfires long before it saw the inside of a geodesic dome. I was nervous as a rabbi in Mecca, knowing that Meta Satterlee was gauging my every move.

Then the com set displayed a pair of apparently identical thumbprints. Eugene confirmed: George Infante had recently driven the transporter—and placed the jacks, too. The OHP man whistled. Satterlee shook her head wonderingly. "This little man has had some busy days, and some luck. How much is the Magnum Seven worth, Mr. Kelley?"

"Six hundred thou," Scortia replied instantly, accusingly.

"Or to some other firms, ten times that," Kelley answered the accusation.

"No telling how much it might be worth to factions of the underworld," Meta Satterlee said. "Keith Ames, I apologize for some reservations about you. I didn't say so, but . . ."

"The hell you didn't, it was all over your face. 'Act natural, Ames, or I'll letcha have it,' " I said, aping the old Bogart style.

She tried not to grin, failed, then sobered. "Sorry. But you have been in rough company. Bear in mind that your Mr. Infante has intimate connections among the Families."

"Meaning?"

"Meaning his reference groups are pretty restrictive," she said. "More simply: he is as likely to care about most human life as he is about a bug on his windshield. I don't want you to be in any doubt about that."

"Why me, especially?"

"Because this weather front is going to impede air search for days. Because Infante might run across dozens of hikers

or workers during that time. And because you're the only
person trained and able to cut that time short, if you're willing
to be deputized to run him down with me.''

It was Satterlee's idea to use the transporter as a jumpoff
point, and mine to run the Magnum Six in wheel mode up
Highway 58. We estimated that Infante could already be
nearing his transporter after several hours' head start in heavy
rains across the Diamond Peak wilderness area. There were
no navigable trails short of the highway, so we'd be unlikely
to cut him off. If we simply trailed him, we could only learn
what he'd done after he'd done it. Better, thought Satterlee,
to intercept him. I had a half-formed notion I could reason
with him if we managed to confront him from a position of
more or less equal footing. I believed as Satterlee did; real or
spurious, the equivalence of the two Magnums might alter
Infante's plans to muscle his way through, leaving still more
grief in his wake.

Kelley was right; with no load but Satterlee and her riot
gun behind me in the bubble, the Magnum Six exceeded
seventy miles an hour on level stretches. An OHP cruiser ran
interference for us most of the way and at two p.m. we were
at Infante's transporter. The lone stakeout man was considerably more nervous when we left him, having seen from
ground level what kind of vehicle he was to stop. Satterlee's
ammunition did not fit his weapon. His orders were to blow
tires if possible, then aim for the air plenums. Without a
prime mover Infante was only a hundred and sixty pounds of
maniac, instead of eight tons of it. Or he could make it sixty
tons if he chose to use a tree for a battering ram. Satterlee put
in an urgent call for more help at the stakeout. They were
promised within the hour.

Satterlee made an obvious target perched up behind me. *If*
he had a weapon capable of penetrating the bubble, and *if* his
own bubble were raised, Infante might bushwhack us from
cover. She saw the logic of hunkering down in the equipment
hopper. She didn't have to like it. I could receive police

frequency, but dared not reply and we had not thought to patch in an extension for Satterlee outside the bubble. Infante could monitor us, and I didn't want him hearing my voice or the strength of my signal.

A damnable dialog kept looping through my head. *What would I do if I were Infante?* The refrain was always . . . *anything at all.* Still, Satterlee made sense. If Infante did something really wild it would probably impede him. If her quarry were smartest he'd be most dangerous—and he'd rendezvous with the transporter.

I went to walk mode en route to a knoll a half-mile from the transporter. Poised on the forty-five-degree talus slope, sliding only a little, I heard a patrol copter pass in the low overcast. A few moments later a strong negative report signal reached my com set. And if they couldn't detect us with our turbine running, they might pass over Infante the same way. The ugly handgun Meta Satterlee gave me seemed like useless weight in my coverall. I had more confidence in the boosted slugs her riot gun carried. Though far from muscular, she handled herself with grace and confidence. The twelve-gauge would be a double armful but she was one smart, tough miz and I never doubted she could use it. If she got the chance. Trouble was, Infante was sheer entropy on wheels; one of those people who lives on uncertainty.

We shifted vantage points twice, getting further from the transporter as we eased toward where we thought Infante might approach. As I walked the Six carefully to keep the pneumatics quiet, my hopes went in both directions. It was like preparing for a race in chancy weather, you don't know whether to count on rain or shine, so you choose your equipment and hope. And get the butterfly-gut syndrome. And you live with it.

I was on the point of suggesting another move when Satterlee made a startled motion. I followed her outstretched hand and saw George Infante scrambling into his harness, not half a mile off in a creekbed. The Seven had been there—how long? I wondered if he knew we were there. It seemed he didn't; he came up from the gully on legs, but cautiously. As the Seven approached the transporter, Infante showed less caution. Satterlee guessed why.

I accelerated for the transporter and saw exhaust pluming from its old diesel. "He has it running," Satterlee shouted, pounding on my bubble. "He took our man out! Go, goddammit, *go!*"

I reached the road and went to wheel mode just as Infante vaulted from his Magnum. It was already on the transporter, but he hadn't chocked or strapped down. When he saw us he stiffened in recognition as if from electric shock. We were already too near for him to reach the cab-over. I wished we'd waited until he got started; a Magnum can outrun a transporter and eat holes through it.

Infante opted for his Magnum, pouring back into his harness as we neared shooting range. Ever see a quarterhorse rear back? When Infante rolled backward off that ramp, he went to walk mode so fast the Seven actually went up on her hind legs before setting off down a ravine.

Satterlee risked a shot and missed, nearly falling with the recoil. We exchanged glances as I whirled the Six on wheels down a gentler incline, hoping to snag Infante with something. Both of us saw the terrible, bleeding lump of meat wearing tatters of a police rain slicker. Infante had run over the stakeout man. I hoped it was after he was already dead.

I broke radio silence and called for everything in Oregon. Then I brodied as hard as I could. Infante had neatly suckered me into building up velocity downhill and had his magnificent, deadly goddamn Seven running *backward* toward the road.

I stayed in wheel mode but without pausing to think about it, momentarily engaged the legs to stilt us over a narrow gully. It saved us a few seconds. I dared not give Infante time to select a tree or he would have a bat and we, the baseball. We reached the road two hundred yards behind Infante and both Magnums went howling toward the main highway, turbines like sirens. Satterlee somehow put a shot directly into Infante's rear video sensor. To me it looked as though the

sensor had simply exploded. Infante raked his duralloy
gangsaw beam back, elbowed it, and made it a shield for his
bubble. I saw a long clean scar appear along the beam as
Satterlee fired again. She might as well have hit a bridge
pillar.

Infante saw the patrol cruiser's flasher before we did; he
crashed off into the brush parallel with the road. I shouted a
warning on my com set. Too late. As the cruiser rushed
toward us, Infante swept his extensor beam out across the
road and the driver barely had time to duck before a set of
wailing gangsaws took away his windshield and roof. They
tell me the officer lived.

I had gained over a hundred yards. On a hunch, I motioned
Satterlee out of the way and manipulated my beam out ahead
about fifteen yards. *What would I do if I were Infante?* Run
that third axle back as a feint to make us swerve, maybe. I
hoped he would, so I could hook onto it and set my brakes.

Craning his head back as he reached the road, his rear
video only a memory, Infante saw my strategy. Then he saw
the campers. Ahead, parked in disarray along the shore of a
small lake, a group of Oregonians were going about the
lovely business of fishing, rain or no rain.

Satterlee shouted something. All I caught was ". . .
hostages!'' If Infante got among those poor devils he could
grind all but one to powder and still have himself a ticket out.
He turned sharply but had to avoid an arroyo. I stilted it, by
God, something I could still teach him. Then I held my breath
and drove straight through a grove of aspen. Both Infante and
I saw that I had the momentum. I might, could, I surely *would*
ram him scant yards from the nearest camper. I shouted for
Satterlee to jump.

Angling his course off behind the parked vehicles, Infante
unlimbered a silenced handgun and fired through his bubble.
A mistake; the polymer turned the slug and gashed his own
bubble. Then he swung his duralloy beam out as if to sweep
three kids and a woman toward him. It probably would kill
them outright, at the rate he was moving. Racing parallel
with him, a covey of horrified campers screaming between

us, I lashed my extensor out and parried his with a jolt that nearly tore me from my harness. With a cry of anger, Satterlee flipped clear of my rear wheels. Her riot gun got thoroughly graunched but it proved one thing: the slug it fired in the process, blew out the right rear tire on my remoting axle.

Infante's gangsaw extensor waved in an arc, bent at its elbow. In one wild swing his gangsaws cut a swath through the back of his bubble. My parry had sideswiped the length of his duralloy beam, taking limit switches with it. For the first time, now, Infante had a real mechanical malf. Those switches prevent the beam from swinging back to hit the vehicle—but only when they work. Infante ducked away from the shards of plastic that spewed around him in his bubble, then turned away from me as he stopped the extensor beam.

I thought he intended to run, but instead, he fired at me through the hole his own gangsaws had made. A hole appeared in my bubble with the toll of a muted bell. The slug stopped on its way out. I thrust my gangsaw beam ahead as a shield and tried to accelerate, intending to ram him from behind. Part of me was scared puckerless, remembering what Infante would do to a man. And part of me, looking past that bullet-hole, just didn't give a good goddamn. Now I saw I could engage his rear axle if he slowed, or pursue him toward the lake if he went ahead. In either case he was beyond taking hostages. I rolled smashing through a litter of unattended camp equipment, boats and all. Infante ran for it in wheel mode, not realizing the trouble I had just to move straight with that deflated rear tire. I saw I would have to give it up, and went to walk mode faster than I thought possible. The Magnum Six leaped up on her legs with hard pneumatic coughs and I ran her straight at him. Still on wheels, looking back without his rear video, Infante laughed as he easily outdistanced me.

And found himself boxed.

He faced the lake on the right side, and an almost straight-up bluff on the left. Fifty yards ahead, the bluff came to the water's edge. It was thirty feet up, much too vertical even for a Magnum. And directly behind, I loped the Six with a spine-jarring stride. She staggered, but she was highballin'.

Infante risked going into the water to get around the bluff. Another mistake. It was a steep dropoff and even with her right-hand legs on full extension, the Seven tilted over at a dizzy, crazy angle. Her turbine swallowed water and seized explosively with a flashing exhaust spray. But he still had his air plenums. Popping his bubble back, Infante set his gangsaws howling as I raced down on him.

I ran my duralloy beam out and above him like a great arm to wave him back as he leaped and clawed up the brush-covered precipice, money spilling from his jacket. His gangsaws moaned just over my bubble and continued the arc Infante had programmed. He saw my beam and made a lightning decision to dive for the lake. With no limit switches, his beam elbowed at precisely the wrong angle, George Infante met his own gangsaws in mid-air.

Kneeling at the lake's edge, I lost the meal Scortia had fed me. Satterlee had the decency to let my brief spasm of heaves and tears pass before she approached. I washed up in the icy clear water and stood shaking, judging the path of Infante's murderous—and suicidal—weapon. It was still swinging in the same arc. There was no danger to me, so I climbed the chassis to the ruined bubble and flicked off the pneumatic valve switches. I did not look at the gangsaws again.

Satterlee refused to let me rig a sling on the Seven until a crew arrived to make the necessary police videotapes. I couldn't argue with a bruised miz who had, in a way, poked out Infante's eye when she obliterated his rear video. I owed her. I would've kissed her if she hadn't been a cop. After the first camera passes, the police asked me to move the Six back a bit, and I made myself think about something else. It had been gnawing at me since my first inkling that Infante himself was erratic.

And in a half-hour I isolated the malf in the Magnum Six. I erased all calibration programs, including mine and Infante's, and carefully recalibrated myself. The campers watched me with suspicion, unaware that I was only making a checkout. Well, maybe I played a little, running backwards and essaying that slanting gait Infante had used.

When Tom Kelley arrived in the police copter, I had good news. "Hey, your new solid-states in the Seven did more than you thought," I hailed him. "They damped out a malf that we put in, ourselves."

As I explained, Kelley furrowed his brow. "But it doesn't work that way," he complained. "Dammit, it won't program a random error, Keith."

I nodded. "I didn't say it was random. In some complex way it was predictable and not a random aberration. It was picked up and integrated by the multigraph functions monitoring his behavior. I checked out in the Six first; but remember, Infante was the first one you calibrated closely because his reflexes were so sharp."

Kelley was silent for a long moment. "So I built in a malf that the damping circuits cured in the Seven. Huh! I'm smarter *and* dumber than I thought I was. Well, we don't know enough about psychophysics, but systems theory should'a told me," Kelley grumbled. "When you have a sane man who overrides a master control, the *real* master control is the man. That's why you were better in the Six than Infante was."

"Come on," I said, remembering Infante's panache in a Magnum

"Infante was flashy; you were predictable, Keith. Your manual override was really a mental override. That makes a malf fundamentally a feedback-correctable item. No wonder Infante thought the Six was nuts, it was feeding his own aberrations back to him amplified—worse than it was for you. That kind of feedback might push a man over the brink; I dunno. I do know that the original malf was Infante."

I gazed out on the lake, where calm gutty Meta Satterlee watched police gather most of eighty-five thousand dollars in bills, like leaves on the quiet water. "I wonder if his malf could've been traced," I said.

But the real world is not a neat circuit. As the OHP captain predicted, we never learned how, or even if, George Infante managed so much by himself. Nor what plans he had for the Magnum Seven.

Kelley's crystal ball wasn't bad, either. By the time I trained Scortia's operators, there were Magnums enough to go around and orders enough to please him. Kelley got his bonus in media coverage. And I got mine. It cost Howard Scortia a bundle to get his pocketwatch duplicated.

Extrapolation is a dangerous game when you have to live on it. My father-in-law, a retired lumberman who used to build his own equipment, had me wagging my tail after he read "Malf". "Why, son," he rumbled, grinning over my fictional machines, "I think a man might downright build a thing like that!" Well—maybe; and he would be that man if anybody could do it. Still, I wasn't worried that anybody might lose a megabuck trying to develop the hardware I roughed out.

In the aerospace industry, though, I used to worry a lot. It's a sobering sight to read a cost proposal for some design you're only half-sure will work; because only then do you fully appreciate that someone is risking ten million dollars on what is, at the moment, science fiction.

My track record at predicting the future of military gadgetry was pretty decent, actually. Bragtime: on one occasion I cobbled up a counterinsurgent weapon design that was ridiculed by a top technical man. Naturally the idea was dropped. A year later, another company savant returned from a government proving ground where he'd watched tests of our competitor's new stuff. "Remember your insurgency gadget, Deano? Supposed to be roughly as effective as a mosquito? Well, I saw it work yesterday." Cynical headshake; chuckle: "Jeez, look out for those mosquitoes!"

And no, I am not going to tell you about the ideas they did fund, that didn't work. A guy's got some pride . . .

If there's one salient trick to designing gadgets of the future, it is probably in setting priorities for performance criteria. I recall a rocket that was developed to maximize specific impulse instead of burnt velocity. I ran a quick-&-dirty mass fraction check on it, shambled babbling to the project engineer, and got shushed for telling him what he already knew, i.e. it could've been improved by a ten-year-old with a hacksaw. Somewhere up the line, at political decision-making levels, the wrong criterion was stressed. That's fact, not guesswork.

And if I had to pick one class of military vehicles in the following article that has the highest potential, I'd say, "Look out for those mosquitoes." But that's guesswork, not fact.

Vehicles for Future Wars

Long before the first ram-tipped bireme scuttled across the Aegean, special military vehicles were deciding the outcomes of warfare. If we can judge from the mosaics at Ur, the Mesopotamians drove four-horsepower chariots thundering into battle in 2500 B.C.; and bas-reliefs tell us that some Assyrian genius later refined the design so his rigs could be quickly disassembled for river crossings. In more recent times, some passing strange vehicles have been pressed into military service—Hannibal's alp-roving elephants and six hundred troop-toting Paris taxicabs being two prime examples. Still, people had seen elephants and taxis before; application, not design, was the surprise element. Today, military vehicle design itself is undergoing rapid change in almost all venues: land, sea, air, space. Tomorrow's war chariots are going to be mind-bogglers!

Well, how will military vehicles of the next century differ from today's? Many of the details are imponderable at the moment, but we can make some generalizations that should hold true for the future. And we can hazard specific guesses at the rest.

It's possible to list a few primary considerations for the design of a military vehicle without naming its specific functions. It should have higher performance than previous vehicles; it should be more dependable; and it should be more cost-effective. Those three criteria cover a hundred others including vulnerability, speed, firepower, maintenance, manufacturing, and even the use of critical materials. Any new design that doesn't trade off one of those criteria to meet others is likely to be very, very popular.

It may be fortunate irony for peace lovers that the most

militarily advanced countries are those with the biggest problems in cost-effectiveness. Any nation that pours billions into a fleet of undersea missile ships must think twice before junking the whole system—tenders, training programs and all—for something radically different. That's one reason why the U.S. Navy, for example, hasn't already stuffed its latter-generation POLARIS missles (after POSEIDON and TRIDENT, what's next?) into the smaller, faster, more widely dispersed craft. A certain continuity is essential as these costly systems evolve; otherwise, costs escalate like mad.

Still, new systems do get developed, starting from tiny study contracts through feasibility demonstrations to parallel development programs. There is probably a hundred-knot Navy ACV (Air Cushion Vehicle) skating around somewhere with an old POLARIS hidden in her guts, working out the details of a post-TRIDENT weapon delivery system. Even if *we* don't already have one, chances are the Soviets do—and if we can prove that, we'll have one, all righty.

The mere concept of POLARIS-packing ACV's says little about the system design, though. We can do better but, before taking rough cuts at specific new designs, it might be better to look at the power plants and materials that should be popular in the near future.

POWER PLANTS

Internal combustion engines may be with us for another generation, thanks to compact designs and new fuel mixtures. Still, the only reason why absurdly powerful Indianapolis cars don't use turbines now is that the turbine is outlawed by Indy officials: too good, too quiet, too dependable. In other words, the turbine doesn't promise as much drama, sound and fury—perfect reasons for a military vehicle designer to choose the turbine, since he doesn't want drama; he wants a clean mission.

Turbines can be smaller for a given output if they can operate at higher temperatures and higher RPM. Superalloy turbine buckets may be replaced by hyperalloys or cermets.

Oiled bearings may be replaced by magnetic types. Automated manufacturing could bring the cost of a turbine power unit down so low that the unit could be replaced at every refueling. In short, it should be possible to design the power plant and fuel tanks as a unit to be mated to the vehicle in moments.

The weapons designer won't be slow to see that high-temperature turbines can lend themselves to MHD (magnetohydrodynamics) application. If a weapon laser needs vast quantities of electrical energy, and if that energy can be taken from a hot stream of ionized gas, then the turbine may become the power source for both the vehicle and its electrical weapons. Early MHD power plants were outrageously heavy, and required rocket propellants to obtain the necessary working temperatures. Yet there are ways to bootstrap a gas stream into conductive plasma, including previously stored electrical energy and seeding the gas stream with chemicals. If the vehicle needs a lot of electrical energy and operates in a chemically active medium—air will do handily—then a turbine or motor-driven impeller of some kind may be with us for a long time to come.

Chemically fueled rockets are made to order for MHD. If the vehicle is to operate in space, an MHD unit could be coupled to a rocket exhaust to power all necessary electrical systems. The problem with chemical rockets, as everybody knows, is their ferocious thirst. If a vehicle is to be very energetic for very long using chemical rockets, it will consist chiefly of propellant tanks. And it will require careful refueling, unless the idea is to junk the craft when its tanks are empty. Refueling with cryogenic propellant—liquid hydrogen and liquid fluorine are good bets from the stored-energy standpoint—tends to be complicated and slow. By the end of this century, rocket-turbine hybrids could be used for vehicles that flit from atmosphere to vacuum and back again. The turbine could use atmospheric oxidizer while the vehicle stores its own in liquid form for use in space. The hybrid makes sense because, when oxidizer is available in the atmosphere, the turbine can use it with reduced propellant expenditure. Besides, the turbine is very dependable and its support equipment relatively cheap.

Some cheap one-shot vehicles, designed to use minimum support facilities, can operate with power plants of simple manufacture. When their backs neared the wall in World War II, the Japanese turned to very simple techniques in producing their piloted "Baka" bomb. It was really a stubby twin-tailed glider, carried aloft by a bomber and released for a solid rocket-powered final dash onto our shipping. The Nazis didn't deliberately opt for suicide aircraft, but they managed something damned close to it with the Bachem "Natter". Bachem hazarded a design that could be produced in under 1,000 man-hours per copy, a manned, disposable flying shotgun featuring rocket ascent and parachute recovery. 'Hazard' was the operative word—or maybe they started with factory seconds. On its only manned ascent, the Natter began to shed parts and eventually blended its pilot with the rest of the wreckage. Yet there was nothing wrong with the basic idea and a nation with low industrial capacity can be expected to gobble up similar cheapies in the future using simple, shortlife power plants.

There's reason to suspect that simple air-breathing jet engines such as the Schmidt pulsejet can also operate as ramjets by clever modifications to pulse vanes and duct inlet geometry. In this way, sophisticated design may permit a small have-not nation to produce air-breathing power plants to challenge those of her richer neighbors, in overall utility if not in fuel consumption. A pulsejet develops thrust at rest, and could boost a vehicle to high subsonic velocity where ramjets become efficient. Supersonic ramjets need careful attention to the region just ahead of the duct inlet, where a spike-like cowl produces exactly the right disturbance in the incoming air to make the ramjet efficient at a given speed. A variable-geometry spike greatly improves the efficiency of a ramjet over a wide range of airspeeds, from sonic to Mach five or so. We might even see pulse-ram-rocket tribrids using relatively few moving parts, propelling vehicles from rest at sea level into space and back.

For a nation where cost-effectiveness or material shortages overshadow all else, then, the simplicity of the pulse-ram-rocket could make it popular. A turbine-rocket hybrid would yield better fuel economy, though. The choice might well depend on manufacturing capability; and before you can complain that rockets absolutely demand exacting tolerances in manufacturing, think about strap-on solid rockets.

MHD is another possible power source as we develop more lightweight MHD hardware and learn to use megawatt quantities of electrical energy directly in power plants. An initial jolt from fuel cells or even a short-duration chemical rocket may be needed to start the MHD generator. Once in operation, the MHD unit could use a combination of electron beams and jet fuel to heat incoming air in a duct, and at that point the system could reduce its expenditure of tanked oxidizer. We might suspect that the MHD system would need a trickle of chemical, such as a potassium salt, to boost plasma conductivity especially when the MHD is idling. By the year 2050, MHD design may be so well developed that no chemical seeding of the hot gas would be necessary at all. This development could arise from magnetic pinch effects, or from new materials capable of withstanding very high temperatures for long periods while retaining dielectric properties.

It almost seems that an MHD power plant would be a perpetual motion machine, emplaced in an atmosphere-breathing vehicle that could cruise endlessly. But MHD is an energy-conversion system, converting heat to electricity as the conductive plasma (*i.e.*, the hot gas stream) passes stationary magnets. The vehicle would need its own compact heat generator, perhaps even a closed-loop gaseous uranium fission reactor for large craft. A long-range cruise vehicle could be managed this way, but eventually the reactor would need refueling. Still, it'd be risky to insist that we'll *never* find new sources of energy which would provide MHD power plants capable of almost perpetual operation.

Whether or not MHD justifies the hopes of power plant people, other power sources may prove more compact, lighter, and—at least in operation—simpler. Take, for example, a kilogram of Californium 254, assuming an orbital manufacturing plant to produce it. This isotope decays fast enough that its heat output is halved after roughly two months; but initially the steady ravening heat output from one kilo of the stuff would be translatable to something like 10,000 horsepower! No matter that a kilo of Californium 254 is, at present, a stupefyingly immense quantity; ways can probably be found to produce it in quantity. Such a compact heat source could power ramjets without fuel tanks, or it could vaporize a working fluid such as water. In essence, the isotope would function as a simple reactor, but without damping rods or other methods of controlling its decay. Like it or not, the stuff would be cooking all the time. Perhaps its best use would be for small, extended-range, upper-atmosphere patrol craft. There's certainly no percentage in letting it sit in storage.

For propulsion in space, several other power plants seem attractive. Early nuclear weapon tests revealed that graphite-covered steel spheres survived a twenty kiloton blast at a distance of ten meters. The Orion project grew from this datum, and involved nothing less in concept than a series of nukes detonated behind the baseplate of a large vehicle. As originally designed by Ted Taylor and Freeman Dyson, such a craft could be launched from the ground, but environmentalists quake at the very idea. The notion is not at all far-fetched from an engineering standpoint and might yet be used to power city-sized space dreadnoughts of the next century if we utterly fail to perfect more efficient methods of converting matter into energy. Incidentally, the intermittent explosion rocket drive was tested by Orion people, using conventional explosives in scale models. Wernher von Braun was evidently unimpressed with the project until he saw films of a model in flight.

This kind of experiment goes back at least as far as Goddard, who tested solid-propellant repeater rockets before turning to his beloved, persnickety, high-impulse liquid fuels. No engineer doubts there'll be lots of glitches between a small model using conventional explosives, and a megaton-sized version cruising through space by means of nuke blasts. But it probably will work, and God knows it doesn't have a whole slew of moving parts. Structurally, in fact, it may be a more robust solution for space dreadnoughts than are some other solutions. It seems more elegant to draw electrical power from the sun to move your space dreadnought, for instance—until we realize that the solar cell arrays would be many square kilometers in area. Any hefty acceleration with those gossamer elements in place would require quintupling the craft's mass to keep the arrays from buckling during maneuvers. The added mass would be concentrated in the solar array structure and its interface with the rest of the craft.

On the other hand, there's something to be said for any system that draws its power from an inexhaustible source—and the Orion system falls short in that department since it must carry its nukes with it. The mass driver is something else again. It can use a nearby star for power, though it must be supplied with some mass to drive. Lucky for dwellers of this particular star system: we can always filch a few megatons of mass from the asteroid belt.

The mass driver unit is fairly simple in principle. It uses magnetic coils to hurl small masses away at high speed, producing thrust against the coils. Gerard O'Neill has demonstrated working models of the mass driver. In space, a mass driver could be powered by a solar array or a closed-cycle reactor, and its power consumption would not be prohibitively high. The thrust of the device is modest—too low for planetary liftoff as currently described. Its use in an atmosphere would be limited, power source aside, by aerodynamic shock waves generated by the mass accelerated to hypersonic velocity within the acceleration coils.

For fuel mass, O'Neill suggests munching bits from a handy asteroid—though almost any available mass would do. The mass need not be magnetic since it can be accelerated in metal containers, then allowed to continue while the metal 'buckets' are decelerated for re-use.

In case you're not already ahead of me, notice that the mass driver offers a solution to the problem of 'space junk' that already litters orbital pathways. The mass-driver craft can schlep around until it locates some hardware nobody values anymore, dice and compact it into slugs, feed it into the mass driver buckets, and hurl the compacted slugs away during its next maneuver. Of course, the craft's computer will have to keep tabs on whatever is in line with the ejected masses, since the slugs will be potentially as destructive as meteorites as they flee the scene. Imagine being whacked by a ten-kilogram hunk of compacted aluminum garbage moving at escape velocity!

Solar plasma, the stream of ionized particles radiated by stars, has been suggested as a 'solar wind' to be tapped by vast gossamer sails attached to a space vehicle—with the pressure of light radiation adding to the gentle 'wind'. Carl Wiley, writing as 'Russell Saunders', outlined the space windjammer proposal in 1951. His sail was envisioned as a parachute-like arrangement of approximately hemispherical shape, made of lithium, many square kilometers in area. Wiley argued that, while such a craft could hardly survive any environment but space, it could be made to revolve with its sail as it circles a planetary mass. By presenting a profile view of the sail as it swings toward the sun, and the full circular view as it swings away again, the craft could gradually build up enough velocity to escape the planet entirely. Even granting this scheme a sail which can be quickly deflated or rearranged into windsock proportions, it seems unlikely that a starsailer could move very effectively into a solar wind in the same way that a boat tacks upwind. The interstellar yachtsman has an advantage, though: he can predict the sources of his winds. He cannot be sure they won't vary in intensity, though; which leads to scenarios of craft becalmed between several stars until one star burns out, or becomes a nova.

It takes a very broad brush to paint a military operation of such scale that solar sails and mass drivers would be popular as power plants. These prime movers are very cost-effective, but they need a lot of time to traverse a lot of space. By the time we have military missions beyond Pluto, we may also have devices which convert matter completely into photons, yielding a photon light drive. In the meantime, nuclear reactors can provide enough heat to vaporize fuel mass for high-thrust power plants in space. So far as we know, the ultimate space drive would use impinging streams of matter and antimatter in a thrust chamber. This is perhaps the most distant of far-out power plants, and presumes that we can learn to make antimatter do as we say. Until recently, there was grave doubt that any particle of antimatter could be stable within our continuum. That doubt seems to be fading quickly, according to reports from Geneva. Antiprotons have been maintained in circular paths for over eighty hours. The demonstration required a nearly perfect vacuum, since any contact between antimatter and normal matter means instant apocalypse for both particles. And as the particles are mutually annihilated, they are converted totally into energy. We aren't talking about your workaday one or two percent conversion typical of nuclear weapon, understand: total means *total*. A vehicle using an antimatter drive would be able to squander energy in classic military fashion!

The power plants we've discussed so far all lend themselves to aircraft and spacecraft. Different performance standards apply to land- and water-based vehicles, which must operate quietly, without lethal effluents, and slowly at least during docking stages. Turbines can be quiet, but they produce strong infrared signatures and they use a lot of fuel, limiting their range somewhat. When you cannot be quick, you are wise to be inconspicuous. This suggests that electric motors might power wheeled transports in the near future, drawing power from lightweight storage batteries or fuel cells. The fuel cell oxidizes fuel to obtain current, but the process generates far less waste heat than a turbine does. The fuel cell also permits fast refueling—with a hydride, or perhaps hydrogen—which gives the fuel cell a strong advantage over conventional batteries. However, remember that the fuel cell 'burns' fuel. No fair powering a moonrover or a submarine by fuel cells without an oxidizer supply on board.

When weight is not a crucial consideration, the designer can opt for heavier power plants that have special advantages. The flywheel is one method of storing energy without generating much heat as that energy is tapped. A flywheel can be linked to a turbine or other drive unit to provide a hybrid engine. For brief periods when a minimal infrared signature is crucial, the vehicle could operate entirely off the flywheel. Fuel cells and electric motors could replace the turbine in this hybrid system. Very large cargo vehicles might employ reactors; but the waste heat of a turbine, reactor, or other heat engine is always a disadvantage when heatseeking missiles are lurking near. It's likely that military cargo vehicles will evolve toward sophisticated hybrid power plants that employ heat engines in low-vulnerability areas, switching to flywheel, beamed power, or other stored-energy systems producing little heat when danger is near. As weapons become more sophisticated, there may be literally almost no place far from danger—which implies development of hybrid power plants using low-emission fuel cells and flywheels for wheeled vehicles.

MATERIALS

Perhaps the most direct way to improve a vehicle's overall performance is to increase its payload fraction, *i.e.*, the proportion of the system's gross weight that's devoted to payload. If a given craft can be built with lighter materials, or using more energetic material for fuel, that craft can carry more cargo and/or can carry it farther, faster.

Many solids, including metals, are crystalline masses. Entire journals are devoted to the study of crystal growth because, among other things, the alignment and size of crystals in a material profoundly affect that material's strength. Superalloys in turbine blades have complex crystalline structures, being composed of such combinations as cobalt, chromium, tungsten, tantalum, carbon, and refractory metal carbides. These materials may lead to hyperalloys capable of sustaining the thermal shock of a nuke at close range.

As we've already noted, graphite-coated steel objects have shown some capcity to survive a nuke at close quarters. There may be no alloy quite as good as the old standby, graphite, especially when we note that graphite is both far cheaper and lighter in weight. Superalloys aren't the easiest things to machine, either. Anybody who's paid to have superalloy parts machined risked cardiac arrest when he saw the bill. Graphite is a cinch to machine; hell, it even lubricates itself.

More conventional alloys of steel, aluminum, and titanium may be around for a long time, with tempering and alloying processes doubling the present tensile strengths. When we begin processing materials in space, it may be possible to grow endless crystals which can be spun into filament bundles. A metal or quartz cable of such stuff may have tensile strength in excess of a million pounds per square inch. For that matter, we might grow doped crystals in special shapes to exacting tolerances, which could lead to turbine blades and lenses vastly superior to anything we have today. Until fairly recently, quartz cable had a built-in limitation at the point where the cable was attached to other structural members. Steel cable terminals can simply be swaged—squeezed—over a steel cable, but quartz can't take the shear forces; you can cut through quartz cable with a pocketknife. This problem is being solved by adhesive potting of the quartz cable end into specially formed metal terminals. Your correspondent was crushed to find himself a few months behind the guy who applied for the first patents in this area. The breakthrough takes on more importance when we consider the advantages of cheap dielectric cable with high flexibility and extremely high tensile strength at a fraction of the weight of comparable steel cable. Very large structures of the future are likely to employ quartz cable tension members with abrasion-resistant coatings.

Vehicles are bound to make more use of composite materials as processing gets more sophisticated. Fiberglass is a composite of glass fibers in a resin matrix; but sandwich materials are composites too. A wide variety of materials can be formed into honeycomb structures to gain great stiffness-to-weight characteristics. An air-breathing hypersonic craft might employ molybdenum honeycomb facing a hyperalloy inner skin forming an exhaust duct. The honeycomb could be cooled by ducting relatively cool gas through it. On the other side of the honeycomb might be the craft's outer skin; say, a composite of graphite and high-temperature polymer. Advanced sandwich composites are already in use, and show dramatic savings in vehicle weight. The possible combinations in advanced sandwich composites are almost infinite, with various layers tailored to a given chemical, structural, or electrical characteristic. Seventeen years ago, an experimental car bumper used a composite of stainless steel meshes between layers of glass and polymer to combine lightness with high impact resistance. A racing car under test that year had a dry weight of just 540 lb., thanks to a chassis built up from sandwich composite with a paper honeycomb core. The writer can vouch for the superior impact and abrasion resistance of this superlight stuff, which was all that separated his rump from macadam when the little car's rear suspension went gaga during a test drive. The vehicle skated out of a corner and spun for a hundred meters on its chassis pan before coming to rest. The polymer surface of the pan was scratched up a bit, yet there was no structural damage whatever. But we considered installing a porta-potty for the next driver . . .

Today, some aircraft use aluminum mesh in skins of epoxy and graphite fiber. The next composite might be titanium mesh between layers of boron fiber in a silicone polymer matrix. The chief limitation of composites seems to be the adhesives that bond the various materials together. It may be a long time before we develop a glue that won't char, peel, or embrittle when subjected to temperature variations of hypersonic aircraft. The problem partly explains the metallurgists' interest in welding dissimilar metals. If we can find suitable combinations of inert atmosphere, alloying, and electrical welding techniques, we can simply (translation: not so simply) lay a metal honeycomb against dissimilar metal surfaces and zap them all into a single piece.

Several fibers are competing for primacy in the search for better composites; among them boron, graphite, acetal homopolymer, and aramid polymers. Boron may get the nod for structures that need to be superlight without a very high temperature requirement, but graphite looks like the best bet in elevated temperature regimes. Sandia Laboratories has ginned up a system to test graphite specimens for short-term high temperature phenomena including fatigue, creed, and stress-rupture. The specimens are tested at very high heating rates. It's easy to use the report of this test rig as a springboard for guessing games. Will it test only graphite? Very high heating rates might mean they're testing leading edges intended to survive vertical re-entry at orbital speeds. Then again, there's a problem with the heat generated when an antitank projectile piles into a piece of Soviet armor. Do we have materials that can punch through before melting into vapor? And let's not forget armor intended to stand up for a reasonable time against a power laser. For several reasons, and outstanding heat conductivity is only one of them, graphite looks good to this guesser. If the Sandia system isn't looking into antilaser armor, something like it almost certainly will be—and soon.

Before leaving the topic of materials, let's pause to note research into jet fuels. A gallon of JP-4 stores roughly 110,000 Btu. Some new fuels pack an additional 65,000 Btu into a gallon. Even if the new fuels are slightly heavier, the fuel tank can be smaller. The result is extended range. It seems reasonable to guess that JP-50, when it comes along, will double the energy storage of JP-4.

VEHICLE CONFIGURATIONS

Now that we're in an age of microminiaturization, we have a new problem in defining a vehicle. We might all agree that a vehicle carries something, but start wrangling over just how small the 'something' might be. An incendiary bullet carries a tiny blazing chemical payload; but does that make the bullet a vehicle? In the strictest sense, probably yes. But a bullet is obviously not a limiting case—leaving that potential pun unspent—when very potent things of almost *no* mass can be carried by vehicles of insect size.

Payloads of very small vehicles could be stored information, or might be a few micrograms of botulism or plutonium, perhaps even earmarked for a specific human target. Ruling out live bats and insects as carriers, since they are normally pretty slapdash in choosing the right target among possibly hundreds of opportunities, we could develop extremely small rotary-winged craft and smarten them with really stupendous amounts of programming without exceeding a few milligrams of total mass. A swarm of these inconspicuous mites would be expensive to produce, but just may be the ultimate use for 'clean room' technology in which the U.S. has a temporary lead.

The mites would be limited in range and top speed, so that a hypersonic carrier vehicle might be needed to bring them within range of the target like a greyhound with plague fleas. The carrier would then slow to disgorge its electromechanical parasites. One immediately sees visions of filters to stop them; and special antifilter mites to punch holes in the filters; and sensors to detect antifilter mite action; and so on.

It's hard to say just how small the mites could be after a hundred years of development. One likely generalization is that the smaller the payload, the longer the delay before the payload's effect will be felt. Take the examples of plutonium or botulism: a human victim of either payload can continue performing his duties for a longer time—call it mean time before failure—if he is victimized by a tinier chunk of poison. Some canny theorists will be chortling, about now, at the vision of a billion mites slowly building a grapefruit-sized mass of plutonium in some enemy bunker. That's one option, for sure. But the blast, once critical mass is reached, would be ludicrously small when compared with other nuke mechanisms.

The best use of mites might be as spies, storing data while hunkered down in an inconspicuous corner of the enemy's

war room, scaring the bejeezus out of the local spiders. Or
would the enemy's spiders, too, be creatures of the clean
room? Pick your own scenario . . .

There is no very compelling reason why mites couldn't
actually resemble tiny flies, with gimbaled ornithopter wings
to permit hovering or fairly rapid motion in any direction.
There may be a severe limitation to their absolute top speed in
air, depending on the power plant. Partly because of square/
cube law problems, a mite could be seriously impeded by
high winds or rain. A device weighing a few milligrams or
less would have the devil's own time beating into a strong
headwind. Perhaps a piezoelectrically driven vibrator could
power the tiny craft; that might be simpler than a turbine and
tougher to detect. Whatever powers the mite, it would probably not result in cruise speeds over a hundred miles an hour
unless an antimatter drive is somehow shoehorned into the
chassis. Even with this velocity limitation, though, the mites
could probably maneuver much more quickly than their organic counterparts—which brings up a second dichotomy in
vehicles.

Information storage is constantly making inroads into the
need for human pilots, as the Soviets proved in their unmanned lunar missions. A military vehicle that must carry
life-support equipment for anything as delicate as live meat,
is at a distinct disadvantage versus a similar craft that can turn
and stop at hundreds of g's. Given a human cargo, vehicle
life-support systems may develop to a point where blood-
streams are temporarily thickened, passengers are quick-
frozen and (presumably) harmlessly thawed, or some kind of
null-inertia package is maintained to keep the passenger
comfortable under five-hundred-gravity angular acceleration. During the trip, it's a good bet that the vehicle would be
under computer guidance, unless the mission is amenable to
very limited acceleration. It also seems likely that women can
survive slightly higher acceleration than men—an old s.f.
idea with experimental verification from the people at Brooks
AFB. Women's primacy in this area may be marginal, but
it's evidently true that Wonder Woman can ride a hotter ship

than Superman. It's also true that your pocket calculator can take a jouncier ride than either of them. In short, there will be increasing pressure to depersonalize military missions, because a person is a tactical millstone in the system.

Possibly the most personalized form of vehicle, and one of the more complex per cubic centimeter, would be one that the soldier wears. Individualized battle armor, grown massive enough to require servomechanical muscles, could be classed as a vehicle for the wearer. The future for massive man-amplifying battle dress doesn't look very bright, though. If the whole system stands ten meters tall it will present an easier target; and if it is merely very dense, it will pose new problems of traction and maneuverability. Just to focus on one engineering facet of the scaled-up bogus android, if the user hurls a grenade with his accustomed arm-swing using an arm extension fifteen feet long, the end of that extension will be moving at roughly Mach 1. Feedback sensors would require tricky adjustment for movement past the trans-sonic region, and every arm-wave could become a thunderclap! The user will have to do some fiendishly intricate rethinking when he is part of this system—but then, so does a racing driver. Man-amplified battle armor may pass through a certain vogue, just as moats and tanks have done. The power source for this kind of vehicle might be a turbine, until heat-seeking missiles force a change to fuel cells or, for lagniappe, a set of flywheels mounted in different parts of the chassis. The rationale for several prime movers is much the same as for the multi-engined aircraft: you can limp home on a leg and a prayer. Aside from the redundancy feature, mechanical power transmission can be more efficient when the prime mover is near the part it moves. Standing ready for use, a multiflywheel battle dress might even sound formidable, with the slightly varying tones of several million-plus RPM flywheels keening in the wind.

For certain applications including street fighting, there may be a place for the lowly skateboard. It's a fact that the Soviets have bought pallet loads of the sidewalk surfers, ostensibly to see if they're a useful alternative to mass transit.

It's also true that enthusiasts in the U.S. are playing with motorized versions which, taking the craze only a step further, could take a regimental combat team through a city in triple time. But if two of those guys ever collide at top speed while carrying explosives, the result may be one monumental street pizza.

No matter how cheap, dependable, and powerful, a military vehicle must be designed with an eye cocked toward enemy weapons. Nuclear warheads already fit into missiles the size of a stovepipe, and orbital laser-firing satellites are only a few years away. A vehicle that lacks both speed and maneuverability will become an easier target with each passing year. By the end of this century, conventional tanks and very large surface ships would be metaphors of the Maginot Line, expensive fiascos for the users.

The conventional tank, despite its popularity with the Soviets, seems destined for the junk pile. Its great weight limits its speed and maneuverability, and several countries already have antitank missile systems that can be carried by one or two men. Some of these little bolides penetrate all known tank armor and have ranges of several kilometers. Faced with sophisticated multi-stage tank killer missiles, the tank designers have come up with layered armor skirts to disperse the fury of a high-velocity projectile before it reaches the tank's vitals. Not to be outdone, projectile designers have toyed with ultrahigh-velocity projectiles that are boosted almost at the point of impact. It may also be possible to develop alloy projectile tips that won't melt or vaporize until they've punched through the tank's skirt layers. Soon, the tanks may employ antimissile missiles of their own, aimed for very short-range kills against incoming antitank projectiles. This counterpunch system would just about *have* to be automated; no human crew could react fast enough. The actual mechanism by which the counterpunch would deflect or destroy the incoming projectile could be a shaped concussion wave, or a shotgun-like screen of pellets, or both. And it's barely possible that a tank's counterpunch could be a laser that picks off the projectile, though there might not be time to readjust the laser beam for continued impingement on the projectile as it streaks or jitters toward the tank.

Given the huge costs of manufacturing and maintaining a tank, and the piddling costs of supplying infantry with tank-killing hardware, the future of the earthbound battle tank looks bleak. It's wishful thinking to design tanks light enough to be ACV's. Race cars like the Chaparral and the formidable Brabham F1, using suction for more traction, are highly maneuverable on smooth terrain. Still, they'd be no match for homing projectiles; and with no heavy armor or cargo capacity for a counterpunch system, they'd almost surely be gallant losers.

All this is not to suggest that the tank's missions will be discarded in the future, but those missions will probably be performed by very different craft. We'll take up those vehicles under the guise of scout craft.

More vulnerable than the tank, an aircraft carrier drawing 50,000 tons on the ocean surface is just too easy to find, too sluggish to escape, and too tempting for a nuclear strike. It's more sensible to build many smaller vessels, each capable of handling a few aircraft—a point U.S. strategists are already arguing. Ideally the aircraft would take off and land vertically, as the Hawker Harrier does. Following this strategy, carriers could be spread over many square kilometers of ocean reducing vulnerability of a squadron of aircraft.

A pocket aircraft carrier might draw a few hundred tons while cruising on the surface. Under battle conditions the carrier could become an ACV, its reactor propelling it several hundred kilometers per hour with hovering capability and high maneuverability. Its shape would have to be clean aerodynamically, perhaps with variable-geometry catamaran hulls.

Undersea craft are harder to locate. Radar won't reveal a submerged craft, and sonar—a relatively short-range detection system unless the sea floor is dotted with sensor networks—must deal with the vagaries of ocean currents, and temperature and pressure gradients as well as pelagic animals. There may be a military niche for large submersibles for many years to come, perhaps as mother ships and, as savant Frank Herbert predicted a long time ago, cargo vessels.

A submerged mother ship would be an ideal base for a fleet of small hunter-killer or standoff missile subs. These small craft could run at periscope depth for a thousand miles on fuel cells, possibly doubling their range with jettisonable external hydride tanks. A small sub built largely of composites would not be too heavy to double as an ACV in calm weather, switching from ducted propellers to ducted fans for this high-speed cruise mode. From this, it is only a step to a canard swing-wing craft, with schnorkel and communication gear mounted on the vertical fin. The sub packs a pair of long-range missiles on her flanks just inside the ACV skirt. The filament-wound crew pod could detach for emergency flotation. High-speed ACV cruise mode might limit its range to a few hundred kilometers. The swing wings are strictly for a supersonic dash at low altitude, using ducted fan and perhaps small auxiliary jets buried in the aft hull, drawing air from the fan plenum.

Heavy seas might rule out the ACV mode, but if necessary the little sub can broach vertically like a POSEIDON before leveling off into its dash mode. With a gross weight of some thirty tons it would require some additional thrust for the first few seconds of flight—perhaps a rocket using hydride fuel and liquid oxygen. The oxygen tank might be replenished during undersea loitering periods. Since the sub would pull a lot of g's when re-entering the water in heavy seas, the nose of the craft would be built up with boron fibers and polymer as a composite honeycomb wound with filaments. The idea of a flying submersible may stick in a few craws, until we reflect that the SUBROC is an unmanned flying submersible in development for over a decade.

On land, military cargo vehicles will feature bigger, wider, low-profile tires in an effort to gain all-terrain capability. Tires could be permanently inflated by supple closed-cell foams under little or no pressure. If the cargo mass is distributed over enough square meters of tire 'footprint', the vehicle could challenge tracked craft in snow, or churn through swamps with equal aplomb. The vehicle itself will probably have a wide squat profile (tires may be as high as the cargo section) and for more maneuverability, the vehicle can be hinged in the middle. All-wheel drive, of course, is *de rigeur*.

It's a popular notion that drive motors should be in the wheels, but this adds to the unsprung portion of the vehicle's weight. For optimal handling over rough terrain, the vehicle must have a minimal unsprung weight fraction—which means the motors should be part of the sprung mass, and not in the wheels which, being between the springing subsystem and the ground, are unsprung weight.

Relatively little serious development has been done on heavy torque transmission via flexible bellows. When designers realize how easily a pressurized bellows can be inspected, they may begin using this means to transmit torque to the wheels of cargo vehicles.

The suspension of many future wheeled vehicles may depart radically from current high-performance practice. Most high-performance vehicle suspensions now involve wishbone-shaped upper and lower arms, connecting the wheel's bearing block to the chassis. A rugged alternative would be sets of rollers mounted fore and aft of the bearing block, sliding vertically in chassis-mounted tracks. The tracks could be curved, and even adjustable and slaved to sensors so that, regardless of surface roughness or vehicle attitude above that surface, the wheels would be oriented to gain maximum adhesion. Turbines, flywheels, fuel cells and reactors are all good power plant candidates for wheeled vehicles.

The bodies of these vehicles will probably be segments of smooth-faced composite, and don't be surprised if two or three segment shapes are enough to form the whole shell. This is cost-effectiveness with a vengeance; one mold produces all doors and hatches, another all wheel and hardware skirts, and so on. On the other hand, let's not forget chitin.

Chitin is a family of chemical substances that make up

much of the exoskeletons of arthropods, including insects, spiders and crabs. The stuff can be flexible or inflexible and chemically it is pretty inert. If biochemists and vehicle designers get together, we may one day see vehicles that can literally grow their skins and repair their own prangs. As arthropods grow larger, they often have to discard their exoskeletons and grow new ones; but who's betting the biochemists won't find ways to teach beetles some new tricks about body armor?

Some cargo—including standoff missiles, supplies, and airborne laser weapons—will be carried by airborne transports. In this sense a bomber is a transport vehicle. Here again, advanced composite structures will find wide use, since a lighter vehicle means a higher payload fraction. Vertical takeoff and landing (VTOL), or at least very short takeoff and landing (VSTOL), will greatly expand the tactical use of these transports which will have variable-geometry surfaces including leading and trailing edges, not only on wings but on the lifting body. Page 75 shows a VSTOL transport. With its triple-delta wings fully extended for maximum lift at takeoff, long aerodynamic 'fences' along the wings front-to-rear guide the airflow and the lower fences form part of the landing gear fairings. Wing extensions telescope rather than swing as the craft approaches multi-mach speed, and for suborbital flight the hydrogen-fluorine rocket will supplant turbines at around thirty kilometer altitude. In its stubby double-delta configuration the craft can skip-glide in the upper atmosphere for extended range, its thick graphite composite leading surfaces aglow as they slowly wear away during re-entry. During periodic maintenance, some of this surface can be replaced in the field as a polymer-rich putty.

As reactors become more compact and MHD more sophisticated, the rocket propellant tanks can give way to cargo space although, from the outside, the VSTOL skip-glide transport might seem little changed. Conversion from VSTOL to VTOL could be helped by a special application of the mass driver principle. In this case the aircraft, with ferrous metal filaments in its composite skin, is the mass repelled by a grid that would rise like scaffolding around the landing pad. This magnetic balancing act would be reversed for vertical landing—but it would take a lot of site preparation which might, in turn, lead to inflatable grid elements rising around the landing site.

Once an antimatter drive is developed, cargo transports might become little more than streamlined boxes with gimbaled nozzles near their corners. Such a craft could dispense with lifting surfaces, but would still need heat-resistant skin for hypersonic flight in the atmosphere. But do we have to look far ahead for cargo vehicles that travel a long way? Maybe we should also look back a ways.

For long-range transport in the lower atmosphere, the dirigible may have a future that far outstrips its past. Though certainly too vulnerable for deployment near enemy gunners, modern helium-filled cargo dirigibles can be very cost-effective in safe zones. Cargo can be lifted quietly and quickly to unimproved dump areas, and with a wide variety of power plants. The classic cigar shape will probably be lost in the shuffle to gain more aerodynamic efficiency, if a recent man-carrying model is any guide. Writer John McPhee called the shape a deltoid pumpkin seed, though its designers prefer the generic term, *aerobody*. So: expect somebody to use buxom, spade-nosed aerobodies to route cargo, but don't expect the things to fly very far when perforated like a collander from small-arms fire. The aerobody seems to be a good bet for poorer nations engaged in border clashes where the fighting is localized and well-defined. But wait a minute: what if the gasbags were made of thin, self-healing chitin? Maybe the aerobody is tougher than we think.

Among the most fascinating military craft are those designed for scouting forays: surveillance, pinpoint bombing sorties, troop support, and courier duty being only a few of their duties. The Germans briefly rescued Mussolini with a slow but superb scout craft, the Fieseler Storch. Our SR-71 does its scouting at Mach 3, while the close-support A-10 can loiter at a tiny fraction of that speed. Now in development in

the U.S., Britain, and Germany is a family of remotely
piloted scout craft that may be the next generation of scout
ships, combining the best features of the Storch and the
SR-71.

The general shape of the scout ship is that of a football
flattened on the bottom, permitting high-speed atmospheric
travel and crabwise evasive action while providing a broad
base for the exhaust gases of its internal ACV fans. The ship
is MHD powered, drawing inlet air from around the underlip
of the shell just outboard of the ACV skirt. The skirt petals
determine the direction of deflected exhaust for omnidirec-
tional maneuvers, though auxiliary jets may do the job better
than skirt petals.

The scout uses thick graphite composite skin and sports
small optical viewing ports for complete peripheral video
rather than having a single viewing bubble up front. The
multiple videos offer redundancy in case of damage; they
permit a stiffer structure; and they allow the occupant, if any,
maximum protection by remoting him from the ports.

The question of piloting is moot at the moment. Grumman,
Shorts, and Dornier are all developing pilotless observation
craft for long-range operations, but a scout craft of the future
would probably have a life-support option for at least one
occupant. The design has an ovoid hatch near its trailing
edge. For manned missions, an occupant pod slides into the
well-protected middle of the ship, and could pop out again for
emergency ejection. For unmanned missions the occupant
pod might be replaced by extra fuel, supplies, or weapons.
Some version of this design might inherit the missions of the
battle tank, but with much-improved speed and maneuverability.

Well, we've specified high maneuverability and a graphite
composite skin. Given supersonic speed and automated evasion programs, it might be the one hope of outrunning an
orbital laser weapon!

Of course the scout doesn't exceed the speed of light. What
it might do, though, is survive a brief zap long enough to
begin a set of evasive actions. Let's say the enemy has an

orbital laser platform (OLP) fairly near in space, not directly overhead but in line-of-sight, four hundred miles from the scout which is cruising innocently along at low altitude at a speed of Mach 1. The laser is adjusted perfectly and fires.

What does it hit? A thick polished carapace of graphite composite, its skin filaments aligned to conduct the laser's heat away from the pencil-wide target point. Sensors in the scout's skin instantly set the craft to dodging in a complex pattern, at lateral accelerations of about 10 g's. At this point the occupant is going to wish he had stayed home, but he should be able to survive these maneuvers.

Meanwhile the OLP optics or radar sense the change of the scout's course—but this takes a little time, roughly two millisec, because the OLP is four hundred miles away. Reaiming the laser might take only ten millisec, though it might take considerably longer. Then the OLP fires again, the new laser burst taking another two millisec to reach the target.

But that's fourteen thousandths of a second! And the scout is moving roughly one foot per millisec, and is now angling to one side. Its change of direction is made at well over three hundred feet per sec, over four feet of angular shift before the second ('corrected') laser shot arrives. The scout's generally elliptical shell is about twenty feet in length by about ten in width. Chances are good that the next laser shot would miss entirely, and in any case it would probably not hit the same spot, by now a glowing scar an inch or so deep on the scout's shell.

Discounting luck on either side, the survival of the jittering scout ship might depend on whether it could dodge under a cloud or into a steep valley. It might, however, foil the laser even in open country by redirecting a portion of its exhaust in a column directly toward the enemy OLP. The destructive effect of a laser beam depends on high concentration of energy against a small area. If the laser beam spreads, that concentration is lost; and beam spread is just what you must expect if the laser beam must travel very far through fog, cloud, or plasma. If the scout ship could hide under a tall,

chemically seeded column of its own exhaust for a few
moments, it would have a second line of defense. And we
must not forget that the laser's own heat energy, impinging
on the target, creates more local plasma which helps to
further spread and attenuate the laser beam.

One method of assuring the OLP more hits on a scout ship
would be to gang several lasers, covering all the possible
moves that the scout might make. The next question would be
whether all that fire-power was worth the trouble. The combination of high-temperature composites, MHD power,
small size, and maneuverability might make a scout ship the
same problem to an OLP that a rabbit is to a hawk. All the
same, the hawk has the initial advantage. The rabbit is right
to tremble.

An unmanned scout ship, capable of much higher rates of
angular acceleration, would be still more vexing to an OLP.
If the OLP were known to have a limited supply of stored
energy, a squadron of unmanned scouts could turn a tide of
battle by exhausting the OLP in futile potshots. It remains to
be seen whether the jittering scout craft will be able to dodge,
intercept, or just plain outrun a locally-fired weapon held by
some hidden infantryman. But given a compact reactor or an
antimatter drive, the scout ship could become a submersible.
In that event the scout craft could escape enemy fire by
plunging into any ocean, lake, or river that's handy. The
broad utility of such a craft might make obsolete most other
designs.

But what of vehicles intended to fight in space? As colonies and mining outposts spread throughout our solar system, there may be military value in capturing or destroying
far-flung settlements—which means there'll be military
value in intercepting such missions. The popular notion of
space war today seems to follow the Dykstra images of
movies and TV, where great whopping trillion-ton
battleships direct fleets of parasite fighters. The mother ship
with its own little fleet makes a lot of sense, but in sheer mass
the parasites may account for much of the system, and battle

craft in space may have meter-thick carapaces to withstand laser fire and nuke near-misses.

Let's consider a battle craft of reasonable size and a human crew, intended to absorb laser and projectile weapons as well as some hard radiation. We'll give it reactor-powered rockets, fed with pellets of some solid fuel which is exhausted as vapor.

To begin with, the best shape for the battle craft might be an elongated torus; a tall, stretched-out doughnut. In the long hole down the middle we install the crew of two—if that many—weapons, communication gear, life support equipment, and all the other stuff that's most vulnerable to enemy weapons. This central cavity is then domed over at both ends, with airlocks at one end and weapon pods at the other. The crew stays in the very center where protection is maximized. The fuel pellets, comprising most of the craft's mass, occupy the main cavity of the torus, surrounding the vulnerable crew like so many tons of gravel. Why solid pellets? Because they'd be easier than fluids to recover in space after battle damage to the fuel tanks. The rocket engines are gimbaled on short arms around the waist of the torus, where they can impart spin, forward or angular momentum, or thrust reversal. The whole craft would look like a squat cylinder twenty meters long by fifteen wide, with circular indentations at each end where the inner cavity closures meet the torus curvatures.

The battle craft doesn't seem very large but it could easily gross over 5,000 tons, fully fueled. If combat accelerations are to reach 5 g's with full tanks, the engines must produce far more thrust than anything available today. Do we go ahead and design engines producing 25,000 tons of thrust, or do we accept far less acceleration in hopes the enemy can't do any better? Or do we redesign the cylindrical crew section so that it can eject itself from the fuel torus for combat maneuvers? This trick—separating the crew and weapons pod as a fighting unit while the fuel supply loiters off at a distance—greatly improves the battle craft's performance. But it also means the

crew pod must link up again very soon with the torus to
replenish its on-board fuel supply. And if the enemy zaps the
fuel torus hard enough while the crew is absent, it may mean
a long trajectory home in cryogenic sleep.

Presuming that a fleet of the toroidal battle craft sets out on
an interplanetary mission, the fleet might start out as a group
of parasite ships attached to a mother ship. It's anybody's
guess how the mother ship will be laid out, so let's make a
guess for critics to lambaste.

Our mother ship would be a pair of fat discs, each duplicat-
ing the other's repair functions in case one is damaged. The
discs would be separated by three compression girders and
kept in tension by a long central cable. To get a mental picture
of the layout, take two biscuits and run a yard-long thread
through the center of each. Then make three columns from
soda straws, each a yard long, and poke the straw ends into
the biscuits near their edges. Now the biscuits are facing each
other, a yard apart, pulled toward each other by the central
thread and held apart by the straw columns. If you think of the
biscuits as being a hundred meters in diameter with rocket
engines poking away from the ends, you have a rough idea of
the mother ship.

Clearly, the mother ship is two modules, upwards of a mile
apart but linked by structural tension and compression members. The small battle craft might be attached to the compression girders for their long ride to battle, but if the mother ship
must maneuver, their masses might pose unacceptable loads
on the girders. Better by far if the parasites nestle in between
the girders to grapple onto the tension cable. In this way, a
fleet could embark from planetary orbit as a single system,
separating into sortie elements near the end of the trip.

Since the total mass of all the battle craft is about equal to
that of the unencumbered mother ship, the big ship can
maneuver itself much more easily when the kids get off
mama's back. The tactical advantages are that the system is
redundant with fuel and repair elements; a nuke strike in
space might destroy one end of the system without affecting
the rest; and all elements become more flexible in their

operational modes just when they need to be. Even if mother ships someday become as massive as moons, my guess is that they'll be made up of redundant elements and separated by lots of open space. Any hopelessly damaged elements can be discarded, or maybe kept and munched up for fuel mass.

Having discussed vehicles that operate on land, sea, air, and in space, we find one avenue left: within the earth. Certainly a burrowing vehicle lacks the maneuverability and speed of some others—until the burrow is complete. But under all that dirt, one is relatively safe from damn-all. Mining vehicles already exist that cut and convey ten tons of coal a minute, using extended-life storage batteries for power. One such machine, only 23 inches high, features a supine driver and low-profile, high traction tires. Perhaps a future military 'mole' will use seismic sensors to find the easiest path through rocky depths, chewing a long burrow to be traversed later at high speed by offensive or defensive vehicles, troop transports, and supply conduits. Disposal of the displaced dirt could be managed by detonating a nuke to create a cavern big enough to accept the tailings of the mole. The present plans to route ICBM's by rail so that enemies won't know where to aim their first strike, may shift to underground routing as the subterranean conduit network expands.

AN ALTERNATIVE TO VEHICLES?

A vehicle of any kind is, as we've asserted, essentially a means to carry something somewhere. So it's possible that the vehicle, *as a category*, might be obsolete one day. The matter transmitter is a concept that, translated into hardware, could obsolete almost any vehicle. True, most conceptual schemes for matter transmitters posit a receiving station— which implies that some vehicle must first haul the receiving station from Point A to Point B. But what if the transmitter needed no receiving station? A device that could transmit people and supplies at light speed to a predetermined point without reception hardware, would instantly replace vehicles for anything but pleasure jaunts. The system would also raise mirthful hell with secrecy, and with any armor that could be penetrated by the transmitter beam. If the beam operated in the electromagnetic spectrum, vehicles might still be useful deep down under water, beneath the earth's surface, or inside some vast Faraday cage.

But until the omnipotent matter transmitter comes along, vehicle design will be one of the most pervasive factors in military strategy and tactics.

REFERENCES

Air Force Times, 12 June 1978

Aviation Week & Space Technology, January 1976, p. 111

Biss, Visvaldis, "Phase Analysis of Standard and Molybdenum-Modified Mar-M509 Superalloys," *J. Testing & Evaluation,* May 1977

Bova, Ben, "Magnetohydrodynamics," *Analog,* May 1965

Clarke, Arthur, *Report on Planet Three and Other Speculations* (N.Y.: Signet Books, 1973)

Committee on Advanced Energy Storage Systems, *Criteria for Energy Storage Research & Development* (Washington, D.C., N.A.S., 1976)

Compressed Air, April 1978

Fairchild Republic Co., Data release on A-10, 1978

Ing, Dean, "Mayan Magnum," *Road & Track,* May 1968

Marion, R.H., "A Short-Time, High Temperature Mechanical Testing Facility," *J. Testing & Evaluation,* January 1978

McPhee, John, *The Curve of Binding Energy* (N.Y.: Farrar, Straus & Giroux, 1974)

O'Neill, Gerard, *The High Frontier* (N.Y.: Bantam Books, 1978)

Owen, J. I. H. (ed.), *Brassey's Infantry Weapons of the World* (N.Y.: Bonanza Books, 1975)

Pretty, R. T. & D. H. R. Archer (eds.), *Jane's Weapon Systems* (London: Jane's Yearbooks, 1974)

Raloff, Janet, "U.S.-Soviet Energy Pact," *Science Digest*, Feb. 1976

Rosa, Richard, *"How To Design A Flying Saucer," Analog*, May 1965.

Saunders, Russell, "Clipper Ships of Space," *Astounding*, May 1951

Singer, Charles *et al, A History of Technology, Vol. I* (N.Y.: Oxford University Press, 1954)

The design exercises of the preceding piece aren't just everybody's piece of baklava, perhaps because they aren't visibly focused on people. What's interesting about a vehicle, anyhow, if it doesn't promote interactions between characters? In the following story, I think the vehicles take their proper places. They didn't, the first time I wrote it.

Only the first time I wrote it, in 1957, it didn't sell. Small wonder: I let the gadgets bulldoze my characters. Then in 1978, I had something entirely different to say and vaguely remembered that old manuscript. Sure enough, I was able to salvage the geography, two major characters, and a crucial confrontation. Other than that, it was back to Square One.

Whatthehell; Square One is the fun part, anyway. (That's what I tell myself beforehand. When I'm ready to advance, I convince myself that Square Two is even better. And so on. A con man's life is not an easy one . . .)

I've already admitted that other writers still influence me, so you may as well know that I was self-consciously wearing a Ted Sturgeon hat while developing my real heavyweight in "Vital Signs". It wouldn't be fair to tell you which of his stories I had in mind, but I can tell you this: Ing under Sturgeon's hat is like a clown under a circus tent. It's a great setting, but you can get lost in there.

Vital Signs

Before July, it promised to be an off-year. Not an election year, nor especially a war year—either of which seems to enrich bail-bondsmen. Early in the summer I was ready to remember it as the year I bought the off-road Porsche and they started serving couscous Maroc at Original Joe's. But it was in mid-July when I learned that the Hunter had been misnamed, and that made it everybody's bad year.

It had been one of those muggy days in Oakland with no breeze off the bay to cool a sweaty brow. And I sweat easily since, as a doctor friend keeps telling me, I carry maybe fifty pounds too many. I'm six-two, one-eighty-eight centimeters if you insist, and I tell him I need the extra weight as well as height in my business, but that's bullshit and we both know it. It's my hobbies, not my business, that make me seem a not-so-jolly fat man. My principal pastimes are good food and blacksmithy, both just about extinct. My business is becoming extinct, too. My name's Harve Rackham, and I'm a bounty hunter.

I had rousted a check-kiting, bail-jumping, small-time scuffler from an Alameda poolroom and delivered him, meek as mice, to the authorities after only a day's legwork. I suppose it was too hot for him to bother running for it. Wouldn't've done him much good anyhow; for a hundred yards, until my breath gives out, I can sprint with the best of 'em.

I took my cut from the bail-bondsman and squeezed into my Porsche. Through the Berkeley tunnel and out into Contra Costa County it was cooler, without the Bay Area haze. Before taking the cutoff toward home I stopped in Antioch. Actually I stopped twice, first to pick up a four-quart butter

churn the antique shop had been promising me for weeks and
then for ground horsemeat. Spot keeps fit enough on the
cheap farina mix, but he loves his horsemeat. It was the least I
could do for the best damn' watchcat in California.

Later, some prettyboy TV newsman tried to get me to say
I'd had a premonition by then. No way: I'd read a piece in
the *Examiner* about a meteorite off the central coast, but what
could that possibly have to do with me? I didn't even have a
mobile phone in the Porsche, so I had no idea the Feebies had
a job for me until I got home to my playback unit. The FBI
purely hates to subcontract a job, anyway. Especially to me. I
don't fit their image.

My place is only a short drive from Antioch, a white
two-story frame farmhouse built in 1903 in the shadow of
Mount Diablo. When I bought it, I couldn't just stop the
restoration at the roof; by the time I'd furnished it in genuine
1910 I'd also become a zealot for the blacksmith shop out
back. By now I had most of my money tied up in functional
antiques like my Model C folding Brownie camera, my
hurricane lamps with polished reading reflectors, swage sets
for the smithy, even Cumberland coal for the forge and a
cannonball tuyere. I had no one else to spend my money on
but before I got Spot, I worried a lot. While I was tracking
down bail-jumpers, some thief might've done a black-bag
job on the place. With Spot around, the swagman would have
to run more than seventy miles an hour.

If I'd had more than five acres, I couldn't've paid for the
cyclone fence. And if I'd had less, there wouldn't've been
room for Spot to run. The fence doesn't keep Spot in; it keeps
sensible folks out. Anybody who ignores the CHEETAH ON
PATROL signs will have a hard time ignoring Spot, who
won't take any food or any shit from any stranger. I'm a
one-cat man, and Spot is a one-man cat.

I saw him caper along the fence as he heard the gutteral
whoosh of the Porsche fans. I levered the car into boost
mode, which brings its skirts down for vastly greater air-
cushion effect. Just for the hell of it, I jumped the fence.

An off-road Porsche is built to take a Baja run, with

reversible pitch auxiliary fans that can suck the car down for high cornering force on its wheels, or support it on an air cushion for brief spurts. But I'd seen Feero on film, tricking his own Baja Porsche into bouncing on its air cushion so it'd clear an eight-foot obstacle. You can't know how much fun it was for me to learn that unless you weigh as much as I do.

Of course, Spot smelled the horsemeat and I had to toss him a sample before he'd quit pestering me. After we sniffed each other around the ears—don't ask me why, but Spot regards that as a kind of backslap—I went to the basement and checked Spot's automated feeder. My office is in the basement, too, along with all my other contemporary stuff. From ground level up, it's *fin-de-siècle* time at my place, but the basement is all business.

My phone playback had only two messages. The first didn't matter, because the last was from Dana Martin in Stockton. "We have an eighty-eight fugitive and we need a beard," her voice stroked me; softly annealed on the surface, straw-tempered iron beneath. "My SAC insists you're our man. What can I say?" She could've said, whatever her Special Agent in Charge thought in Sacramento, she hated the sight of me. She didn't need to: ours was an old estrangement. "I can come to your place if you'll chain that saber-toothed animal. And if you don't call back by five PM Friday, forget it. I wish they'd pay me like they'll pay you, Rackham." Click.

My minicomputer terminal told me it was four-forty-six. I dialed a Stockton number, wondering why the FBI needed a disguising ploy to hunt a fugitive fleeing from prosecution. It could mean he'd be one of the shoot-first types who can spot a Feebie around a corner. I can get close to those types but I'm too easy a target. The hell of it was, I needed the money. Nobody pays like the Feebies for the kind of work I do.

Miz Martin was out mailing blueprints but was expected shortly. I left word that I'd rassle the saber-tooth if she wanted a souffle at my place, and hung up chuckling at the young architect's confusion over my message. Time was, brick agents didn't have to hold down cover jobs. Dana did

architectural drafting when she wasn't on assignment for her
area SAC, who's in Sacramento.

I took a fresh block of ice from the basement freezer and
put it in my honest-to-God icebox upstairs. I had nearly a
dozen fertile eggs and plenty of cream, and worked up a
sweat all over again playing with my new butter churn until
I'd collected a quarter-pound of the frothy cream-yellow
stuff. It smelled too good to use for cooking, which meant it
was just right. After firing up the wood stove, I went outside
for coolth and companionship.

I'd nearly decided La Martin wouldn't show and was
playing 'fetch' with my best friend when, far down the
graveltop road, I heard a government car. When you hear the
hum of electrics under the thump of a diesel, it's either a
conservation nut or a government man. Or woman, which
Dana Martin most assuredly is.

Spot sulked but obeyed, stalking pipe-legged into the
smithy as I remoted the automatic gate. Dana decanted herself from the sedan with the elegance of a debutante, careless
in her self-assurance, and stared at my belt buckle. "It's a
wonder your heart can take it," she sniffed. Dana could well
afford to twit me for my shape. She's a petite blonde with the
face of a littlest angel and a mind like a meat cleaver. One of
those exquisite-bodied little charmers you want to protect
when it's the other guy who needs protection.

I knew she worked hard to keep in shape and had a
fastidious turn of mind so, "We can't all have your
tapeworm," I said.

I thought she was going to climb back into the car, but she
only hauled a briefcase from it. "Spare me your ripostes,"
she said; "people are dying while you wax clever. You have
an hour to decide about this job."

Another slur, I thought; when had I ever turned down
Feebie money? I let 'no comment' be mine, waved her to my
kitchen, poked at the fire in the stove. Adjusting the damper
is an art, and art tends to draw off irritation like a poultice. I
started separating the eggs, giving Dana the cheese to grate.
She could've shredded Parmesan on her attitude. "I can

brief you," she began, "only after you establish an oral commitment. My personal advice is, don't. It needs an agile man."

"Hand me the butter," I said.

She did, shrugging. "All I can tell you beforehand, is that the fugitive isn't human."

"Spoken like a true believer, Dana. As soon as somebody breaks enough laws, you redefine him as an unperson."

Relishing it: "I'm being literal, Rackham. He's a big, nocturnal animal that's killed several people. The Bureau can't capture him for political reasons; you'll be working alone for the most part; and it is absolutely necessary to take him alive."

"Pass the flour. But he won't be anxious to take *me* alive; is that it?"

"In a nutshell. And he is much more important than you are. If you screw it up, you may rate a nasty adjective or two in history books—and I've said too much already," she muttered.

I stirred my supper and my thoughts, adding cayenne to both. Obviously in Bureau files, my dealings with animals hadn't gone unnoticed. They knew I'd turned a dozen gopher snakes loose to eliminate the varmints under my lawn. They knew about my ferret that kept rats away. They knew Spot. I'd taken a Kodiak once, and they knew that, too. But true enough, I was slower now. I postulated a Cape Buffalo, escaped while some South Africans were presenting it to a zoo, worth its weight in krugerrands to antsy politicians. "I think I'll give this one a 'bye," I sighed and, as afterthought: "but what was the fee for taking it *a la* Frank Buck?"

"Who the devil is Frank Buck?"

"Never mind. How much?"

"A hundred thousand," she said, unwilling.

I nearly dropped the dry mustard. For that, I could find Spot a consort and dine on escargot every night. "I'm in," I said quickly. "Nobody lives forever."

While the souffle baked, Dana revealed how far afield my

guess had gone. I fed her flimsy disc into my office computer downstairs and let her do the rest. The display showed a map of Central California, with a line arching in from offshore. She pointed to the line with a light pencil. "That's the path of the so-called meteorite last Saturday night. Point Reyes radar gave us this data." Now the display magicked out a ream of figures. "Initial velocity was over fifteen thousand meters per second at roughly a hundred klicks altitude, too straight and too fast for a ballistic trajectory."

"Would you mind putting that into good old feet and miles? I'm from the old school, in case you hadn't noticed," I grinned.

"You're a goddam dinosaur," she agreed. "Okay: we picked up an apparent meteorite coming in at roughly a forty-five degree angle, apparent mass um, fifty tons or so, hitting the atmosphere at a speed of about—fifty thousand feet per second. Accounting for drag, it should've still impacted offshore within a few seconds, sending out a seismometer blip, not to mention a local tsunami. It didn't.

"It decelerated at a steady hundred and forty g's and described a neat arc that must've brought it horizontal near sea-level."

I whistled. "Hundred and forty's way above human tolerance."

"The operative word is 'steady'. It came in so hot it made the air glow, and it was smart—I mean, it didn't behave as though purely subject to outside forces. That kind of momentum change took a lot of energy under precise control, they tell me. Well, about eleven seconds after deceleration began it had disappeared, too low on the horizon for coverage, and loafing along at sub-mach speed just off the water."

"Russians," I guessed.

"They know about it, but it wasn't them. Don't they wish? It wasn't anybody human. The vehicle came in over the Sonoma coast and hedge-hopped as far as Lake Berryessa northwest of Sacramento. That's where the UFO hotline folks got their last report and wouldn't you know it, witnesses claimed the usual round shape and funny lights."

I sprinted for the stairs, Spot-footed across the kitchen floor, snuck a look into the oven. "Just in time," I called, as Dana emerged from below.

She glanced at the golden trifle I held in my potholder, then inhaled, smiling in spite of herself. "You may have your uses at that."

"Getting up here so fast without jolting the souffle?"

"No, cooking anything that smells this good," she said, and preceded me to the dining room. "I don't think you have the chance of a cardiac case on this hunt, and I said as much to Scott King."

She told me why over dinner. The scrambled interceptors from Travis and Beale found nothing, but a Moffett patrol craft full of sensor equipment sniffed over the area and found traces of titanium dioxide in the atmosphere. Silicon and nox, too, but those could be explained away.

You couldn't explain away the creature trapped by college students near the lake on Sunday evening. Dana passed me a photo, and my first shock was one of recognition. The short spotted fur and erect short ears of the quadruped, the heavy shoulders and bone-crunching muzzle, all reminded me of a dappled bear cub. It could have been a terrestrial animal wearing a woven metallic harness but for its eyes, small and lowset near the muzzle. It looked dead, and it was.

"The pictures were taken after it escaped from a cage on the Cal campus at Davis and electrocuted itself, biting through an autoclave power line. It was evidently a pet," Dana said, indicating studs on the harness, "since it couldn't reach behind to unlock this webbing, and it wasn't very bright. But it didn't need to be, Harve. It was the size of a Saint Bernard. Guess its weight."

I studied the burly, brawny lines of the thing. "Two hundred."

"Three. That's in kilos," Dana said. "Nearly seven hundred pounds. If it hadn't got mired in mud near a student beer-bust, I don't know how they'd have taken it. It went through lassos as if they were cheese, using this."

Another photo. Above each forepaw, which seemed to

have thumbs on each side, was an ivorylike blade, something like a dewclaw. One was much larger than the other, like the asymmetry of a fiddler crab. It didn't seem capable of nipping; slashing, maybe. I rolled down my sleeves; it wouldn't help if Dana Martin saw the hairs standing on my forearms. "So how'd they get it to the Ag people at Cal-Davis?"

"Some bright lad made a lasso from a tow cable. While the animal was snarling and screeching and biting the cable, they towed it out of the mud with a camper. It promptly chased one nincompoop into the camper and the guy got out through the sliding glass plate upfront—but he lost both legs above the ankle; it seems the creature ate them.

"The Yolo County Sheriff actually drove the camper to Davis with that thing fighting its way through the cab in the middle of the night." Dana smiled wistfully. "Wish I could've seen him drive into that empty water purification tank, it was a good move. The animal couldn't climb out, the Sheriff pulled the ladder up, and a few hours later we were brought into it and clamped the lid down tight."

"Extraterrestrial contact," I breathed, testing the sound of a phrase that had always sounded absurd to me. The remains of my souffle were lost in the metallic taste of my excitement—okay, maybe 'excitement' wasn't quite the right word. "If that's the kind of pets they keep, what must *they* be like?"

"Think of Shere Khan out there," Dana jerked a thumb toward a window, "and ask what *you*'re like."

Why waste time explaining the difference between a pet and a friend? "Maybe they're a race of bounty hunters," I cracked lamely.

"The best guess is that the animal's owner is hunting, all right. Here's what we have on the big one," she said, selecting another glossy. "Four men and a woman weren't as lucky as the fellow who lost his feet."

I gazed at an eight-by-ten of a plaster cast, dirt-flecked, that stood next to a meter stick on a table. Something really big, with a paw like a beclawed rhino, had left pugmarks a foot deep. It might have been a species similar to the dead pet, I thought, and said so. "Where'd this cast come from?"

"Near the place where the beer-bust was busted. They're taking more casts now at the Sacramento State University campus. If the hunter's on all-fours, it may weigh only a few tons."

"Davis campus; Sac State—fill it in, will you?"

It made a kind of sense. Once inside a chilled-steel cage, the captive pet had quieted down for ethologists at Davis. They used tongs to fumble a little plastic puck from a clip on the harness, and sent it to Sacramento State for analysis, thinking it might be some kind of an owner tag. It turned out to be a bug, an AM/FM signal generator—and they hadn't kept it shielded. The owner must have monitored the transmitter and followed it to Sacramento. More guesswork: its vehicle had traveled in the American River to a point near the Sac State labs where the plastic puck was kept.

And late Tuesday evening, something big as a two-car garage had left a depression on the sand of an island in the river, and something mad as hell itself had come up over the levee and along a concrete path to the lab.

A professor, a research assistant, a top-clearance physicist brought in from nearby Aerojet, and an FBI field agent had seen the hunter come through a pumice block wall into the lab with them, but most of the information they had was secure.

Permanently.

Dana Martin didn't offer photos to prove they'd been dismembered, but I took her word for it. "So your hunter got its signal generator back," I prompted, "and split."

"No, no, and yes. It's *your* hunter, and our man had left the transmitter wrapped in foil in the next room, where we found it. But yes, the hunter's gone again."

"To Davis?"

"We doubt it. Up the river a few klicks, there's an area where a huge gold dredge used to spit its tailings out. A fly-fisher led us to remains in the trailings near the riverbank yesterday. A mighty nimrod type who'd told his wife he was going to sight in his nice new rifle at the river. That's a misdemeanor, but he got capital punishment. His rifle had

been fired before something bent its barrel into a vee and—
get this—embedded the muzzle in the man's side like you'd
bait a hook.''

"That's hard to believe. Whatever could do that, could
handle a gorilla like an organ grinder's monkey.''

"Dead right, Rackham—and it's loose in the dredge tailings.''

Well, she'd warned me. I knew the tailings area from my
own fishing trips. They stretch for miles on both sides of the
American River, vast high cairns of smooth stones coughed
up by a barge that had once worked in from the river. The
barge had chewed a path ahead of it, making its own lake,
digesting only the gold as it wandered back and forth near the
river. Seen from the air, the tailings made snaky patterns
curling back to the river again.

This savage rape of good soil had been committed long ago
and to date the area was useless. It was like a maze of gravel
piles, most of the gravel starting at grapefruit size and pro-
gressing to some like oval steamer trunks. A few trees had
found purchase there; weeds; a whole specialized ecology of
small animals in the steep slopes. The more I thought about it,
the more it seemed like perfect turf for some monstrous
predator.

I took a long breath, crossed my arms, rubbed them briskly
and stared across the table at Dana Martin. "You haven't
given me much to go on,'' I accused.

"There's more on the recording,'' she said softly.

I guessed from her tone: "All bad.''

Shrug: "Some bad. Some useful.''

I let her lead me downstairs. She had an audiotape sal-
vaged from the lab wreckage, and played me the last few
minutes of it.

A reedy male expounded on the alien signal generator.
"We might take it apart undamaged,'' he ended, sounding
wistful and worried.

"The Bureau can't let you chance it,'' said another male,
equally worried.

A third man, evidently the Aerojet physicist, doubted the

wisdom of reproducing the ar-eff signals since what looked like junk on a scope might be salient data on an alien receiver. He offered the use of Aerojet's X-ray inspection equipment. A young woman—the research assistant—thought that was a good idea at first. "But I don't know," she said, and you could almost hear her smile: "it looks kinda neat the way it is."

The woman's sudden voice shift stressed her non sequitur. It sounded idiotic. I tossed a questing frown at Dana and positively gaped as the recording continued.

The Feebie again: "I suppose I could ask Scott King to let you disassemble it. Hell, it's harmless," he drawled easily in a sudden about-face. King, as I knew, was his—and Dana Martin's—SAC in the region.

The reedy older voice was chuckling now. "That's more like it; aren't we worrying over trifles?"

The physicist laughed outright. "My sentiments exactly." Under his on-mike mirth I could hear the others joining in.

And then the speaker overloaded its bass response in a thunderous crash. Several voices shouted as the second slam was followed by clatters of glass and stone. Clear, then: "Scotty, whatthehell—", ending in a scream; three screams. From somewhere came a furious clicking, then an almost subsonic growling *whuffff*. Abrupt silence. Posterity had been spared the rest.

I glowered at Dana Martin. "What's good about that?"

"Forewarning. Our man wasn't the sort to vacillate, and the professor was known as a sourball. It's barely possible tht they all were being gassed somehow, to hallucinate during the attack."

"Maybe," I said. "That would explain why your man thought he saw Scotty King coming through the wall. Ah,— look, Dana, this just about tears it. You need a covey of hoverchoppers to find this, this hunter of yours. I get a picture of something that could simply stroll up to me while I grinned at it, and nothing short of a submarine net could stop it. Won't I even have a brick agent to help?"

"Every hovercraft we can spare is quartering the Ber-

ryessa region. And so are a lot of chartered craft," she said
softly, "carrying consular people from Britain, France, the
Soviets, and the United Chinese Republics. *They know,*
Rackham, and they intend to be on hand from the first
moment of friendly contact."

"Some friendly contact," I snorted. I realized now that the
air activity over Lake Berryessa was a deliberate decoy.
"Surely we have the power to ground the rest of these
guys . . ."

"The instant our government makes contact, we are committed by treaty to sharing that confrontation with the rest of
the nuclear club," Dana said wearily. "It's an agreement the
Soviets thought up last year, of which we have been forcibly
reminded in the past days."

I showed her my palms.

"*You're not government,*" she hissed. "We're a laissez
faire democracy; we can't help it if a private U.S. citizen does
the first honors. Could we help it if he should dynamite the
spacecraft in perfectly understandable panic?"

"Destroy a diamond-mine of information? Are you nuts?"
For the first time my voice was getting out of hand.

"Perfectly sane. We've got a kit for you to record the
experience if you can get into the craft—maybe remove
anything that looks portable, and hide it. We don't want you
to totally wreck the vehicle, just make it a hangar queen until
another civilian friend has studied the power plants and
weaponry, and then he might blow it to confetti."

I was beginning to see the plan. Even if it worked it was
lousy politics. I told her that.

"This country," she said, "has an edge in communications and power plants at the moment. We'd a whole lot
rather keep that edge, and learn a few things to fatten it, then
take a chance that everybody—including Libya—might get
onto an equal technological footing with us overnight. *Now*
will you drop the matter?"

"I may as well. Am I supposed to ask the damn' hunter for
some thermite so I can burn his ailerons a little?"

"We've sunk a cache of sixty per cent dynamite in the river shallows for you—common stuff you could buy commercially. We've marked it here on a USGS map. Best of all, you'll have a weapon."

I brightened, but only for a moment. It was a gimmicked Smith & Wesson automatic, a bit like a Belgian Browning. Dana took it from her briefcase with reverence and explained why the special magazine carried only seven fat rounds. I could almost get my pinkie in the muzzle: sixty calibre at least. It was strictly a short-range item rigged with soluble slugs. Working with the dead pet and guessing a lot, Cal's veterinary science wizards had rendered some of its tissues for tallow and molded slugs full of drugs. They might stop the hunter.

On the other hand, they might not.

If I couldn't make friends with it I would be permitted to shoot for what, in my wisdom, I might consider noncritical spots on its body.

Finally, *if* I hadn't been marmaladed and *if* I had it stunned, I was to punch a guarded stud on the surveillance kit which looked like an amateur's microvid unit with a digital watch embedded in its side. At that point I could expect some other co-opted civilian to 'happen' onto me with his Hoverover.

I wondered out loud how much money the other guy was getting for his part in this, and Dana reminded me that it was none of my damned business. Nor should I worry too much about what would happen after the beast was trussed up in a steel net and taken away. It would be cared for, and in a few days the Feebies would 'discover' what the meddling civilians had done, and the rest of the world could pay it homage and raise all the hell they liked about prior agreements which, so far as anyone might prove, would not have been violated. It was sharp practice. It stank. It paid one hundred thousand dollars.

I collected the pitifully small assortment of data and equipment, making it a small pile. "And with this, you expect me to set out?"

''I really expect you to *crap* out,'' she said sweetly, ''in which case you can expect to be iced down for awhile. We can do it, you know.''

I knew. I also knew she had the extra pleasure of having told me not to commit myself. There was one more item. ''What if I find more than one hunter?''

''We only need to bag one. For reasons I'm not too clear on, we don't think there's more. Something about desperation tactics, I gather.'' She frowned across the stuff at me. ''What's so funny—or are you just trembling?''

I shook my head, waved her toward the stairs. ''Go home, Dana. I was just thinking: it's our tactics that smack of desperation.''

She swayed up the stairs, carrying her empty case, talking as she went. It was no consolation to hear that nobody would be watching me. The little foil-wrapped AM/FM bug would be my only bait, and of course they'd be monitoring that; but it was essential that I dangle the bait only in some remote location. Lovely.

Spot ambled out as he heard my automatic gate energize, chose to frisk alongside Dana Martin's sedan as she drove away. I called him back, closed the gate, and felt Spot's raspy tongue on the back of my hand. I shouted at him and he paced away with injured dignity, his ears back at half-mast. How could I explain it to him? I knew he was enjoying the salt taste of sweat that ran down my arm in defiance of the breeze off Mount Diablo. It might have been worse: some guys get migraines. I'd known one—a good one, too, in my business—who'd developed spastic colon. All I do is sweat, without apologizing. You can't explain fear to a cheetah . . .

I spent the next hour selecting my own kit. In any dangerous business, a man's brains and his equipment are of roughly equal quality. Nobody has yet worked out a handier field ration than 'gorp', the dry mix of nuts, fruit bits and carob I kept—but I tossed in a few slabs of pemmican, too.

Water, spare socks, a McPhee paperback, and my usual stock of pills, including the lecithin and choline.

I considered my own handguns for a long time, hefting the Colt Python in a personal debate, then locked the cabinet again and came away emptyhanded. In extremis, my own Colt would've been too great a temptation—and I already had a weapon. Whether it would work was something else again.

When the Porsche was loaded I spent another hour in my office. The maps refreshed my memory, corrected it in a few cases. A new bridge over the American River connected Sacramento's northeast suburb of Orangevale with Highway Fifty, cutting through the dredge tailings. Gooseflesh returned as I imagined the scene at that moment. Dark as a hunter's thoughts, not enough moon to help, the innocent romantic gleam of riffles on water between the tailings to the south and the low cliffs on the north side. More tailings on the other side too, upriver near Orangevale. This night—and maybe others—it would be approximately as quiet, as inviting, as a cobra pit. I pitied anyone in that area, but not enough to strike out for it in the dark. I needed a full day of reconnaissance before setting out my bait, and a good night's sleep wouldn't hurt.

Usually, sleep is no problem. That night it was a special knack. And while I slept, a pair of youthful lovers lay on a blanket near the river, too near the Sac State campus, and very nearly died.

Saturday morning traffic was light on the cutoff to Interstate Five. I refueled just south of Sacramento, then drove across to the El Dorado Freeway and fought the temptation to follow it all the way to Lake Tahoe. A part of my mind kept telling me I should've brought Spot along for his nose and ears, but I liked him too much to risk him.

I left the freeway east of the city and cruised slowly toward the river, renewing auld acquaintance as I spotted the river parkway. Nice: hiking and bridle trails paralleled the drive, flowing in and out of trees that flanked the river. I didn't wonder why the area was deserted until I saw the road crew lounging near their barricade. The flagman detoured me to a road that led me to a shopping center. I checked a map, took an arterial across the river, spotted more barricades and flagmen barring access to the drive along the north bank of the river as well.

That flagman's khakis had been creased; and who irons work khakis these days? Also, he'd been too pale for a guy who did that every day. I found a grocery store and called Stockton from there, cursing.

Dana Martin answered on the first ring, bright and bubbly as nearbeer and twice as full of false promise. "Hi, you ol' dumplin'," she cascaded past, after my first three words. I stammered and fell silent. "I won't be able to make it today, but you have Wanda's address; she's really dynamite. Why don't you call on her, shug, say around noonish, give or take an hour? Would you mind just terribly?"

I'd worked with Dana enough to know that the vaguer she sounded, the exacter she meant. Wanda at twelve on the dot, then—except that I didn't know the lady or her address. "Uh, yeah, sure; noonish more or less. But I've mislaid her address. You got her phone number?"

Slow, saccharine: "She hasn't got a phone, honeybuns. Must you have a map for such a dynamite lady?"

Map. Dynamite. Ahhh, shee-it, but I was dull. "Right; I must have it somewhere. The things I do for love," I sighed.

Dana cooed that she had just oodles of work to do, and hung up before I could object that the whole goddam river area was crawling with fuzz in false clothing.

I went back to the Porsche and studied my map. The explosive cache was fairly near a dead-end road, only a few miles downriver. I found the road led me past a few expensive homes to a turnaround in sight of the river. No barricades or khakiclads that I could see, but the damned dredge had committed some of its ancient crimes nearby. I guessed there were so many dead-end roads near the river it would take an army to patrol them all. It was nearly two hours before noon and it occurred to me that the time might best be spent checking available routes to and from the tailings areas.

Shortly before noon I hauled ass from a bumpy road near Folsom and headed for my tryst with Wanda. I'd marked several routes on the map, where I could get very near tailings or sandbars from Sacto to Folsom. It was the sort of data the Feebies couldn't have given me, since they didn't really know what the Porsche could do.

At eleven fifty-three I realized I was going to be late if I kept to the boulevards. I checked my route, turned right, zipped on squalling tires to a dead end, and shifted to air cushion mode. A moment later the Porsche was whooshing over the lawn of some wealthy citizen, scattering dandelion puffs but leaving no tracks as it took me downslope and over a low decorative fence.

Using the air cushion there's always the danger of over-speeding the Porsche's primary turbo, but I kept well below redline as I turned downriver just above the ripples. In air cushion mode, the legendary quick response of a Porsche is merely a myth. The car comes about like a big windjammer and tends to wander with sidewinds, so I had my hands full. But I navigated five miles of river in four minutes flat.

Triangulating between bridges, eyeballing the map, I estimated that the cache of dynamite was at the foot of a bush-capped stone outcrop that loomed over the river. I slowed, eased onto a sandbar, let the car settle and left the turbo idling. At exactly noon by my watch, I stood over a swirl of bubbly river slime as long and broad as my kitchen. It had sticks and crud in it, and reminded me of the biggest pizza in town, which made my belly rumble. Junk food has its points too.

I was thirty feet from the Porsche, and past my grumbling gut and the turbo whistle I could hear the burbling hiss of the river. Nothing else. It was high noon on a sandbar on a hot Saturday in the edge of Sacrabloodymento, perfect for a meal and a snooze, and there I stood feeling properly unnerved, waiting for a woman to tell, or bring, or ask me something. I put one hand to my jacket, feeling the automatic in my waistband for cold-steel comfort, and to nobody at all I shook my head in disgust and said, "Wanda."

"Mister Rackham," said the voice above me, and I damned near jumped into the river. He was decked out in waders and an old fishing vest of exactly the right shades to blend with the terrain. He had a short spinning rig, and behind the nonglint sunglasses he was grinning. He'd sat inside those bushes atop that jumble of rocks and watched me from above the whole time, getting his jollies. I'd busted my hump to be punctual but judging from this guy's demeanor, fifteen minutes one way or the other wouldn't've mattered. No wonder people learn to scoff at government orders!

He'd done nothing for my mood, or my confidence. I cleared my throat. "Would you mind telling me—" I trailed off.

"I'm Agent Wanda. And there can't be two car-and-mercenary combos like you, *any*where." He didn't climb down but made a longish cast into the river; began to reel in. "New developments," he said casually. "Fortunately all the white noise around us should raise hob with any shotgun mikes across the water."

I waited until he'd reeled in, changed his spinner for another lure, and flashed me the I.D. in his lure wallet as though by accident. Wanda explained that while the decoy action at Lake Berryessa still seemed to be working on the foreign nationals, some of that cover might be wearing thin. The night before, a lovestruck couple had been thoroughly engaged—even connected, one might infer—near the river when something, surely not boredom, added a religious touch to their experience. According to the girl it seemed to be a great guardian angel, suddenly transformed into a moving rock of ages wielding a terrible swift sword.

Agent Wanda broke off to tell me the girl was a devout fundamentalist, evidently a newcomer to the oldest sport, who'd been overcome by her sense of the rightness and safety of it all—until a huge boulder nearby became a winged angel, gave a mighty chuff, flashed a scimitar in the faint moonlight, and glided into the river like a stone again to sink from sight. It left pugmarks. It probably weighed five tons.

To the girl it had been a powerful visitation. To her boyfriend, who also got a set of confused images of the thing, it had been a derailment. But the girl was the niece of the Sacramento County Sheriff who had—and here fisherman Wanda drawled acid—not been told of the security blanket. The girl trusted her uncle, called him in hysterics. He knew an explosion had taken its toll at a campus lab, and had heard from Yolo County where his counterpart had delivered a wild woolly package to another campus, and like any good lawman he put some things together. By now, elements of the city, county, state and United States were gradually withdrawing the cordon of bozos he had deputized and strung along the river. It was quick action, but far too obvious to suit the feds. Worse still, the campus radio station at Sac State had already got an exclusive from the young man.

School media, Wanda told me, have their own news stringers and an alternative network in National Public Radio. When KERS-FM ran its little hair-raiser on Saturday morning, it scooped the whole country including the FBI. The Feebies had only managed by minutes to quash a follow-up story which, in its usual ballsy aggressive way, NPR's network headquarters in Washington had accepted from Sacramento. It described a huge version of the dead specimen, complete with silvery harness and flaming sword. As a dogdays item for summer consumption, it had almost been aired coast-to-coast over NPR. It would have blown the government's cover from hell to lunch. As it was, KERS had already aired too much of the truth in Sacramento but with TV, Wanda sighed, fortunately almost nobody listens to NPR.

I resolved, in the future, to pay more attention to National Public Radio; it was my kind of network. Meanwhile, the national government was drawing off the protective net along the river, to avoid tipping our hand to other governments—while casually allowing hundreds of nature lovers to wander into harm's way. When officialdom up and down the line conspires to endanger a thousand people, I reasoned, it must be balancing them against a whole lot more. Millions, maybe. It was a minimax ploy: risk a little, save a lot. I began to feel small, like the lure on the end of Wanda's monofilament line: hurled into deep water and very, very expendable.

I watched Wanda cast again, the line taking a detour into the deepest part of the channel. "I expect my explosives are under all that crap," I said, jerking a palm toward the slowly wheeling green pizza in the lee of the stone outcrop.

"Sure is. Looks natural, doesn't it? Just grab the edge and pull it in when you need it. It's anchored on a swivel to a weighted canvas bag. And you know what's in the bag."

I stared at the spinning pizza, and damned if it wasn't a work of plastic camouflage. Real debris, polyurethane slime and bubbles, gyrating in an eddy. I said, "Never know what's real along the river, I guess."

"That's the point," Wanda replied, pulling against a snag almost below him. "The hunter was in plain sight last night, not ten meters from those kids, and the girl claims she never felt so safe. Even thought she saw an approving angel for a few seconds."

"Like your man thought he saw his SAC coming through that wall on the campus?"

"Could be," he nodded. "We thought you should know that, and the part about your quarry being at home in the water."

He frowned at the river; his rod bent double until he gave it slack. I touched my sidearm for luck as his line moved sideways, then began a stately upstream progression. "Jesus, I must have a salmon," he said, his face betraying a genuine angler's excitement.

With the bright July sun and the clear sierra water, I saw a dark sinuous shape far below the surface and grinned. I knew what it was; it wasn't salmon time, and salmon don't move with the inexorable pace of a finned log moving upstream. "No, you have a problem," I said. "And so do I, if a gaggle of Soviet tourists come snooping around here in copters."

"Just keep it in mind," said Wanda, scrambling up, reluctantly letting more line out. "Play it safe and don't have a higher profile than necessary." Then, plaintively, as I turned to go: "What the hell do I have here?"

"Sturgeon."

Pause as the upstream movement paused. Then, "How do I land it?"

I nodded toward the plastic pizza. "Try some sixty per cent dynamite. Or wait him out. Some of 'em get to be over ten feet long; don't worry, they're domestic."

He called to me as I trudged to my Porsche: "Domestic, *schmomestic;* what's that got to do with it?"

I called back: "I mean it's not a Soviet sturgeon. At least you needn't worry about catching an alien."

When I drove away he was still crouched there, a perfect metaphor of the decent little guy in a big government, jerking on his rod and muttering helplessly. I kept the Porsche inches off the water en route downriver as far as the county park and thrilled a bunch of sporty car freaks as I hovered to the perimeter road, trying to let the good feeling last. It wouldn't; all the Feebie had to do was cut his line and he'd be free of his problem. All I had to do was unwrap an alien transmitter and my problem would come to me in a hurry. Maybe.

For sure, I wasn't about to do it in full view of a dozen picnickers. I hadn't yet seen a piece of ground that looked right for me, and I'd covered a lot of river. To regain the low profile I drove twenty miles back upriver on the freeway without being tailed, and to exercise my sense of the symbolic I demolished a pizza in Folsom. Thus fortified, I found a secondhand store in the restored Gay Nineties section of Folsom and bought somebody's maltreated casting rig with an automatic rewind. Wanda had been right to use fishing as a cover activity. I was beginning to grow paranoid at the idea of foreign nationals watching me—and drawing sensible conclusions.

I drove from Folsom to a bluff that overlooked the river and let my paranoia have its head as I studied the scene.

Somewhere, evidently downriver, lay my quarry. I'd assumed it was nocturnal simply because it hadn't shown in daylight. But for an instant, just before I caught a glimpse of that sturgeon, I'd realized the hunting beast might have been on the other end of Wanda's line. Truly nocturnal? Not proven . . .

I'd also assumed, without thinking it out, that the hunter was strictly a land animal. Scratch another assumption; it apparently could stroll underwater like a hippo. Gills? Scuba?

The report about the sword led me to a still more worrisome train of thought. A saber was hardly the weapon I'd expect from an intelligent alien. What other, more potent, weapons did it carry? Its harness might hold anything from laser weapons to poison gas—unless, like the smaller animal, it too was a pet. Yet there had been no evidence of modern weapons against humans. The fact was, I hadn't the foggiest idea what range of weapons I might run up against.

Finally there was the encounter with the lovers, sacrificial lambs who weren't slaughtered after all. Why? They could hardly have been more vulnerable. Maybe because they were mating; maybe, for that matter, because they *were* vulnerable. All I could conclude was that the hunter did discriminate.

One thing sure: he knew how to keep a low profile with his own vehicle. So where do you hide a fifty-ton spacecraft? Surely not where it can be spotted from the air. The likeliest place seemed to be in the river itself, but I could think of a dozen reasons why that might not be smart. And if the Feebies couldn't track it by satellite from Berryessa to Sacramento, the hunter was either damned smart, or goddam lucky.

I decided to make some luck on my own by being halfway smart, and eased the Porsche down to the river. It takes less fuel to hover on the water if you're not in a big hurry, and I cruised downstream slowly enough to wave at anglers. Mainly, I was looking for a likely place to spend the night.

A glint from the bluffs told me someone was up there among the trees in heavy cover. Birdwatcher, maybe. From the British Embassy, maybe. I swept across to a banana-shaped island in plain sight and parked, then unlimbered my spinning rig and tried a few casts. I never glanced toward the bluffs and I still don't know if it was perfidious Albion or paranoia that motivated me. But while sitting on a grassy hummock I realized that I couldn't choose a better stakeout than one of these islands.

It required a special effort for me to scrunch through the sand at the water's edge. If I'd weighed five tons it should slow me a lot more. Even a torpedo doesn't move through water very fast; if I chose an island with extensive shallows and a commanding view, I'd have plenty of warning. Well, that was the theory . . .

By the time I'd found my island, the sun was nearing trees that softened the line of bluffs to the west, and dark shadows crept along the river to make navigation chancy. It's no joke if the Porsche's front skirts nose into white water, especially if the turbo intake swallows much of it. I floated upslope past clumps of brush and cut power as my Porsche nosed into tall weeds at the low crest. I stretched my legs, taking the fishing equipment along for protective coloration, and confirmed my earlier decision. It was the best site available.

The island was maybe two hundred yards long; half that in width. Tailings stretched away along both sides of the river. Sand and gravel flanked the island on all sides and the Porsche squatted some twenty feet above the waterline. The nearest shallows were thirty yards from me and, accounting for the lousy traction, I figured Spot might cover the distance in four or five seconds. Surely, surely the hunter would be slower: In that time I could jump the Porsche to safety and put several rounds into a pursuer.

Then I bounced my hand off my forehead and made a quick calculation. If I hoped to be ready for damnall at any second, I absolutely *must not* let the turbo cool down. It takes roughly twelve seconds before the Porsche can go from dead cold to operational temperature, but if I kept it idling I'd be okay. Fuel consumption at idle: ten quarts an hour. I sighed and

trudged back to the car, and went back to Folsom and refueled. Oh, all right: and had Oysters Hangtown with too
much garlic and synthetic bacon. Hell; a guy's gotta eat.

I cruised back to the island again by way of the tailings. I'd
been half afraid the air cushion wouldn't work along those
steep piles of river-rounded stone. Now I was all the way
afraid, because it only half worked. You can't depend on
ground effect pressure when the 'ground' is full of holes and
long slopes. It was like roller-coasting over an open cell
sponge; controlling it was a now-you-have-it, now-you-don't
feeling. As sport it could be great fun. As serious pursuit it
could be suicide.

Back among the tall weeds atop the island, I let the Porsche
idle as I walked the perimeter again, casting with my pitiful
used rig now and then for the sake of form. How any trout
could be so naive as to hit my rusty spinner I will never know;
I played the poor bastard until he finally threw the hook.
Ordinarily I would've taken him home for an Almondine.
But they spoil fast, and I wasn't planning on any fires, and if
Providence was watching maybe It would give me a good-
guy point. God knows I hadn't amassed many.

There were no pugmarks or prints in the sand but mine, and
the tic tac toeprints of waterbirds. I returned to the Porsche
and unwrapped the foil shielding from the rounded gray disc
that had already cost too many lives. It was smaller than a
hockey puck, featureless but for a mounting nipple. It didn't
rattle, hum, or shine in the lengthening shadows, but it had
been manufactured by some nonhuman intelligence, and it
damned well gave me indigestion. I knew it was broadcasting
as it lay in my hand even if I couldn't detect it: calling like
unto like, alien to alien, a message of—what? Distress?
Vengeance? Or simply a call to the hunt? I imagined the
hunter, responding to the call by cruising upriver in its own
interstellar Porsche, as it were, and got busy with an idea that
seemed primitive even to me, while the light was still good
enough to work by.

I cut a pocket from my jacket, a little bag of aramon fiber
that held the alien transmitter easily. Then, using a fishhook as

a needle, I sewed the bag shut and tied it, judging the monofilament line to be twenty pound test. Finally I jammed the rod into the crotch of a low shrub, took the bag, and walked down the gentle slope kicking potential snags out of the way. I laid the bag in the open, hidden by weeds fifteen yards from the water's edge, and eyeballed my field of fire from the Porsche that whined softly to me from above. It was ready to jump. So was I.

A light overcast began to shoulder the sun over the horizon, softening the shadows, making the transition to darkness imperceptible. I retreated to the car, grumbling. I knew there were special gadgets that Dana Martin's puppeteers could have offered me. Night-vision glasses, mass-detector bugs to spread around, constant two-way tightband TV between yours truly and the feds—the list became a scroll in my head. The trouble was, it *was* all special, the kind of equipment that isn't available to private citizens. The microvid was standard hardware for any TV stringer and its 'mayday' module could be removed in an instant. If I wound up as a morgue statistic surrounded by superspy gadgetry, my government connection would be obvious. I didn't know how Dana's SAC would explain the alien hockey puck, but I knew they'd have a scenario for it. They always do.

I cursed myself for retreating down that mental trail, practically assuming failure, which could become a self-fulfilling prophecy. Night birds called in the distance, and told me the whispering whine of my turbo was loud only in my imagination. I released the folding floptop on the Porsche and let it settle noiselessly behind me, something I should have done earlier. I might be more vulnerable sitting in the open, but my eyes and ears were less restricted. My panoramic rearview commanded the upriver sweep, the big-bore automatic was in my hand, and the Porsche's tanks were full—well, nearly full. What was I worried about?

I was worried about that standing ripple a stone's throw off; hadn't it moved? I was spooked by the occasional plash and plop of feeding trout; were they really trout? I was antsy as hell over the idea that I might spend the next eight hours this way, nervous as a frog on a hot skillet, strumming my own nerves like a first-timer on a fruitless stakeout.

Recalling other vigils, days and nights of boredom relieved only by paperbacks and the passing human zoo with its infinitely varied specimens, I began to relax. The trout became just trout, the ripple merely a ripple, the faint billiard-crack of stones across the channel to my left, only a foraging raccoon. Soon afterward, another series of dislodged stones drew my interest. I decided my 'coon was a deer, and split my attention between the tailings and the innocent channel to my right. I'd been foxed once or twice by scufflers who melted away while I was concentrating on a spider or a housecat.

A third muffled cascade of stones, directly across on my left, no more than fifty yards away across the narrow channel. With it came a faint odor, something like a wet dog, more like tobacco. I hoped to see a deer and that's what I saw, the biggest damn' buck I'd ever seen in those parts. It relieved me tremendously as it picked its way down toward the water. Though they're actually pretty stupid, deer know enough to stay well clear of predators. The buck that moved to the shoreline hadn't got that big by carelessness, I figured, which meant that the alien hunter almost certainly couldn't be nearby.

Well, I said 'almost'. In the back of my mind I'd been hoping to see something like that big buck; some evidence that the locale was safe for the likes of me. He picked his way along the shore, staring across in my general direction. As part of the dark mass of the Porsche among the scrub and weeds, I moved nothing but my eyes, happy to have him for a sentry on my left, and alert for anything that might be moving through the channel to my right.

It took the animal perhaps a minute to disappear up a ravine in the tailings—but long before that I began to feel a creeping dread. It came on with a rush as I strained to see the path of the buck along the water's edge. Where the 'buck' had made his stately promenade there was a new trail that gleamed wet in the overcast's reflection from the city, and instead of dainty hoofprints I saw deep pugmarks in the patches of sand.

They seemed the size of dinner plates. I had wanted to see something safe, and I had seen it, and somewhere up in the tailings a fresh rumble told me the alien hunter was not far off.

I let the adrenal chill come, balled my fists and shuddered hard. If I couldn't trust my eyes or instincts, whatthehell *could* I trust? My ears; the hallucination had been visual, my eldritch buck larger than life, the clatter of stones a danger sign I had chosen to misinterpret.

I knew that my hunter—and the deadly semantics of that phrase implied 'the one who hunted me'—would make another approach. I didn't know when or how. Damning the soft whistle of the turbo, I fought an urge to put my foot to the floor, idly wondering what my traitor eyes would offer next as a talisman of safety. I'd made some new decisions in the past minutes: one, that the first thing I saw coming toward me would get seven rounds of heavy artillery as fast as I could pull the trigger.

I waited. I heard a swirl of water to my right, thought hard of trout, expected a shark-sized rainbow to present itself. Nothing. Nothing visual, at least—but in the distance was an almost inaudible hollow slurp as if someone had pulled a fencepost from muck. I opened my mouth wide, taking long silent breaths to fuel the thump between my lungs, and made ready to hit the rewind stud that would reel in the transmitting bait a few feet. I was leaning slightly over the doorsill, the spinning rig in one hand, the Smith & Wesson in the other, staring toward the dim outlines of weeds near my lure. I saw nothing move.

I could hear a distant labored breathing, could feel an errant breeze fan the cold sweat on my forehead, yet the stillness seemed complete. A cool and faintly amused corner of my mind began to tease me for my terror at nothing.

The truth telegraphed itself to the tip of my spinning rod; the gentlest of tugs, the strike of a hatchery fingerling, and in a silent thunderclap of certainty I realized that despite the breeze I had not seen the high grass move either, was hallucinating the visual tableau. To see nothing was to see safety. Not only that: I felt safe, so safe I was smiling. So safe there was no danger in squeezing a trigger.

I fired straight along the fishing line. Yes, goddammit; blindly, since my surest instinct told me it was harmless fun.

When firing single rounds at night, you're wise to fire blindly anyway. I mean, blink as you squeeze; the muzzle flash blinds anyone who's looking toward it and by timing your blinks, you can maintain your night vision to some extent. In this case, I heard a hell of a lot, thought it all hilariously silly, but still I saw nothing move until after my second blink and the round I sent with it.

The second round hit something important because my vision and my sense of vulnerability returned in a flicker. Straight ahead of me, a great dark silvery-banded shape rolled aside with a mewling growl and crunch of brush, and I knew it would be on me in seconds. I floored the accelerator, hit the reel rewind stud, let the Porsche have its head for an instant holding the steering wheel steady with my knee.

Subjectively it seemed that the car took forever to gain momentum, pushing downslope through that rank tobacconist's odor. I dropped the automatic in my lap to steer one-handed, desperately hoping to recover the tiny transmitter.

As my Porsche whooshed to the water's edge I saw the hunter's bulk from the tail of my eye, its snuffling growl louder than its passage through the brush. I was twenty feet out from the shore when it reached the water and surged into the shallows after me. Only the downward slope of the channel saved me in that moment as the hunter submerged. A flash of something ivory-white, scimitar-curved, and the Porsche's body panel drummed just behind the left front wheel skirt. Then I scooted for the far shore.

I turned upstream at the water's edge, grasping the spinning rig, unwilling to admit that the spring-loaded rewind mechanism had reeled in nothing but bare line. The hunter had taken my lure; now I had no bait but myself. At the moment, I seemed to be enough.

Furious at my own panic, I spun the Porsche slowly so that

it backed across the shallows. Apparently I could outrun the hunter, but it wasn't giving up yet. A monstrous bow wave paced me now, a huge mass just below the water. It was within range of my handgun but you can't expect a slug to penetrate anything after passing through a foot of water. I took my bearings again, seeing a sandbar behind me, and hovered toward it.

I saw massive humped shoulders cleave the bow wave, grabbed for my weapon, fired two more rounds that could not have missed, marveled at the hunter's change of pace as it retreated into deeper water. There was nothing for me to shoot at now, no indication of the hunter's line of travel. I angled out across the channel, knowing my pursuer was far too heavy to float and hoping 'deep' was deep enough. Every instant I had the feeling that something would lash up through the Porsche's bellypan until I heard the heavy snort from fifty yards downstream. I'd been afraid the damned thing could breathe underwater, but apparently it had to surface for breath just like any mammal. Chalk up one for my side.

Moving far across the sandbar, I settled the car and let it idle, waiting for the next charge, straining to hear anything that might approach. Under the whirl of possibilities in my head lay the realization that the hunter had lost or abandoned its habit of fooling me; since my second shot, my vision and hearing had agreed during its attacks. All the same, I didn't entirely believe my senses when the hunter splashed ashore a hundred yards downriver, bowling over a copse of saplings to disappear into the darkness.

The overcast was my ally, since it reflected the city's glow enough to reveal the terrain. I wondered where the hunter was going, then decided I might follow its wet trail if I had the guts. And since I didn't, that was when I thought of backtracking its spoor.

I traversed the river, guided my car up a tailings slope, cut power to a whisper. Standing to gaze over the windshield I could see where the 'deer' had moved over the tailings, leaving a dull dark gleam of moist trail on the stones. In a few minutes the stones would be dry. I spotted more damp stones just below the crest of the tailings ravine and followed.

Hardly half a mile downstream the trail petered out, the stones absorbing or losing their surface moisture. But the trail led me toward a bend in the river, and I could see a set of monster pugmarks emerging from the shallows.

I guessed I'd find more pugmarks directly across the river, but I didn't want to bet my life on it. The hunter could be anywhere, on either side of the river. I estimated that the brute couldn't travel more than thirty miles an hour over such terrain, and knew it had been within fifteen minutes of me when I unwrapped the transmitter. A seven-mile stretch? No, wait: I'd heard its original approach over a period of a minute or two, so it had been moving slowly, cautiously. My hunter had probably been holed up within a couple of miles of me—perhaps in its own vehicle somewhere deep in the river.

The Porsche was not responding well and, climbing out with my weapon ready, I inspected the car for damage. There was only one battle scar on it, but that one was a beaut: a clean slice down through the plastic shell, starting as a puncture the size of a pick-axe tip. It allowed the air cushion skirt to flap a bit behind the wheel well, and it told me that the stories about the hunter's sword hadn't been hogwash.

I tested my footing carefully, moved off from my idling machine, then squatted below the hillock crest so I could hear something besides the turbo. Again there came the lulling murmur of the river, a rustle of leaves applauding a fidget of breeze. No clatter of stones, no sign of stealthy approach. I wondered if I had been outdistanced. Or outsmarted.

A subtle movement in the tailings across the river drew my attention. I wasn't sure, but thought I'd caught sight of stones sliding toward the river. Why hadn't I heard it? Perhaps because it was two hundred yards away, or perhaps because it suggested safety. I obeyed the hackles on my neck and slipped back to the Porsche.

As I was oozing over the doorsill I saw above the rockslide and watched a small tree topple on the dim skyline. An instant later came the snap of tortured green wood; I judged that the hunter was more hurried than cautious. Its wet trail would be fresh. I applied half throttle down the slope, passed across the river near enough to spot telltale moisture climbing the tailings, and gunned the turbo.

Twice I felt the car's flexible skirts brush protruding stones as I moved up the adjoining pile of tailings. I was trying to see everything at once: clear escape routes, dark sinister masses of trees poking up through the stones, my alien adversary making its rush over treacherous footing. When the Porsche dipped into the vast depression I nearly lost control, fought it away from the steep downward glide toward a hidden pool. I wasn't quite quick enough and my vehicle slapped the water hard before shuddering across the surface. I tried to accelerate, he felt the vibration through my butt and knew I'd drawn water into the air cushion fans. I'd bent or lost a fan blade—the last thing I needed now. Traveling on wheels was out of the question in this terrain; walking wasn't much better, and if I tried to move upslope again the unbalanced fan might come apart like a grenade.

I brought the Porsche to a stop hovering over water, checking my position. I'd found a big water pocket, one of those places where a rockslide shuts off a small valley in the tailings and, over the years, becomes a dead lake. The tarn was fifty yards or so long, thirty yards wide; the water came up within fifteen yards of the crest. That was a hell of a lot higher than the river, I thought. The stones around the water's edge were darker for a foot or so above the water—whether from old stain or fresh inundation, I couldn't tell. Yet.

I felt horribly vulnerable, trapped there at the bottom of a sloping stone pit, knowing I couldn't be far from an alien hunter. The fan warning light glowed, an angry ruby eye on the dashboard. I let the car settle until its skirts flung a gentle spray in all directions, trying to stay afloat with minimum fan speed. If the fans quit, my Porsche would sink—and if I tried to rush upslope I would blow that fan, sure as hell. Nor could I keep hovering all night. Idle, yes; hover, no.

My own machine was making so much racket, I couldn't

immediately identify the commotion coming from somewhere beyond my trap. Then, briefly, came a hard white
swath of light through treetops that were just visible over the
lip of the pit. A hovering 'copter—and a big one, judging
from the *whock-whock* of its main rotors—was passing
downriver with a searchlight.

The big machine lent momentum to the hunter: the huge
beast came tearing over the lip of my pit in a sudden avalanche
of stones large and small, twisting to lie flat, watching back toward a new enemy that shouted its way downriver.

The hunter was simply awesome, a quadruped the size of a
shortlegged polar bear with the big flat head of an outsize
badger. Around its vast middle, crossing over the piledriving
shoulders, ran broad belts that could have been woven metal.
They held purses big as saddlebags on the hunter's flanks.
The beast's weight was so tremendous that the stones beneath
it shifted like sand when it moved suddenly; so powerful that
it had plowed a furrow through the tailings crest in its haste to
find shelter. But with such a mass it couldn't travel in this
terrain fast unless it made a big noise and a furrow to match. It
hadn't, until now. Once again I revised my estimate of its
den, or vehicle. The hunter couldn't have started toward me
from any great distance.

I had a clear field of fire as the searchlight swept my
horizon again, but the hunter was fifty yards away; too far to
risk wasting a single round. It was intent on the big 'copter
and hadn't seen me yet. I gunned the Porsche directly across
the water, intending to make one irrevocable pass before
angling upslope on my damaged fans toward the river. There
should be time for me to empty the Smith & Wesson.

There should have been, but there wasn't.

Alerted by the scream of the turbo and the squall of galled
fan bearings, the hunter rolled onto its back, sliding down in
my direction, forepaws stretched wide. I saw a great ivory
blade slide from one waving forepaw, a retractable dewclaw
as long as my forearm, curved and tapered. The hunter
scrambled onto its hind legs, off-balance on the shifting
stones but ready for battle.

I wrenched the wheel hard, trying to change direction. Crabbing sideways, the Porsche slid directly toward certain destruction as the hunter hurled a stone the size of my head. I was already struggling upright, trying to jump, when the stone penetrated body panels and cannoned into the chassis.

I think it was the edge of my rollbar that caught me along the left breast as the Porsche shuddered to a stop under the staggering impact. That was when the forward fan disintegrated and I fell backward into the pool. Blinding pain in my left shoulder made me gasp. I shipped stagnant water, almost lost my grip on the weapon in my right hand, but surfaced a few yards from the great beast. It was at the pool's edge as I raised the Smith & Wesson, but the convulsion of my spluttering cough made me duck instead of firing.

The hunter had another stone now, could have pulped me with it, but poised motionless over me; immeasurably powerful, looming too near to miss if it chose to try. I jerked a glance toward the Porsche, which had slowly spun on its aft fan cushion toward deeper water before settling into the stuff. My car began to sink, nose tilted down, and the hunter emitted a series of loud grinding clicks as it watched my car settle. It didn't seem to like my car sinking any better than I did.

Since I'd originally intended to simply immobilize the brute, why didn't I fire again? Probably because it would've been suicide. The hunter held one very deliberate forepaw out, its palm vertical, then lobbed the stone behind me. It was clearly a threat, not an attack; another stone, easily the size of a basketball, was tossed and caught for my edification. When the dewclawed paw waved me nearer, I came. There was really no choice. The effort to swim made my shoulder hurt all the way down to my belly, and the grating of bone ends told me I had a bad fracture.

The damned shoulder hurt more every second and, standing in the shallows now, I eased my left hand into my belt to help support my useless left arm. No good. Without releasing the drenched Smith & Wesson which might or might not fire when wet, I ripped a button from my shirt and let the gap become a sling. Not much better, but some. The hunter towered so near I was blanketed by the rank bull durham odor; could actually feel the heat of its body on my face.

Again the hunter slowly extended both forepaws, digits extended, palms vertical. There was enough cloud reflection for me to see a pair of flat opposable thumbs on each paw, giving the beast manipulation skills without impeding the ripping function of those terrible middle digits.

I stuck the pistol in my belt and held up my right hand, and not all of my trembling was from pain. But I'd got it right: my enemy had signaled me to wait. I was willing enough. Just how much depended on that mutual agreement, I couldn't have imagined at that moment; I figured it was only my life.

Still moving with care and deliberation, the hunter retracted the swordlike dewclaw and fumbled in a saddlebag, bringing forth a wadded oval the thickness of a throw rug. It glowed a dim scarlet as it unfolded and became rigid, two feet across and not as flimsy as it had looked. Around the flat plate were narrow detents like a segmented border. I squinted at it, then at the bulk of the hunter.

The glow improved my vision considerably; I could see three smallish lumps through the bristly scant fur of the hunter's abdomen, and a greatly distended one, the thickness and length of my thigh, ending in a pouch near the hind legs. I took it to be a rearward-oriented sex organ. In a way, I was right.

The hunter sat back with a soft grunt, still looming over me, watching with big eyes set behind sphincter-like lids. I didn't make a move, discounting the sway when I yielded to a wave of pain.

The hunter propped the glowing plate against one hind leg and ran its right 'hand'—obviously too adroit to be merely a paw—along the edge of the plate. I saw a slow rerun of myself squinting into my own face, looking away, trying not to fall over. It made me look like a helpless, waterlogged fat man.

Then the display showed a static view of me, overlaid by others, as a series of heavy clicks came from the plate. The picture became a cartoonish outline of me. After more manipulation by the hunter, the cartoon jerkily folded into a sitting position. The hunter looked at me, thumbed the margin of the plate again. The cartoon sat down again. So did I.

The hunter placed its left 'hand' to its chest and made a big production of letting its eyelids iris shut.

"What the hell does that mean," I said.

Instantly the eyes were open, the dewclaw extended and waving away in what I took to be a slashing negation.

I knew one sign: 'wait'. I raised my empty hand, palm out, and thought hard. Humans have a lot of agreed-upon gestures that seem to be based on natural outcomes of our bodies and their maintenance. But we're omnivores. Pure predators, carnivores like the great cats, have different gestural signs. I didn't *know* the hunter was in either category but you've got to start somewhere.

I cudgeled my memory for what I'd read of the ethologists, people like Tinbergen and van Iersel and Lopez, whose books had helped me live with a cheetah. The slashing motion was probably a mimed move of hostility, a rejection. Maybe it was hunterese for 'no'.

To test the notion, I made an obvious and slow gesture of reaching for the automatic in my belt. The eyes irised, the dewclaw slashed the air again as easily as it could have slashed me. I started to say something, suddenly suspected that the hunter didn't want me to talk. I remembered something about speech interfering with gestural language, then pointed to the weapon with my finger and made a throwing-away gesture of my own.

Distinctly and slowly in the red glow, the hunter folded its left hand to its breast and closed its eyes in a long blink. I brought my good hand to my breastbone and blinked in return. It made sense: if an intelligent predator closes its eyes and withdraws its natural weapon from sight, that compound gesture should be the opposite of hostility. Unless I was hopelessly—maybe fatally—wrong, I had signs for 'no' and 'yes' in addition to 'wait'.

The hunter's next attempt with the display took longer,

with several evidently botched inputs. It seemed to breathe
through a single sphinctered nostril in its muzzle, and the
snuffling growl of its breath was irregular. I began to wonder
if any of those drugged bullets was having an effect; tried not
to cough as I watched. My chest hurt, too—not with the
spectacular throb of my collarbone but enough to make me
short of breath.

The dimness of the display suggested that the hunter could
see infrared, including the heat signatures of prey, better than
I could. That display was now showing a cartoon of the
hunter and of me, gesturing, while clouds of little dots
migrated from each head to the other. Germs? Were we
infecting each other?

The hunter pointed a thumb at the display. Sign: 'yes'.
Then the display, under the hunter's guidance, stopped the
gestures and the dots flowing from my side. The next cartoon
was pellucid and coldblooded, as the figure of the hunter
slashed out at the me-figure. The human part of the display
disintegrated into a shapeless mass of dots. The hunter tapped
the display plate and signed, 'no'.

If the hunter wanted those dots to pass between us, they
must mean something useful. If not germs, then what? If I
stopped gesturing, the dots stopped. Uh-huh! The dots were
communications; messages. There was an assumption built
into the display sequence: it assumed that our brains were in
our heads. For all I'd known, the hunter's brain might've
been in its keester.

So I was being warned to cooperate, to talk or I'd be dead
meat. I signed 'yes' twice and coughed once, tasting salt in
my mouth.

The display went blank, then showed the hunter sketch
without me. Not alone, because from its bulging pouch a
small hunter's head protruded, biting on the prominent sex
organ of the big beast. Not until then did I harbor a terrible
surmise. I pointed from the display to the hunter, and I was
close enough that I could point specifically at the big swollen
organ.

She lifted the long dribbling teat from her pouch, and she signed, 'yes'.

She. Oh sweet shit. The hunter was a huntress, a female with a suckling babe, and I'd mistaken the lone functioning teat for a male organ. But she had no suckling babe, as she indicated by patting the empty pouch. No, and she wouldn't ever have it again. The little one had been an infant, not a pet. It hadn't been entirely our fault but I felt we, the human race, stumblebums of the known universe, had killed it. Or let it kill itself, which was almost as bad.

My fear of the revenge she might take—and a pang of empathy for a mourning mother of any species—conspired to make me groan. That brought on a cough, and I ducked my head trying to control the spasm because it hurt so goddam much to cough. I wasn't very successful. Luckily.

When I looked up again, the huntress was staring at me, her head cocked sideways in a pose that was almost human. Then she spread the short fur away from her belly with both hands and I saw a thick ooze of fluid that matted the fur there. When she pointed at the weapon in my belt, then at the puncture wound, I knew at least one slug had penetrated her flesh. But it might have been from the guy she'd met with the new rifle. Not likely: she had specifically indicated my weapon. When she ducked her head and grunted, I cocked my own head, waiting. She repeated the charade, complete with the series of coughing grunts and ducked head, as if imitating me.

By God, she *was* imitating me. It didn't take a Konrad Lorenz to know when an animal is in pain, and she was generating a sign for 'hurt' that was based on my own behavior.

I signed 'yes'. Staring at the woven belt that bandoliered over her shoulders, I saw that another slug had been deflected by a flat package with detent studs—pushbuttons for a big thumb. The studs were mashed, probably deformed by the slug's impact, and while I may never know for sure, I suspect that little package had been responsible for the hallucinations before I put it out of commission.

The huntress was punching in a new display. Images fled across the screen until she had the one she wanted, a high-resolution moving image. Somehow I knew instantly it was a family photo, my huntress lounging on a sort of inflated couch while another of her species, slightly smaller and with no pouch, stood beside her leaning on a truly monstrous dewclaw like a diplomat on his umbrella. Proud father? I think so. He—it—was looking toward the infant that suckled in her protective custody.

The huntress pointed at her breast, then at the image to assure me that the image was indeed of her.

I gave a 'yes', managing to avoid another cough which could have been misinterpreted. I was beginning to feel cold; on hindsight I suppose it was mild shock. If I fainted, I'd stop communicating. The huntress had made it very clear what would happen if I stopped communicating.

From a saddlebag she drew the little transmitter she'd stolen back from me, still in the sewn-up pocket. She developed a cartoon of the disc, gestured to show it represented the real one, adjusted the display. The disc image floated across the display to the now-still-shot of the infant. She stared at me, unmoving.

Of course I understood. I signed 'yes'.

She patted her empty pouch, held both hands out, drew them toward her. In any language, a bereft mother was imploring me for the return of her baby.

I signed 'no', then gritted my teeth against the fit of coughing that overtook me, and this time I knew the salt taste was blood in my throat. When I looked up, I knew the cough had saved my life; the dewclaw was in inch from my belly, and she was dribbling something like dark saliva from her fanged mouth while she insisted 'yes', and 'yes' again.

I ducked my head and formally grunted. I was hurt, I was sorry. I pointed to the image of the infant hunter, made the negative sign again, again the sign for my pain. Anguish can be mental, too; we seemed to agree on that.

She withdrew the threatening scythe, wiped her mouth, changed the display again. Now it was an image of the infant with an image of me. Expectant stare.

I denied it, pointing off in the distance. She quickly multiplied the image of me, made them more slender. Other men had her baby? I agreed.

She showed another swarm of dots moving between her baby and the men's images, waited for my answer.

Negative. Her baby wasn't communicating with us. I don't know why I told the truth, but I did. Eventually she'd get around to the crucial question. If I lied she might take me hostage. If I told the truth she might mince me. She sat for a long moment, swaying, staring at me and, if the dark runnel meant what I think it did, sobbing. I also think she was as nearly unconscious as I was.

At last she fumbled the display into a single outline of her baby, then—with evident reluctance—made an adjustment. The image collapsed into shapeless fragments.

I started to make the 'pain' sign, but it developed into the real thing before I could recover. Then I signed 'yes'. Her baby was dead.

She tucked her muzzle into forearms crossed high, soft grinding clicks emanating from—I think—some head cavity, swayed and snuffled. Not a message to me or anyone else. A deeply private agony at her loss.

My next cough brought enough blood that I had to spit, and I put one hand out blindly as I bowed to the pain. I felt a vast enveloping alien hand cover my own, astonishingly hot to the touch, and looked up to find her bending near me. Her tobaccolike exhalation wasn't unpleasant. What scared me was the sense of numbness as I tried to get my breath. I slumped there as she withdrew her big consoling hand, watched dully as she pointed to the image of the infant's remains.

She motioned that she wanted the body. I thought if I stood up, I could breathe. I signed 'yes' and 'no' alternately, then tried an open-handed shrug as I struggled to my feet. It helped, but even as I was making the sign for her to wait, she kept insisting. Yes, yes, give me my baby. The big dewclaw came out. I couldn't blame her.

But the only way I could get her baby back was by calling a mayday, and my microvid with its transmitter was in the sunken Porsche. As I turned, intending to gesture into the pool, I saw that the Porsche hadn't completely sunk after all, was floating still. Maybe I could find the microvid. I stumbled backward as the huntress lurched up to stop me, signing negation with murderous slashes.

She came as far as the shallows, erect, signing for me to wait as I kicked hard in the best one-armed sidestroke I could manage. I was giddy, short of breath, felt I wasn't going to make it; felt the grating in my collarbone, told myself I *had* to, and did.

My next problem was getting into the car and, as my feet sank, they touched something smooth below the car. My mind whirled, rejecting the idea that the bottom was only two feet down. But a faint booming vibration told me the bottom was hollow. Then I knew where the huntress kept her vehicle. My Porsche had settled squarely atop an alien ship, hidden beneath the surface of that stagnant pool.

I got the door open, sloshed inside, managed to find the microvid with my feet and brought it up from the floorboards with my good hand, coughing a little blood and a lot of water. The car's running lights worked even if the headlights were under water, and I found the mayday button before I aimed the gadget toward the huntress. She had staggered back to shore, dimly lit by the glow of the Porsche's rear safety lights, and was gesturing furiously.

As near as I could tell, she was waving me off with great backhanded armsweeps. She pointed down into the pool, made an arc with her dewclaw that ended in a vertical stab. I could barely see her but thought I understood; it wouldn't be healthy for me to stay there when she lifted off. I agreed and signed it, hoping her night vision could cope with my message, showing her my microvid and signing for her to wait.

The last I saw of her, the huntress was slowly advancing into the depths of the pool. She was signing, 'No! Clear out'.

I wanted to leave, but couldn't make my muscles obey. I was cold, freezing cold; bone-shivering, mind-numbing cold, and when I collapsed I lost the microvid over the side.

Not far out from the Porsche, a huge bubble broke the surface, a scent of moldy cavendish that must have come from an alien airlock. *They aren't really all that different from us,* I thought, and *I wish I could've told somebody that and ohjesus I can feel a vibration through the chassis. Here we go . . .*

Olfactory messages have got to be more basic than sight or sound. By the smell of starch and disinfectant, I could tell I was in a hospital long before I could make sense of the muttered conversation, or recognize that the buttercup yellow smear was featureless ceiling. In any case, I didn't feel like getting up right then.

Just outside my private room in the hall, a soft authoritative female voice insisted that she would not be pressured into administering stimulants at this time, exclamation point. Rackham had bled a lot internally from his punctured lung, and the ten-centimeter incision she'd made to reposition that rib was a further shock to his system, and for God's sake give the man a chance.

Other voices, one female, argued in the name of the national interest. If the good doctor watched newscasts, she knew Harvey Rackham was in a unique position vis-a-vis the human race.

The doctor replied that Rackham's position was flat on his arse, with a figure-eight strap holding his clavicle together and a pleurovac tube through his chest wall. If Miz Martin was so anxious to get stimulants into Rackham, she could do it herself by an old-fashioned method. Evidently the doctor had Dana Martin pegged; that was the first time I ever knew that caffeine can be administered as a coffee enema.

A vaguely familiar male cadence reminded the doctor that

Rackham was a robust sort, and surely there was no real risk if his vital signs were good.

The doctor corrected him. Vital signs were only good considering Rackham's condition when the chopper brought him in. His heartrate and respiration were high, blood pressure still depressed. If he carried twenty less kilos of meat on him—at least she didn't say 'flab'—he'd be recovering better. But the man was her patient, and she'd work with what she had, and if security agencies wanted to use Rackham up they'd have to do it after changing physicians. Then she left. I liked her, and I hadn't even seen her.

Dana Martin's trim little bod popped into view before I could close my eyes; she saw I was awake. "Harve, you've given us some anxious hours," she scolded cutely.

I'd heard some of that anxiety, I said, and flooded her with questions like the time of which day, how long would I be down, where was the alien, did they know it was a female.

"Hold on; one thing at a time, fella." Scott King stepped near, smiling, welcoming me back as if he meant it. Scotty, Dana's area SAC, was an ex-linebacker with brains. I'd met him years before; not a bad sort, but one who went by the book. And sometimes the book got switched on him. From his cautious manner I gathered he was thumbing through some new pages as he introduced me to Señor Hernen Ybarra, one of the non-permanent members of the U.N. Security Council. Ybarra, a somber little man in a pearl-grey summer suit that must have cost a fortune, showed me a dolorous smile but was barely civil to the two Feebies, managing to convey that there was nothing personal about it. He just didn't approve of the things they did for a living.

·I put my free hand out, took Ybarra's. I said, "Security Council? Glad to meet a man with real clout."

The eyes lidded past a moment's wry amusement. "A relative term," he assured me. "Our charter is to investigate, conciliate, recommend adjustments, and—" one corner of his mouth tried to rebel at the last phrase, "—enforce settlements."

"What's wrong with enforcement, *per se?* I've been in the business myself."

With softly accented exactness: "It is an egregious arrogance to speak of *our* enforcing a Sacramento settlement."

"The clout is with the hunting people," Dana chimed in, patting my hand, not letting it go. Her sex-appeal pumps were on overdrive, which meant she was on the defensive.

I let her think I was fooled. "Hunting people? You've found more, then?"

"They found us," King corrected me, "while we were draining that sinkhole in the middle of the night. Smart move, immobilizing that shuttle craft by parking on it. We owe you one."

I thought about that. "The huntress didn't lift off, then," I said, looking at King for confirmation.

A one-beat hesitation. "No. Paramedics realized you were lodged on top of something when they found you. The most important thing, right now, is whether you had any peaceful contact with the female hunter before you zapped each other."

"Is anybody taping us now?"

Ybarra and King both indicated their lapel units with cables snaking into coat pockets. "Rest assured," King said laconically.

I told them I'd managed a couple of lucky hits with the medicated slugs. When I mentioned that the visual hallucinations and the shallow whatthehell feeling stopping after I hit a piece of the huntress's equipment, a sharp glance passed between Ybarra and King.

"So: it would seem not to be an organic talent," Ybarra mused with relief. "Go on."

I gave a quick synopsis. The hovercraft that passed downriver—chartered by Chinese, Ybarra told me—, the way I'd managed to get myself walloped when falling from my Porsche, my sloppy sign language with the huntress, my despairing retreat to the half-sunken car to find my microvid.

"So you made no recording until you were safely distant,"

Ybarra muttered sadly, sounding like a man trying to avoid placing blame. "But still you were making sign language?"

"Mostly the huntress was doing that. She wanted me the hell out of there. I wanted to, believe me."

King, in hissing insistence: *"But where is the microvid unit?"*

"You'll find it in the pool somewhere," I said. The shrug hurt.

King shook his head. "No we won't. Maybe the hunting people will." At my glance he went on: "Pumping out the pool must have given them a fix. They came straight down like a meteorite and shooed us away before dawn this morning. No point in face-to-face negotiation; anybody that close, acts like he's on laughing gas. But they've been studying us a while, it seems."

"How'd they tell you that?"

"Clever system they have," Ybarra put in; "a computer-developed animation display that anyone can receive on VHF television. The hunting people make it clear that they view us as pugnacious little boys. The question before them, as we understand it, is whether we are truly malign children."

"You can ask the huntress. She's reasonable."

"That is what we cannot do," Ybarra said. "They acknowledge that the female came here mentally unbalanced."

Scotty King broke in, waving his hand as if disposing of a familiar mosquito: "Spoiled young base commander's wife; serious family argument. She takes their kid, steals a jeep, rushes off into cannibal country. Kid wanders off; distraught mother searches. Soap opera stuff, Harve. The point is, they admit she was nuts."

"With her baby dead from cannibal incompetence," I added, spinning out the analogy. "Who *wouldn't* be half crazy? By the way, what base do they command?"

King looked at Ybarra, who answered. "Lunar farside; the Soviets believe their site is just beyond the libration limit in the Cordillera chain. The hunting people are exceedingly tough organisms and could probably use lunar mass to hide a fast final approach before soft-landing there.''

"You don't have to tell me how tough they are," I said, "or that we reacted like savages—me included.''

"It is absolutely vital," Ybarra said quietly, "that we show the hunting people some sign that we attempted a friendly interchange. If we cannot, our behavior is uniformly bad in their view. Some recording of your sign talk is vital," he said again.

"Find the microvid. Or bring me face to face with the huntress, since she didn't lift off after all.'' I brightened momentarily, trying to be clever: "The vital signs are hers, after all.''

Silence. Stolid glances, as Dana withdrew her hand.

"You may as well tell him," Ybarra husked.

"I wouldn't," Dana warned. She knew me pretty well.

Scotty King: "It took a half-hour to find you after your mayday, Harve; and two hours more to pump the water down to airlock level. The female had turned on some equipment but she never tried to lift off. There were no vital signs when we reached her.''

Dana Martin cut through the bullshit. "She's dead, Rackham. We don't know exactly why, but we learned that much before their second ship came barreling in.''

I made fists, somehow pleased at the fresh stabbing twinge through my left shoulder. "So I killed her. No wonder you're afraid of a global housecleaning.''

King: "Not much doubt they could do it.''

"And they might exercise that option," Ybarra added, "without a recording to verify your story.''

Dana Martin sought my gaze and my hand. "Now you see our position, and yours," she said, all the stops out on her Wurlitzer of charm.

I pulled my hand away. "Better than you do," I growled. "You people have taped this little debriefing. And the flexible display the huntress used seemed to have videotape capability, or it couldn't have developed an animation of me on the spot. She was taping, too, out there on the rockpile.''

King, staccato: "Where is her recording?"

"Ask the hunting people." My voice began to rise despite my better judgment. "But don't ask anything more from *me*, goddam you! Take your effing debrief tape and run it for the hunting people. Or don't. Just get out and leave me alone."

Scott King cleared his throat and came to attention. "We are prepared, of course, to offer you a very, very attractive retainer on behalf of the State Department—"

"So you can pull more strings, hide more dynamite, slip me another weapon? Get laid, Scotty! I've had a gutful of your bloody mismanagement. My briefings were totally inadequate; your motives were short-sighted; the whole operation was half-assed, venal and corrupt."

Dana abandoned the cutesypie role; now she only looked small and cold and hard. "How about your own motives and venality?"

"Why d'you think I'm shouting," I shouted.

King became stiffly proper. "Let me get this straight for the record. You won't lift a hand for the human race because you're afraid to face the hunting people again."

"Don't you understand *any*thing, asshole? I'm not afraid: I'm *ashamed!* That grief-stricken predator showed more respect for life processes than all of us put together. In the most basic, vital way—the huntress was my friend. You might say yes when your friend says no, but once you've agreed to defer a selfish act you've committed a friendly one."

Ybarra had his mouth ready. "Don't interrupt," I barked. "The first agreement we made was to hold back, to confer; to wait. I know a cheetah named Spot who wouldn't waste a second thought on me if he thought I'd had anything to do with killing one of his kits. He'd just put me through Johnny Rubeck's machine. And I wouldn't blame him."

Ybarra's face revealed nothing, but King's was flushed. "You're inhuman," he said.

"Jesus, I hope so," I said, and jerked my thumb toward the door.

Well, I've had a few hours to think about it, mostly alone. What hurts a lot more than my collarbone is the suspicion that the huntress waited for me to clear out before she would move her ship. Okay, so she'd wasted some lives in her single-minded desperation to recover her child. In their ignorance those killed had been asking for it. Me? I was begging for it! It was no fur off her nose if I died too, and she was lapsing into a coma because I'd shot her full of drugs that may have poisoned her, and other humans had used her own baby's tissues to fashion weapons against her. And there she sat, for no better reason than an uncommon decency, waiting. And it killed her.

It's bad enough to get killed by enmity; it's worse to get it through friendship. In my friend's place, I know what I'd have done, and I don't like thinking about that either. When you're weak, waiting is smart. When you're strong, it's compassion. Compassion can kill you.

As soon as I get out of here I'm going into my smithy in the shadow of Mount Diablo and pound plowshares for a few weeks, and talk to Spot, and mull it over.

If I get out of here. Nobody seems very anxious to stick to the hospital routines; they're all watching the newscasts, essentially doing what I'm doing.

What the hunting people are doing.

Waiting.

In the last story, I made the point that our most vital signs are nonverbal. Few behavioral scientists would argue against that, but they'll go to the mat over ways to quantify it! I still entertain a vagrant hope that someday a specialist in nonverbals will rediscover my doctoral dissertation, which quantified the errors made by people observing nonverbals in field settings.

But the Master's thesis was in Amerind sign talk, where I found that gestural language can be powerfully verbal; not oral, but verbal in the sense that it's as symbolic as letters of an alphabet. At the time, I was introduced to studies on Washoe and other chimps; and then came Lilly's work with dolphins—which was only an intuitive leap away from the story below.

Maybe cetaceans need one thing to communicate with us, maybe another, maybe both or neither. In any case we may be wise to keep it down to basics. Karel Capec told us why a long time ago . . .

Liquid Assets

Because she'd had an exhausting week training a young bottlenose, Vicki Lorenz dallied in her bungalow over the standard Queensland breakfast of steak and eggs. And because it was Saturday, the Aussie marine biologists had trooped off to Cooktown, leaving Cape Melville Station to her for the weekend. Or maybe they just wanted to avoid her fellow Americans scheduled to fly in; she couldn't blame them for that. She did not know or care why a research site near the nor-east tip of Australia had attracted visiting honchos.

Though it was midmorning in September, the sun had not yet forced its way through the pile of cumulus that loomed eastward over the Barrier Reef like the portent of a wet summer. She chose her best short-sleeved yellow blouse as concession to her visitors, and faded denim shorts as refusal to concede too much. She flinched when the sun searchlighted through her bedroom window to splash her reflection in the full-length mirror. Short curls, intimidated toward platinum by tropical summers, complemented the blouse, bright against her burnt-bronze skin. In two years, she thought, she'd be as old as Jack Benny, and her deceptive youthful epidermis would begin its slow sea change into something like shark leather. She tucked the blouse in, assessing the compact torso and long thighs that gave her a passable, if angular, figure with less than average height. It would do, she thought. If Korff had liked it so much, it had to be in good taste.

Against her will, her eyes searched out the curling poster she had tacked against the bedroom wall two years ago, after Korff's boat had been found. Sunlight glinted off the slick

paper so that she saw only part of the vast greenish tube of a
surfer's dreamwave which some photographer had impris-
oned on film. At the lower left was a reprinted fragment from
Alec Korff's *'Mariner Adrift'* :

> *The wave is measured cadence*
> *In the ocean's ancient songs*
> *Of pélagic indifference*
> *To mankind's rights and wrongs . . .*

And knowing that indifference as well as anyone, he'd
made some trifling mistake along the treacherous reef, and it
had cost him. Correction: it had cost *her*. Well, no doubt it
benefited the reef prowlers. Korff would have been pleased,
she thought, to know that his slender body had finally become an offering to the flashing polychrome life among the
coral. She turned then, self-conscious in the sliver of light,
and made a mocking bow toward the sun. Scuffing into
sandals, she padded out to her verandah. It was then that she
saw Pope Pius waiting before the sea gate far below, a
three-meter torpedo in grey flesh.

She called his name twice, trotting down the path. She
knew it was her old friend Pius even though his identifying
scars were below the water's surface. The slender mass of the
microcorder, on its harness just ahead of the high dorsal fin,
was unmistakable. He heard and greeted her, rearing vertically, the sleek hairless body wavering as tail flukes throbbed
below. He was an adult *griseus,* a Risso's dolphin, with
exquisite scimitar flippers and a beakless prominent nose that
made the name *Pius* inevitable. Inevitable, that is, if you had
Korff's sense of the absurd.

Soon she had activated the pneumatics, the stainless grate
sliding up to permit free passage from Princess Charlotte Bay
into the concrete-rimmed lagoon. She whistled Pius in, whistled again. Then she clicked her tongue and spanked the
water to urge him forward. The cetacean merely sidled near
the planking outside the sea gate, rolled to view her with one
patient eye, and waited.

Vicki sighed and fetched the lightly pickled squid, tossed
one of the flaccid morsels just inside the gate. No

response—perhaps the slightest show of impatience or wariness as if to say, *I'm jack of it, mate; it's dicey in there.* Except that Pius was cosmopolitan, no more Aussie than he was Japanese or Indonesian. As usual, she tended to append false values to the people of the sea, and then to chide herself for it.

Eventually Vicki went outside the sea gate and knelt on the wood. Pius rolled to assist her, breathing softly to avoid blowhole spray that could soak her with its faint alien rankness. She fed him one small squid, earning a rapid burst of friendly Delphinese complaint at her stinginess, and she knew he would wait for her to return.

The videotape was fully spent. The batteries should be good for another cartridge but Vicki took fresh nicad cells from the lab with a new blank tape cartridge just to be on the safe side. She was hurrying back to Pius when she saw the aircraft dip near. Sure enough, it was one of the Helio Couriers which, everybody knew, meant that the passengers had clout with American cloak-and-dagger people. On the other hand, there'd been a lot of that kind of air traffic in the area for the past fortnight. She was increasingly glad that McEachern and Digby had gone to Cooktown to get shickered. *Plastered,* she told herself; *must revert to American slang for the day.*

Something seemed to be bothering the big *griseus,* she thought, fumbling to replace the equipment on Pius's backpack. He had never refused to enter the sea gate before. *Don't get shirty,* she thought; *if I'm late it's my bum, not yours.* And because of Pius, she was clearly going to be late. The fact of his early return made the tape important, though. The microcorder operated only when triggered by calls made by Pius himself, and it pinged to remind him of squid when the cartridge was expended. That meant he might return once a month—though he was very early this time. Two years ago it had been once a week, and no one was sure why Pius communicated with his fellows less as time passed. Perhaps he was growing laconic with age, she thought, giving him a pat before she upended the squid bucket.

Pius whirled and took a mouthful of delicacies in one
ravening swoop, pausing an instant to study Vicki, then
seemed to evaporate into the bay, leaving only a roil of salt
water in his wake. Water and uneaten squid. *Boy, you must
have a heavy date,* she mused. It did not occur to Vicki
Lorenz that the big cetacean might be hurrying, not toward,
but away from something.

She wheeled the decrepit Holden sedan onto the taxi strip,
chagrined to see that the pilot had already set his chocks and
tiedowns. The portly fellow standing with the attache case
would be Harriman Rooker, from the cut of his dark suit and
the creases in his trousers which might have been aligned by
laser. The little weatherbeaten man sitting on the B-four bag,
then, had to be Jochen Shuler.

Vicki made breathless apologies. "I had a visitor who
wouldn't wait," she smiled. "Dolphins can be a surly lot."

So could State Department men. "At least you make no
secret about your priorities, Dr. Lorenz," Rooker said. "It *is*
Dr. Victoire Lorenz?" The hand was impeccably manicured,
its grip cool and brief, the smile a micron thick.

"I truly am sorry," she said, fighting irritation, and turned
toward the smaller man. Shuler wore rumpled khakis and no
tie, his voice a calm basso rasp leavened with humor.
"Forget it," he said, with a shoulder pat that was somehow
not patronizing. "It's not as if we were perishable."

The imp of extravagance made her say it: "Everybody's
perishable in tropical salt. You come here all bright and
shiny, but you leave all sheit and briny." Shuler's control
was excellent; his wiry frame shook silently but he only put
his head down and grinned. Rooker was plainly not amused.
Well, at least she could relate to one of them.

The pilot, Rooker explained, was prepared to stay and take
care of the Courier. He looked as though he could do it, all
right. The bulge in his jacket was no cigarette case. Rooker
selected three of his four pieces of luggage for the Holden's
boot (*trunk, dammit; trunk,* Vicki scolded herself). One, a
locked leather and canvas mail sack, required both men to

lift. Shuler lugged his one huge bag into the rear seat. The bag clinked. Perrier water? Booze?

Vicki appointed herself tour guide without thinking and drove along access roads until she was pointing out the salt water pens where young dolphins and other cetaceans were monitored. "We knew Delphinese has dialectal differences, just as people and honeybees have local variants of language. We're using recorders to identify various subspecies by sonic signatures. I've made friends with a big Risso's dolphin that roams around loose with a video recorder, sort of a linguistic shill. Maybe we can get some idea whether a *grampus orca*, a killer whale, sweet-talks a little *tursiops* before he swallows it. Generally, larger species communicate in lower frequencies—." She broke off, glancing at Harriman Rooker who sat erect beside her, his right arm lying precisely along the windowframe. *Straightens pictures*, she guessed. His left hand was in his lap and—inexcusable for a trained observer—Vicki realized only then that a wrist manacle bound the man to his equipment. She pulled to a stop, killed the engine. "You didn't come here for a tour," she accused. With sudden intuition, she did not want to know why they had come.

Rooker's pale eyes swept her face, hawk-bright, unblinking. "No," he agreed. "We are here for an exchange of information—and other valuables. A matter of the most extreme urgency, Dr. Lorenz."

"Vicki, please," she urged with her most engaging smile.

"If I must. I suggest that *you* tell *us* what our next move should be."

She searched the implacable features, puzzled, then faintly irked. She felt as if she had been thrust into the middle of a conversation she hadn't been listening to. "Well, you could try telling me what information you need, and why the urgency."

He stared until she grew positively uneasy. And that made her, unaccountably, angry. Then, "Tell us about Agung Bondjol," he said. Softly, but cold, cold.

"Uh. A kid from Djakarta, wasn't he? Right; he was with

that Wisconsin senator on the *R. L. Carson* when she sank a few hundred miles south of here last month. One of the four people lost."

From the back seat: "Some kid."

"Thank you, Jo," Rooker said quickly, in that'll-be-enough tones. "Nothing more, Dr.—Vicki?"

"If there was, I didn't read it. I don't pay much attention to the news on any medium, you know."

"Apparently. Now tell us about Alec Korff." The transition was verbally smooth, but for Vicki it was viciously abrupt.

She took a deep breath. "Poet first, I suppose; that's how he liked it. And because he could be acclaimed at that and starve at the same time, he made his living as a tooling engineer.

"Korff got interested in interspecies communication between cetaceans and humans; his mystic side, I guess. He didn't give two whoops about explicit messages. Just the emotional parts."

Low, but sharp: "You're sure of that?"

Long pause, as Vicki studied the sea for solace. Then she said, "Certain as one person can be of another. He once said that the truth is built from gestures, but words are the lumber of lies. He hated phonies and loved cetaceans.

"You know, of course, that I lived with Korff. Met him while I was getting my doctorate at Woods Hole and he was designing equipment for whales and dolphins. Prosthetic hands they could work with flipper phalanges, underwater vocoders, that sort of thing. When I landed the job here, he came with me."

She waited for Rooker to respond. When he did not, she sighed, "Korff was happy here. I knew when he was really contented because he'd compose doggerel on serious topics and laugh his arse off about it. Hiding his pearls like a swine, he said. Everybody's heard *'Mariner Adrift'*, but did you ever hear *'Fourteen Thousand Pounds Of God'*? Pompous *and* self-deprecating, and hides a great truth right out in the open.

'The orca's fangéd dignity
Fills me with humility.
One is wise to genuflect
To seven tons of self-respect.'

The killer whale doesn't really have fangs, of course. Just teeth a tyrannosaur would envy. Korff knew that. He knew a hell of a lot about cetaceans.''

Still no response. Rooker was not going to let her off the hook. ''And two years come November,'' she recited quickly, fingernails biting her palms, ''Korff took his goddam sloop along the goddam Barrier Reef and caught a goddam tradewind squall or something and goddammit, *drowned!* Is that what you wanted to hear?''

''Quite the contrary,'' Rooker said, still watching her.

Instantly she was out of the car. ''I don't know why I let the consulate talk me into this pig-in-a-poke hostess job on my own time, and now it's become cat-and-mouse insinuation, and I won't have it! If you know anything, you know how I felt about Korff and—and you can go piss up a rope, mate,'' she stormed. She slammed the door so hard the Holden groaned on its shocks.

Halfway to her bunglaow afoot, she looked back to see Shuler patiently following. He had a bottle in each hand, so she waited. It seemed a good idea at the time.

Given that they knew her fondness for mezcal, how did they know she couldn't get it locally? Vicki considered many such nuances in the next hour, sitting cross-legged with Jo Shuler while they plastered themselves into a thin film on her verandah. At first he answered nearly as many questions as he asked. She learned that he was detached from the U.S. Mine Defense Labs in Panama City, Florida; an expert in experimental sonar video and no ignoramus on dolphin research either. He had read her papers on cetacean language, but his own papers were classified. He did not elaborate.

Shuler even managed to explain his companion's cryptic manner, after a fashion. It wasn't nice, Vicki decided, but it made sense. ''Okay,'' she said, stifling a belch, ''so some nit at Rand Corporation figured Korff was alive and that I knew it. I'm sure he isn't, and if he is, I don't.'' She shrugged: "You know what I mean. So much for heavy thinkers at Rand.''

Shuler regarded her gravely, listing to port a bit. "Why are you so sure?''

"You want it straight?'' Why was she so willing to bare these intimacies? Something beyond her normal candor was squeezing her brains. "Okay: Alec Korff had a few leftover sex hangups, and very tough standards, but he was highly sexed. Me, too. My mother hated him for his honesty about it. She was a tiny little thing, always trying to prove something by vamping him. Then one day she phoned—I was on the extension and I don't think either of them knew it. She implied she might fly up to see him alone. Korff suggested she could ride a whiskbroom and save the price of a ticket.'' She spread her hands wide. "How could I not love a man like that? Anyway, the point is that we clicked. It was like finding the other half of yourself. He played poet for me and I played floozy for him.'' With a sly grin: "It'd take him years to develop a replacement, I think. Oh yes, he'd have got in touch with me, all righty.'' She took a mighty swig, remembering. "You can go back to the car and tell Mr. stiff-corset Rooker all about it.''

"I bet he's blushing about the corset,'' Shuler laughed, then looked abashed.

Vicki squinted hard. "You're bugged, aren't you? He's been listening!'' She saw guilt, and a touch of truculence, and went on. "You two have been rough-smoothing me, haven't you? He's really the rough and you're really the smooth. How many of my old friends did you bastards interview before I fitted into your computers?'' She stared grimly at her bottle; she had consumed over a pint of the stuff and now she had a good idea why Shuler was drinking from another bottle.

"I dunno about that, Vicki, I was briefed just like Rooker was. He's used to representing the government, negotiating with some pretty weird groups. I'm just a technician like you. Lissen, lady, we're hip-deep in hockey—all of us.''

She flung the bottle far out over the turf, watched it bounce. "Not me, I feel bonzer."

"You're just high."

"High? I could hunt kookaburra with a croquet mallet," she boasted, then went down on hands and knees near the immobile Shuler, shouting, "That's a bird, Rooker, you twit!" Then she saw past Shuler's foolish grin, realized that he carried a shoulder holster too, and sat back. "You people scare me. Go away."

"We're scared too," he said, no longer playing the drunk. As though Rooker were standing before them he went on, "She's about to pass out on us, Harriman. Why can't we drop this interrogation farce and accept her at face value? Or d'you have any nasty little questions to add to mine before the drug wears off?"

Australian slang is compost-rich with unspeakable utterance. Vicki Lorenz had heard most of it, and found it useful now. She had not exhausted her repertoire when she began to snore.

Jo Shuler waited for a moment, moved near enough to tap his forefinger against her knee. Snores. "Drive that heap on over here," he said to his signet ring. "She's out. We can put a call through while she sleeps it off. For the record, I say we take a chance on her." Then he managed to carry Vicki inside to the couch, and waited for Harriman Rooker.

Late afternoon shadows dappled the verandah before Vicki had swept the cobwebs from her mind. To Rooker's apology she replied, "Maybe I could accept those vague insinuations if I knew what's behind them. What's so earth-shaking about that kid, Bondjol?"

"He's small loss in himself," Rooker agreed. "He's a renegade Sufi Moslem—pantheist, denied the concept of evil, embraced drugs to find religious ecstasy, learned he could purchase other ecstasy from the proceeds of his drug-running—tricks that's get him arrested in Djakarta if he weren't the pampered son of an Indonesian deputy premier."

"I take it a deputy premier's a real honcho."

"Oh, yes; roughly equal to half a vice president for openers. But the elder Bondjol is quite the pivotal figure. He's made it very clear: if the United States wants to keep some leased bases, Bondjol gets his son back."

Vicki considered this. "If you think I can round up a million dolphins and send them out to find the body—forget it. I'm not sure I could even get such complicated messages across in Delphinese—"

"Somebody sure as hell can," Jo Shuler put in.

Rooker: "You still don't understand. Western media haven't broken the story yet, but it's all over Indonesia: Agung Bondjol is alive, sending notes on driftwood—or was, ten days ago. I think you'd better view this tape," he added, patting the attache case.

It took an interminable twenty minutes to locate a compatible playback machine in the lab. The men stood behind Vicki as she sat through the experience. The *R. L. Carson* had been a four-hundred tonner, a small coastal survey vessel inside the great Barrier Reef with Australian permission, under contract to the United States Navy. The vessel carried unusual passengers: the swarthy young Bondjol with two camp followers and Bondjol's host, Wisconsin Senator Distel Mayer. This part of the tape, chuckled Jo Shuler, had been surreptitious film footage saved by a crew member. The good senator had paid more attention to one of Bondjol's young ladies than he had to the wonders of the reef. Thus far it was an old story, a junketeering politican with a foreign guest on a U.S. vessel far from home.

Shuler cut through Vicki's cynical thoughts: "Now you know why Mayer's so helpful in persuading our media to hold the story. The next stuff, I put together at M.D.L. from the ship's recordings. It's computer-enhanced video from experimental sonar equipment."

The scene was panoramic now, a vertical view of sandy bottom and projecting coral heads with preternatural color separation. Visually it seemed as if animation had been projected over a live scene. It was a hell of a research tool, she thought longingly. The audio was a series of clicks and coos, with a descending twitter. Vicki punched the tape to 'hold' and glanced toward the Navy civilian. "Don't ask," Shuler said quickly. "I promise you'll be the first nonmilitary group to get this enhancement rig. It may take a year or two, we're working on better . . ."

"That's not it," she said. "The audio, though: isn't it ours?" She re-ran the last few seconds as Rooker shrugged his ignorance.

"The Great White Father signal," Shuler nodded. "Sure. It's becoming standard procedure for the Navy in such treacherous channels, when they don't mind making the noise. But it won't be any more," he added darkly.

Cape Melville Station had developed two messages in Delphinese that, in themselves, justified every penny spent on research. The first message was a call for help, repeatedly sent by a battery-powered tape loop whenever a modern life jacket was immersed in salt water. During the past year, over a hundred lives had been saved when cetaceans—chiefly the smaller dolphins but in one documented case, a lesser rorqual whale—towed shipwrecked humans to safety. The device had come too late for Korff, though.

The Great White Father signal had a very different effect. It seemed to make nearby cetaceans happy, to provoke playful broachings and aerobatics as though performing for a visiting dignitary. "I hope you don't let whalers get a copy of this," Vicki said ominously. "It was intended as a friendly greeting. The people of the sea are too trusting for their own good."

"Is that a fact," murmured Harriman Rooker, his eyebrows arched. "Roll the tape."

The tape repeated its record, then proceeded as the *Carson* swept over sandy shallows, reef fish darting into coral masses that projected nearly to the hull. Then Vicki saw a thin undulating line of bright brown cross the video screen, rising slightly as the ship approached. Something darted away at the edge of the screen; something else—two somethings, then others, regular brown cylindrical shapes—swerved into view, attached to the brown line like sodden floats on a hawser. One of the cylinders disappeared, suddenly filled the screen, moved away again. Then the varicolored display turned brilliant yellow for an instant.

"Concussion wave," Shuler explained.

Nearby coral masses seemed to roll as the picture returned, hunks of the stuff crumbling away with the reef flora and fauna.

Vicki stopped the tape again. "Did the boilers explode?"

"The *Carson* was diesel," said Shuler. "It took us hours to identify those drums and the cable, but there's not much doubt it was some of our old munitions. A mine cable barrier, the kind we used in the Philippines forty years ago. Five hundred pound TNT charges intended against assault boats. We're not sure exactly how it got to Australia, but we're not ruling out your cetaceans, Vicki."

A silent *ahh*, then quick re-runs of the underwater explosion. Vicki's fingers trembled as she flicked the tape to 'hold' again. "Much as I hate to say it," she poked a finger against an ovoid gray blur on the screen, "that could be a cetacean. Big one, maybe a *pseudorca*—false killer whale."

"The sonar says it was live flesh," Shuler responded, "possibly big enough to haul a cable barrier into position."

Vicki drummed her fingers against the screen, then flicked off the display. "Could this be the work of terrorists?"

"I was picked because of modest experience in that arena," Rooker said. "Yes, it obviously *is*. But up 'til now we've counted on human leadership."

"Didn't someone take Bondjol away? You said he was alive."

"We thought you might have some ideas," Rooker said apologetically. "There are thousands of islands to check, and not enough aircraft. We've tried. The witnesses—all citizens of the United States except for Bondjol and his two child concubines—agree on some uncanny points the Indonesians don't know. One: there was a second blast while they were filling the inflatable lifeboats. Perhaps the *Carson* wasn't sinking fast enough?

'In any case, two: almost the moment she went down,

every one of the lifeboats was capsized. Not by sharks, in spite of what some of the crew claimed. No one drowned or sustained a shark attack. Two nonswimmers have toothmarks proving they were carried *back* to the lifeboats by dolphins. Distel Mayer himself says he was buffeted, ah, rudely, by something godawfully big and warm. He shipped a bit of water while it was happening, I'm happy to say.''

''Same thing happened to most of the crew,'' Shuler added.

Vicki, to the stoic Shuler: ''You think they were being visually identified?''

Rooker: ''Don't *you?*''

''Maybe.'' Vicki stared blindly at the video screen, testing hypotheses, thinking ahead. ''But this presupposes that a big group of cetaceans knew exactly whom they were after, and culled him out of a mob. That's—it's not very credible,'' she said politely.

''We are faced by incredible facts,'' Rooker agreed. ''Of course Bondjol's junket on the *Carson* was previously announced on Radio Indonesia. And in the non-Moslem press, his picture is better known than his father would like.''

Vicki was tempted to offer acid comment on pelagic mammals with radios and bifocals, then recalled that Pius had a video recorder of the latest kind. She tried another last-ditch devil's advocacy: ''What proof do you have that Bondjol didn't drown?''

Jo Shuler moved to retrieve the classified tape from her. ''Show her the glossies, Harriman.'' Then, as Rooker exchanged items in his tricky attache case, Shuler went on, ''Out of fifty-six people, four were missing when they got to the mangroves near shore. Three were crewmen. They were found in the *Carson* when divers retrieved the ship recordings. Bondjol wasn't found. Nobody saw him go under, or knows how he was taken away. But if you can believe our Indonesian friends, here's what was tossed from the sea into a little patrol boat off Surabaya a week later when everybody figured young Bondjol was only a bad memory.'' He flicked a thumb toward the photographs that Rooker held.

The first three photographs showed a scrap of metal, roughly torn from a larger sheet. It looked as though it had been subjected to salt corrosion, then roughly scrubbed, before someone covered it with cryptic marks. Vicki took a guess: ''Malayan?''

''Bahasa, the official Indonesian language,'' said Rooker. ''Roughly translated, 'Saved from American plot by whales. I am on island in sight of land, but sharks cruise shoreline. Living on coconut milk and fish that come ashore, I am, et cetera, Agung Bondjol, son of et cetera, et cetera.' I hardly need add that there was no American plot that we know of.''

She ignored his faint stress on his last four words. ''I'll bet there aren't any sharks around, either. Some dolphin dorsal fins look awfully suspicious to most people.'' In spite of herself, she was beginning to accept this awesome scenario. ''Dolphins often scare whole schools of fish ashore, right here in Queensland. The aboriginals divide the catch with them, believe it or not.''

Silent nods. She turned her attention to the other glossies, fore and obverse views of a second metal fragment. It looked much like the first one, except for a pattern of dots and lines incised on the obverse side, and Vicki admitted as much.

''The jagged edges appear to fit together,'' Rooker said, using a finger to trace torn and evidently matching sides of the metal sheets. ''This piece showed up a week ago. Poor little rich boy: 'Third day, sick of fish and coconuts; small whales will not let me swim. Death to evil Senator Mayer and American imperialists responsible. Finder please remit to Deputy Premier Bondjol, et cetera, signed Agung Bondjol, ad nauseaum.' At least he seems to be rethinking his ideas about evil,'' Rooker finished. His eyes held something that could have been cold amusement.

Vicki tapped the last photograph. ''How was this one delivered?''

''Thought you'd never ask,'' Shuler said. ''It was literally placed in the hands of a research assistant near the study pens at Coconut Island, last Saturday. By a bottlenose dolphin.''

Vicki could not avoid her yelp. "Oahu? The marine labs?"

"You got it. Halfway across the Pacific at flank speed—maybe just to prove they could do it. The pattern on the back is the simplest code you could imagine: one for 'a,' two for 'b,' but in binary. Easier to peck it out that way. It reads in clear American English."

As gooseflesh climbed her spine: "Bondjol didn't encode it?"

"No-o *way!* Analysis shows Bondjol scratched his message with sharp coral fragments, but our metal sheet was torn and the obverse incised with some tool. The tool was an alloy of iron, lots of chromium, some manganese, a little selenium—in other words, austenitic stainless steel."

"Now," Rooker put in, "do you see why we wonder about Korff?"

She nodded, letting her cold chills chase one another. More than once, cetaceans wearing Korff's experimental manipulators had escaped the pens—a fact she had mentioned in scholarly papers. "But you're implying a lot of—of subtlety. For one thing, that they've somehow learned much more about human languages than we have about theirs."

"Unless Alec Korff, or someone like him, is behind it," Rooker insisted softly. "He could have two motives: money; politics."

Vicki moved away to the lab's crockery tea service because it gave her hands something to do while she considered these bizarre ideas. The men accepted the strong brew and waited until she met Rooker's gaze. With fresh assurance: "Not big money, because he ran from it. Believe me, I know," she smiled ruefully. "Politics? He didn't want anyone governing anyone, which is why he used to say ours was the least of a hundred evils. No," she said with conviction, "I wish—God, you don't know how I wish—I could believe you. But Korff is—dead. I know it here," she added, placing a small fist near the hard knot just under her heart.

A searching look passed between the men. "She's probably right, you know,'' Shuler muttered at last.

"So much the worse," said the diplomat. "We are forced to concede the possibility that cetaceans must be classed as hostile, tool-using entities who can interdict us across three-quarters of the globe.''

"Oh, surely not hostile," Vicki began, then paused. "All the same, if I were whaling I might seriously consider some less risky line of work. Starting today. Oh: what was the binary message?''

Rooker's mirth was faint, but it came through. "Assurance that young Bondjol was safe, and a demand for ransom in exchange for his whereabouts.''

"What do they demand, a ton of pickled squid?'' Vicki was smiling back until she thought of the gradual attenuation of data on the Pius tapes. If cetaceans were getting subtler, they would reveal only what they wanted to reveal. And Pius had behaved strangely—. She strode to the forgotten tape she had taken from Pius that morning, but paused in disbelief as Rooker answered her question.

"They demand ten million Swiss francs, in hundreds. They promised to contact us again, and gave Melville Station's co-ordinates.''

In a near-whisper, Vicki Lorenz held up the Pius cartridge between thumb and forefinger. "I have a terrible suspicion,'' she said, and threaded the tape for playback.

She was right, as she had known she would be. Not only did they see an unshaven Bondjol from the viewpoint of Pius just offshore; they could hear the man's excited cries as he struggled with his dinner. The rest was sunlight filtered through deep water, eerie counterpoint to a long series of flat tones and clicks. Vicki shared unspoken surmise with Shuler as they listened: binary code.

Vicki and Jo Shuler easily programed the lab computer to print out the simple message as Harriman Rooker stood by. There were a few mistakes in syntax, but none in tactics. They would find a red-flagged float, attach the ransom to it, and tow the float into the bay. They would find Bondjol's co-ordinates on the same float, after the ransom was examined.

"I've been going on the assumption that it's counterfeit," Shuler grinned to his companion.

"Unacceptable risk," Harriman Rooker said blandly. "We don't know how much they know. It's marked, all right—but it's real." Shuler's headshake was quietly negative, but Vicki saw something affirmative cross his face.

It was not yet dark. Vicki hurried from the lab and was not suprised to spy a small channel marker buoy bobbing just outside the sea gate, a crimson cloth hanging from its mast.

Vicki drove the Holden to the sea gate with Harriman Rooker while Shuler, in a dinghy, retrieved the buoy. Rooker unlocked the mail bag, shucked it down from the sealed polycarbonate canister, and smiled as Vicki glimpsed the contents. Vicki mentally estimated its weight at a hundred kilos, obviously crammed with more liquid assets than she had ever seen. The clear plastic, evidently, was to show honest intentions. She turned as Jo Shuler, breathing hard from his exertions, approached them from behind. Something in her frozen attitude made Harriman Rooker turn before, silently, they faced the little man holding the big automatic pistol.

Shuler was not pointing it at anyone in particular. A sardonic smile tugged at his mouth as Jo Shuler, staring at the equivalent of nine million dollars in cash, took one long shaky breath. Then he flung the weapon into the dusk, toward the tall grass, as hard as he could. "Let's get this crap onto the buoy," he grunted as the others began to breathe again.

They towed the world's most expensive channel marker into the bay, hurrying back without conversation, half expecting some dark leviathan to swallow them before they reached shore. They had all seen the buoy plunge beaneath the surface like a tiny cork float above a muskellunge.

The trio stood very close on the wharf, sharing a sense of common humanity and, a little, of deliverance as they peered across the darkling water. "Don't worry," Vicki said finally. "They'll keep their end of the bargain."

"That's what I was thinking," Jo Shuler replied, "back at the car. I couldn't very well do less."

As though to himself, Rooker murmured, "The most adept seafarers on the globe, and they could have been such an asset. I don't share your optimism, Vicki. Isn't it time you finally gave up on them?"

"I'm more worried about how they intend to use *their* assets," Vicki said softly. "And how they'll raise more money when they want it. Anyway," she said, turning back toward the Holden, "you ask the wrong question. The real question is, have *they* finally given up on *us?*" She wondered now if Korff had outlived his usefulness to the sea people. One thing sure: his surviving work included more than poetry.

Given language, she had said, cetaceans would develop other tools. But given other tools, Korff had argued, they'd develop further linguistically. Since she and Korff had worked to develop cetacean assets at both ends, she knew the argument would never be resolved. But which species would be caught in the middle?

She could almost hear the laughter of Alec Korff.

By now you may have noticed that a fair percentage of my work invites you to reflect on doomsday scenarios, without invoking the U.S.S.R. Ah, but there is a U.S.S.R., and it is not your friend if you value truly unfettered discussion. It's big and smart and its offensive power is matched by its civil defense. Have you spotted the area in which we don't even begin to compete? If you have, congratulations; they have, too. Now then: what in the hell have you done about it?

Gimme Shelter!

A generation ago, Herman Kahn urged us to think about the unthinkable: nuclear war. He then proceeded to scare the hell out of us with his own scenarios on megadeath and civil defense (CD). Soon afterward we were deluged with plans, arguments for and against fallout shelters, and an open letter to the public by then-President John Kennedy. The President, New York Governor Nelson Rockefeller, Kahn, and many others were strongly in favor of public shelter programs in view of the awesome destructive power of nuclear weapons.

A loyal opposition quickly emerged, notably from a phalanx of educators in the Boston area and in the pages of the Bulletin of the Atomic Scientists. Freeman Dyson's argument was succinct: nuclear nations should *not* build shelters on a large scale because, while a lack of effective shelters may mean death for a warring nation, effective shelters may mean death for the entire human race. Dyson reasoned that effectively sheltered antagonists would go on pounding away at each other until not only the duelists, but the whole world, was fatally contaminated. Better that the warring nations die alone, he concluded, than to drag all mankind down with them.

Dyson did not deal with the obvious, e.g., what happens when one duelist is protected and the other is not. We must deal with it now. Relatively speaking, the USSR is effectively protected. The USA is not.

Now that we have your full attention, let us remind you that Dyson warned us against shelters *on a large scale*. If a few thousands or millions of us choose to survive on a small scale, it shouldn't affect first-order terms of the megadeath equation very much.

No one can know today whether our lives would be worth living after a nuclear war, and we don't dwell on the moral questions of the individual's responsibility to oneself and to others. For the ultimate amorality, the survivor who envies the dead can join them any time he chooses. But you ought to have the option of nuclear survival, and that option starts with information. We can't expect to be as effective as the USSR has been in training tens of millions of Soviet citizens as a survival cadre, but we can help a few to train themselves. Much of the information is basic. For many of us, particularly urbanites, it begins *before* we step into a fallout shelter. This article is a beginning. Subsequent articles will show how, with a little foresight, you might reverse the odds against yourself once a shelter is reached.

In the 1950's we knew that the 20KT (equivalent to twenty thousand tons of TNT) Hiroshima blast was almost insignificantly small compared to 20 MT—*mega*ton—and larger weapons then in development. Was the public interested? Not much, until Kahn popularized the mathematics of annihilation and helped provoke the great shelter debate of the sixties. Suddenly in 1961 we were more than interested; we were fascinated, and then inundated by a tsunami of articles, pamphlets and books. Like the European tulip craze of the 17th Century and our Muckraker Era after 1900, the topic blazed into focus. It didn't stay long; anyone can see by checking the Reader's Guide to Periodicals that by 1963, the topic was plummeting from public view. By 1979 it had fallen almost out of sight.

For several reasons, the U.S. public largely abandoned civil defense matters until very recently; and now the rules have changed! Government agencies spent most of a billion dollars locating and stocking potential fallout shelters in urban areas. With all those signs telling us where to go, we'd be okay when we got there; right?

Wrong. Language sets its own tripwires, and in our focal effort to find fallout shelters, we concentrated altogether too much on only one danger, i.e., fallout. Quick, now: how many victims in Hiroshima and Nagasaki succumbed to fallout? Evidently none. The bombs were detonated high in the air for maximum effect against the two cities. An air burst does its damage as a one-two-three-four punch. First comes the thermal radiation, moving out from the fireball core at light speed and lasting something under one minute. Next comes the blast wave, a hammerblow of air moving a bit faster than Mach 1 that can reduce nearby concrete structures to powder, the range of blast destructiveness weakening with the cube root of the bomb's energy. This means that a 20 MT bomb's blast effect reaches only (!) ten times as far as that of a 20 KT bomb. Third comes the firestorm, a genuine meteorological event caused by the burning of everything ignitable within range—and that encompasses many square miles—of the initial heat effects. Last and most lingering comes the fallout, a rain of deadly radioactive ash from the mushroom cloud that moves downwind.

The bigger the bomb, the more preponderantly it is an incendiary weapon. Victims of conventional Allied incendiary air raids in World War II were found suitably protected from blast effects in shelters—suffocated and cremated by the firestorms that ensued. Even without nukes the toll was 200,000 in Tokyo, 300,000 in Dresden. In New York City fallout shelters, the toll might be twenty times as high, because the first bomb targeted against a big city will almost certainly be an air burst with appalling incendiary effects. Suburbanites far downwind may live long enough to worry about fallout.

The ground burst is the one that punches a vast depression in the earth and sends thousands of tons of vaporized dirt into the air. We can expect ground bursts against deeply-buried military installations and other 'hard' targets. The fallout from a ground burst may be lethal hundreds of miles downwind, because the vaporized dirt will condense and drift down as radioactive ash—thousands of tons of it.

Incidentally, because so much of the ground burst's energy goes into punching that hole in the ground, the blast and initial radiation effects of a ground burst will not be as widespread. Your chances a few miles from a ground burst can be better than the same distance from an air burst, if you're far enough upwind, or sheltered well enough, to avoid fallout from the ground burst. But that mushroom cloud will be miles across; and if I'm near it, gimme shelter!

But what *is* effective shelter? Not an ordinary urban basement. Probably not even a subway tunnel, unless the tunnel can be hermetically sealed against the firestorm. Imagine a gopher in his tunnel, with openings fifty feet apart—under a bonfire a hundred feet across. The fire will rage for hours, causing updrafts of hurricane force toward the center that suck air right out of the tunnels. It simply withdraws the little varmint's oxygen while the heat gradually builds up deep beneath the bonfire. Well, a big firestorm is a miles-wide bonfire, and our subway commuter is the gopher. The Soviets have given that a lot of thought. Unlike us, according to Leon Gouré, they've done something about it.

Gouré, a RAND Corporation man, emigrated from Moscow in infancy and revisited the USSR in 1960. He found huge blast doors set into the floors of Moscow subway tunnels—and we can take hermetic seals for granted. Moscow might burn, but a million or so Muscovites can keep on breathing. Gouré also learned that Soviet civil defense officials, the MPVO (for Mestnaia Protivovoz-dushnaia Oborona, so from now on we'll just give acronyms; trust us, okay?), can call on twenty or thirty million members of a paramilitary civilian cadre called DOSAAF. DOSAAF people correspond roughly to a national home guard, and they all get compulsory training as population leaders in evacuation and shelter exercises.

The Soviets, with total control over the architecture of apartment buildings as well as municipal structures, have very special building codes for urban basements. Many apartment building basements have specially reinforced, thick ceilings and walls with load-bearing partitions and airtight steel doors. In addition, ventilation tunnels filter incoming air and provide remote emergency escape passages. Gouré cited toilet facilities, stored food and water with other supplies, and implied that bottled air may be provided.

Thus protected, Soviet apartment dwellers just might live through all but the fiercest firestorm.

It's possible for us to build better urban shelters than these, but we do not appear to be doing it. Our civil defense posture has regeared itself more toward evacuation than to digging in. More accurately, at the moment we're between gears, idling in neutral.

A recent Boeing study revealed to a Congressional committee that, with its low-key, continuing civil defense; its carefully dispersed industry; and its less centralized population, the USSR might recover from a war in two to four years while the U.S. might need twelve years for recovery. Two per cent of the Soviets might die. Sixty per cent of Americans might die. *Now* do you see why the Soviets marched into Afghanistan with such confidence?

Anecdote time: we know a scientist who fled the Soviet bloc some years ago. Her eyewitness report on Soviet civil defense is more recent than Gouré's, and perhaps more scarifying. She insists that the USSR and its satellite countries feel confident that their people would easily survive a nuclear war because of their massive compulsory CD programs. Now in the U.S., our scientist friend moved as far from local target areas as she could, and modified her basement into an acceptable fallout shelter. She's still dismayed that her American friends have no hermetically sealed public tunnels and that they consider her efforts, in word, weird.

China has her tunnels, too. Less elaborate than Moscow subways, Peking's tunnels are only a few meters below the surface and probably would be employed as an escape route to the countryside. Dairen, a big shipping port, is a likely target and its deep tunnels are stocked for 80,000 evacuees. The tunnels criss-cross like a bus network and might be marginally suitable if they are effective conduits beyond the firestorm area.

Canada has her National Shelter Plan, several years in arrears of our own and still geared to identifying mass fallout shelters for urbanites. Undeniably, Canada harbors fewer prime targets than we do in both major categories; the hardened military sites for which ground bursts are slated, and the soft population targets so vulnerable to air bursts. But Canada's cities are just as vulnerable as ours. She needs an urban public that's drilled as well in evacuation as in cellar-dwelling, just as we do.

From all evidence, both U.S. and USSR civil defense officials count on being alerted many hours or even days before Time Zero, apparently on the basis of judgments of political events and evidence that the other side is battening down its hatches. This is a gamble we take collectively; but you, *personally*, don't have to take all of that gamble.

So how do you reduce the gamble to your immediate family? Being painfully aware that you may find some of the answers very unpleaant, we'll start with some generalizations, and some specifics.

1. Talk to your local CD coordinator, who may be making do with absurdly low federal and local funding. Local officials usually have expert guesses as to the nearest target area. What common carriers are earmarked for evacuation? What should you carry with you? Where will you go and what facilities will you find there? Ask for a copy of the 1977 booklet, *Protection in the Nuclear Age,* or borrow theirs and copy it. The booklet strongly reflects the shift in emphasis toward evacuation—or in CD jargon, 'Crisis Relocation'. Among other things the booklet describes home shelters of several kinds, a source of free shelter plans, and your best tactics in evacuating a target area.

2. If you live or work in a primary target area, for God's sake seek other stomping grounds. This is far and away the best item in improving your chances—and the toughest one to implement.

3. Do your homework on fallout, prevailing winds, and target areas upwind of you. The November 1976 *Scientific American* is a good departure point.

4. More homework. Make a low-key, consistent hobby of studying survival and technology. Oldies like *Fortunes in Formulas* and any decent encyclopedia set may be more helpful than books on woodcraft. If you wind up in the woods

you either know your stuff already, or you're up the creek without a scintillator. Mel Tappan's column on survival has been a fixture in *Guns & Ammo* magazine since December, 1976, and Tappan is no wild-eyed troglodyte. His argument in favor of living in a smallish town, rather than metropolis or mountaintop, is eloquent.

5. Fill a scruffy rucksack with raisins and jerked meat, transistor radio, masking tape and monofilament line, first-aid equipment including water purification tablets, a few rolls of dimes, leather gloves, vitamins, steel canteen, thermally reflective mylar blanket from any outfitter, good multipurpose clasp knife, and so on. You might have to change plans and relocate without notice. We spend an evening once at Poul Anderson's place with several writers, arguing the merits of a survival kit that was originally stored in a certain specially-stiffened Porsche coupe. Basically, our kit was intended to get a tinkerer across country. It didn't look worth stealing. That's a vital point: when you can't expect a policeman to help, keep a low profile.

The kit had some of the items mentioned above, plus small slide rule, pliers, drill bits, wire and needles, compass, fishhooks, wax-coated matches and candle stub (a plumber's candle is high in stearic acid and burns very slowly), thick baggies, pencils and pad, all wrapped in heavy aluminum foil so that it could be swung like a short club. Huge half-inch-wide rubber bands looped around the handle end. Never forget that a slingshot with big rubber bands is quiet and flashless, and ammunition for it is everywhere. Why the masking tape? Whether you stay put or evacuate, you may need to tape cracks around openings to make your quarters as airtight as possible. Freshen the kit annually.

Pamphlets suggest you may have two days' warning. Don't bet your life on it.

No booklet can possibly cover all the problems you're likely to find if you choose crisis relocation, i.e., evacuation after the alert sounds. But another brief list might help you.

1. Keep detailed county and state maps. Decide where

you'll go and learn alternative routes; chances are, major arterials will soon be clogged. Consider strapping bikes onto your car as second-stage vehicles. Roads that become impassable by car might still be navigable on a bike.

2. When you already have a good idea which way you will probably go, polish up your friendships with acquaintances who live in that presumably safer region. Establish agreements that they'll accept you, and do your part ahead of time. For example: buy a 100-gallon water storage tank and let them have it on permanent loan; furnish them with a survival library; help them build their shelter; and/or *be* an encyclopedia of survival lore which they'd rather be with, than without.

3. Get in shape. Stay that way. Regular exercise, particularly jogging, hiking, and bicycling, gives you stamina for that extra klick or edge of alertness when you need it. Physical exhaustion has its corollary in emotional exhaustion, and a sense of futility is a heavier load than a full backpack. Besides, if you use a cycle regularly you'll keep your bike in good repair. How long since you patched a bike tire at the roadside?

4. Collect a first-stage kit and a second-stage kit in your garage or storage shed, and be ready to stow both in your car. First-stage kits include saw, pick, and shovel, plastic tarps, extra bedding and clothes, all the food you can quickly pack into rugged boxes, a spare fuel supply for your car (store it wisely in the meantime), the contents of your medicine cabinet, tools, sanitation items, and any books you may think especially useful. Second-stage kits include the rucksack we described earlier, small ax or hatchet, sleeping bag, plastic tarp, maps, and medication or other essentials according to your special needs. If you must abandon your car later, you can grab your second-stage kit and keep going afoot or on a bike.

5. Move quickly without panic if the time comes to relocate. Drill your family in details, and obey officials in face-to-face encounters. Law officers coping with the crisis may not be willing to put up with much argument when

you're en route. Choose the clothes you'll wear beforehand, and dress for a hike.

6. Pretend you've gone halfway to your destination, abandoned your car, and are afoot in a sparsely populated area when you perceive that you're downwind of a mushroom cloud. You may have several hours before you must have shelter, but the time to seek it is right *now!* A homeowner may take you in, especially if you look like you'll be more help than hindrance. If not, don't risk getting shot. Keep going until you find some structure that will shelter you. The more dirt or concrete above and around you, the better; a dry culvert could be much better than a bungalow. Establish your location on the map, seal yourself in for what may be days, and attend to your radio for information on local conditions. If you're one of the few with a radiation counter, you'll know when to stay put and when to move on. Fallout is like lust; it isn't forever, but it colors your decisions.

7. If you're heeled—carrying weapons—cache them securely before you enter any public or communal shelter. You'll almost certainly be required to give them up anyhow, and you'd be dangerously unpopular if it were known that you didn't surrender them. And you probably wouldn't get them back once you surrendered them. For most of us, weapons are more harmful temptation than useful tools. Of course, a tiny pocket canister of Mace is another matter. Ever notice how some defensive items look like cigarette lighters—especially if spray-painted silver or white?

It's probably not necessary to justify all the points we've listed, but you'll find a rationale behind any advice that's worth hearing. Our embedded biases aren't hard to pin down. We believe that mass evacuation from target areas is a more viable response than most shelters in those areas. We know that our present CD planning is underfunded for the goals it is planning. Translation: your local officials probably won't be able to cope with the evacuation after they call for it.

We also believe that, the more actively you study the problems and consider prudent means to avoid bottlenecks in your own relocation, the more likely it is that you'll become a part of CD solutions.

And consider the rationales in the details, e.g., bicycling. It does more than improve your stamina and speed your relocation. It can be equipped with a tiny generator and light; it requires no stored fuel; it can be bodily carried or even hauled through water; it is almost noiseless in use; and ultimately it can be abandoned without great financial or emotional loss. It's part of that low profile we mentioned.

By now it should be obvious that, for many of us, crisis relocation will precede effective shelter. Once you've relocated to an area where shelter can be effective, you'll need to focus on such things as fallout shielding; air filtration and pumping; hygiene; and other basic life-support needs. In the next article we'll show you how to build simple air filtration and pump units with a minimum of effort and time.

In the meantime, do yourself a favor. Talk with your local CD people, and visit your library for the articles we've mentioned. After you've studied the problem a bit, you'll be prepared to make a better response to an alert than to stand on the courthouse lawn bawling, "Gimme shelter!"

There's an old joke to the effect that the best way to revitalize a culture is to let it lose a war to a civilized opponent. When you're knee-deep in rubble, there's no need to patch up your old structures—so you can build brand-new and better ones. For examples, compare German and Japanese to American industry in late 1945, and look at them today.

Well, I only said it was a joke. I didn't promise it'd be funny.

Unfunnier still, the end of urban life as we know it may not depend on hostile acts from the outside. God knows, our internal stresses are explosive enough! In my opinion, you can't even isolate one special category of villain. Look at it from an engineering standpoint: we've built incredibly complex social structures with human parts that are increasingly interdependent. We know the parts are fragile; we see them crumbling, and know that they are subjected to as-yet-unquantified stresses. Some of our best analysts predict imminent collapse of some of these structures—and still we're making them taller, more vulnerable. Can it be that we have some subliminal desire to see how thunderous a crash we can make?

I don't think that's it. I think most of us just don't consider it much. But what of those who do, and who feel unable to delay the inevitable despite a brim-full measure of courage and altruism?

Why Must They
All Have My Face?

Some of the squad was already in full body armor when Morse darted up, pulling his sweater off as he approached his locker. "Lookit him," Norm Weintraub cackled, waving a shinguard at Morse; "too little and too late, and too nookie-whipped for rollcall. Hey, Slope: we gonna have to hold our gumba up by his beltpac today?"

Burgess Ngo, trading glances with the hurrying Morse, saw through the frown. Gary Morse had his moody mornings, but today the brown eyes were dancing. "Nah, he bears all the earmarks of a quickie this ayem," Ngo piped, his voice curiously high for a man of his bulk. "In another month, Gary'll be a twice-a-week man."

"Never," Morse said, deadpanning as he shucked his civvy trousers. "Fran and I took an extra vow: once a newlywed, always a newlywed."

Morse stepped aside as a fully-dressed gumba trio paced down the aisle, already in lockstep and nearly identical in their massive streetsuit armor. But you could tell by the little things, thought Morse, even from behind if they were on your squad. Sadler carried the mob-control staff with the dent, Torre rolled like a sailor as he walked, and the great height of McEachern was unmistakable. Anyway, if you made one of a trio, you knew who the others had to be.

Of course, once you had your helmet on you could read the infrared-sensitive ID on each helmet. That way you knew which name to call on your streetsuit intercom, in case you had to call a fast warning. Or call for help; sometimes that happened too. In a pitched battle on the street you had to know every other cop at a glance, but it could be tough-

shitsville if you were identified by some scumbag. Scumbags, mob leaders, had been known to wear IR-sensitive
cheaters. That was why possession of such equipment by a
private citizen was a felony.

Weintraub and Ngo stood waiting, trading insults impar-
tially as Morse adjusted his streetsuit conditioner. Too cold in
summer, too hot in winter, the damned thing was like a bad
cop; always overreacting. Morse had the knack of monitoring
his thoughts, caught himself oversimplifying, smiled. It
wasn't as simple as good cop/bad cop, either/or, scumbag/
lawful citizen. On the other hand you had Sadler, a downright
bad case who seemed to be on the force for the single purpose
of kicking ass. Offsetting Sadler—validating him, in a
way—was Ngo. Burgess Ngo of the ready smile, the easy
response to slope jokes, the solid belief in the country that
had adopted his father a generation back. Ngo, the true
believer in the system. Gary Morse envied his gumba that
almost religious certainty that a cop, particularly a strike
force cop, was part of the solution, not part of the problems.

Problem: Life support for City Center, where the council
and the tax and licensing people and urban service engineers
and their clerks and secretaries huddled behind thick earth-
filled walls, insulated from street people. Too much life. Too
little support.

Problem: Protection for convoys that kept City Center
supplied. With luck, the central nervous system of the self-
besieged city might continue desperate efforts to save something, anything, of its gangrenous body. Last month a
bottleneck had emerged in printout software. A flying wedge
of students had surprised a convoy, had 'liberated' pallet-
loads of paper for outlying schools. This month it was food.

Problem: Housing. City Center could not provide living
quarters for its own strike force. If a cop's seniority was low,
he couldn't live in a safe zone. He had to make do, somehow,
on the outside where he was just as vulnerable to theft and
water contamination and shortages as the next citizen. More
vulnerable, really, if some scumbag figured out which lucky

workers were disappearing into conduits toward checkpoints near City Center, as Morse did.

Problem: Fran.

Cancel that. For Gary Morse, Fran was the nexus of calm in a city gone spastic with its agony. Before the government imposed a city quarantine, very few people were worried enough, and wealthy enough, to get out. Choice terms were reserved for those who did: *bugout, candyass, noballs*. The social pressure generated by those terms was simply incalculable. A few optimists were still trickling into cities on the day their quarantines were announced.

Even after he found his parents trashed in the wreckage of their home, Gary Morse had never considered a bugout. He could have joined the army, probably to wind up with a night-scoped carbine outside a quarantine area—Newark or San Antonio or Detroit, for example—where escapees got hard labor if they weren't shot first. Or he could have joined a mob; soldiering in the gutter trenches of his own city. Or he could take police exams; fight the good fight.

Morse was not a tall man. Not tall enough for the job, one academy instructor had warned. But the tenacity was there, and the shoulders were wide and thick, sloping into a heavily corded neck. If Gary Morse stood half a head shorter than his gumbas, the muscular upper torso could still inspire respect. Fran always claimed she'd singled him out because she was a neck-and-shoulders girl. Well then, solution: Fran.

Annafrances Kohler, tousled locks gleaming velvety umber on a high forehead, blue eyes melancholy as she had waited in a job applicant line two years before. Morse had tried to ignore the lithe girl, obviously fresh from the country in her clean frock (too short) and her farmgirl legs (too strong). But he couldn't ignore the pimp who was jiving her. Neither could she; when the jiver touched her elbow it became a weapon and the man needed Morse's help to find the exit. Morse returned to pay his respects, and one thing led to another, and—.

Fran Kohler, defusing his anger when Gary saw the condi-

tion of her hands, the first day when she returned from work
in a suburban berry thicket. "No one forced me to do it," she
had whispered into the hollow beneath his jaw.

He had kissed the ravaged fingers, juice-dyed and bitter-
slick under synthoderm that stopped the bleeding. Voice
tight, hoarse: "No one forces you to eat, either. You've got
to go home, Fran. Now, while you still can."

She hadn't quite lost her naivete. "I'll always be welcome
back home," she'd said, nipping at his ear.

He'd turned, regarding her with one eye, so near she was a
fragrant blur of honey-tints. "If you can get there. Rumor in
the Academy, Fran: they'll be forming street control squads
soon."

"That means a full-time position for you," she'd said,
pleased.

"It means they know the city's going under quarantine
soon."

Her mouth an *Oh,* silent, gravely waiting.

"I give us a month, six weeks at most," he said.

"Then you'll just have to come away with me."

"You know I can't. I'm signed up, and they're already
checking ID's at the terminals. God *dam*mit, honey, it'll be
hand-to-mouth for you here in a month. No contacts, no
family,—"

"No husband. Well," her grin was enterprising, "I'll just
have to find one."

"I couldn't do that to you."

And she had transmuted the grin into a whore's leer, her
special joke for him, tonguetip provocative between her
teeth. And after she'd found an apartment—

Fran Morse, *nee* Kohler, self-assured and regal in their
shabby digs a week after the wedding. Ngo and Weintraub
had failed to hide their amazement when they arrived and
quickly gave up trying.

From Norm Weintraub, indicating the whole room with
arms outflung: "Wine and canapes and a lady from the Lido:
magic, by God!"

"Dandelion wine and zucchini pizza," she'd said, pleased but coloring slightly under the Weintraub appraisal.

Burgess Ngo: "You two just got in under the wire, y'know. Gary was the last gumba on the force to get permission to marry."

They had drunk to that, then to early revocation of the new quarantine, and then to advancement that could lift Morse from the ranks. And then to other brave dreams.

Late that evening, all of them fuzz-brained from dandelion wine, Ngo in all innocence had committed an unpardonable sin. He'd broached the really insoluble problem with, "Here's to schizophee—uh, schizophreniacs," surprised that he could still pronounce it.

Fran didn't understand; Gary winced.

Glancing around him at the suddenly morose Weintraub and Morse: "You know, Gary on the strike force and Fran hustling the necessaries—"

"Let it lie, Burgess," from Weintraub.

"There's a key word, if I can say it," Morse had begun. "*An-on-ymity;* and thanks a bunch for bringing it up, pal." By now, Ngo understood his faux pas; a cop didn't say 'pal' if he was in a good mood. It had been the gentlest of warnings.

"I know what you mean," from Fran in slow cadence, each syllable deliberate and clear and earnest. "We've worked it all out, Burgess. At home, Gary is a man without a job. On duty, he is a man without a wife. Me, too—I mean, you know. But I won't take crazy chances. And Gary won't ask where I get the sirloins."

The very idea of sirloin had been too ludicrous, had produced helpless guffaws from them all. Finally, from Ngo who was still trying for a comic effect: "Okay, you've worked it all out." Shrug. "And it still spells schizo."

That was when Norm Weintraub yelled at him. It was two interminable minutes before Fran discovered how to quell the two of them. She merely went about building another pizza, claiming that there was plenty more, her lie opaque beneath a dandelion-yellow glow.

And long after the others had gone, sharing the pallet and their bodies in eager communion, they had heard a single despairing cry from somewhere outside. Someone was hustling his necessaries.

The sleep that Fran found so easily was denied Gary Morse. He fought back to wakefulness, recoiling from a nightmare image that would not wait, that fled as he pursued it. It seemed that he gazed down on some great stone wheel that rolled endlessly in a circular groove. Filling the groove, in the path of the rust-stained wheel, lay countless granules too small to be clearly discerned. Morse had never seen a millstone, but the imagery had plagued his sleep before.

Eventually he came to a conclusion. *The mills of God,* he remembered. Had it been Whitman? Longfellow? Thus deflected, he had fallen asleep.

To make a liar of Weintraub, Morse made it to rollcall— barely. Lieutenant Rawlins would not keep them long with the briefing, he said; and then kept them too long. The gist of it was, Squads One and Three would provide security for the convoy coming eastward into City Center. Squad Two, he said, was slated for special duty.

Weintraub vented a moaning grunt without parting his lips and Morse, standing just ahead of him, agreed with the faintest of gestures. Special duty meant the shitty end of the stick, a breakneck race in armored vehicles to some crucial strongpoint beyond City Center, timed to coincide with small supply convoys. Today it was the main power station.

When Rawlins dismissed them, Ngo moved to Weintraub's side as they unhinged their helmets. "You have a microfiche map of the power station, gumba? I don't know the area."

"Morse won't need his," Weintraub said. "He knows that part of town backwards."

Morse nodded, fumbling for a microfiche card in his beltpac. "Big gray building down the hill from my place, about two klicks," he said. "Tall smokestack; looks like a fort.'' He handed over the card, watched Ngo don his helmet to study the brow-level display inside.

The voice even thinner through the visor: "Got it. Yeah.'' Reflective: "When I was a kid I used to wonder why city buildings looked like fortifications.''

"Be glad they do,'' from Weintraub.

"Civil engineers were thinking 'way ahead,'' Morse sighed. In unspoken agreement they strode toward the staging area. You didn't want to be the last trio on a strike force van; the lumbering vehicles hadn't been designed to take the weight of the armor. You could lose your breakfast sitting near the tailgate, the way the van swayed on overloaded springs.

The drivers careened out from the Center with self-conscious brio, each taking a different route, each making tires squall at the limit of adhesion around corners, swerving past old roadblocks. Some of the roadblocks had been their own. Some, identifiable by the ragtag ends of furniture dragged from office buildings, had been the work of mobbers. A few scumbags had the knack of fitting hardwood furniture into barricades of appalling toughness.

"Uh-oh,'' Ngo muttered, nudging Morse. "Sadler looks a little barf-baggish.'' Sadler, near the tailgate, was paying the price. You weren't supposed to stand up or hang over the chest-high tailgate, but you weren't supposed to barf inside the vehicle either.

Weintraub, in muttered fraudulence: "Couldn't happen to a nicer guy.''

Without a word, Morse worked his way past the others, touched Sadler on the shoulder, jerked a thumb back toward his vacated seat. After a moment. Sadler nodded, his face blank, and left Morse to lean on the tailgate alone. Now and again, Morse saw the jagged gray fingernail of the power station smokestack pointing skyward over a gutted building in the foreground. He squinted back at the occasional bright sparkle of glass shards in the street, enjoying the sensation, disdaining the polarized visor. Once he saw a boy standing immobile on a corner, watching the truck in its headlong progress. Morse waved. The boy did not wave back.

Morse recognized the market where he sometimes shopped, on days off, and when the plywood facing was removed to imply that food was available. Today the plywood was up in place and there were very few people in sight. Not nearly enough people in sight, he thought. That was something Morse could allow himself to think about, though perilously near things he could not afford to think about.

The ready signal flashed. Morse was staring across the city and did not see the signal. He knew it had flashed when he sensed the change in the others. Psych-up time: time for rousing the inner man, for quickening the adrenal flow before battle was joined. Morse wondered if it was pan-cultural, if it had really worked for Sioux, Zulu, North Koreans. Assuredly it worked for his gumbas. He heard Sadler, whose curses grew stronger by the moment; felt a flutter in his own guts; smiled because he knew he could not lose his own breakfast. There had been no breakfast to lose.

The trio swung from their van two blocks from the power station, the vehicle lurching forward again to disgorge others fifty meters beyond. Ngo stumbled, cursed, hurried to take his position. He was leaning on his mob-control staff, Morse saw.

Weintraub, by intercom: "Geez, you slopes are clumsy."

Ngo: "Turned my ankle. It'll be okay." He wriggled the heavy boot tentatively. They waited at parade-rest stance, scanning blank storefronts. Silence.

Presently, Morse laughed. "So here we are in the late movie. The wagons are in a circle and it's midnight. I say, 'it's quiet.' Give me the next line, Norm."

"And I say, 'yeah, *too* quiet.' Right?"

"You two are real bundles of sunshine," said Ngo, still favoring the ankle, chortling through it.

Two minutes later the convoy arrived, speeding stealthily past on purring electrics. It was not as foolproof as supply by helicopter, but the choppers guzzled too much fossil fuel and the electrics were ideal for heavy cargo carriers. The last was a squad pickup van, slowing to take on gumba trios. Morse and Weintraub helped Ngo scramble onto the pickup platform, hauled him aboard, joked as they moved down the street toward the power station.

A cop in a full streetsuit cannot perform stevedore chores easily. By the time they unloaded the last crate in the power station, most of the squad reeked of sweat despite their conditioners. Weintraub, standing next to Morse, let his helmet swing from its hinges as he cocked his head toward his gumba. "What was that? What?"

Morse, grinning: "Just a gut-rumble. Something I ate."

"Bullshit; something you didn't eat."

"Sounds to me like he's smuggled a pet coon into his suit," said Ngo.

Sadler, his dark face gleaming with honest perspiration, was not quite out of earshot. "Who said *coon?* Whothefuck said that?"

"Poon, Sadler, poon," Weintraub said quickly. "Relax, pal; save your hostility for after lunch."

"What for? It was a cool operation, we go back to Center after lunch."

"Shit we do," from an amused Torre. "Gumba, don't you ever listen to the loo-tenant? We deploy here again for the rest of the supplies."

"Two convoys to the same place, same day," said Sadler, shaking his head. "It's not ess-oh-pee."

"Scumbags know that too. That's why we're doing it, I imagine," Morse explained.

"I guess." With his easy agreement, Sadler discharged the small obligation he felt to Morse. Then he sauntered in the general direction of the food serving line.

No one actually hurried to be served. It was a point of honor to deny hunger, though a third of the squad would miss at least one meal on any given day. But you never missed lunch on your shift. The city took care of its finest—once a day.

Weintraub made his patented funny-wry face at his tray.
"Exigencies of the service," he sighed, and wolfed his clam
strips along with the creamed potatoes, the mystery custard,
the green salad. Morse had an outsized portion of everything.
He ate methodically, dropping most of the meat into his lap
without looking. He glanced to his right and caught Burgess
Ngo covertly watching him.

"Don't say it," Morse muttered.

A scrutable smile: "Nothing to say, gumba," in mild
protest. "Personally I can't stand the stuff either. I don't
suppose you'd take my tray back, let me rest this ankle. . . ."

Ngo's clam strips lay artfully hidden in cream sauce.
Morse grunted and took both trays. He had time to stuff
Ngo's clams into his little stash bag. Well, it was a minor
infraction. It might also be supper enough for—more than
enough for one.

In the john, Morse tucked the bag into a pocket sewn into
his shorts. The precious contraband made a heartbreakingly
small package. It was not the first nor the tenth time Morse
had done it.

As they redeployed on the street, Weintraub was surly.
"You're more trouble than you're worth, Slope. Should'a
reported in with that ankle."

"And lose a half-day? No way."

"Here they come," Morse called. Far down the street,
now rounding a corner, a cargo vehicle picked up speed
toward them. Three others followed, including the empty
pickup van. Morse opened his mouth to make a
suggestion—and kept it open. He felt the thump through his
feet, saw the shockwave fling its ghostly dust-ring, before he
heard it. The pickup van caught a concussion device squarely
on its armored sidewall and toppled like a toy, fell on its side,
slithered to a stop trailing sparks. Morse was running toward
the explosion before he realized it.

The second concussion was nearer and heavier, less audi-
ble, a distinct slap against boot soles. A section of the street

erupted, mined from beneath. Some scumbag had put an old sewer to good use.

The first two supply vehicles had already passed but the third, irrevocably committed by its mass and velocity, skidded into the gaping trench that now spanned the street. Its entire front suspension was swept away as it encountered the trench, slammed down, the inertia of its load carrying it forward, spinning crazily as it came to rest. Cargo crates spilled into the street and even from a hundred meters away, Morse recognized the tinned beef labels.

Morse took cover until the rain of debris subsided, jerked his head around at Torre's call: "Not yet, Sadler! Appropriate force, the man said." Sadler had been reaching for his carbine.

Sadler cursed and complied. The doctrine of appropriate force had peculiar applications. You could throw a stun grenade, which might do more harm than a plastic bullet, because the enemy had demonstrated his willingness to use explosives. But if some scumbag intended to deploy his people openly, he knew better than to issue firearms. The sheer firepower and the dye of strike force ammunition created too many problems for mobbers to handle. So they thought up tactics that were nastier than bullets.

Morse sprinted up the street, outdistancing his gumbas, pacing the long-legged McEachern who was bawling into his intercom for a support vehicle. Both men saw the stream of jelly that lofted across the street ahead of them and splattered on macadam. McEachern veered toward the doorway from which the high-pressure stream had come, but he was a heartbeat too late with his staff.

A towering barricade of flame emerged from the doorway and raced across the street an instant after Morse leaped across the treacly stuff. Morse calculated that the napalm would burn away in half a minute. He did not yet know about the phosphorus and the titanium compound that would mask him from his fellows by a wall of white smoke.

Heart pounding, Morse loped to the supply van, clipping

the long staff to his shoulder. First priority: victims of mob violence. He wrenched at the driver's door, ignoring the half-dozen mobbers who had already materialized, were throwing goods from the rear of the van.

The driver was a woman, inert against the windshield, a chunky flaccid burden in her police coverall. The damn' fool had not been wearing her helmet. She was breathing but a trickle of blood issued from one ear. Morse lifted her with a standard fireman's carry, lashed out with one arm as a mobber ran past, trotted quickly to the curb and eased his burden to the sidewalk.

"McEachern, get the other driver," Morse shouted. The big man was flailing with his activated mob control staff at the rear of the van. Two mobbers lay stunned underfoot. McEachern wasn't listening. Behind them, a barrier of white billowed up from a sizzle of bright flame. Nobody was coming through it.

A streetsuited figure lay silent, sprawled grotesquely in police armor, and nearby a mobber of medium height moved frantic hands over a mob control staff, trying to activate it. Morse ignored him-or-her; mobbers usually wore handmade padding under coveralls, and some wore respirators under their rubber halloween masks. Thank God, Morse thought, the safety catch on that staff was a strike force secret.

The pickup van was empty. Morse found the driver lying in the street, beyond help, and turned toward the fray where McEachern now battled three mobbers while several more escaped with food.

"Help is on the way," Morse shouted on the loudhailer circuit. Even if it wasn't true, the idea might cause the mobbers to scatter. He used his staff on one mobber who'd circled around McEachern, oblivious to Morse himself. The man went jerking and shuddering to the macadam with one jolt.

Then Morse felt a tingling tremor, simultaneous with a heavy blow over his rib pads. The suit protected him from most of the amperage, but as Morse turned to face his assailant he knew the stolen staff was activated. If it caught him on a zipper or a metal joint it could jolt him unconscious.

Morse whirled, dropped into approved combat stance, feinted with his own staff and then tried for a quick disarming sweep. He often practiced the maneuver as a calisthenic when off duty.

His enemy seemed almost to expect his move, avoided his sweep, dodged with balletic grace. Morse waited for the next blow and, when it came, let his opponent's staff slide down his own. His gauntlets were insulated, and that was his great advantage. In an instant he gripped the mobber's staff with both hands, jerked it toward him, then flung it back without letting go.

For a fleeting aeon the mobber's face was against his visor, eyes slitted through mask eye-holes. They stared in mutual murderous rage until Morse began his abrupt savage push-pull that shook the mobber like a doll, long hair spilling from the neck of her coverall, half obscuring the woman's mask with its rictus of hatred and despair and, in the blue eyes, something else.

Abandoning the unequal contest she leaped away, rolled, managed to parry Morse's savage kick with her hand, scuttled away holding her battered mask more or less in place. With her good hand she paused to fumble several cans of food into capacious pockets, keeping well clear of Morse as he shambled back to McEachern's side carrying both staffs.

Then Morse saw a broad armored figure hobble through the smoke, knew that Slope Ngo had taken extra chances to atone for his injury. The heel of his boot was on fire, but the heavy insulation might protect him.

McEachern went down, a mobber lasso encircling his staff. The cord snaked around the big man's legs as two husky mobbers hauled him writhing on his back from the vicinity of the van.

Ngo waded into the two mobbers with his staff, evidently using it without the jolter, as always the last man on the squad to escalate to appropriate force.

Morse took a stand before the rear of the van, calling for reinforcements as he waved a skulking mobber away. With Ngo's help, McEachern struggled to his feet again, pawing at his visor. The fall had ruined his suit conditioner and without it, a streetsuit got stuffy very fast.

"Your boot's still on fire, Slope," Morse warned, slowly advancing on two of the remaining three mobbers who seemed uncertain, now, whether to continue the raid. Ngo allowed one mobber to haul the other away. He leaned on his staff, peered down at the boot, levered his visor up to get a better look. That was when the third mobber, the woman, flung the tin of beef.

Her missile took Ngo under the edge of his visor, impacted into his unprotected face. Ngo went down instantly, silently, sprawling on a scatter of food tins. The woman scrambled to secure several more tins, then fled with the springing leap of a doe as Morse drew near. He took a stun grenade from his beltpac, judged that it would land far enough from his gumbas, hurled it. The mobbers were on the run now but, with a good toss, Morse could flatten the woman and two others.

But the fight had sapped his strength and his will. The grenade fell short, its shocking blast no more than a heavy push speeding the woman in her flight. Morse saw Weintraub and others advancing through the smoke then, and knelt beside his fallen gumba.

Clumsy in his gauntlets, Morse thrust Ngo's visor away; saw the ruined cheek, the nose torn apart, the broken teeth. He ripped off his gauntlet, laid his naked palm on Ngo's still unbloody forehead, and fought the shakes that threatened to consume him.

Morse was only half aware, automatically going through the right motions, when he helped Weintraub shift Ngo onto a stretcher. All the time, and during most of the trip to City Center, Morse remained numb with his waking nightmare. The great millstone churned in its track behind his eyes, unstoppable, filling his awareness, and now he saw that the vast wheel was much larger, infinitely larger, than he had thought. It was taller than trees; mountainous. And it ground exceedingly small.

When she saw that Gary had finished his clam strips, Fran Morse put down her fork. "So soon, greedy gut? Don't tell me you want more."

"Lounging around all day in the park is hard work," he said, trying to grin.

She gave him her I've-got-a-secret smile: "What if I told you there was mincemeat pie?"

"I'd figure you finally got a package from your folks, or more likely just setting me up for a gagline."

He watched as she went to the jury-rigged evaporation cooler, lifted its damp canvas flap, reached into the cool dark recess. She was turned away from him but he detected the patchwork cunning in her voice. "I got lucky at—the market today," she said, busy with her slicing. Then she turned with a demi-pirouette, revealing a saucer, and placed it before him. She returned for a second saucer. Each was piled with a dark mass of mincemeat pie, the glorious olfactory tang of autumn spices making him salivate even before he tasted it.

Fran grasped her fork awkwardly, drew a hissing breath, changed hands. She surrounded her first bite in mock ferocity.

Gary held the first bite in his mouth. He always made his first bite a small one, to make good things last. He'd forgotten how good—how deliriously, almost sexually delicious—food could taste. "Ah lordy, it tastes homemade," he marveled. "I wonder where they get the meat."

"What's all this 'they' business? It *is* homemade, with these two maladroit hands," Fran said, carving another bite. "Even if I did have to start with Spam."

Somehow, forcing himself to chew, he managed to swallow the stuff. He looked up to find her eyes on him, unflinching, all-accepting; and when he put down the fork with, "Too rich to eat all at once," he knew his lie was obvious.

She accepted the lie too; stood quickly when she saw the change come over his face; moved to his side. Gary buried his face against the firm swell of her belly. He felt the strong slender hands sweep through his hair, moved his own hands up and lifted Fran as he stood. The pallet was only steps away and he summoned enough strength to get there, unaware of the need to summon that strength.

For long minutes they lay together in the shadows, making no demands, sharing. "There will be better days," she whispered at last. "How are—the others?"

After a pause he husked, "Burgess will probably make it. Talk about *your* day, okay?"

"Let's just say it was profitable." She held her hands out in a *comme ci, comme ça* flutter. He caught one hand gently by the wrist, studied the shadings of an angry sunset in the dreadful bruise that spanned her thumb and forefinger.

With infinite tenderness, he brushed the swollen flesh with his lips.

She chuckled, "Just be glad you didn't catch me in the side of the head," and realized her mistake only when she felt him shudder.

"I *am* glad, and I'm sorry, and for God's sake *don't talk about it,*" he muttered, shaking. Again he pleaded, "Tell me about your day."

She knew a moment of terror as she stroked the heavy shoulders, recalled the power they could command. Yet the moment passed as Fran Morse began, crooningly, to spin a tale of the day she might have had.

Gary Morse closed his eyes and tried to concentrate on Fran's account. Anything—her most desperate fantasy—was better than a return to his own inner recesses and the millstone that churned inside him. He could understand it now that he knew its size, recognized the grist beneath it as a billion upturned faces soundlessly screaming. He understood it all but one detail.

Why, he wondered, *must they all have my face?*

The scenario just before this began with my plebeian guess that too many of us will continue to crowd and foul our urban nests. It said nothing about the alternatives in space habitats, because it was set in a future too near for any reasonable hope that people of average education could wangle a berth on a shuttle ship. My personal belief is that competition will still be fierce, fifty years from now, for ecological niches in space.

But the people who do manage to get to a space colony will be a motley lot; highly motivated and, I suspect, not especially tractable. Ben Bova and others had already done in-depth studies of space colony pioneers before I became seriously interested in the manmade colonies that will probably be erected in stable, near-earth Lagrangian orbits in our lifetimes. No one had written much about countercultures in L-5 colonies. It happens that I've spent some time studying what I call infracultures, stable groups living below the parent culture in some respect. Are they necessarily parasitic? The hell they are! Sometimes they know things we don't, and knowledge can be a great gift.

Certainly the story owes a lot to Eric Arthur Blair, an exquisite stylist more familiar to us as George Orwell. His autobiographical Down And Out In Paris And London *gave us a unique view of an English gentleman on the bum. No wonder he wrote* Animal Farm *and* 1984. *No wonder I was so pleased when, visiting friends in Hampstead, I found that Blair's digs had been two blocks from ours. And no wonder there was never any question about the title of the story below.*

Down And Out On Ellfive Prime

Responding to Almquist's control, the little utility tug wafted from the North dock port and made its gentle pirouette. Ellfive Prime Colony seemed to fall away. Two hundred thousand kilometers distant, blue-white Earth swam into view; cradle of mankind, cage for too many. Almquist turned his long body in its cushions and managed an obligatory smile over frown lines: "If that won't make you homesick, Mr. Weston, nothing will."

The fat man grunted, looking not at the planet he had deserted but at something much nearer. From the widening of Weston's eyes, you could tell it was something big, closing fast. Torin Almquist knew what it was; he eased the tug out, watching his radar, to give Weston the full benefit of it.

When the tip of the great solar mirror swept past, Weston blanched and cried out. For an instant, the view port was filled with cables and the mirror pivot mechanism. Then once again there was nothing but Earth and sharp pinpricks of starlight. Weston turned toward the engineering manager, wattles at his jawline trembling. "Stupid bastard," he grated. "If that'll be your standard joke on new arrivals, you must cause a lot of coronaries."

Abashed, disappointed: "A mirror comes by every fourteen seconds, Mr. Weston. I thought you'd enjoy it. You asked to see the casting facility, and this is where you can see it best. Besides, if you were retired as a heart case, I'd know it." *And the hell with you,* he added silently. Almquist retreated into an impersonal spiel he knew by heart, moving the tug back to gain a panorama of the colony with its yellow lengend, *L-5'*, proud and unnecessary on the hull. He moved the controls gently, the blond hairs on his forearm masking the play of tendons within.

The colony hung below them, a vast shining melon the length of the new Hudson River Bridge and nearly a kilometer thick. Another of its three mirror strips, anchored near the opposite South end cap of Ellfive Prime and spread like curved petals toward the sun, hurtled silently past the view port. Almquist kept talking. ". . . Prime was the second industrial colony in space, dedicated in 2007. These days it's a natural choice for a retirement community. A fixed population of twenty-five hundred—plus a few down-and-out bums hiding here and there. Nowhere near as big a place as Orbital General's new industrial colony out near the asteroid belt."

Almquist droned on, backing the tug farther away. Beyond the South end cap, a tiny mote sparkled in the void, and Weston squinted, watching it. "The first Ellfive was a General Dynamics-Lever Brothers project in close orbit, but it got snuffed by the Chinese in 2012, during the war."

"I was only a cub then," Weston said, relaxing a bit. "This colony took some damage too, didn't it?"

Almquist glanced at Weston, who looked older despite his bland flesh. Well, living Earthside with seven billion people tended to age you. "The month I was born," Almquist nodded, "a nuke was intercepted just off the centerline of Ellfive Prime. Thermal shock knocked a tremendous dimple in the hull, from inside, of course; it looked like a dome poking up through the soil south of center."

Weston clapped pudgy hands, a gesture tagging him as neo-Afrikaner. "That'll be the hill, then. The one with the pines and spruce, near Hilton Prime?"

A nod. "Stress analysts swore they could leave the dimple if they patched the hull around it. Cheapest solution—and for once, a pretty one. When they finished bringing new lunar topsoil and distributing it inside, they saw there was enough dirt on the slope for spruce and ponderosa pine roots. To balance thousands of tons of new processed soil, they built a blister out on the opposite side of the hull and moved some heavy hardware into it."

The fat man's gaze grew condescending as he saw the great

metal blister roll into view like a tumor on the hull: "Looks
slapdash," he said.

"Not really; they learned from DynLever's mistakes. The
first Ellfive colony was a cylinder, heavier than an ellipsoid
like ours." Almquist pointed through the view port. "Dyn-
Lever designed for a low ambient pressure without much
nitrogen in the cylinder and raised hell with water transpira-
tion and absorption in a lot of trees they tried to grow around
their living quarters. I'm no botanist, but I know Ellfive
Prime has an Earthside ecology—the same air you'd breathe
in Peru, only cleaner. We don't coddle our grass and trees,
and we grow all our crops right in the North end cap below
us."

Something new and infinitely pleasing shifted Weston's
features. "You used to have an external crop module to feed
fifty thousand people, back when this colony was big in
manufacturing—"

"Sold it," Almquist put in. "Detached the big rig and
towed it out to a belt colony when I was new here. We didn't
really need it anymore—"

Weston returned the interruption pointedly: "You didn't
let me finish. I put that deal over. OrbGen made a grand sum
on it—which is why the wife and I can retire up here. One
hand washes the other, eh?"

Almquist said something noncommittal. He had quit wondering why he disliked so many newcomers. He *knew* why. It
was a sling-cast irony that he, Ellfive Prime's top technical
man, did not have enough rank in OrbGen to be slated for
colony retirement. Torin Almquist might last as Civil Proj-
ects Manager for another ten years, if he kept a spotless
record. Then he would be Earthsided in the crowds and smog
and would eat fish cakes for the rest of his life. Unlike his
ex-wife, who had left him to teach in a belt colony so that she
would never have to return to Earth. And who could blame
her? *Shit*.

"I beg your pardon?"

"Sorry; I was thinking. You wanted to see the high-g
casting facility? It's that sphere strapped on to the mirror

that's swinging toward us. It's moving over two hundred
meters per second, a lot faster than the colony floor, being a
kilometer and a half out from the spin axis. So at the mirror
tip, instead of pulling around one standard g, they're pulling
over three g's. Nobody spends more than an hour there. We
balance the sphere with storage masses on the other mirror
tips.''

Restive, only half-interested: ''Why? It doesn't look very
heavy.''

''It isn't,'' Almquist conceded, ''but Ellfive Prime has to
be balanced just so if she's going to spin on center. That's
why they filled that blister with heavy stored equipment
opposite the hill—though a few tons here and there don't
matter.''

Weston wasn't listening. ''I keep seeing something like
barn doors flipping around, past the other end, ah, end cap.''
He pointed. Another brief sparkle. ''There,'' he said.

Almquist's arm tipped the control stick, and the tug slid
farther from the colony's axis of rotation. ''Stacking mirror
cells for shipment,'' he explained. ''We still have slag left
over from a nitrogen-rich asteroid they towed here in the old
days. Fused into plates, the slag makes good protection
againt solar flares. With a mirror face, it can do double duty.
We're bundling up a pallet load, and a few cargo men are out
there in P-suits—pressure suits. They—''

Weston would never know, and have cared less, what
Almquist had started to say. The colony manager clapped the
fingers of his free hand against the wireless speaker in his left
ear. His face stiffened with zealot intensity. Fingers flicker-
ing to the console as the tug rolled and accelerated, Almquist
began to speak into his throat mike—something about a Code
Three. Weston knew something was being kept from him. He
didn't like it and said so. Then he said so again.

''. . . happened before,'' Almquist was saying to someone, ''but this time you keep him centered, Radar Prime. I'll
haul him in myself. Just talk him out of a panic; you know the
drill. Please be quiet, Mr. Weston,'' he added in a too-polite
aside.

"Don't patronize me," Weston spat. "Are we in trouble?"

"I'm swinging around the hull; give me a vector," Almquist continued, and Weston felt his body sag under acceleration. "Are you in voice contact?" Pause. "Doesn't he acknowledge? He's on a work-crew scrambler circuit, but you can patch me in. Do it."

"You're treating me like a child."

"If you don't shut up, Weston, I *will*. Oh, hell, it's easier to humor you." He flicked a toggle, and the cabin speaker responded.

". . . be okay. I have my explosive riveter," said an unfamiliar voice; adult male, thinned and tightened by tension. "Starting to retro-fire now."

Almquist counted aloud at the muffled sharp bursts. "Not too fast, Versky," he cautioned. "You overheat a rivet gun, and the whole load could detonate."

"Jeez, I'm cartwheeling," Versky cut in. "Hang tight, guys." More bursts, now a staccato hammer. Versky's monologue gave no sign that he had heard Almquist, had all the signs of impending panic.

"Versky, listen to me. Take your goddamn finger off the trigger. We have you on radar. Relax. This is Torin Almquist, Versky. I say again—"

But he didn't. Far beyond, streaking out of the ecliptic, a brief nova flashed against the stars. The voice was cut off instantly. Weston saw Almquist's eyes blink hard, and in that moment the manager's face seemed aged by compassion and hopelessness. Then, very quietly: "Radar Prime, what do you have on scope?"

"Nothing but confetti, Mr. Almquist. Going everywhere at once."

"Should I pursue?"

"Your option, sir."

"And your responsibility."

"Yes, sir. No, don't pursue. Sorry."

"Not your fault. I want reports from you and Versky's cargo-team leader with all possible speed." Almquist flicked toggles with delicate savagery, turned his little vessel around, arrowed back to the dock port. Glancing at Weston, he said, "A skilled cargo man named Yves Versky. Experienced man; should've known better. He floated into a mirror support while horsing those slag cells around and got grazed by it. Batted him hell to breakfast." Then, whispering viciously to himself, "God*damn* those big rivet guns. They can't be used like control jets. Versky knew that."

Then, for the first time, Weston realized what he had seen. A man in a pressure suit had just been blown to small pieces before his eyes. It would make a lovely anecdote over sherry, Weston decided.

Even if Almquist had swung past the external hull blister he would have failed to see, through a darkened view port, the two shabby types looking out. Nobody had official business in the blister. The younger man grimaced nervously, heavy cords bunching at his neck. He was half a head taller than his companion. "What d'you think, Zen?"

The other man yielded a lopsided smile. "Sounds good." He unplugged a pocket communicator from the wall and stuffed it into his threadbare coverall, then leaned forward at the view port. His chunky, muscular torso and short legs ill-matched the extraordinary arms that reached halfway to his knees, giving him the look of a tall dwarf. "I think they bought it, Yves."

"What if they didn't?"

Zen swung around, now grinning outright, and regarded Yves Versky through a swatch of brown hair that was seldom cut. "Hey, do like boss Almquist told you. Relax! They *gotta* buy it."

"I don't follow you."

"Then you'd better learn to. Look, if they recover any pieces, they'll find human flesh. How can they know it was a poor rummy's body thawed after six months in a deep freeze? And if they *did* decide it's a scam, they'd have to explain how we planted him in your P-suit. And cut him loose from the blister, when only a few people are supposed to have access here; *and* preset the audio tape and the explosive, *and* coaxed a decent performance out of a lunk like you, *and*,'' he spread his apelike arms wide, his face comically ugly in glee, ''nobody can afford to admit there's a scam counterculture on Ellfive Prime. All the way up to Torin Almquist there'd be just too much egg on too many faces. It ain't gonna happen, Versky.''

The hulking cargo man found himself infected by the grin, but: ''I wonder how long it'll be before *I* see another egg.''

Zen snorted. ''First time you lug a carton of edible garbage out of Hilton Prime, me lad. Jean Neruda's half-blind; when you put on the right coverall, he won't know he has an extra in his recycling crew, and after two days you won't mind pickin' chicken out of the slop. Just sit tight in your basement hidey-hole when you're off duty for a while. Stay away from crews that might recognize you until your beard grows. And keep your head shaved like I told you.''

Versky heaved a long sigh, sweeping a hand over his newly bald scalp. ''You'll drop in on me? I need a lot of tips on the scam life. And—and I don't know how to repay you.''

''A million ways. I'll think of a few, young fella. And sure, you'll see me—whenever I like.''

Versky chuckled at the term *young fella*. He knew Zen might be in his forties, but he seemed younger. Versky followed his mentor to the air lock into the colony hull. ''Well, just don't forget your friend in the garbage business,'' he urged, fearful of his unknown future.

Zen paused in the conduit that snaked beneath the soil of Ellfive Prime. ''Friendship,'' he half-joked, ''varies directly with mutual benefit and inversely with guilt. Put another way,'' he said, lapsing into scam language as he trotted toward the South end cap, ''a friend who's willing to be understood is a joy. One that demands understanding is a pain in the ass.''

''You think too much,'' Versky laughed. They moved softly now, approaching an entry to the hotel basement.

Zen glanced through the spy hole, paused before punching the wall in the requisite place. ''Just like you work too much.'' He flashed his patented gargoyle grin. ''Trust me. Give your heart a rest.''

Versky, much too tall for his borrowed clothing, inflated his barrel chest in challenge. ''Do I *look* like a heart murmur?''

A shrug. ''You did to OrbGen's doctors, rot their souls—which is why you were due to be Earthsided next week. Don't lay that on *me*, ol' scam: I'm the one who's reprieved you to a low-g colony, if you'll just stay in low-g areas near the end caps.'' He opened the door.

Versky saw the hand signal and whispered, ''I got it: Wait thirty seconds.'' He chuckled again. ''Sometimes I think you should be running this colony.''

Zen slipped through, left the door nearly closed, waited until Versky had moved near the slit. ''In some ways,'' he stage-whispered back, ''I do.'' Wink. Then he scuttled away.

At mid-morning the next day, Almquist arranged the accident report and its supporting documents into a neat sequence across his video console. Slouching behind his desk with folded arms, he regarded the display for a moment before lifting his eyes. ''What've I forgot, Emory?''

Emory Reina cocked his head sparrowlike at the display. Almquist gnawed a cuticle, watching the soulful Reina eyes dart back and forth in sober scrutiny. ''It's all there,'' was Reina's verdict. ''The only safety infraction was Versky's, I think.''

''You mean the tether he should've worn?''

A nod; Reina started to speak but thought better of it, the furrows dark on his olive face.

''Spit it out, dammit,'' Almquist goaded. Reina usually thought a lot more than he talked, a trait Almquist valued in his assistant manager.

''I am wondering,'' the little Brazilian said, ''if it was really accidental.'' Their eyes locked again, held for a long moment. ''Ellfive Prime has been orbiting for fifty years.

Discounting early casualties throughout the war, the colony has had twenty-seven fatal mishaps among OrbGen employees. Fourteen of them occurred during the last few days of the victim's tour on the colony.''

"That's hard data?''

Another nod.

"You're trying to say they're suicides.''

"I am trying not to think so.'' A devout Catholic, Reina spoke hesitantly.

Maybe he's afraid God is listening. I wish I thought He would. "Can't say I'd blame some of them,'' Almquist said aloud, remembering. "But not Yves Versky. Too young, too much to live for.''

"You must account for my pessimism,'' Reina replied.

"It's what we pay you for,'' Almquist said, trying in vain to make it airy. "Maybe the insurance people could convince OrbGen to sweeten the Earthside trip for returning people. It might be cheaper in the long run.''

Emory Reina's face said that was bloody likely. "After I send a repair crew to fix the drizzle from that rain pipe, I could draft a suggestion from you to the insurance group,'' was all he said.

"Do that.'' Almquist turned his attention to the desk console. As Reina padded out of the low Center building into its courtyard, the manager committed the accident report to memory storage, then paused. His fingers twitched nervously over his computer-terminal keyboard. Oh, yes, he'd forgotten something, all right. Conveniently.

In moments, Almquist had queried Prime memory for an accident report ten years past. It was an old story in more ways than one. Philip Elroy Hazen: technical editor, born 14 September 2014, arrived on L-5 for first tour to write modification work orders 8 May 2039. Earthsided on 10 May 2041: a standard two-year tour for those who were skilled enough to qualify. A colony tour did not imply any other bonus: the tour *was* the bonus. It worked out very well for the owning conglomerates that controlled literally everything on their colonies. Almquist's mouth twitched: *well, maybe not literally . . .*

Hazen had wangled a second tour to the colony on 23 February 2045, implying that he'd been plenty good at his work. Fatal injury accident report filed 20 February 2047.

Uh-*huh;* uh-*huh!* Yes, by God, there was a familiar ring to it: a malf in Hazen's radio while he was suited up, doing one last check on a modification to the casting facility. Flung off the tip of the mirror and—*Jesus, what a freakish way to go*—straight into a mountain of white-hot slag that had radiated like a dying sun near a temporary processing module outside the colony hull. No recovery attempted; why sift ashes?

Phil Hazen; Zen, they'd called him. The guy they used to say needed rollerskates on his hands; but that was envy talking. Almquist had known Zen slightly, and the man was an absolute terror at sky-bike racing along the zero-g axis of the colony. Built his own tri-wing craft, even gave it a Maltese cross, scarlet ploymer wingskin, and a funny name. The *Red Baron* had looked like a joke, just what Zen had counted on. He'd won a year's pay before other sky bikers realized it wasn't a streak of luck.

Hazen had always made his luck. With his sky bike, it was with young seasoned spruce and foam polymer, fine engineering and better craftsmanship, all disguised to lure the suckers. And all without an engineering degree. Zen had just picked up expertise, never seeming to work at it.

And when his luck ran out, it was—Almquist checked the display—only days before he was slated for Earthside. Uh-*huh!*

Torin Almquist knew about the shadowy wraiths who somehow dropped from sight on the colony, to be caught later or to die for lack of medical attention or, in a few cases, to find some scam—some special advantage—to keep them hidden on Ellfive Prime. He'd been sure Zen was a survivor, no matter what the accident report said. What was the phrase?

A scam, not a bum; being on the scam wasn't quite the same. A scam wasn't down and out of resources: he was down and out of sight. Maybe the crafty Zen had engineered another fatality that wasn't fatal.

Almquist hadn't caught anyone matching the description of Zen. Almost, but not quite. He thought about young Yves Versky, whose medical report hadn't been all that bad, then considered Versky's life expectancy on the colony versus his chances Earthside. Versky had been a sharp, hard worker too.

Almquist leaned back in his chair again and stared at his display. He had no way of knowing that Reina's rainpipe crew was too late to ward off disaster. The rain pipe had been leaking long before Grounds Maintenance realized they had a problem. Rain was a simple matter on Ellfive Prime: You built a web of pipes with spray nozzles that ran the length of the colony. From ground level the pipes were nearly invisible, thin lines connected by crosspieces in a great cylindrical net surrounding the colony's zero-g axis. Gravity loading near the axis was so slight that the rain pipes could be anchored lightly.

Yet now and then, a sky biker would pedal foolishly from the zero-g region or would fail to compensate for the gentle rolling movement generated by the air itself. That was when the rain pipes saved somebody's bacon and on rare occasions suffered a kink. At such times, Almquist was tempted to press for the outlawing of sky bikes until the rabid sports association could raise money for a safety net to protect people and pipes alike. But the cost would have been far too great: It would have amounted to a flat prohibition of sky bikes.

The problem had started a month earlier with a mild collision between a sky bike and a crosspiece. The biker got back intact, but the impact popped a kink on the underside of the attached rain pipe. The kink could not be seen from the colony's axis. It might possibly have been spotted from floor level with a good, powerful telescope.

Inspection crews used safety tethers, which loaded the rain

pipe just enough to close the crack while the inspector passed. Then the drizzle resumed for as long as the rain continued. Thereafter, the thrice-weekly afternoon rain from that pipe had been lessened in a line running from Ellfive Prime's Hilton Hotel, past the prized hill, over the colony's one shallow lake, to work-staff apartments that stretched from the lake to the North end cap, where crops were grown. Rain was lessened, that is, everywhere but over the pine-covered hill directly below the kink. Total rainfall was unchanged; but the hill got three times its normal moisture, which gradually soaked down through a forty-year accumulation of ponderosa needles and humus, into the soil below.

In this fashion the hill absorbed one hundred thousand kilograms too much water in a month. A little water percolated back to the creek and the lake it fed. Some of it was still soaking down through the humus overburden. And much of it—far too much—was held by the underlying slope soil, which was gradually turning to ooze. The extra mass had already caused a barely detectable shift in the colony's spin axis. Almquist had his best troubleshooter, Lee Shumway, quietly checking the hull for a structural problem near the hull blister.

Suzanne Nagel was a lissome widow whose second passion was for her sky bike. She had been idling along in zero-g, her chain-driven propeller a soft whirr behind her, when something obscured her view of the hill far below. She kept staring at it until she was well beyond the leak, then realized the obstruction was a spray of water. Suzy sprint-pedaled the rest of the way to the end cap, and five minutes later the rains were canceled by Emory Reina.

Thanks to Suzy Nagel's stamina, the slope did not collapse that day. But working from inspection records, Reina tragically assumed that the leak had been present for perhaps three days instead of a month. The hill needed something—a local vibration, for example—to begin the mud slide that could abruptly displace up to two hundred thousand tons of mass downslope. Which would inevitably bring on the nightmare more feared than meteorites by every colony manager: spin-quake. Small meteorites could only damage a colony, but computer simulations had proved that if the spin axis shifted suddenly a spinquake could crack a colony like an egg.

The repair crew was already in place high above when Reina brought his electrabout three-wheeler to a halt near a path that led up to the pines. His belt-comm set allowed direct contact with the crew and instant access to all channels, including his private scrambler to Torin Almquist.

"I can see the kink on your video," Reina told the crew leader, studying his belt-slung video. "Sleeve it and run a pressure check. We can be thankful that a leak that large was not over Hilton Prime," he added, laughing. The retired OrbGen executives who luxuriated in the hotel would have screamed raw murder, of course. And the leak would have been noticed weeks before.

Scanning the dwarf apple trees at the foot of the slope, Reina's gaze moved to the winding footpath. In the forenoon quietude, he could hear distant swimmers cavorting in the slightly reduced gravity of the Hilton pool near the South end cap. But somewhere above him on the hill, a large animal thrashed clumsily through the pines. It wasn't one of the half-tame deer; only maladroit humans made that much commotion on Ellfive Prime. Straining to locate the hiker, Reina saw the leaning trees. He blinked. No trick of eyesight; they were really leaning. Then he saw the long shallow mud slide, no more than a portent of its potential, that covered part of the footpath. For perhaps five seconds, his mind grasping the implication of what he saw, Reina stood perfectly still. His mouth hung open.

In deadly calm, coding the alarm on his scrambler circuit: "Torin, Emory Reina. I have a Code Three on the hill. And," he swallowed hard, "potential Code One. I say again, Code One; mud slides on the main-path side of the hill. Over." Then Reina began to shout toward the pines.

Code Three was bad enough: a life in danger. Code Two was more serious still, implying an equipment malfunction that could affect many lives. Code One was reserved for colony-wide disaster. Reina's voice shook. He had never called a Code One before.

During the half-minute it took for Almquist to race from a conference to his office. Reina's shouts flushed not one but two men from the hillside. The first, a heavy individual in golf knickers, identified himself testily as Voerster Weston. He stressed that he was not accustomed to peremptory demands from an overall-clad worker. The second man emerged far to Reina's right but kept hidden in a stand of mountain laurel; listening, surmising, sweating.

Reina's was the voice of sweet reason. "If you want to live, Mr. Weston, please lie down where you are. Slowly. The trees below you are leaning outward, and they were not that way yesterday."

"Damnation, I know that much," Weston howled; "that's what I was looking at. Do you know how wet it is up here? I will not lie down on this muck!"

The man in the laurels made a snap decision, cursed, and stood up. "If you don't, two-belly, I'll shoot you here and now," came the voice of Philip Elroy Hazen. Zen had one hand thrust menacingly into a coverall pocket. He was liberally smeared with mud, and his aspect was not pleasant.

"*O demonio,* another one," Reina muttered. The fat man saw himself flanked, believed Zen's implied lie about a weapon, and carefully levered himself down to the blanket of pine needles. At this moment Torin Almquist answered the Mayday.

There was no way to tell how much soil might slide, but through staccato interchanges Emory Reina described the scene better than his video could show it. Almquist was grim. "We're already monitoring an increase in the off-center spin, Emory, not a severe shift, but it could get to be. Affirmative on that potential Code One. I'm sending a full emergency crew to the blister, now that we know where to start."

Reina thought for a moment, glumly pleased that neither man on the slope had moved. "I believe we can save these two by lowering a safety sling from my crew. They are directly overhead. Concur?"

An instant's pause. "Smart, Emory. And you get your butt out of there. Leave the electrabout, man, just *go!*"

"With respect, I cannot. Someone must direct the sling deployment from here."

"It's your bacon. I'll send another crew to you."

"Volunteers only," Reina begged, watching the slope. For the moment it seemed firm. Yet a bulge near cosmetically placed slag boulders suggested a second mass displacement. Reina then explained their predicament to the men on the slope, to ensure their compliance.

"It's worse than that," Zen called down. "There was a dugout over there," he pointed to the base of a boulder, "where a woman was living. She's buried, I'm afraid."

Reina shook his head sadly, using his comm set to his work crew. Over four hundred meters above, men were lashing tether lines from crosspieces to distribute the weight of a sling. Spare tethers could be linked by carabiners to make a lifeline reaching to the colony floor. The exercise was familiar to the crew, but only as a drill until now. And they would be hoisting, not lowering.

Diametrically opposite from the hill, troubleshooters converged on the blister where the colony's long-unused reactor and coolant tanks were stored. Their job was simple—in principle.

The reactor subsystems had been designed as portable elements, furnished with lifting and towing lugs. The whole reactor system weighed nearly ten thousand tons, including coolant tanks. Since the blister originally had been built around the store reactor elements to balance the hill mass, Almquist needed only to split the blister open to space, then lower the reactor elements on quartz cables. As the mass moved out of the blister and away from the hull, it would increase in apparent weight, balancing the downward flow of mud across the hull. Almquist was lucky in one detail: The reactor was not in line with the great solar-mirror strips. Elements could be lowered a long way while repairs were carried out to redistribute the soil.

Almquist marshaled forces from his office. He heard the

colony-wide alarm whoop its signal, watched monitors as the colony staff and two thousand other residents hurried toward safety in end-cap domes. His own P-suit, ungainly and dust-covered, hung in his apartment ten paces away. There was no time to fetch it while he was at his post. *Never again,* he promised himself. He divided his attention among monitors showing the evacuation, the blister team, and the immediate problem above Emory Reina.

Reina was optimistic as the sling snaked down. "South a bit," he urged into his comm set, then raised his voice. "Mr. Weston, a sling is above you, a little north. Climb in and buckle the harness. They will reel you in."

Weston looked around him, the whites of his eyes visible from fifty meters away. He had heard the alarm and remembered only that it meant mortal danger. He saw the sling turning gently on its thin cable as it neared him.

"Now, steady as she goes," Reina said, then, "Stop." The sling collapsed on the turf near the fat man. Reina, fearful that the mud-covered stranger might lose heart, called to assure him that the sling would return.

"I'll take my chances here," Zen called back. The sling could mean capture. The fat man did not understand that any better than Reina did.

Voerster Weston paused halfway into his harness, staring up. Suddenly he was scrambling away from it, tripping in the sling, mindless with the fear of rising into a synthetic sky. Screaming, he fled down the slope. And brought part of it with him.

Reina saw apple trees churning toward him in time to leap atop his electrabout and kept his wits enough to grab branches as the first great wave slid from the slope. He saw Weston disappear in two separate upheavals, swallowed under the mud slide he had provoked. Mauled by hardwood, mired to his knees, Reina spat blood and turf. He hauled one leg free, then the other, pulling at tree limbs. The second man, he saw, had slithered against a thick pine and was now trying to climb it.

Still calm, voice indistinct through his broken jaw, Reina

redirected the sling crew. The sling harness bounced upslope near the second man. "Take the sling," Reina bawled.

Now Reina's whole world shuddered. It was a slow, perceptible motion, each displacement of mud worsening the off-center rotation and slight acceleration changes that could bring more mud that could bring worse. . . . Reina forced his mind back to the immediate problem. He could not see himself at its focus.

Almquist felt the tremors, saw what had to be done. "Emory, I'm sending your relief crew back. Shumway's in the blister. They don't have time to cut the blister now; they'll have to blow it open. You have about three minutes to get to firm ground. Then you run like hell to South end cap."

"As soon as this man is in the sling," Reina mumbled. Zen had already made his decision, seeing the glistening ooze that had buried the fat man.

"Now! Right fucking *now*," Almquist pleaded. "I can't delay it a millisecond. When Shumway blows the blister open it'll be a sudden shake, Emory. You know what that means?"

Reina did. The sharp tremor would probably bring the entire middle of the slope thundering down. Even if the reactor could be lowered in minutes, it would take only seconds for the muck to engulf him. Reina began to pick his way backward across fallen apple trees, wondering why his left arm had an extra bend above the wrist. He kept a running fire of instructions to the rain-pipe crew as Zen untangled the sling harness. Reina struggled toward safety in pain, patience, reluctance. And far too slowly.

"He is buckled in," Reina announced. His last words were, "Haul away." He saw the mud-spattered Zen begin to rise, swinging in a broad arc, and they exchanged "OK" hand signals before Reina gave full attention to his own escape. He had just reached the edge of firm ground when Lee Shumway, moving with incredible speed in a full P-suit, ducked through a blister airlock and triggered the charges.

The colony floor bucked once, throwing Reina off stride. He fell on his fractured ulna, rolled, opened his mouth—

perhaps to moan, perhaps to pray. His breath was bottled by mud as he was flung beneath a viscous gray tide that rolled numberless tons of debris over him.

The immense structure groaned, but held. Zen swayed sickeningly as Ellfive Prime shook around him. He saw Reina die, watched helplessly as a retiree home across the valley sagged and collapsed. Below him, a covey of Quetzal birds burst from the treetops like jeweled scissors in flight. As he was drawn higher he could see more trees slide.

The damage worsened; too many people had been too slow. The colony was rattling everything that would rattle. Now it was all rattling louder. Somewhere, a shrill whistle keened as precious air and more precious water vapor rushed toward a hole in the sunlight windows.

When the shouts above him became louder than the carnage below, Zen began to hope. Strong arms reached for his and moments later he was attached to another tether. "I can make it from here," he said, calling his thanks back as he hauled himself toward the end-cap braces.

A crew man with a video comm set thrust it toward Zen as he neared a ladder. "It's for you," he said, noncommittal.

For an instant, an eon, Zen's body froze, though he continued to waft nearer. Then he shrugged and took the comm set as though it were ticking. He saw a remembered face in the video. Wrapping an arm around the ladder, he nodded to the face. "Don Bellows here," he said innocently.

Pause, then a snarl: "You wouldn't believe my mixed emotions when I recognized you on the monitor. Well, *Mister* Bellows, Adolf Hitler here." Almquist went on, "Or you'll think so damned quick unless you're in my office as fast as your knuckles will carry you."

The crewman was looking away, but he was tense. He knew. Zen cleared his throat for a whine. "I'm scared—"

"You've been dead for ten years, Hazen. How can you be scared? Frazer there will escort you; his instructions are to brain you if he has to. I have sweeping powers right now. Don't con me and don't argue; I need you right here, right now."

By the time Zen reached the terraces with their felled, jumbled crops, the slow shakes had subsided. They seemed to diminish to nothing as he trotted, the rangy Frazer in step behind, to an abandoned electrabout. Damage was everywhere, yet the silence was oppressive. A few electrical fires were kindling in apartments as they moved toward the Colony Center building. Some fires would be out, others out of control, in minutes. The crew man gestured Zen through the courtyard and past two doors. Torin Almquist stood looming over his console display, ignoring huge shards of glass that littered his carpet.

Almquist adjusted a video monitor. "Thanks, Frazer; would you wait in the next room?" The crewman let his face complain of his idleness but complied silently. Without glancing from the monitors, Almquist transfixed the grimy Zen. "If I say the word, you're a dead man. If I say a different word, you go Earthside in manacles. You're still here only because I wanted you here all the time, just in case I ever needed you. Well, I need you now. If you hadn't been dropped into my lap we'd have found you on a Priority One. Never doubt that.

"If I say a third word, you get a special assistant's slot—I can swing that—for as long as I'm here. All I'm waiting for is one word from *you*. If it's a lie, you're dead meat. Will you help Ellfive Prime? Yes or no?"

Zen considered his chances. Not past that long-legged Frazer. They could follow him on monitors for some distance anyhow unless he had a head start. "Given the right conditions," Zen hazarded.

Almquist's head snapped up. "My best friend just died for you, against my better judgment. *Yes or no.*"

"Yes. I owe you nothin', but I owe him somethin'."

Back to the monitors, speaking to Zen: "Lee Shumway's crew has recovered our mass balance, and they can do it again if necessary. I doubt there'll be more mud slides, though; five minutes of spinquakes should've done it all."

Zen moved to watch over the tall man's bare arms. Two crews could be seen from a utility tug monitor, rushing to repair window leaks where water vapor had crystallized in space as glittering fog. The colony's external heat radiator was in massive fragments, and the mirrors were jammed in place. It was going to get hot in Ellfive Prime. "How soon will we get help from other colonies?"

Almquist hesitated. Then, "We won't, unless we fail to cope. OrbGen is afraid some other corporate pirate will claim salvage rights. And when you're on my staff, everything I tell you is privileged data."

"You think the danger is over?"

"Over?" Almquist barked a laugh that threatened to climb out of control. He ticked items off on his fingers. "We're losing water vapor; we have to mask mirrors and repair the radiator, or we fry; half our crops are ruined and food stores may not last; and most residents are hopeless clods who have no idea how to fend for themselves. *Now* d'you see why I diverted searches when I could've taken you twice before?"

Zen's mouth was a cynical curve.

Almquist: "Once when you dragged a kid from the lake filters I could've had you at the emergency room." Zen's eyebrows lifted in surprised agreement. "And once when a waiter realized you were scamming food from the Hilton service elevator."

"That was somebody else, you weren't even close. But okay, you've been a real sweetheart. Why?"

"Because you've learned to live outside the system! Food, shelter, medical help, God knows what else; you have another system that hardly affects mine, and now we're going to teach your tricks to the survivors. This colony is going to make it. You were my experimental group, Zen. You just didn't know it." He rubbed his chin reflectively. "By the way, how many guys are on the scam? Couple of dozen?" An optimist, Torin Almquist picked what he considered a high figure.

A chuckle. "Couple of hundred, you mean." Zen saw slack-jawed disbelief and went on: "They're not all guys. A few growing families. There's Wandering Mary, Maria Polyakova; our only registered nurse, but I found her dugout full of mud this morning. I hope she was sleepin' out.''

"Can you enlist their help? If they don't help, this colony can still die. The computer says it will, as things stand now. It'll be close, but we won't make it. How'd you like to take your chances with a salvage crew?''

"Not a chance. But I can't help just standing here swappin' wind with you.''

"Right.'' Eyes bored into Zen's, assessing him. The thieves' argot, the be-damned-to-you gaze, suggested a man who was more than Hazen *had* been. "I'll give you a temporary pass. See you here tomorrow morning; for now, look the whole colony over, and bring a list of problems and solutions as you see 'em.''

Zen turned to leave, then looked back. "You're really gonna let me just walk right out.'' A statement of wonder, and of fact.

"Not without this,'' Almquist said, scribbling on a plastic chit. He thrust it toward Zen. "Show it to Frazer.''

Inspecting the cursive scrawl: "Doesn't look like much.''

"*Mais, que nada,*'' Almquist smiled, then looked quickly away as his face fell. *Better than nothing;* his private joke with Emory Reina. He glanced at the retreating Zen and rubbed his forehead. Grief did funny things to people's heads. To deny a death you won't accept, you invest his character in another man. Not very smart when the other man might betray you for the sheer fun of it. Torin Almquist massaged his temples and called Lee Shumway. They still had casualties to rescue.

Zen fought a sense of unreality as he moved openly in broad daylight. Everyone was lost in his own concerns. Zen hauled one scam from his plastic bubble under the lake surface, half dead in stagnant air after mud from the creek swamped his air exchanger. An entire family of scams, living as servants in the illegal basement they had excavated for a resident, had been crushed when the foundation collapsed.

But he nearly wept to find Wandering Mary safe in a secret conduit, tending to a dozen wounded scams. He took notes as she told him where her curative herbs were planted and how to use them. The old girl flatly refused to leave her charges, her black eyes flashing through wisps of gray hair, and Zen promised to send food.

The luck of Sammy the Touch was holding strong. The crop compost heap that covered his half-acre foam shell seemed to insulate it from ground shock as well. Sammy patted his little round tummy, always a cheerful sign, as he ushered Zen into the bar where, on a good night, thirty scams might be gathered. If Zen was the widest-ranging scam on Ellfive Prime, Sammy the Touch was the most secure.

Zen accepted a glass of potato vodka—Sammy was seldom *that* easy a touch—and allowed a parody of the truth to be drawn from him. He'd offered his services to an assistant engineer, he said, in exchange for unspecified future privileges. Sammy either bought the story or took a lease on it. He responded after some haggling with the promise of a hundred kilos of "medicinal" alcohol and half his supply of bottled methane. Both were produced from compost precisely under the noses of the crop crew, and both were supplied on credit. Sammy also agreed to provision the hidden infirmary of Wandering Mary. Zen hugged the embarrassed Sammy and exited through one of the conduits, promising to pick up the supplies later.

Everywhere he went, Zen realized, the scams were coping better than legal residents. He helped a startlingly handsome middle-aged blonde douse the remains of her smoldering wardrobe. Her apartment complex had knelt into its courtyard and caught fire.

"I'm going to freeze tonight," Suzy Nagel murmured philosophically.

He eyed her skimpy costume and doubted it. Besides, the temperature was slowly climbing, and there wouldn't *be* any night until the solar mirrors could be pivoted again. There were other ways to move the colony to a less reflective position, but he knew Almquist would try the direct solutions first.

Farmer Brown—no one knew his original name—wore his

usual stolen agronomy-crew coverall as he hawked his pack load of vegetables among residents in the low-rent area. He had not assessed all the damage to his own crops, tucked and espaliered into corners over five square kilometers of the colony. Worried as he was, he had time to hear a convincing story. "Maybe I'm crazy to compete against myself," he told Zen, "but you got a point. If a salvage outfit takes over, it's kaymag." KMAG: Kiss my ass good-bye. "I'll sell you seeds, even breeding pairs of hamsters, but don't ask me to face the honchos in person. You remember about the vigilantes, ol' scam."

Zen nodded. He gave no thought to the time until a long shadow striped a third of the colony floor. One of the mirrors had been coaxed into pivoting. Christ, he was tired—but why not? It would have been dark long before, on an ordinary day. He sought his sleeping quarters in Jean Neruda's apartment, hoping Neruda wouldn't insist on using Zen's eyesight to fill out receipts. Their arrangement was a comfortable quid pro quo, but please, thought Zen, not tonight!

He found a more immediate problem than receipts. Yves Versky slumped, trembling, in the shambles of Neruda's place, holding a standard emergency oxygen mask over the old man's face. The adjoining office had lost one wall in the spinquake, moments after the recycling crew ran for end-cap domes.

"I had to hole up here," Versky gasped, exhausted. "Didn't know where else to go. Neruda wouldn't leave either. Then the old fool smelled smoke and dumped his goldfish bowl on a live power line. Must've blown half the circuits in his body." Like a spring-wound toy, Versky's movements and voice diminished. "Took me two hours of mouth-to-mouth before he was breathing steady, Zen. Boy, have I got a headache."

Versky fell asleep holding the mask in place. Zen could infer the rest. Neruda, unwilling to leave familiar rooms in his advancing blindness. Versky, unwilling to abandon a life, even that of a half-electrocuted, crotchety old man. Yet

Neruda was right to stay put: Earthside awaited the OrbGen employee whose eyes failed.

Zen lowered the inert Versky to the floor, patted the big man's shoulder. More than unremitting care, he had shown stamina and first-aid expertise. Old Neruda awoke once, half-manic, half just disoriented. Zen nursed him through it with surface awareness. On another level he was cataloguing items for Almquist, for survivors, for Ellfive Prime.

And on the critical level a voice in him jeered, *bullshit: For yourself*. Not because Almquist or Reina had done him any favors, but because Torin Almquist was right. The colony manager could find him eventually; maybe it was better to rejoin the system now, on good terms. Besides, as the only man who could move between the official system and the scam counterculture, he could really wheel and deal. It might cause some hard feelings in the conduits, but . . . Zen sighed, and slept. Poorly.

It was two days before Zen made every contact he needed, two more when Almquist announced that Ellfive Prime would probably make it. The ambient temperature had stabilized. Air and water losses had ceased. They did not have enough stored food to provide three thousand daily calories per person beyond twenty days, but crash courses in multicropping were suddenly popular, and some immature crops could be eaten.

"It'd help if you could coax a few scams into instructing," Almquist urged as he slowed to match Zen's choppy pace. They turned from the damaged crop terraces toward the Center.

"Unnn-likely," Zen intoned. "We still talk about war-time, when vigilantes tried to clean us out. They ushered a couple of nice people out of airlocks, naked, which we think was a little brusque. Leave it alone; it's working."

A nod. "Seems to be. But I have doubts about the maturing rates of your seeds. Why didn't my people know about those hybrid daikon radishes and tomatoes?"

"You were after long-term yield," Zen shrugged. "This

hot weather will ripen the stuff faster, too. We've been hiding a dozen short-term crops under your nose, including dandelions better than spinach. Like hamster haunch is better'n rabbit, and a lot quicker to grow.''

Almquist could believe the eighteen-day gestation period, but was astonished at the size of the breeding stock. ''You realize your one-kilo hamsters could be more pet than protein?''

''Not in our economy,'' Zen snorted. ''It's hard to be sentimental when you're down and out. Or stylish either.'' He indicated his frayed coverall. ''By the time the rag man gets this, it won't yield three meters of dental floss.''

Almquist grinned for the first time in many days. What his new assistant had forgotten in polite speech, he made up in the optimism of a young punk. He corrected himself: an *old* punk. ''You know what hurts? You're nearly my age and look ten years younger. How?''

It wasn't a specific exercise, Zen explained. It was attitude. ''You're careworn,'' he sniffed. ''Beat your brains out for idling plutocrats fifty weeks a year and then wonder why you age faster than I do.'' Wondering headshake.

They turned toward the Center courtyard. Amused, Almquist said, ''You're a plutocrat?''

''Ain't racin' my motors. Look at all the Indians who used to live past a hundred. A Blackfoot busted his ass like I do, maybe ten or twenty weeks a year. They weren't dumb; just scruffy.''

Almquist forgot his retort; his desk console was flashing for attention. Zen wandered out of the office, returning with two cups of scam ''coffee.'' Almquist sipped it between calls, wondering if it was really brewed from ground dandelion root, considering how this impudent troll was changing his life, could change it further.

Finally he sat back. ''You heard OrbGen's assessment,'' he sighed. ''I'm a God-damned hero, for now. Don't ask me about next year. If they insist on making poor Emory a sacrificial goat to feed ravening stockholders, I can't help it.''

Impassive: "Sure you could. You just let 'em co-opt you." Zen sighed, then released a sad troglodyte's smile. "Like you co-opted me."

"I can unco-opt. Nothing's permanent."

"You said it, bubba."

Almquist took a long breath, then cantilevered a forefinger in warning. "Watch your tongue, Hazen. When I pay your salary, you pay some respect." He saw the sullen look in Zen's eyes and bored in. "Or would you rather go on the scam again and get Earthsided the first chance I get? I haven't *begun* to co-opt you yet," he glowered. "I have to meet with the Colony Council in five minutes—to explain a lot of things, including you. When I get back, I want a map of those conduits the scams built, to the best of your knowledge."

A flood of ice washed through Zen's veins. Staring over the cup of coffee that shook in his hands: "You *know* I can't do that."

Almquist paused in the doorway, his expression smug. "You know the alternative. Think about it," he said, and turned and walked out.

When Torin Almquist returned, his wastebasket was overturned on his desk. A ripe odor wrinkled his nose for him even before he saw what lay atop the wastebasket like an offering on a pedestal: a lavish gift of human extrement. His letter opener, an antique, protruded from the turd. It skewered a plastic chit, Zen's pass. On the chit, in draftsman's neat printing, full caps: I THOUGHT ABOUT IT.

Well, you sure couldn't mistake his answer, Almquist reflected as he dumped the offal into his toilet. Trust Zen to make the right decision.

Which way had he gone? Almquist could only guess at the underground warrens built during the past fifty years, but chose not to guess. He also knew better than to mention Zen to the Colony Council. The manager felt a twinge of guilt at the choice, truly no choice at all, that he had forced on Zen—but there was no other way.

If Zen knew the whole truth, he might get careless, and a low profile was vital for the scams. The setup benefited all of

Ellfive Prime. Who could say when the colony might once
more need the counterculture and its primitive ways?

And that meant Zen had to disappear again, genuinely
down and out of reach. If Almquist himself didn't know
exactly where the scams hid, he couldn't tell OrbGen even
under drugs. And he didn't intend to tell. Sooner or later
OrbGen would schedule Torin Almquist for permanent
Earthside rotation, and when that day came he might need
help in his own disappearance. *That* would be the time to
ferret out a secret conduit, to contact Zen. The scams could
use an engineering manager who knew the official system
inside out.

Almquist grinned to himself and brewed a cup of dandelion coffee. Best to get used to the stuff now, he reasoned; it
would be a staple after he retired, down and out on Ellfive
Prime.

As we saw a few pages back, there will probably always be a need for a few do-it-yourselfers, no matter how advanced our technology becomes. Most likely, your own kitchen is a high-tech area where, without thinking about it, you develop much of your manual skill. Think about it. Assuming you don't already have basic life-support systems for a fallout shelter, could you build the absolute essentials in half a day? I'm sure you could; I suspect you may have to, someday. The piece below shows you how you might go about it on the spur of the moment.

Please understand that I faced a nasty little ethical choice in doing this (and other) material. Could I show you how to make last-minute preparations that meet commercial standards? Good God, no! At best I could only show you how you might be able to stay alive–exhausted, filthy, possibly ill–but alive. Asking the next question, then: how many people are at the point of buying good reliable equipment, but will read the piece below and decide to save money by doing it my way?

Well, listen: this isn't my way. Build the units I describe, just for practice. Then you'll fully realize that they are the equivalent of tying your trousers into waterwings, when you should've invested in a raft. Get the bloody raft!

But the raft might leak. Don't forget the primitive ways . . .

Living Under Pressure

In the previous issue of *Destinies,* * we began this series of articles to update and alert you on the problems of survival after an all-out nuclear exchange. Briefly summarized: in "Gimme Shelter" we explained that twenty-mile-wide, thermonuclear-kindled firestorms would render many U.S. urban areas utterly uninhabitable. The government—much too quietly, in my opinion—now favors mass evacuation from high-risk areas following an alert. The problems with this new and more sensible civil defense (CD) posture lie in educating us about it; in the likelihood of clogged routes during the evacuation; in improvising shelters in low-risk areas; and in doing anything on a large scale with damnably low CD budgets. We also referenced some publications and promised to give you some tips on making a shelter more effective, starting with air filtration and pump units that you can make on short notice. We're making good on that promise now. In a phrase, one key to clean air is living under pressure.

We assume that you have your free copy of the government's CD pamphlet of February, 1977, *Protection In The Nuclear Age,* which admits the wisdom of 'crisis relocation' and suggests that you find a shelter completely surrounded by two or three feet of masonry or dirt. But even if you have such shelter, you still aren't safe from fallout unless you can make the place airtight.

If you've ever fretted through a dust storm, you know how air supports dust particles, and how a breeze sifts the finest ones past infinitesimal cracks around doors and window-frames. While a lot of fallout will be large visible ash, too much of the stuff will be invisibly small hunks of airborne

*See page 144 of this volume. —Editor

grit, settling hundreds of miles downwind of a nuclear strike. They are lethal dustmotes if you breathe enough of them during the first two or three weeks after a nuclear strike. That's why a shelter should be stocked with caulking material and tape; so that every crevice in the shelter can be sealed. In short, you must turn the shelter into a pressure vessel and bottle yourself up in it.

Which means that you could swelter in your body heat and asphyxiate in your own carbon dioxide waste if you stayed inside very long without a fresh air supply. We'll give figures later in this article; for the moment, the rationale's the thing.

If your supplies are adequate, you might stay in the shelter for weeks—but almost nobody will have a week's supply of bottled air. What you need is a means for pumping cool filtered air from the outside, and for exhausting the stale humid air from your shelter. Believe it or not, the solution isn't necessarily very complex once you've practice doing it, even on a small scale model.

We infer from sources on Soviet CD that the first stage of their civilian shelter filters is through something called a 'blast attenuator'—a wide vertical conduit pipe filled with big rocks and gravel. The pipe has a raincap on top, above-ground, and a removable grille covering one side of its bottom end. The grille is sturdy enough to hold the gravel and coarse enough to let air through. Notice that a conduit of twenty-four-inch diameter can be used as an emergency exit, once the grille is removed and the gravel drained out. The gravel lets air through while trapping large fallout particles and baffling concussion waves from any nearby explosions. The Soviets use finer filters for the air that is sucked down through the gravel by pumps. Incidentally, if you're building such a 'blast attenuator' for a shelter, specify rounded quartz gravel. Hunks of limestone can eventually become cemented together to become a rigid sponge that impedes airflow.

In extremis, you could build a medium-mesh filter by taping a towel over a square-foot-sized inlet into the shelter. You might find it clogged after a day or so. A finer-mesh filter can be made with corrugated cardboard, large juice cans, replaceable rolls of toilet paper, and tape.

Our demonstration rig was designed to provide air for two adults. It uses a standard household furnace filter element taped securely over the intake hole of the filter box—because we assume that you *won't* have a yards-long gravel-filled conduit. After you build your air filtration unit, you'll have to place it in some weatherproof spot just outside the sealed shelter. Thus, you can get to the unit quickly in case filter elements become clogged.

The standard furnace filter has a coarse fiberglass element. Particles that get past it will be small, but many would be visible to the naked eye. That calls for a second and finer element.

For its second element, our model uses the same stuff employed by a great many industrial air filters: nothing more than a piece of flannel. As it happens, we spent a dollar on a yard of cotton outing flannel, enough for a one-square-foot filter element with eight spares. That might be enough for two weeks, depending on how much fallout is in your area. We could've used a new diaper or a flannel shirt; it's the soft fuzzy nap of the flannel that traps so much dust. Flannel that's been washed until its fuzz has gone the way of all lint is, ah, washed up. Don't use it, or use two layers. Terrycloth could be used, but to less effect.

So far our scheme calls for a coarse fiberglass filter element taped over a shallow frame of some sort and, right behind it, one fuzzy flannel element. In a pinch, these elements would probably protect you from 95% of the fallout without finer filtration. But the particles that get past these two coarse elements might still zap you if fallout is heavy. What we really need is a still finer element, or a set of them in parallel, to take out particles of micron size. That's where toilet paper rolls come in.

For many years, some engine oil filters employed a roll of toilet paper as the filter element. The oil was forced under pressure to pass between the many circular layers of paper—and the central hole was, of course, plugged. Note well: the oil didn't pass from one *side* of the paper cylinder to the other;

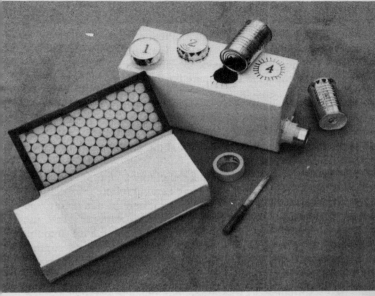

it passed from one circular *face* to the other. In the process, even very small solid particles in the oil were trapped in the paper. Only the smallest particles, reportedly on the order of a half-micron, could get through such a filter element.

The same kind of filtration works in extracting tiny fallout particles from air. However, we assume that your air pump (like ours) will be the sort that provides high volume but not much pressure. Since a paper roll restricts the airflow somewhat, it's necessary to use at least four of the rolls simultaneously, in parallel, to allow enough airflow for two adults. It's worth repeating: a four-roll filter is minimal. Use more if you have the materials.

In Figure 1 we see the filtration unit during assembly. The coarse filter elements with their shallow cardboard frame are ready for mounting, the fiberglass element hinged by masking tape and ready to swing down over the flannel element. The shallow frame will fit over the canisters holding the (fine) paper elements. Our small model uses only four paper roll elements, fitted into juice cans. The can with Fine Element #1 is already taped in place; Fine Element #2 is in place, ready for taping; Fine Element #3 is ready to be thrust into its hole; and the hole for Fine Element #4 hasn't yet been cut. Element #4 lies beside the filter box with the paper roll inside its canister. To prepare the hole for Element #4, first cut out the central hole; then cut the radiating slits; and finally fold the slit tabs of cardboard outward so that the hole allows passage of the juice can, in the same manner as Element #3. The white paint on the unit isn't just cosmetic; a gallon of quick-drying latex paint will seal the pores of lots of corrugated cardboard.

You'll probably find that a roll of toilet paper won't fit in a juice can until some paper has been unrolled. Strip off the necessary layers and stuff some of it into the can before you insert the roll. Stuff the rest of the paper tightly into the central hole of the tissue roll. Lastly, insert the roll into the can so that it's a snug, but not crush, fit. Of course there must be holes in the other end of the canister through which air can be drawn. In the demo model we've punched four triangular holes next to the closed end of each can, orienting the holes so that when the filter box lies in its normal position, air must rise up through the holes. This gives fallout particles one more chance to drop out. In Figure 1, the filter box stands upended so that you can see assembly details.

In Figure 2, the filter box lies in its normal operating position. The coarse elements and their cardboard frame have been taped in place on the filter box. Hidden within the coarse filter frame are the four canisters with the fine-filter rolls, taped securely in place. Every seam on the unit has been double-taped, and you can see its size from the meter-sticks in the illustration. The small soup can inserted at one rear corner of the filter box has both its ends removed. It merely provides a connection to the air conduit tube leading from your filter unit to the pump in your shelter.

Our pump unit is a simple bellows pump, made from another cardboard box. Obviously, if you have a hand-cranked blower, a battery-powered automobile heater

blower, or some other commercial pump, you're way ahead. We're taking the position that, like almost everybody else, you failed to buy such equipment and must either make your own at the last minute or die trying.

Before starting on the pump body, make its conduit tube. If you don't have the equivalent of a three-inch-diameter cardboard tube, grab a thick section of old newspaper and roll it into a tube. Tape the long seam and tape the ends to prevent fraying, then slather latex paint over it. Make it no longer than necessary, remembering that the longer it is, the more resistance it has to airflow. Ideally your filtration unit will be only a step from your shelter, so you'll need only a few sections of newspaper conduit. Our demo model uses one section, just to show how simple it is.

Chances are, a newspaper conduit won't be sturdy enough on its own to withstand the partial vacuum created when the pump is working. So why didn't we use a heavy cardboard tube or, more efficient, smooth-walled metal stovepipe? Only because we assumed you won't *have* any. As it happens, there's a quick remedy for the 'collapsing conduit' problem. You make a long cruciform stiffener of cardboard, or several short ones, and insert it into the conduit. The conduit might still buckle a bit, but it won't collapse. If you can make conduit that's stiffer, without incurring a heavy time penalty, do it.

Now cut a round hole in your shelter wall near the floor and run the conduit through, taping around the hole, and tape the conduit to the filter unit outside (as we did in Figure 2). At this point you can retreat into your shelter and seal yourself in with tape. You're only half-finished, but you can breathe shelter air while you build the pump.

The pump unit is absurdly simple, really, even with its two flapper valves. In Figure 3 it's half-finished, the inked lines showing where you must fold and cut, including the flat piece that eventually becomes our admittedly gimmicky pump handle. For our bellows material, we used transparent flexible sheeting so that we could see through it to watch the inlet valve operate; but plain translucent, or even black, polyethylene sheeting would do. You should choose four-mil-thick or thicker sheeting.

You can see that the pump begins as a rugged corrugated cardboard box, with seams taped to make it airtight. As the dotted lines show, one rectangular face and the adjoining triangular halves of two other faces must first be cut away. The removed cardboard can be used as a pattern to cut the flexible plastic bellows material. Or you can cut the flexible plastic free-hand, as we did. In Figure 3 the flexible stuff is folded double, lying between the box and the pattern for the pump handle.

Next make the pump handle. We like to play with cardboard, so we built a rigid cardboard handle that locked into the top of the pump with tabs, and we taped it around the tab slits to prevent air leakage. It probably would've been quicker to merely punch two holes in the box and to run a rope handle through the holes. Knots in the ends of the rope handle would keep it from pulling through, and tape around the holes

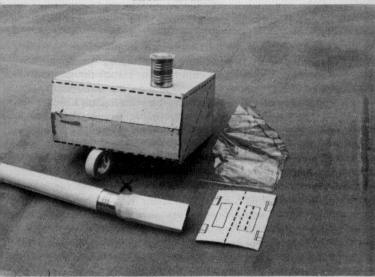

would minimize air leaks. The point is, you can do it any of several ways—so long as you don't leave sizeable holes in the pump box which would dramatically lower the pump's efficiency.

Now for the moving parts: the two flapper valves. Here again, we deliberately made them of different materials only to demonstrate that you can use whatever's handy. In Figure 3, the valves aren't yet in place. The outlet valve is sitting atop the pump. The body of the inlet valve has been mated to a conduit tube via a soup can. We made the inlet valve from an empty macaroni carton; a sloppily-cut rectangle of cardboard slightly larger than the mouth of the carton; and a piece of masking tape as a hinge. Simply tape the cardboard rectangle—the flapper—at the top only, so that it hangs down over the mouth of the carton. Blow through the carton and the cardboard flapper swings out to let the air pass. Blow against the face of the flapper and it swings shut, preventing airflow. That's it; a one-way flapper valve. It isn't completely air-tight, of course, but so long as it fits neatly over the mouth of the carton it's close enough. And it only takes a moment to make.

Cut a hole through the rear face of the pump box to accept the carton; shove the carton halfway through; and tape it in place. The valve works better if you mount the carton at a slight angle, protruding upward into the box. That way, gravity makes the flapper lie flat over the carton's mouth. In Figure 4 you can see the inlet valve flapper through the transparent bellows—about which, more later.

Make the outlet valve and install it the same way, except that the outlet valve flapper is mounted on the outside of the box. *Inlet flapper inside; outlet flapper outside*. In our model, we made the outlet valve from a soup can and a throwaway plastic lid. Even at the risk of boring you, I repeat: there was no special reason why the inlet and outlet valves were different shapes and made from different materials, except to prove that there are lots of ways to do it. For you perfectionists: with rubber faces between flapper and valve body, and with very slight spring-loading to help them close, you could make better valves than we made. But it

would take longer. Our model worked so well that the observer's typical first response was delighted laughter. The little bugger'll blow your hat off!

You're almost finished when you cut a long trapezoidal piece of flexible plastic sheeting (the same size and shape as the piece of cardboard you cut away along the dotted lines) and then tape the sheeting onto the box in place of the missing cardboard. When you finish double-taping and latex-painting the pump box (you don't have to paint the handle), grab the handle and raise the lid of the box. You should hear the pump draw a mighty breath, then a faint 'clack' as the cardboard flapper of the inlet valve drops back into place inside the pump box. Now push down firmly on the handle. The pump should exhale with a whispery 'whoosh', followed by another 'clack' as the outlet flapper drops back into place. Check for air leaks; if air is expelled from anyplace besides the outlet valve, those leaks must be sealed. In Figure 5, the complete pump is in 'inhale' position and the tape-hinged outlet flapper is visible.

Our small model displaces about two-thirds of a cubic foot

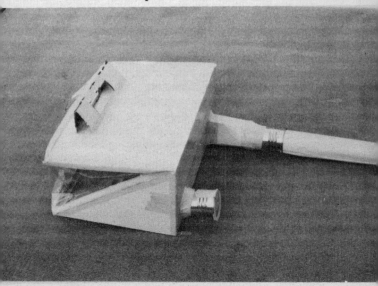

of air with every inhale/exhale cycle. If you can start with a bigger box, naturally your pump will move more air—which is all to the good, as we'll explain later.

The last step before drawing clean air is simply to mate the conduit from the filter unit to the pump inlet; tape the joint; and start pumping. It may not keep absolutely all radioactive particles out of your shelter, but the little rig assembled for testing in Figure 6 should make your breathing air cleaner than outside air by several orders of magnitude—a thousand times as clean. For somebody who started three hours ago, you're doing pretty well! If two of you are building the units together it could be closer to two hours. Incidentally, in Figure 6 you can see cruciform conduit stiffeners of various lengths—the longest one not yet assembled—and a stale air valve we haven't yet discussed because, when minutes count, it should be built last.

Though you now have a means to pump clean air into the shelter, you still need to consider how you'll get rid of the stale air you've already breathed. That stale air will normally

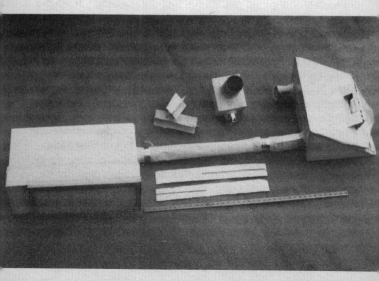

be a bit warmer than it was when it entered the shelter but it'll be more moist, too, from water vapor given off by every animal in the shelter. The stale air will also be loaded with your exhaled carbon dioxide, which is slightly heavier than air. All in all, you can expect the moist, carbon dioxide-laden stale air to lie near the floor. Therefore, the stale air exhaust valve inlet should be placed at floor level, and far away from the fresh air squirting into your shelter from the pump.

Before you ask how much more mickey-mouse gadgeteering we need for the system, a glance at Figure 7 will show you. The job of the stale air exhaust valve is to permit the escape of stale air when the shelter air pressure is raised by a very small fraction of a pound per square inch—in fact, by a fraction of an *ounce*. This little exhaust valve is the last part of our air supply system.

Our stale air exhaust valve consists of a small box for the valve body; a perforated soup can sticking up into the box from below as an inlet and flapper support; a piece of styrofoam taped atop the soup can as the valve flapper; and a cardboard tube leading from the side of the valve box, through a hole in the shelter wall, to the 'outside'. Note the penny glued atop the styrofoam flapper. Styrofoam is so light, it needed a tiny weight to ensure that the flapper would always close. The flapper will rise when shelter pressure is very slightly elevated above ambient, i.e., outside, air pressure. If a windstorm brews up outside and gusty winds try to blow in through the exit tube, the flapper stays put. Little or no unfiltered, fallout-laden air gets in.

By studying Figure 7 you can see that, like the other parts of our system, the stale air exhaust valve can be made from whatever's handy, so long as it's airtight. We punched triangular holes around the bottom of the soup can for stale air to enter. We taped the can securely into the box, then did the same with the cardboard exit tube. We tape-hinged the styrofoam flapper atop the soup can, then taped the box shut so that any air passing out of the shelter must pass through the

triangular vents at floor level, up through the flapper, and then out of the shelter via the exit tube.

Finally, in Figure 8, we pushed the end of the exit tube through a hole in the shelter wall and taped it in place so that the valve stands on its inlet tube.

Unlike the valves in the pump, the stale air exhaust valve won't clatter much during operation. In fact, you might want to install a piece of plastic or glass as a window into the little box so that you can inspect it now and then while someone operates the pump. If it never opens at all, start looking for leaks in the shelter while the pump is in operation. A few wisps of cigarette smoke might help you trace a leak. Otherwise, don't smoke!

You now have all the necessary elements for a minimal air supply system for two adults in a small shelter. It's a far cry from an automated system. In fact, if alone in your shelter, you could still be in serious trouble if you fell asleep for many hours.

Engineering texts on ventilation systems call for two or more air changes per hour in a meeting room—more for lavatories, locker rooms or assembly halls. They also call for roughly a thousand cubic feet of air, per person, *per hour*. Frankly, this approaches the upper airflow limit of our small demo unit even if you kept it going all the time. Luckily, as the texts admit, these figures are greatly in excess of general practice.

How much in excess? Well, you probably needn't worry about CO_2 poisoning or sticky-wet humidity if you manage to get 400 cu. ft. of fresh air into the shelter per person, per hour. It's my personal suspicion that you could get by on a fraction of that when sleeping, or sitting quietly. But if you begin to feel headachy, dizzy, or drunk, get to work on the pump.

For a rough approximation of your pump's output, measure the outside dimensions of the pump when it is fully open, then find the volume inside. Next, bearing in mind that the pump doesn't entirely close down to half of its maximum volume, multiply the maximum by 0.4; in other words, take 40% of the pump's maximum volume. That's roughly how much air the pump gives you every time you open and close it fully.

Example:

Our pump box dimensions are 20″ x 14″ x 10″.
Maximum volume, then, is 2,800 cubic inches.

40% of 2,800 cu. in.	=	1,120 cu. in
And since 1 cu. ft	=,	1,728 cu. in.,
each pump stroke yields		$\frac{1,120}{1,728}$ cu. ft. of air,

which is roughly ⅔ cu. ft. per stroke.

For those of you who think these calculations are too elementary: please knock it off, you guys. We want to make this clear enough for a smart sixth-grader.

Since we can operate our pump at about 20 strokes per minute without tearing it up, we find that our little demo unit will give us 14 cu. ft. of fresh air per minute, or 800 cu. ft. per hour. I think—but with so many variables of shelter, valve seals, and such I wouldn't swear to it—that you might get by with three adults in a shelter using this little rig half the time. To put it another way: each of you three would probably have to operate our little pump for four or more hours every day to assure a decent air supply. That implies a lot of work, which means heavy breathing, which means elevated humidity.

As we said before, the pump provides more than just oxygen; it also keeps the humidity and temperature down to bearable levels in the sealed shelter by forcing out the stale air.

What if you're alone? There's no one to pump while you sleep, so you should choose a shelter that contains a thousand cubic feet of air, or more. And bring an alarm clock with you. Far better to be awakened by a clattering bell every two hours to pump for awhile, than never to wake at all.

No alarm clock? Lordy, what are we gonna do with you! Just remember that sand or water can be metered to trickle slowly into a container on a teeter-totter. When the teeter-totter shifts, it can knock something over noisily in approved Rube Goldberg fashion. Sure, this is all a lot of trouble. Why didn't you invest in good, commercially available equipment *before* the klaxon tooted?

No one is suggesting that the primitive life-support system illustrated here is any match for a commercial unit. To repeat: this article is for the ninety-five per cent of us who may know what we ought to do, but aren't doing it. It's easy to critique the system—and to make this one better.

The filter unit could be improved several ways: by being larger with more fine paper roll elements; by having a quickly resealable panel for fast replacement of paper rolls in case they become clogged; and by being more rugged than cardboard. Duct tape is stronger than the masking tape we used, but much more expensive. Buy some anyhow; tell yourself you're worth it.

The pump is the weakest link in our model; it should've been bigger. But even using the box we used, you could increase its capacity by altering the pattern for the bellows so the pump would open wider. We found that a single thickness of cardboard is almost too flimsy for the top face (the one with the handle) of the pump. A double sheet of cardboard, plywood, or even thin wooden slats taped across the flimsy top face would make it last longer.

You'll find that the pump's light weight can be a problem. It creates so much suction, the whole box wants to rise up when you lift the handle. If you don't want to wedge the pump in place on the floor, you could weigh it down. Just unseal the bellows, lay several bricks down on the pump's bottom face between the valves, then reseal the bellows. In that position the bricks won't reduce the pump's output, and they'll keep the pump from jumping around while you use it.

When we characterized this model as 'minimal', we weren't kidding. With only four paper rolls in the filter unit, airflow is so restricted that you must exert some effort to lift the pump handle. You'll be dogtired after using it awhile. You'll wish you'd built a filter box with more roll elements so you could pump more easily. Well, you still can! Just build another filter unit, go outside briefly, and connect the filter units by a short conduit.

You could elect to build a filter without the paper roll elements. It won't purify the air as much, but it's much quicker and it makes pumping much easier. Of course, the flannel element can be quite large.

We won't go into great detail on the subject of negative-pressure shelters because they aren't as secure. But you could opt for such a system, in which the shelter air pressure is very slightly *lower* than ambient. Essentially, you install a stovepipe from your shelter to the roof and install a simple, commercial wind-driven rotating ventilator atop the pipe. When the wind blows, the ventilator sucks air up and out of the shelter. If you taped a couple of layers of flannel over a window-sized opening into your shelter, the ventilator would do your pumping for you, drawing fresh air in past the flannel elements. The pressure differential in the shelter would be too low, however, for you to hope it could suck air in through paper roll elements.

Summarizing the low-pressure shelter scheme: it's attractive because it doesn't require you to pump by hand. On the other hand, it won't pull air through a really fine filter element—and besides, the low shelter pressure can draw unfiltered air in through crevices. Moreover, when the wind isn't blowing your air gets stale anyway.

Whatever sytem you use to provide fresh clean air in your shelter, what do you do if it proves less than adequate? Well, you trouble-shoot it to check for something clogging any part of the system. You breathe through a flannel (or something better) mask while the shelter is open to ambient air. You remind yourself that you're buying time during the hours when your system *is* working, because day by day the radioactivity of fallout particles should diminish. In forays outside the shelter, you wear gloves and all-enveloping raingear, leaving it just outside the shelter when you seal yourself in again. You treat clogged elements as radioactive.

Now we're getting into hygiene. What do we do about hygiene in a shelter, including disposal of body waste? How about lights and other niceties? We'll get to those topics in subsequent articles; for the moment, it's enough to know you can live under pressure.

There are lots of ways to live under pressure. Perhaps the limiting case is a full pressure-suit, under the crushing awareness that the future of homo sapiens rides your shoulders. "Banzai" talks about that. It's pure happenstance that the plot depends on pressure suits, among other things. Because it's really a story about the many faces of altruism.

Now and then someone writes to say, "Obviously you've lived in the place where you set your story," when I've never been there—or "Obviously you've never seen the place," when I've lived there for years. It's true that I beat my buns off to make a certain locale work for a certain story. That partly explains why my background notes for a story make a taller stack than the story itself. It's also true that, if a certain locale seems pluperfect for a story, I'll schlep down there if I can to soak up its ambiance before writing the story. I know a guy who does that and hates it. I don't fathom that; if I didn't love it, I wouldn't do it much.

I couldn't go to Guam. I did the best I could though, shuffling big maps and little postcards and accounts of a recent discovery on the island that I recap in the story. It was all secondary to the theme, but it was a primary enjoyment in writing the story.

Banzai

The landing module groaned under the buffets of Earth's hostile atmosphere. Diana Moi, shrinking even smaller into her couch, saw the star-flecked black segue to familiar blue as their automatics, backed by Hauser's deft corrections, steadied the wingless aerobody high above the Philippine Sea. Another jolt, and Diana mouthed a silent *O* through her fullsuit visor toward Paul Evans. Paul smiled in reassurance; he had no inkling that the nose gear hatch had already begun to curl.

Carrol Hauser knew. No warning light pinpointed the failure, but the much-modified lander's precarious trim was off and with the return module heavy on its back, Hauser suddenly had an unstable platform. He adjusted a tab actuator, held his breath, saw the visual display record a return to optimum glide path.

"Coming up on ten klicks altitude," he informed Grissom Base, which by now had sailed beyond them toward Hawaii in permanent orbit. "A little trim problem, no big deal—I'm high; going to run an early gear-down," he added, prescient with his flight experience. He activated the hydraulics. Three seconds later the little trim problem became a big deal.

"We have you eighty klicks west of Agana, four minutes to final bank maneuver." Grissom was still with them, Diana thought. They wouldn't let anything happen. Would they?

The main gear slid from their hatches with siamesed precision. "Main gear lock," Hauser grunted. The nose gear, four steel-wrapped rubber doughnuts flanking their metal strut, locked a moment later. Hauser could not see the folded titanium skin slice through both starboard tires as they swung past. One layer of steel cord still held the enormous pressure

in the tires. It would not be enough. "Nose gear lock,"
Hauser said happily. "It's looking like candy, Grissom."
Diana smiled.

The big craft banked northeastward, nose arrogantly high
on the only pass it could ever make, gliding down to the
island of Guam. Andersen Air Force Base had a crash crew.
They had all been dead for nearly a year, in common with six
billion others. But pilot Hauser, medic Evans, and linguist
Moi did not expect a welcoming throng. They had heard the
tapes of the last known Earthsiders in Riga, who had succumbed to plague when their air scrubbers, electrolysis, and
virus filters proved inadequate like everything else, six
months before in April, 1991.

Agnostic Hauser prayed the lander down, now on direct
visual approach, not thinking about the past. If his feeling
about this big tub was wrong, if all went well on the month-
long mission, if they could erect the return module, they
might have a future.

The lander touched with leviathan grace, drogue chutes
billowing as the nose gear dropped toward the runway. "We
have a touchdown, Grissom," Diana heard, then: *"Christ!
Hang on."*

The slashed tires both exploded on second contact, their
initial spin adding velocity to hunks of rubber and steel that
shrapneled into the ship. The adjacent tires, grossly over-
stressed, blew in separate blasts, flattening essential hy-
draulic lines. The naked strut plowed a deepening furrow into
the runway before it folded, and Hauser saw they must
cartwheel if the craft's nose caught any obstruction. He
managed to cycle the main gear up before titan forces
wrenched his fingers from the controls.

The entire lander spun once as a strut hesitated in retrac-
tion, the spin adding friction while it spewed pieces of ship.
Pyrotechnic sensors energized the sprays that kept white-hot
metal from igniting the craft as it thundered out of control, off
the runway, and into a water-filled depression. The lander
rocked once, settled a few meters before its belly struck
bottom on the pond.

It was ten meters down to the pond but Diana and Paul Evans leaped without pause. Only after surfacing did she wonder how deep it was. Diana did not swim.

Her suit was an encumbrance, but helped her float. As near an absolute protection as human minds could craft, its pack recycled a breathing mix before exhausting it, so the walk-around 'air' bottles were merely inconvenient. Sterile positive-flush umbilicals made it possible to ingest, excrete, and perform work in modest misery without exposure to plague. The virus did its work quickly, had killed every known anthropoid, including those on every satellite but Grissom Base. Grissom's 1,351 humans were in their last ditch; not quite self-supporting, able to mount one round-trip mission, they had chosen its elements carefully and without much ballyhoo about volunteers. There would be no rescue party.

Diana floundered onto grass, wiping water from her visor. "We can't say here," she whimpered.

"We have to," Paul said, grasping her sleeve. "Look."

High on the lander's back, a strapping figure emerged from the cargo hatch. "Air," said Hauser's voice in her headset, as he tossed the life-sustaining cylinders into the pool.

Diana misread the fire-retardant vapors. "It's going to burn, Cal," she cried.

Cal Hauser's voice grew and dwindled as he moved through the broken ship. "If it does, we're almost certainly dead when our air runs out. Otherwise we have a month, and first things first," he finished. More cylinders splashed and bobbed in the pond.

Numb, relieved beyond belief yet fearing some small rip in her suit, Diana hurried away with air bottles and fought the urge to keep running. It was not until she was carrying food reserves that she realized they had made it down, might see another day.

But Paul, swimming to the forward cargo hatch, put limits on her relief. "May as well go after a truck," he said. Something more than exhaustion tinted his voice.

"Good heavens, there's lots more," Diana said.

"The rest is smeared all over the bulkheads, and—never mind." A prolonged sigh. Then softly, "All the rest is contaminated."

Diana turned to study the pathetic little hoard she had carried to the runway, and wondered if it would last a week.

She had never felt so pressured and useless. Inventory proved that, borrowing from the return module, they might have nine days' food, fifteen of water, sixteen of air. With unbelievable luck they might lift off in sixteen days. Very hungry. Nor did Cal's faintly sardonic conversation help much as he cut away the buckled fairing over the return module. He sensed her anxiety and chuckled. "Don't worry, Moi; we'll get you back to the big sugartit in the sky."

"Must you be vulgar?"

"Sometimes. Quit nagging and relax. Even with those sunspots blanketing the AM bands, our FM link to Grissom is fine here. If there's anything to be found, Paul and I will find it. Then, enter Diana Moi," he intoned, "—if milady will pardon the expression." The fairing shifted under his urging. Not enough.

"Am I the only one who's been here before?" Diana saw in her helmet readout that Cal was switching to a private, though inferior, channel. She followed suit.

"I can hear 'why me' if I listen carefully, Diana." The big man strained at a fitting. "You, because you were evacuated to Guam as a kid from Vietnam. You command oriental languages better than most—even speak the local Chamorran, a little." He grunted; she saw the fairing's edge protrude like a flaccid tongue, wondered if he hoped to splash her with filthy water. "Anyhow, frankly you had no real use on Grissom and you were altogether too goddam fastidious for some. Nobody minded risking you."

"Not since Joel died."

"Joel Marcus was a better politician than biologist, he had no business wangling a place for his lady-fair on Grissom. English is a lingua franca and you know it." He heard the stifled sob, paused. "I'm sorry he bought it, Diana. But he was thinking of his gonads and not your future."

Angrily: "We weren't—he wasn't sleeping with me." In haste, then, "I wanted to be sure."

"More fool, he. You aren't half-homely, outside these ambulatory coffins that make us all look alike."

To change the subject from gentle dead Joel she said, "All right; I never asked, but now I know why me. But why you?"

"Because I'm a McGill anthropologist who plays politics too, in a minority party. Also, since nobody on Grissom has flown the Lockheed quiet ships, they figure an old Canadian bush-pilot like me would have the best chance. And there's supposed to be a Qship over there," he nodded across the field. "It'd be ideal for close air support when we start hunting—whatever is out there." He fell silent. Diana glanced to the serrated southern mountains and felt gooseflesh.

"Or try this one," and now Hauser was laughing easily. "I'm here because if the Guamanian Devil is real, and if we should somehow succeed, our names will be in history books a thousand years from now!"

It was far more likely that there would be no history books at all, but she could not miss the zeal that burned in his labored breathing. "You're saying you volunteered?"

"No, but my physician could have, um, faked a medical hitch."

"Paul? He wouldn't do that." Diana remembered Hauser as she had first seen him on Grissom, the great squared shoulders and muscular buttocks impressive under his coverall. A coterie of Grissom personnel had a secret label for him: *Lonranger-san*. Hauser might be growing older, but it was impossible to think of him as a medical case.

"Paul would do a lot of things," Cal snorted, "if the right man asked. He's a good mechanic, a better pathologist, and an embarrassment to a very old, and *very* very dear," he softly expectorated the final word, "friend."

Diana watched a coil of quartz cable arc from Cal to the

grass near her. "I can't pull that fairing," she complained.

The response was carefully flat. "You can with me pushing, m'love. We'll skate it out along the leading edge to the fin."

She bit off a sarcasm, seeing his long, strong legs flex. Wordless, puffing together, they maneuvered the fairing along the deltoid shell of the lander until it overhung the grass. When the fairing dropped, it formed a makeshift ladder. Hauser sank to his knees, breathing hard. Diana heard the life-support alarm and trudged away for an air bottle. Her own supply was still good; she knew Cal Hauser's work was extracting a toll.

When Paul Evans returned in a pickup truck he brought local charts, good news, and bad news. "The Qship is in its hangar and I got a jaypee fuel truck running, so we can fuel the Qship and the strap-on turbine bladders, too." A pause. "Let's erect the return mod and sleep here tonight. It isn't pretty over there."

"But at briefing they said the pilot's ready room was nice," Diana objected. "I thought . . ."

"Did you, lady? That's where I got the charts. I also walked ankle-deep in what the rats left of the deaders in there. I saw—never mind," he finished, with a phrase Diana was learning to respect.

She replaced her air bottle, then Paul's, laid the empties aside, and realized they would need recharging from the return module. Well, that was *some*thing she could do. *All in good time*, she thought, watching Paul prepare the gas generators that would swing the return module into vertical stance.

Hauser initiated the vertical sequencing alone while Diana and Paul fretted from a safe distance. Diana blanched to see the hot gas exhaust, expecting an almighty fireball to consume their mission. But the squat return module pivoted on its trunnions, accompanied by the screech and shudder of buckling belly structure within the lander. Paul loosed a shout of triumph and moments later, they heard Cal Hauser on the FM. "We concut on the angle, Grissom," he said.

"And you're right, we'll fill the bladders simultaneously."

Soon the three were regrouped in the erected module. Diana stared thoughtfully at Cal Hauser's back, grateful that such brawn could be expended. Wishing she were that strong, that masculine, that capable. She did not wonder why he was so quiet.

Paul turned from the console, his ruddy young face alert, his helmet obscuring tight blond curls that gave him the profile of a Greek athlete. "So much for the day's work," he grinned. "We can fuel the bladders tomorrow. Now we can—not you, Cal," his hand gently restrained the big Canadian. "Diana, help me get air and water into the pickup while we still have some sun."

He was already at the hatch. Diana followed, mystified. "But the day's work is over."

"So it is," was the reply as Paul helped her negotiate their 'ladder'. "And Cal and I have the night's work to do. You can help."

As they shuttled to and from the pickup, Diana caught the edge of frayed patience in Paul's explanations. Grissom was not pleased that they had erected the return module first but could hardly enforce a countermand. Now they must push themselves to regain schedule—and Diana could extend Cal's endurance in small ways. Paul was briefed on the Qship preflight procedure, but he was no test pilot. "Still, I should be able to taxi the thing," he said airily, hunched in the pickup with their gear. "Climb in."

Hauser did not enjoy being left behind and said as much. As the pickup roared off Paul answered, "Just doing a preflight, Cal. Catch a wink, I'm not gonna run off with the damn thing."

"He's tired," Diana murmured. Paul switched to direct audio.

"Don't show sympathy," she heard him warn.

"He deserves it," she countered in their now-private argument.

"Dead right, but he doesn't want it. And if he sees or hears much of it, your sympathy could abort this mission."

"Well my goodness, why . . ."

"You don't have to know everything. I'm edgy and I'm sorry, and if that's sniffling I hear, I'm going to feed you to whatever we find out there in the—what, toolies?"

"Boonies," she corrected, glad to contribute her knowledge of the area. "A hike is a boonie-stomp since *sumasaga zo' giza* Guam."

"I didn't get that."

"You mean, *ti hu comprende;* Chamorran's a mix of Spanish and islander. Never mind." The phrase worked as well for her as against her.

The Lockheed craft, its slender wing no higher than her breastbone, was a revelation to Diana. "The wings seem to stretch forever," she said, captivated.

"Thirty meters to the outriggers. Seats two, quiet as mice, and can land at forty klicks. That's *crawling*. Fitted with infrared scan and side-looking radar. Now you see how we'll sneak up on our boonie beast." He began to laugh as fuel poured into the tank. "That is, if it doesn't outrun us. With those whopping mufflers, this engine couldn't outpull a popcorn fart. Wup—"

Diana seemed oblivious to accidental gaffes. "It almost seems as if a vehicle designed to use the least energy is bound to be beautiful," she mused.

After a long wait: "By God, I think you're right. Very perceptive," he said, begrudging it.

The preflight routine took Diana's mind from the polychrome delirium of a sunset on Guam. She clambered from the svelte Qship to let Paul essay a short taxi test, and heard him ask if she could drive a fuel truck. "Why, I—I suppose so," she stammered.

"You're elected, then," was the reply. Stunned, Diana watched him ghosting away, the wings seeming almost to flap though the Qship never lifted. She found herself forgotten.

Spares from the pickup to the truck, she thought. *Well, does he have to tell me everything?* Curiously lighthearted, Diana piled their gear into the truck before ascending the cab.

She looked at the manual transmission, intimidated, then recalled that no one would hear the squall of gears but Diana Moi. She could not fathom her own elation when she arrived at the lander before Paul Evans.

Diana knew enough to be frightened when Cal Hauser gunned the Qship away from them in near darkness. "He'll be okay," Paul said, reading her fidgets precisely. "It's almost stallproof unless you work at it, and it's very slow."

A subtle black shape eased up from the runway on swaying pinions, disappeared. Standing on the concrete, direct audio circuits open, they could hear only the whisper of breezes. "If there *is* somebody in the mountains," Diana asked, "won't he see the landing lights?"

Paul chuckled. "No, and we won't either. We can't see him but Cal can see everything. That image intensification stuff is lovely."

Cal's voice crackled: "I do believe this thing is idiot-proof. Passing over you at three hundrd meters." They waited. Nothing—perhaps a hint of windsong.

Evans: "We'd never know it, Cal. A good ship?"

Hauser: "I think I'm in love." Minutes later he taxied up near the lander, his mood cutting through exhaustion in his voice. "The brakes wouldn't stop a flexible flyer, but I can live with it," he said. Hauser was no prophet. "Ready for a hunting party?"

Paul and Diana stowed air and water in the Qship before the smaller man eased himself into the aft seat. "Hand me the sensors, Diana," he said. "We'll talk to you on line-of-sight FM channels. That puts us in relay to Grissom—if you don't monkey with anything."

She nodded, knowing her gesture was lost in the dark. This time she saw nothing at all of the quiet ship as it slowly gained airspeed. Feeling the awesome uncertainty of their mission as though it were some evil presence, she climbed to the return module.

Idly, she listened to talk between the distant pilot and his 'bombardier'—for Paul carried hundreds of tiny audiovisual sensors to be dropped, looking like so many pebbles, into the precipitous mountains of Guam. She understood little of what she heard. Diana's education spanned a Vietnamese hill country childhood, displacement to Guam and then California under the bumbling blanket of American goodwill, then a period of false security as a translator in the United Kingdom where she had met Joel Marcus in 1987. Despite all that, partly because of it, Diana had never mastered details that most could readily absorb. She could operate calculators but not a sportscar, could deal with an idiom yet not a rebuff. She found it a crushing irony to be left alone on feral Earth while her technical and medical experts skimmed the low southern mountains in search of an enigma.

The mystery was simple enough to describe. While one group on the surviving polyglot satellite worked to develop better filters in hopes of straining out the viral killer of billions, a second strived to make Grissom self-supporting until, hopefully, they could outlast the virus and repopulate their home that lay so tantalizingly below. But a third group, decoding the data they accumulated with every sweep over the globe, found a striking anomaly on Guam.

The island's shape reminded Diana of a broaching whale, with a mountain lake where the creature's eye would be. She recalled the picturesque Talofofo River spilling toward its bay in a series of steep declivities. Somewhere near a tributary stream, a series of heat emissions kept triggering Grissom's sensors.

Philippine deer, wild pigs, even a few horses and cattle roamed the island—but these infrared signatures were intense, smaller than a close-knit herd of animals. Possibly a volcanic vent—except that it never occurred after dark. Vulcanism of that sort simply did not belong there, nor did the repeated trace of hot vapors that were sometimes found, almost *always* at night, always in the same vertical fastness of interior Guam. Analysts dared one another to say it aloud: *survivors on Guam?*

Grissom would have mounted a larger mission, had that been possible with return potential. The two reserve landers

would be used as one-way passenger liners or not at all.
Occam's razor sliced away all but the most transparently thin
chance that a search would find humans alive, learn how they
kept that way, and provide crucial data for mankind huddled
on Grissom. Several volunteers did come forward. None had
the necessary skills. Those skills, Diana knew, were mostly
invested in a sleek Prussian-blue aircraft flitting over the
southern jungle. Then she remembered the empty air bottles
and set about a task on her own initiative.

Wrestling with the positive-flush adaptors to the module
air supply, she continued to eavesdrop. The men had swung
westward from the bay, climbing a valley alive with night
birds. Turning at the lake, they had swept the next valley.
Their charts marked locations of old IR emissions but they
found no suggestive heat signatures. Then they began to
quarter the area near Talofofo Falls.

"What was that? Deer?" Paul's voice.

"Probably coming down for a drink," from Cal.
"They—hey, over at three o'clock, look at . . ."

Paul cut him off. "Smoke! This display is like daylight;
Jesus, look out for those trees!"

Diana had an image of the silent craft plunging into the
jungle. Her hands trembled on the fittings. Too much.

"I'll drive the goddam taxi," she heard Hauser grumble.
"You throw the rocks." This, she knew, involved nothing
more complicated than distributing camouflaged sensors
from the opened canopy by hand. Some were pronged and
sticky, intended to lodge in trees. Others would tumble to the
ground. Their chief limitation was that the tiny audiovisuals
operated on FM, which was line-of-sight, so that they must
be monitored from nearby or from overhead—and flights
could be risked only at night. One essential criterion of the
mission was maximum data from a naive subject. Theirs to
observe, not to *be* observed.

Diana saw that she had begun to cross-thread an air fitting
and tried to undo the damage using pliers. A curl of
aluminum, unseen, rotated down inside the fitting to lodge
within the valve's nozzle and pintle. Caught between worry

and surmise, she finished unscrewing the air bottle hose and
elected, a wisdom one step too late, to leave the rest to better
mechanics. Tuned to FM and not direct audio, Diana could
not hear the steady rush of precious breathing mix from the
jammed supply valve.

She listened in growing hope to airborne dialogue when
they found a steady emission from a hole in a cliff face.
Below and to one side was a lesser emission from a larger
hole.

"Could be a cave entrance and smoke hole," Paul judged.

"Hell of a funny way for people to live," was the reply.
"No predators on Guam bigger than a coconut crab. Dogs,
maybe. If you're right, they want to stay hidden. I suggest a
line of sensors down the stream there."

"Right. How's your air, Cal?"

Diana glanced at the troublesome air valve near her,
smiled—and saw clipboard papers fluttering. *Inside the
module?* She flicked to direct audio, grabbed the hose, stared
at it. She felt the cold outrush against her gloved palm and
pushed frantically on the valve. It might have freed the
obstruction. It did not.

". . . ciful God," her voice knifed through on FM, and
was lost as the Qship dipped below a peak. Rising quickly,
they emerged from microwave shadow to hear Diana's
agonized, tearful, ". . . and I don't know how to stop it! Dr.
Evans, Major Hauser, pleasepleeeease . . ."

Hauser was banking to the north before he knew the
problem. Diana calmed enough to explain. Paul, with profes-
sional calm, said, "If you can't get the cap on, tape over it.
Your glove and quickset—no, forget that. Try to plug it,
Diana. We're on the way."

A half-hour later she cringed into her couch while a stern-
faced Paul Evans pried at the valve seat. Arms folded, Cal
Hauser glared from her to the gauges. In another minute the
valve had sealed, far too late to save most of the breathing
mix.

Paul studied the console display, his mouth a prim blood-
less line behind the visor. "So we can forget the half-ra-

tions,'' he said bitterly. ''Nine more days of food, but now only ten of air.'' He seemed not to see the reddened almond eyes, the mucus-stained pad at her chin. ''I'll gloss it over with Grissom. And then I think we need sleep.''

They did find sleep at last. First Hauser, who was clearly at the end of his strength for the day. Then Evans, quietly furious at everything, especially Diana. Next Diana, terrified and lost in her thoughts. And finally a fourth, who lay for hours, forty kilometers away. He had seen the enormous nightbird, spanning more than many men, pass down his valley. He wondered if it could be a creature of his mind. Perhaps an omen . . .

The next morning they fueled the strap-on bladders, shuttling between the booster turbines that would be jettisoned with the emptied bladders. Fueling was completed on schedule, the sun still low on its climb out of the Pacific. The trio enjoyed a moment of optimism.

Logistics was a fresh irritation. Paul sat astride the fuselage as Diana and Cal rode in the Qship while they taxied to the abandoned pickup. There Paul dismounted for his lone foraging trip. It was just possible, Grissom had agreed, that he could locate a storage of oxygen or compressed air with filler stamps over a year old.

Diana's heart leaped with apprehension as she saw the fragile wing behind her. It flexed slowly as Cal Hauser sought altitude. The altimeter responded and Diana remembered the device in her lap. ''May I try the sensor display?''

''We're too far for the little buggers, but—maybe not. Hell, what do I know?'' The great shoulders lifted in consent.

They wafted higher. Diana flicked tentative fingers over the display control and, when she remembered to patch in the audio, instantly heard a faint shrill cacophony. ''What on Earth is that?''

''Palm leaves, birds, water. Guamanian devils,'' Hauser cracked.

She spied a complex of low white buildings set back from shore and, with keen *déjà vu,* recognized the University of

Guam. Then they were dropping lazily along the eastern shore, curving inland. She tried not to notice as the land soared up to meet them.

"The Cross Island Road coming up," Hauser gestured ahead. "We'll put down here at the Country Club."

The landing was perfect. Hauser taxied over rank grasses near utility buildings, avoiding the stately palms. A gaunt animal loped away, Diana's first recent sighting of a live Guamanian, and she realized that most dogs had already starved without their human meal tickets. *And those that haven't—look out,* she thought.

Then Diana saw dead men, or tatters of them, and could not go nearer to the main buildings. In a dull rage, Cal Hauser stalked off in search of a quiet vehicle. He returned in an open rig that was half convertible, half electric golf cart, and together they discarded the gay candy-striped canvas top. Its little diesel thrummed merrily, generating current to restore the languished batteries. The cart had not been intended for skulking but, on battery mode, would serve well.

"Can you read a map?" Hauser's tone bore conspicuous doubt. She nodded. "Then let's transfer some air to this thing and you direct me up the Cross Island Road. We have to set an FM relay on a high point so we can read those sensors from here."

Diana began to realize how tenuous were the threads of modern communication. Two hills near Andersen Air Force Base made it difficult to contact Paul unless they were aloft. And the sunspots made hash of AM channels, as Cal had warned.

They hummed along the broad drive, lurched up a macadam road, soon found a promontory. Lush green valleys dropped away on each side of them and, querying the sensor display, Diana found over a hundred sensors operating. With Cal's aid she arranged the videos roughly in order of their distribution. Audio noise was bewildering, most of it the abrasive hiss of jungle growths amplified with each breeze. The video was worse, with many closeups of stones and palm fronds. But in one quadrant they found a view that Hauser recognized.

"That's it, the place where we found those emissions. Now you sit there and monitor every God-blessed one of those things while I arrange this relay."

Fascinated by the display, she scanned videos by fours, then by sixes. Presently a repeated sound made her turn. Cal was gone afoot; the noise was undeniably coming from her sensor display. It sounded like someone paddling in water. She began to isolate the sensors. "Cal," she called, "I have something on audio."

"Some animal; pig, maybe."

"Do pigs swim? It's on three sensors along that creek, not far from your cliff." She enlarged them in line, one elevated and two worm's-eye views of a swift stream. "It's getting louder. I think you might come and look."

Tiredly: "Diana, I can only move so fast. Record the goddamned thing."

She was already recording, looking steadily at the display. "You don't have to be surly; good lord—MY GOD!" Her graceful asiatic eyes were round as a tarsier's, her mouth working silently.

A slender oriental of mature years moved with slow certain steps up the creek, stirring the water ahead of him with a pole. He wore a loincloth so brief that Diana felt shame for him, and nothing else but thong sandals. With a sudden practiced motion he tossed the pole aside and hopped forward, reaching into a shallow pool. And instant later he lifted a woven net aloft, staring impassively at the wiggling creatures he had trapped.

Diana saw him brush his catch into a small basket. "Maj—Cal Hauser, I've got a man, you come here this minute," she babbled. As she watched, the man strode to a rock and retrieved a short robe which lay in plain sight, unnoticed before. The robe draped over his slight, tendon-corded shoulder, the man disappeared into the jungle with almost no sound. She realized that he made commotions when he liked, and none when he chose. He was obviously adept at his business.

When Cal Hauser trotted to the cart she replayed the sequence, watching his face covertly. The cynical mask evaporated: it was Hauser's turn to gawk. He analyzed details Diana had missed, repeatedly viewing the scene. Then he arranged its relay to Grissom and, after several tries, contacted Paul Evans. It was evident that Paul could use some cheer.

"By Christ, it didn't take long," Hauser exulted. "Diana, as she puts it, has a man."

"Absurd," she flashed, then shuddered. "I—he's repulsive!"

"Not to me," Cal smiled. "My first impressions: slender mesomorph, dolichocephalic, male; looks about fifty but I'd bet my commission he's sixty-five. Got a good closeup of his eyes; pronounced inner epicanthic fold says he's Japanese, and that Mortimer Snerd haircut says he does it himself or his barber hates his guts.

"Ah, let's see: very practiced with a freshwater shrimp trap. Thongs and net, in fact all his clothes, look handwoven from local fiber. That little tool at his waist may be a steel knife. He carries a short robe, like a judo *gi* but thinner—and he's one wary customer. Doesn't jerk his head but those eyes rove like uncaged gyros." Diana had missed that in her mixture of revulsion and excitement. Why did the little man repel her so?

Paul was infected with Hauser's rare good spirits. "D'you think he's alone, and what makes you think he's so old?"

"I don't know if he's alone, but: Japanese, has uniquely survived, with a travel range and actions suggesting a fugitive, entirely self-dependent. This sounds crazy but it isn't, Paul: the guy is exactly what you'd expect to find if you looked for a World War Two Japanese holdout!" Now Cal was laughing at his own notion.

"Aw, Cal, that was before I was born."

"He's no spring chicken. They found holdouts like him

well into the eighties, one here on Guam in eighty-two. With this ground cover, it's no wonder.''

"Then we're lucky we have Diana."

Hauser jerked as though bitten, glanced at his small companion who affected concentration on her display. "Eh?"

"If and when we meet him, he'll speak Japanese. Diana's our only direct contact," was the amused response, "if you're right. Which seems ve-ry unlike-ly."

"I'd say he is Japanese," Diana put in. "Now what?"

After a moment, Paul: "I've wasted the morning here, guys. All I can think of now, is building an electrolysis plant for more oxy."

"Isn't that what they did at Riga?"

"It is, and somehow it snuffed them all. Even if I tried it, I'd be here and not there. But it's up to you, Cal."

Diana was glad the decision was not hers. She saw Hauser's helmet shake as he considered the options. "Okay," he said, "fuel that pickup and bring everything you'll need—including a rope. Our little character could be a handful if it comes to that. We'll operate from here whether Diana likes it or not. The deaders seem to've congregated at the clubhouse anyhow, and on the greens. And I always thought golf mania was exaggerated," he finished drily.

As Cal drove back toward the country club, Diana watched the monitor. She stayed in the cart as he sought an outbuilding which could protect them from weather and roaming dogs. She knew that Cal talked chiefly to assure radio contact and did not care, so long as she felt the security of his presence.

"This guy," he told her, "may be the only experimental animal we'll ever get. We can't sic you on him until we know every possible detail on his daily routines, his *modus operandi*. When we have his em-oh, maybe we'll learn how he keeps suckin' wind."

"I don't suppose you could just ask him," she offered.

"Sure we could." A snort. "You think he knows? No, we won't change his routines 'til we have to. But we'll have to take a look in that cave, for sure. God knows how we'll do

that without putting him wise. What d'you think we should
do, Paul?''

No answer. They learned why shortly afterward, while
they moved spares into the club's toolshed. Paul had driven
the pickup into a revetment area where he found and rifled
medical supplies. Hauser, breathing heavily, took over the
monitor, content to let Diana make the place livable while he
rested. Before the sun stood at its zenith Paul had located
their cutoff from the eastern coastal highway. Diana thought
his good spirits seemed forced as the lithe medic prowled
through their new quarters.

Their link to the satellite was acceptable. Most of Grissom's personnel were in a predictable ecstasy, had deliberately mislabeled their discovery 'the Ainu' in some
turgid whimsy. It seemed that a party was underway on
Grissom; toasts to the men, jokes for Diana.

The afternoon was endless. They did not dare approach
afoot in daylight, though an unimproved road meandered less
than two kilometers from the cave. It was decided that Paul
could venture up the road in the near-silent electric cart, if
Diana could notify him the moment their 'Ainu' appeared.
Paul, with their spare sensor display clamped to the cart's
windscreen, could emplace another FM replay and many
more sensors before dark.

But the steep terrain required Cal to put the Qship aloft to
assure constant relay between Paul and Diana, wherever the
road might lead. He flew the little craft high and far to the
west, beyond a chance sighting by their watchful quarry.
Thus Diana was alone again, frightened as always.

Afternoon shadows stretched as Diana lazed at her post.
Paul finished his work, drove up an uncharted trail for better
elevation, and promptly dropped one of the cart's little
wheels into a hole. "I'm maybe a klick from the cave," he
muttered between curses. "I can dig myself out but I can't
use the diesel. Too loud."

"This is as good a time as any," Hauser said, "to refuel.
I'll need it tonight. Over the city of Agana now; give me, oh,
thirty minutes to get back on station."

The refueling came very nearly too late. Diana could not

say when she first realized the Ainu was staring at her. It was a process of suspicion: a suggestion of motion near the cave, a line that could be flexed legs; and then she saw, as one sees an optical illusion reverse itself, the man squatting behind ferns. Immobile as a painting, he stared toward the sensor fifty meters away. He could not possibly know the pebble was looking back at him, but nevertheless Diana felt apprehended.

She began in a whisper, then more loudly: "Paul, check your display. Sensor one-oh-six, to the left of the cave."

After a moment, Paul's reply: "Jesus, is he made of stone?"

"He may've been there for hours, Paul. Could he be dead?"

"Boy, you're just a little ray of sunshine. Nope, his eyes moved. You think he heard me working here?" He answered himself with, "Doubtful, but I can't risk it."

Hauser's baritone cut in on them. "Risk what? Can't I leave you two alone for a minute?"

"Thirty-two minutes, and evidently not," Paul said, explaining the problem. Paul and Diana exclaimed at once, then, as the graven image abruptly came to life and walked to the stream. Without a wasted motion, he continued down the little watercourse and was soon lost in deep shadow, moving quickly.

From Hauser: "Which way's he going?"

"Away from me, thank God. Downstream, and making good time."

"He doesn't seem worried," Diana judged. "There! On seven-three, Paul."

"He's carrying a stick and a big cloth, Cal. Sandals but no robe," Paul announced. "It's getting too dark for these sensors. You may have to pick him up—you have a better rig."

"Bearing one-niner-five," Hauser replied. "I'm en route."

"He may have heard me working on this miserable velocipede," Paul said angrily.

"If he did, he may be running for it," said Hauser, making

his voice unemotional. They all knew his implication.

"You think he has another hiding place?" Diana hated to ask, but had to know.

"Good point," Paul answered. "If we lose him for a week—well, let's not." She heard him puffing as he dug around the cart.

Twice the Qship investigated IR signatures. Both were deer. Once, her display a mosaic, Diana caught movement and expanded the tiny rectangle in time to see the Ainu fade into dense jungle. He was moving along the river, still downstream, which cheered Hauser as the light faded. "If he keeps this up he'll end in Talofofo Bay and I'll see him."

"Doing what," Paul asked. "It could be important! *Damn* this little rig, this little road, this little time . . ." He began to remove the batteries so that he could wedge the little cart out.

It was full dark when Hauser spotted the solitary man. He moved along the southern edge of the bay, engaged in some sort of gathering ritual. The Qship, its engine nearly below operating speed, passed as low as Hauser dared. The Canadian admitted his defeat in a series of sizzling curses.

"I'm hurrying as fast as I can," Paul huffed. "I have to get down there and see what he's doing."

"Without the IR scope?"

"God*dammit*," Paul raged, "Diana's got it! So I'd have to drive past the effing bay to get the scope. Cal, any ideas?"

Again that unruffled confidence. "Only the obvious. With its more obvious drawback: have Diana take the scope, drive down nearby in the pickup, and try to get near without being seen."

Diana, tremulously: "What's the drawback?"

"Never mind," from both men. *Your incompetence,* she heard.

The job seemed an easy one. She grabbed a spare air bottle, tried the simple IR scope, and found she could easily drive while peering through its circular display. She stopped once to obey an order. "If you don't smash those brake lights, Moi, I will land this thing and strangle you with my bare hands," Hauser warned.

Abashed, she did it with a stone. "That's better," said the voice from the Qship somewhere above. She resumed the drive, stopping short of the bay as Hauser directed.

She skirted the narrow inlet afoot. "Cross the bridge," said Hauser. "That's where the river takes its dump in the bay. Your man is two hundred meters out on the south shore. See him?"

She did, but faintly. She hurried along the road, cut through a gate to move along a low cliff. Through direct audio she heard the lonely bittersweet rhythm of waves aswirl in the rocks below.

"Stay there," said Hauser, startling her. "Sneak a peek. You can see him just below you."

Diana inched forward, scanning the shore. She took a fierce glee from Hauser's error; his own angle permitted a view, but hers did not. She shifted in a gambit of her own, eased between crumbly footing until she was braced only a few meters above the salt spray. Then she saw the Ainu, and realized what he was collecting, and averted her face in abhorrence. And slipped.

Her first thought, on caroming from the ledge into the bay, was *I've lost the scope,* which was true enough. Her second was *my suit is torn,* which narrowly evaded truth. Her third was, *I'll drown.*

The worst of it was humiliation as she heard her plight described by the inevitable, invisible Hauser who circled above. "So much for stealth, Paul; our dumb broad belly-flopped right beside the Ainu. He's scared shitless, up against the rocks, and she's in the shallows and can't even stay on her feet. Thanks, Grissom, you sure pick winners . . ."

Hauser saw her stagger to her feet, hands beseeching, saw the little man kneel with arms extended toward her. He was beyond describing the travesty of a woman literally covered in advanced technology, rescued by a cave dweller.

Nor could he understand a word of the conversation between them. It was brief, and it ended in mutual retreat. Hauser guided Diana toward the road again, half-persuaded to talk her off a higher cliff. She managed to steer the pickup back up the road by starlight. Hauser followed the Ainu, lost him in the retreat upriver, then located Paul Evans who had at last got underway.

It was another half-hour before they convened in the toolshed. "I don't believe this," Hauser snarled. "Life is a dirty joke, and the joke is on me, and I don't get it."

"Sure simplifies our options," Paul grinned ruefully at the big man's frustration. "Diana, what's the idea of the Ainu calling you 'Commie'?"

Still trembling, reliving the storm of emotions that had clashed in her during the encounter, she steadied her voice. "A *kami* is a local spirit—a sort of Shintoist deity. He wasn't reaching for me, he was doing obeisance and I just grabbed his hands," she said.

Hauser grunted with new interest. "A magic woman? May be useful."

"Gender isn't essential to a *kami*," she said. "Lord, that awful little man . . ." and shuddered, wiping her hands for the hundredth time.

The gesture was not lost on Hauser. "That's your own childhood you're trying to wipe away, Moi."

"Don't psychoanalyze me," she spat.

"Don't bullshit me," he said evenly. In kindlier tones he continued, "I saw your dossier, Diana. 'Moi' isn't even a real surname, it's a Vietnamese tribal tag you got saddled with. We can't help it if you're still running from a label; hick, savage—" he shrugged, "—whatever it means to you."

She fought her tears and won. "It means grinding poverty. Apologizing for your existence—and having the apology rejected." She straightened small shoulders and faced him squarely. "Maybe I'm doing some rejecting of my own. Maybe I've had enough of people who, who,—who eat filth!"

"Just because he was gathering bloody palolo worms," Hauser sniffed. "Moi, people do that all over the Pacific. Or did."

"It's a polychaete that swarms about this time every year," Paul explained, retreating from Diana's personal quandary. "Perfectly good nourishment, Diana. If he dries and smokes them, it may be a diet supplement factor we're looking for."

Hauser stretched out on the floor, flexing his limbs. "At least it didn't happen in his front yard. He's probably holed up in his cave by now." The pilot began slow pushups, difficult maneuvers in the heavy suit.

"Well, we're certain he's Japanese," the physician mused, then flicked an irritated glance at Hauser. "Stop that, Cal. It wouldn't help if you did a million."

Hauser lay prone, his voice muffled. "Just keeping fit."

"Just wasting air—and killing yourself." The words were Paul's. The faint groan, Diana realized with a shock, was Hauser's. "Sorry," Paul added softly. "I might've chosen a better phrase."

Mystified, Diana shifted the topic. "He said his name is Shigeo," she said. "He has the oddest phrasing and accent, but he's certainly Japanese. We have his language, his beliefs, and his name."

"We don't have diddly-squat yet," Hauser rasped. He was holding a troche under his tongue, the chin dispenser still ajar under his visor. "But you, blithe spirit, will solve that. And more."

"I haven't helped much so far."

The long, endorsing silence was broken by the pilot. "Tomorrow will be your day, Diana. I think we're agreed it's a waste of time to cruise the Qship around tonight over— uh—Shigeo, is it?" Two nods. "So let's get some sleep. Suit alarms for five ayem. When our little man comes out tomorrow morning he's going to find you all set for a nice long chat. Paul? You concur?"

No one asked Diana's opinion. She lay awake, listening to the men breathe, hoping she could control her aversion to the worm-smeared animal. No, she must think of him as a person. *Shigeo–Shigeo–Shigeo*. It would not be easy.

Sitting quietly, a spare bottle slung at her side, Diana Moi waited before the cave. She resisted the urge to look behind her, knowing that Paul was too distant and well-concealed. Hauser had stayed at the shed to conserve air and assure their relay to Grissom, just in case. She had both FM and direct audio on-line, and slowly cultivated a headache trying to localize sounds. When the little Japanese emerged, then, she mingled relief with her loathing.

"*Konnichi wa,*" she greeted him, and wisely allowed him to complete rituals of obeisance. His assumption of inferiority suited her perfectly.

"The *kami* is welcome, I am unworthy," he said in that curiously inflected but clear Japanese. She saw that he was scrubbed clean, his loincloth meticulously mended. Diana knew that she did not have to maintain eye contact because he would not dare establish it.

She forced herself to comment favorably on his prowess in the jungle, his tailoring, his health. The voice of Cal Hauser jarred her with, "Whatever happens, don't admit ignorance." She nodded in irritation. Little Shigeo, plainly mystified by the gesture, seemed about to ask a question but thought better of it. Diana smiled; she would seem more inscrutable by the second.

"It pleases me," she began, resuming her seat on the stone, "to observe you at closer range than usual." He bobbed his head quickly, eager to please. In a flash of empathy she added, "It would please me to hear a civilized tongue. Speak."

"What would the *kami* hear?"

"A song, perhaps. And then a story, Ai—Shigeo." Well, maybe he thought her slip was *hai,* yes. So far, so good.

He begged the *kami's* pardon, his singing was a caterwaul, he had not the talent. She said he was modest and suggested two stories instead. To this he readily agreed, adding, "Which tales would the *kami* prefer?"

"Tell me of the things I see you do in daily life; and the things you seldom do. Which foods you like the most, the things you dislike doing. *Dozo,* Shigeo," she wheedled politely. "Tell me truly; an untruth is *kinjir',* forbidden."

She ended with an amicable teasing inflection to avoid offense.

Squatting before her, his private parts ludicrously exposed, he began a halting monologue. His life was steeped in small drudgeries. Weaving fibers on a bow loom; mending his shrimp net; catching a huge fruit bat; feasting on a pig; absorbing a sunset. These were his pleasures. He was less pleased with the robber crab, which invaded his lair; and with the *taifun,* which threatened to drown him in it.

From time to time she injected the, *"ah, so des'ka,"* you don't say, or *"shigata ga nai,"* too bad but that's the way it goes, of a good listener.

Once, Paul Evans interrupted her. "Is all this germane?"

Hauser: "Anything's germane; shut up, Paul. We're lucky he's taking this contact so calmly."

The fugitive's greatest trial had been a great *taifun,* many years before. A towering tree had fallen across his burrow, collapsing the earth upon him. He had fought his way out, found another home. But he had been forced to steal new fire from a party of the islanders who, he said, were eaters of men. At this he rolled his eyes and, to Diana's amazement, made the sign of the cross. He saw her start and misconstrued it. He clenched his eyes shut, ducked his head and drew an inward hissing breath. He hoped the *kami* was not offended, he said, by the *Deus Catolico.*

"Iye'," she denied. In English she said, "Merciful heavens, this animal has been converted—I supposed by Spanish-speaking priests. And they filled him with lies about the Guamanians."

"Maybe; and maybe he's testing you. Take nothing for granted on a first contact," the anthropologist chanted his faith.

Shigeo was watching her, perhaps wondering at the sounds that emanated from the gleaming head of this strange *kami.* Yet his eyes did not stray above her knees. She made no explanation for her behavior, even when she made the switch to a fresh air bottle with carefully slow movements, talking all the while. "It would please me," she lied, her voice shaking at the thought, "to visit your home."

Only his eyes showed fear. It was too wretched in his hovel, he said; too unworthy. She persisted. He made fresh protestations of its unsuitability, unspeakably polite, unshakably firm. The little man did not want the *kami* in that hole. Period.

She changed the subject. "The other story, Shigeo. Tell me how you came here."

For the first time, he really smiled. His teeth were remarkably good. "The *kami* is not far-ranging, *neh?* Forgive me, I forgot it could not know me before I came here. *Wakarimas'*, I understand."

"*Hai, domo,*" she thanked him, and waited.

He had been a mere foot-soldier on Kyushu where the good fathers were accepted by a powerful *daimyo*. Shigeo had been conscripted from his fishing boat at Nagasaki to fight in the great war. When it appeared that the enemy must inevitably conquer, they had returned to Nagasaki. A shipload of soldiers escaped, helped by a priest. To her question, he replied that he had not reached this island early in the war. *Iye'*, no, it was panic flight from Kyushu the day before the planned surrender.

Was it not dangerous to land? *Hai,* indeed it was, but he had little choice in the line squall that swamped his ship as she beat toward a little bay on the island's western flank. Some of his companions were caught. He soon found that his chances were better alone and, except for brief and terrifying trips in earlier days, he had rarely left the sanctuary of the interior jungle since them.

But recently he had seen no people, and let the season and the Moon tell him when to gather sea worms. The *kami's* miraculous emergence from the sea had left him shaken. But honored, he amended quickly. *Hai,* covered with honor.

"Let me think aloud on this," Diana said, and began a rapid-fire translation. Grissom would provide analysis later, but she knew that much of a translation depended on nuance, small gestures, malfluencies; all the communication lying below the symbols.

"I never knew there were so many escapees after the bomb the Americans laid on Nagasaki," Cal murmured. "Ask him about it."

She did so. *Go mennasai,* he was sorry, but he had seen only the fires started by enemy weapons. He had experienced no great thunder and slap. She passed this on.

"Then he wasn't there on *that* day," Hauser rumbled. "This isn't getting us anywhere, Diana. Ask him how long he's been alone and what he does to keep healthy. Maybe he does have some ideas," he sighed.

She asked the necessary questions. He had long ago ceased reckoning the length of loneliness, he said, and added a shrewd point: unlike Kyushu, this island had little climate variation but for the rains and storms. Why keep a calendar?

As for keeping fit, he stayed clean, toyed with carvings to ward off depression, and had great confidence in an herb tea which he had developed over the years. The wrong herb, as the *kami* knew, could kill quickly. Two wrong herbs, however, could be beneficial.

The right herbs? "*Banzai,*" he smiled shyly, almost sadly.

Diana knew she had already slid into the trap of asking things any intelligent spirit should know. But he had perhaps felt himself tested. She risked another test. It would please the *kami* if he would offer a sample of the herb tea. A large sample. Now? Yes, she husked, and realized how long she had been talking. In an hour she would need another air bottle.

The slender Japanese whisked between two stones, pulled a decayed log across the hole, and was gone. Diana quickly added her new information and heard a jubilant Paul Evans curse happily.

"This could be it," Hauser agreed. "Get the stuff in a sample container, Diana. You're sure he won't let you into that hole?"

"Yes, and almost as sure I couldn't do it," she quavered.

"I wouldn't know what to do in there anyway, Cal."

"Hold on," Paul cautioned. "Don't count on this herb infusion; it may be all, part, or none of the answer. And if you can't go in the cave, I'll have to. I need blood and tissue samples from him. Keep the aerosol handy, Diana. We'll tell you if it's necessary."

The aerosol had been intended as a defensive weapon, or so Paul had told her. She listened to the men argue tactics, noticing a wisp of smoke from a hole several meters up the cliff. In a few minutes, Shigeo returned.

The 'tea' was dark amber, presented in a crudely handsome piece of raku pottery. She thanked him, dipped a gloved finger in it, and pronounced it excellent. She sensed his disappointment at her odd method of enjoying it, and let him stare as she poured it into a container. And then she saw the toy he had carved.

"Your fishing boat," she guessed, genuinely pleased, hearing the exclamations in her headset.

"*Iye', kami-san;* the *barco* of the priests *Catolico*." He moved nearer, pointing out the high sterncastle where the white men stayed. This was the vessel which had carried him to Guam. Diana held the model up, turned it this way and that for the watching sensors. She began to murmur her translation as Shigeo explained that the three tiny triangular sails were the membranes of bat wings. A gnawing sense of disbelief tugged at her mind, as little as she knew of sailing craft. Wooden threemasters in 1945?

"Hold everything, Moi," came Hauser's reply. "Oh, Christ on rubber crutches, this can't—" With an effort he began again, speaking very slowly. "Ask him who the enemy was in his great war, and what the weapons were."

She returned the model with great care. "I believe, Shigeo, you did not say how your enemy fought. Nor his name."

"We called him the ugly peasant, *kami-san,* even we who were only *ronin,* common soldiers. His men fought as we did with arrows and great swords, sweeping over all the islands until they came to Kwanto and Kyushu. There was great killing. Those of us who had accepted the *Deus Catolico* feared we were marked for special torture. Ah, *mate,'* wait: his name was Hideyoshi.'' She was a phrase behind in her translation when the last word emerged.

The yell in her headset came with the name. It almost rattled her into overlooking the other word for the second time. *Deus,* from Latin, was not Spanish at all. It was close. It was Portuguese.

"Paul, goddammit Paul, you realize what this means?'' Cal Hauser was chortling, his voice almost a whisper. "Barring the possibility that Shigeo is the greatest actor and scholar of our time, you're looking at a frigging sixteenth-century mercenary. The sonofabitch is over four hundred years old!''

The little man gazed more frankly now at Diana, who knew her actions must seem odd. Then from Paul she heard, "He is either feeding us a long thin line, or he has antibodies older than dirt. In either case I have to check him out as soon as humanly possible. Zonk him with the aerosol, Diana. Zonk him *right now.''*

Diana could not bring herself to such direct action. Instead she began, "I see into your *hara,* the core of your soul, Shigeo.'' As she arose, hands outstretched and high, he knelt as to a priest. It was so easy, she thought, *and why do I feel like a cheat?* The little aerosol spray was in her hand. *That's why.* "I approve your *hara,* and I offer you a dream.'' With that she triggered the aerosol. His head jerked up in a brief astonishment; then he began to grovel backward until his legs failed him. Finally he lay still.

While she waited for Paul, Diana heard Cal relay news from the satellite. "Diana, why didn't you tell us *'banzai'* means 'long life'? Grissom's confirming our wildest hypothesis. Paul, that model is an early lateen-rigged caravel. He even has the big mast up forward. Broad beam, holier-than-thou sterncastle, all of it. The guy must've worked on ships, all right; he made a fair copy of a Portuguese ship of 1585.

"Oh; there were Jesuits on Kyushu when Hideyoshi

finally subdued and unified Japan. He was a famous
general—but just an ugly peon to poor Shigeo. Hey, Diana,
that was no mistake about early Chamorros being cannibals.
Some were, before 1600. It seems that Magellan found a
good anchorage on the western side of Guam.''

"That tallies," Diana replied, "with something Shigeo
said about his ship being wrecked near an old port. I think he
tried to go back later but—Paul, over here," she broke off
abruptly.

Paul Evans stumbled up, loaded with equipment, too excited to talk. He knelt beside the unconscious Shigeo, rolled
him over with gentle hands to begin his work. The trained
hands seemed to fly, pause motionless, fly again. Diana
could not watch it all. Biopsies, blood samples and smears,
even stool samples, all obtained with a dispatch almost as
incredible as their discovery of Shigeo's age. There was a
hoax somewhere, she felt. No four-hundred-year-old man
should have good teeth, black bristly hair, nearly smooth
golden skin and a monkey's agility. She concentrated on the
monkey angle, afraid that she was beginning to think of him
as a person. She did not consider the irony of that.

"There," Paul said, returning lab samples to his kit.
"Give me the holocamera and canisters, I'm going into that
cave."

She helped him squeeze between the big stones, worn
smooth by many passings, and watched him disappear. "Better talk on direct audio," she warned. "And one more thing:
have you considered that he may have booby-trapped the
place?"

Utter silence for long seconds. "No, by God, I hadn't. But
what can I—oh. Maybe this will help." A moment's
wordless grunting, then: "Shoving this collection bag ahead
of me. Bouncing it around. It goes down here; drainage hole,
maybe. Then—" A muffled impact, another silence.

"Paul?" It was a scream.

"Oh, I'm here," came an echoing sheepish voice. "Damn
near permanently; you were right. A weighted spike, like a

deadfall. No wonder he didn't want you in here. I can get around it, though."

At length Paul returned. "Wish Cal could've been down there. So many variables! A wick he uses to keep his fire going; food of all sorts, breadfruits, dried shrimp, herbs and medicines in little pots; roots—I don't know." He hefted the canisters with their stolen samples. "I just don't know . . ."

"He'll know you've been in his cave," Diana accused.

"Tell him you did it," Paul said, "or—Cal, what *does* she say?"

"Whatever fits a *kami*," Hauser answered. "I'm on shaky ground too. Best thing is to learn what he wants that we have. Or what he *thinks* we have. We need bargaining power, Diana, and interaction. Anything to—to—"

"To keep me underfoot here instead of there," she finished for him.

"If you want to put it that way," Paul nodded, darting a glance at the twitching Shigeo. "I'll be waiting; don't be long." He hurried off with his booty.

Shigeo awakened slowly with all the signs of a hangover. He struggled to his squatting position, holding his head briefly.

She donned her most innocent act. "Did you dream?"

Impassive: "Perhaps. I do not know. The sleep brought pain; but not so bad as the pain a year past."

Intuition creased her thoughts. "Tell me of the pain last year."

"The *kami* knows I journeyed three days. Does it know I found no people but dead ones? I felt gladness at first, but at last only sorrow. While returning I fell ill." He described the sudden dizziness, the blinding headaches and sores, the cramps and bleeding throat that waxed and waned as plague began to ravage a human body.

Diana translated the essentials, including the crucial, "The *kami* knows I returned and lay here ill for days. Has the sickness returned?" He felt his temples gingerly.

"No," she guessed, hoping she was right—then spoke a phrase too many. "You returned in time."

He studied the ground for several moments. "I may make the journey again," he said at last.

"If you do, you will surely die," she replied. *And so will we all*. "But let us think on pleasant things. Think, Shigeo: for your pain, what compensation would please you?"

"Death."

His reply had been shatteringly simple. For an instant Diana had a glimmering of the man's life, and his weariness with it. "That is Shinto," she said, "but you are Catholic."

"Even a *ronin* can be both." A hint of challenge. Something close to a smile crossed his face. "It would not be fitting to ask a Shinto *kami* for—*nani mo*, never mind," he shrugged.

"Ask, Shigeo."

"For a Catholic priest."

She laughed. He seemed not offended. "This might not be possible. But," she added quickly, "I will think on it. Nothing else?"

Bitter longing, hopelessness, remembered pleasures, all crowded into the word: *"Onna,* woman."

A pause. "Yes. I see. Nothing else?"

"I have named three things." Unspoken was the charge that the *kami* seemed unable to provide anything worth having.

Paul's voice jerked her from the fruitless confrontation. "Diana, I *have* to get this stuff back to my equipment. Hurry."

"I will think on it," she said again to Shigeo. "Live here as always and wait for my return soon. Do not follow. It pleases me to walk as you do," she added, and turned to go.

"It also pleased you to enter my home," he said sullenly, noting the bootprints.

Different sized prints, at that. "I assumed different shapes to accomplish it," she said, knowing the lie was silly. "It did you no harm."

He made no response, but moved slowly toward the cave on unsteady feet. Diana knew the interview had ended badly.

When they returned to Cal Hauser, the spirited three-way conversation lasted until Paul, engrossed in dyes and microscopy, began to utter asides to himself. Then Hauser dozed, and Diana saw the rugged face in complete repose. The heavy strain lines were permanent creases, the eyes deeply recessed under their lids. She wondered how long it would take Cal to become his old vital self again, once the mission was complete. *Cal looks so tired.*

"Shut up, Diana," was Paul's whispered reply, and she realized she had voiced her concern. "Just keep your mind on your monitors."

Shigeo was near the cave, drying flat baskets of palolo worms in the sun. Without turning from the display she asked, "Are you sure it was plague Shigeo had, last year?"

Long, long pause. "No. Symptoms could've been jungle rot, plus food poisoning, plus strep. Only where'd he catch strep?" Another silence. Then, "If only we had time to let him try again. Boy, this is old tissue. Too bad we're not up to cloning him." Longer silence. "Whatever's working for him at the cave, it evidently wasn't working when he changed venue. What does he leave behind that he ought to take? Well—at a guess, if I did everything he does at the cave, I could be here this time next year."

"Or a thousand years from now." Hauser's wakefulness startled them both.

"Maybe." Paul continued to work. "But no maybe about this: we'll save air if you sleep, Cal. Diana can handle the display."

Presently, as Hauser lay under his blanket of medicated sleep, Paul brought up the subject of Shigeo's desires. Death was the one thing they could not deliberately give him. A priest might be managed, if Shigeo would accept a video link to Grissom's sole bishop who, in any case, spoke no Japanese. Still, the priest was a possibility. Paul stared at nothing. "The woman is a nice problem."

"Over my dead body," Diana countered.

Paul grinned. "A straight line I could follow two ways," he said, "one being that if you weren't already dead, you soon might be. I wonder about his acculturation. Would he accept a man instead?"

"Only you would think of that," she grumbled.

He replied quietly, "My preferences aren't your problem. His are. Don't forget that."

"All right, I'll ask. When?"

"I don't know, it may never be important. Right now, saving air is important. Take a pill; I'll wake you."

But it was Carrol Hauser whose thundering curses brought Diana up from sleep.

The big man shook with rage, grasping Paul's air bottle as though it had committed some terrible offense. "If I hadn't seen the telltale, how long before you'd have told me?"

"Just before the bottled air runs out," was the too-quiet reply. Paul did not cringe but seemed ready to ward off a blow. Diana, still sleep-drugged, lay quietly confused.

"By what right did you decide you were so fucking expendable that *you* could try the filters?" Hauser dropped his hands, raised them high again. Dropped them again.

"I've done my job," Paul said. "There are lots more things we can do with extra days of air for you two. At worst, I could treat myself for days, and at best we can all be breathing filtered air in a week. It's a risk I had to take."

"ONE of us had to take," Hauser shouted. "I'm still commanding—all right, *lead*ing—this mission. I could've been the guinea pig!"

"So who pilots us back to Grissom if the filters fail?"

Hauser dropped heavily into a chair. "If I have to spell it out for you, I will. The return sequence is so automated even Moi could initiate it. You knew I plugged it into the console for her. I'm the only one who could stay behind *and* pilot the Qship *and* run a longitudinal study on Shigeo. I could've been experimental subject number two," he finished, nearly crooning his agony.

"Admit it, Cal. You wanted to justify that in hopes you'd get a remission." Diana saw the look of mutual understanding pass between the men. "And there's absolutely no evidence it would work for you. It might for—for an average specimen."

"Nor any evidence it *wouldn't* work! Tell me, *doc*tor, where do I have the better chance, on Grissom with the best modern facilities, or here with this impossible Japanese Methuselah?"

Paul turned away. "Don't ask, Cal. As a friend."

"You mean no chance either way." The thunder was dying, now, the lightning spent. Hauser's voice was old. Old.

"I don't know." Softly, lovingly.

"But in your vast wisdom," Hauser continued, "you removed my justification for taking the risk."

"That's true," Paul nodded, studying his gloves as though some answer were written on them. "I swear I never thought you'd want to."

"I still might, if those filters seem to work." Hauser grabbed for a spare bottle, missed, grabbed again, then collected a pocket illuminator. "I'm going for the refills."

"Okay, let's leave it at that," Paul said as the larger man moved into the darkness beyond their shed. "Should I go along?"

Cal Hauser refused the offer and kept walking. Diana could not believe her suit's temperature readout; it suggested a comfortable level but her marrows had frozen through, twice in the past minute. First, Paul had opted for ambient air, which might not only kill him but would leave her without medical aid. Second, Hauser was threatening to do the same—which could place her utterly alone, thirty kilometers from a return module she had never dreamed of piloting.

She listened until Hauser's gruff transmissions reported him headed toward Andersen in the Qship, bearing thirty-five degrees. Then she spoke on direct audio. "Does this mean Cal has plague?"

"You heard, then." He sat loosely, emptied from hours of

mental and physical effort. Eyes closed, he continued. "No. I may have it, though these filters just may do the job. We'll know in a day or so. But Cal Hauser has something more cruel, in some ways. We call it Korsakoff's syndrome."

"Meaningless to me," she prompted.

"Of course. It's a form of accelerated aging. Tissue loss, muscular weakness, eventual early senility. Cal could've gone on, under Grissom's half-gravity, without serious trouble for a long time. Until brain tissue loss became severe, anyhow. That's what toxic chemicals can do to you.

"I knew it. We just didn't realize he'd tire so quickly down here. Not so soon. Not to a specimen like Cal Hauser." Paul bored his gaze into Diana's face. "Can you imagine how this wasting, inexorable disease would affect a man like Cal?"

"And there's nothing anybody can do?" Her throat constricted as she heard a scientist chipping away at the pedestal where she had enshrined Modern Science. "Medicines? Surgery?"

"Oh, some chemicals to help the body take nutrition. A tall order when your cells are shot through with collagen—fibrous tissue that blocks other tissue functions. But," he shook his head, "it's not as simple as an arterio-sclerotic process. When he begins to lose brain mass you'll see true senility. With luck, he has a few months."

Diana nodded. "That's why he's been so quiet, sleeping so much?"

"He's bone-tired, Diana. All the time." Paul reached to his equipment, brought out a vial of amber liquid, swirled it reflectively. "And he thinks Shigeo's patent herb tea can send all that into remission."

"Why couldn't it?"

Another long, slow headshake. "Too many processes to reverse. Even if Shigeo has stumbled onto an antiviral better than the amantadines, it just isn't likely to cure senility. I suppose it might've somehow prevented it." He replaced the vial.

Diana rechecked her monitors, trying to divert her mind. She selected a mosaic and watched idly until Hauser's call.

He was apologetic, the voice almost reedy. He dared not
risk a return while clumsy with exhaustion, he said. He was
in the module with air bottles and would stay until morning.
"Grissom reports some heavy weather building that might
affect us. And another thing, Paul," he said after a moment.
"You'd better tell Moi about me and the big bad K. My
vanity isn't worth her confusion. It might help."

Paul had the grace to pretend he had not already acquainted
Diana with Korsakoff's syndrome. She saw moisture in
Paul's eyes as they ganged their air bottles for sleep. There
would be no Qship sortie that night. Nor any other night.

It was almost noon when Hauser radioed that he had
rechecked the automated liftoff sequence with Grissom and
had stowed fresh bottles in the Qship. Some of his vitality had
returned, or so it sounded to Diana's ears. For the first time in
her memory she welcomed jovial curses.

"Getting breezy out," Paul observed through a begrimed
window. "Stick with the monitors, Diana. I'll help Cal
unload."

She heard Cal announce his arrival overhead, was later
glad she had sent him a cheery greeting. Paul flooded the
carburetor on the pickup, quickly switched to the cart, and
steered the little open vehicle toward the golf course.

Diana was disposing of an excreta bag when she heard
Hauser's cry of alarm. A grating thump sounded in his
headset and she raced outside to see Paul Evans sprawled in a
sand trap, a stone's throw distant. The cart, now twenty
meters from Paul, was slowing. But the slim-winged Lockheed bounced over the grass between breeze-swept palms.
Its drooping wing would almost certainly pass over the re-
cumbent Evans. And then Paul struggled to his feet, hands
out, obviously disoriented as he moved forward.

She heard Hauser shout for Paul to drop flat, heard Paul's
mumbled apology, and saw the Qship fight for altitude as
Paul, erect in a shambling run, headed toward the cart—and
toward the Qship that approached at a ludicrous, stately,
deadly pace.

There could have been no real question in Cal's mind that the underpowered craft might soar aloft. The best he could do was to swoop the Qship into a brief stall, nose high, airspeed disastrously near zero as he passed over Paul Evans—who fell again, would have passed safely beneath in any case, as Hauser clawed the ship to a sharp angle.

For one unforgettable beat there was silence, the Qship balanced on her tail, one wing tilting from a sudden gust of wind. Then the splintering frenzy of polymer and wood as the aircraft fell tail-first, safely beyond Paul, folding the starboard wing which absorbed much of the impact as it crumpled against the turf less than fifty meters from the shed. The port wing slashed across the electric cart, carrying away its windscreen, demolishing its sensor display in the same instant.

Diana started to run, then stopped. She was very near fainting. She saw Cal Hauser relax in the cockpit as if overtaken by a great weariness. There was no fire yet. But Diana's breakfast was rising, a potential calamity in her sealed environment. "I'm sick," she gasped, and sat down facing away from the scene.

"Then stay away," she heard the medic snarl. "I'll help him."

She was still pale and frightened when Paul returned minutes later, the cart still functioning and laden with air bottles. Body shaking, he stumped past her, dropped a ruined water container in the doorway. She whirled toward the crash, then managed to follow Paul into the shed.

"Goddamned idiot," he faltered, swinging to face the doorway. She thought the comment was for her, but: "Tried to cram an extra ration of water into his lap. Punctured. Wasted. Like him."

"His suit is punctured, Paul? Cal's hurt?"

Evans stared away toward the wreck that now began to send smoky tendrils into the sky. "It was a massive frontal skull fracture."

Fists balled, he fell to his knees. "Cal, *dammit* Cal,—oh Jesus *Christ!* Why didn't you just run me down? Now I've killed the ship and you too!"

An icy stolid steadiness gripped her as Diana knelt behind him, laid her arms along his, sorrowing that the helmets prevented closer contact. She knew now why Paul would not extract Hauser from the wreckage. They watched the Qship burn, a pyre for *Lonranger-san* who would never know senility now, who had wanted to take a gamble that was not really a sacrifice but, on an instant's decision, had chosen a sacrifice that was not even a gamble.

They felt the muffled impact of concussion as the fuel tank finally exploded. Fragments of spruce and plastic showered the area. Huddled in the doorway with Paul, she saw the bathhouse begin to burn from the roof. In minutes, the flames would reach out for them across the intervening breezeway.

Her priorities were short-ranging: Paul in the cart already piled with air bottles, his medical kit next, then more air and food from the shed. She moved the load to another shanty nearer to the access road, solicitous of her human burden, undisturbed by the cursing until she realized it was her own.

She left Paul to retrieve more gear and precious samples, only to find the searing heat too great for close approach. No Qship, no herb tea, no sensor display or comm set outside their suit units. But the scorched pickup truck started for her. She drove it back to Paul careful to park it on a downslope, and tried to shrug off their new vulnerability as she spied Paul slumped against their supplies.

She felt anger at Carrol Hauser, and shame at her anger. his last act had been selfless—but not wise. Even Cal could make a fatal error under pressure. Her dependence on male competence was crumbling. Beneath it, she saw dimly, lay the self-assurance she had hidden away so well, so long ago, with her pride in her primitive people. Shigeo had not made that mistake, she reflected. From this insight she accorded Shigeo a certain respect.

Then, sorting her memories of the crash: "Paul? What's wrong with you?" She had misinterpreted his gasps as emotion.

"I've really done it, killed myself too." He retched with graphic results. She leaned against his back, helping him sit up, trying to deny the truth. "A lot of crap about treating

myself. A fool for a patient. True.'' He cramped again, a dry
heave that shook his wiry body. ''Though I'd have more
resistance. Some do. But I was candy. Twenty-four hours
almost on the dot. Candy,'' he repeated.

''What can I do?''

''That's quite a riddle. Sorry,'' and he rolled forward on
hands and knees. ''Get this suit off me,'' he mumbled. ''No
use now. I can deal with the nausea, at least.''

In a forced calm that caged her fear and served as de-
tachment, Diana struggled with the seals until Paul lay prone,
the suit peeling away like rabbit skin. She could not tell if he
was fevered, could only lend support as he found his way to
the single bunk in the place.

Between spasms of colic and an evident splitting
headache, Paul directed her to capsules in his kit. When he
could not swallow, she broke a capsule into his slack mouth.
She detached a water flask from his suit, dribbled a bit into
his mouth.

Bustling about in efforts to make him comfortable, she
stopped to say, ''If we can move you in with Shigeo,
then . . .''

''No! He's already spooked. He'd just disappear.'' Paul
was racked by coughs. ''God, my throat hurts.''

A million lost opportunities assailed her. Cal's air and
water left plugged into his suit; comm sets in the Qship and
the burned shed; her own clumsiness with the air valve, and
for that matter with Shigeo.

Lost; all lost. Every new contact prodded Shigeo toward
retreat. He would never agree to nurse a dying stranger.
Unless it was a geisha, she thought wryly.

Or a priest. ''Paul?'' He was conscious, his pallor leaving
him for the present. ''Could you pose as a Catholic priest?''

''In my skivvies?''

''I'll find something for you to wear. I'll translate—uh—
freely. It could work, Paul! All you have to do is be a good
listener.''

''And give him plague.'' Paul shook his head hopelessly.

''Think, damn you! He's had it already. Do you want his
help or don't you?''

Paul managed a wan smile, then an inexpert sign of the cross.

"No, left side, then right," she corrected.

"A lot can change in four hundred years," he said, still smiling.

"I'm going now. I'll be back soon." Forgetting caution, forgetting even a spare air bottle, she hurried to the pickup and began her unique scavenger hunt.

The town of Ylig was only a few kilometers up the coast. From a thickwalled traditional church there, Diana took several carven crosses, candles, a small cast madonna, and a sadly frayed little velvet cloth. She tried not to see the remains of worshipers, shriveled husks lying in endless abasement for some global sin. She tried but failed to locate priestly vestments in other rooms, racking her memory for an image of a priest in the solemn splendor of his rank. There were so many denominations and variations!

A lot can change in four hundred years, Paul echoed in her mind, as she stared at a row of choir robes on hangers. Quickly she gathered up several of the white garments, ignoring the dust that rose wraithlike in the stillness. Within the hour she was struggling into their shed with her ecclesiastical trappings, gasping the last of her air bottle's reserve.

Late in the afternoon, Diana found herself plucking at the false surplice now draped over Paul Evans, and knew that the setting was as realistic as she could manage. Paul was coherent, propped in the bunk, even amused in his drug-induced fog. "Don't forget Dr. Shigeo's celebrated herb elixir," he said. "And anything else he'll share. That sennit wick or whatever he burns—who knows?"

Diana promised, pausing in the doorway. She knew better than to relax; exhaustion would consume her in that moment. Paul's skullcap of blond curls, sweat-plastered to his forehead, lent a priestly cast to his features. She wished she knew more about Catholicism. "What religion are you, Paul? I never thought to ask."

"Lapsed athiest," he said, then brightened. "Make that *pro*lapsed," he added in mincing burlesque and began to laugh, playing to some internal audience of his own. Diana slipped out, uncomprehending, willing that he should indulge his harmless pleasures.

Shigeo heard her approach the cave, came down the creek to meet her. He dropped the shrimp netting and did formal honors. She caught wariness in his expression and wondered if Paul's tests had meant lasting pain for Shigeo. She made formal thanks for the welcome before proceeding to business.

"It is possible, Shigeo, for you to see a priest." The wariness stayed, now mixed with new interest. "Yet he is ill and will die unless you help him. It would please me if you came to his aid."

"What does the *kami* wish me to do?"

He brightened as she enumerated her simple requirements. Careful to avoid any hint that he would also be helping her, Diana requested a feast for the *padre Catolico*, complete with herb tea brewed in Shigeo's fashion. It was important that he bring his own fire, she added.

Shigeo bowed himself into the cave, returning with a woven bag full of oddments. In his other hand was a cunning contrivance that held a coil of coarse fiber rope, the smouldering end well-protected. "If the father is ill, perhaps my medicines will help, as well," he said, then asked craftily, "or will they? Will he die?"

She paused, affected a haughtiness she could not feel. "*Kinjir'*, Shigeo; do not ask." She motioned him to follow.

Shigeo showed great curiosity but little fear at the growling contraption that Diana drove. He had seen automobiles many times. *Hai, wakarimas'* he understood that the priest spoke no Japanese or even Portuguese. *Hai,* many things change in time. *Iye',* he had not visited this area since the new people came with their growl-machines and heavy, ungainly buildings. Chagrined to hear that his own people had occupied the island for a short time less than fifty years before, he chided himself for a fool. And all the while, he watched the sun and the hills.

Keeping your bearings, eh, she approved. *Alone with a lying kami, so would I.*

Diana led Shigeo to the shed, not deigning to look toward the still-smoking rubble in the distance. But she could not suppress a cry of alarm, seeing Paul in a fetal crouch on the floor.

Paul had obviously been up and around again, feverishly tallying the precious store of air and water, now hers alone. Together, the ancient Japanese and the young Moi woman placed Paul Evans on the bunk. Diana kept one eye on Shigeo as he set about coaxing a tiny blaze on the bed of sand he prepared. The balance of her attention was on Paul, breathing noisily as he fought his losing battle with a pitiless antagonist that was no farther from Diana than the thickness of her glove.

Shigeo displayed his small hoard of foods, making of it an oddly attractive arrangement. She elected not to repeat the capsule she had given Paul earlier, fearing overdosage, and kept a silent vigil as darkness overtook the island. She lit votive candles from the fire, which Shigeo seemed to approve. Then she saw the small hypodermic syringe on the floor near Paul's head, its semitranslucent contents reflecting the flicker of the candles.

She placed it on a windowsill, watched Shigeo husband his embers, and then heard Paul say, "My lord, fella, but you're ripe."

He stared at Shigeo in open, friendly curiosity.

Shigeo moved near, murmuring devotions. Diana knelt to one side, half-listening, yet straining to hear Paul as he spoke around the pain in his body. In Japanese she said, "The priest hears you, and surely God does." Softly she continued in English, "The cross in your hand, Paul. Hold it up if you can." Shigeo kissed the talisman with reverence. "He's brought the herb tea and lots more. Can you eat or drink?"

A slow nod. "Soon. Fixed—syringe with—soup of my own. Over there," he tried to point toward his kit which was in disarray on the floor. "Can you—find a vein?"

She remembered the little hypodermic from the floor. Paul lay with eyes closed, frowning at each breath's fiery effort. She fumbled the cover from the needle, remembered to clear its barrel of air, then probed for the blue line at his elbow juncture.

"Florence Nightingale—you ain't," he grunted, trying to smile. His eyes were bright with hope as the lids fluttered back. Shigeo had ceased his murmur, watched spellbound as she located the vein and eased the plunger home. For a moment there was no response from Paul. Then a slow ecstatic inhalation, a lambent smile. Followed by a gasp as Diana withdrew the needle. "Oh, my Christ," Paul said. He blinked twice, slowly, a dawning horror in his face as he spied the syringe. "Where'd you—find that?"

"Why, on the floor. What's wrong?"

He seemed to sink in upon himself, breathing easily now, staring at the ceiling. "Supposed to be—under my pillow. Hoped I wouldn't need it. You were supposed to—use the big ten ceecee job over there." He nodded toward his kit.

Her eyes sought and found the second loaded hypodermic, lying in the gloom. She inhaled deeply to avoid screaming. "Paul. What did I do?"

"Ah, God, it's good not to hurt." Then quick, lucid: "Diana, stick with him as long as you can. Give yourself a day to get to the module. Liftoff access word is 'klutz'; sorry 'bout that. You may not hit Grissom exactly, but they can get you home. You won't like the sterilization process, but—"

She gripped his arm. *"What was in that hypo?"*

"Had it hidden, in case things got too bad. I'm no hero. Morphine sulfate and—something else. Never mind. It's faster than plague, and a whole lot kinder." He peered into her visor, searching for credibility. "I didn't intend this, Diana. I swear to God."

In ghastly self-recrimination: "I've poisoned you."

"My own stuff, my own fault. I must say it's a gentle slide, honey." He was smiling now, his nose wrinkling. "Boy, this little guy has an air about him. What's he waiting for? What do I do for him?"

"He's confessed four hundred years of solitary sin, Paul. I think he wants absolution."

He chuckled, a clean healthy sound that ravished her with irony. "Don't we all?"

"Not me," she said. "I've done nothing to merit that."

Paul closed his eyes, fought them open, mumbled, "What do I say to him?"

Diana gently took Paul's hand, laid it over the bristly scalp of Shigeo. "These phrases may do it. Say them aloud." She spelled them out for Paul.

"Ego te absolvo," Paul whispered. *"In nomine Patri, et Fili, et Spiritus Sancti.* Sorry I can't—try your smorgasbord, Shigeo."

At the sound of his name, the little man looked at Paul; to Diana. She controlled her voice with difficulty. "You are forgiven, Shigeo. For everything; your sloth, your desires, your anger at God. Everything," she said again in Japanese.

She did not know the moment when Shigeo slipped out into the enveloping dark, did not care. She was not crying. She was much too empty for that. He murmured a word. "What, Paul? What?"

"Banzai," he repeated. "Long life, right?" His eyes were on her again, calm, young, unaccusing.

"Yes."

He fumbled for a gloved hand. She gave him both *"Ego te absolvo,"* he said.

"He's gone now."

The gentlest of squeezes. "I know. That was for you, love."

At last the hands no longer pulsed, respiration ceased, the flutter of tiny muscles halted their play across the face. Once she murmured, "It would be, wouldn't it? The last word you ever spoke . . ."

Diana roused herself at last to arrange air bottles for the long night, pausing only once in her slow rituals. She stared at the medical kit, at the life-giving, death-bestowing mysteries of a science beyond her knowing. She could not explain why she gathered it all up, made the kit tidy, and then smashed it into junk with an empty air bottle.

By the time Diana awoke, the great satellite had completed its direct pass, as it did every few days, over the island. She could not know that the shed was a barrier between her headset and the anguished transmissions from Grissom. She knew only that she was more alone than Shigeo. He at least had his God. Her faith in the mass of interlocked sciences was dead. They had proven a false malevolent deity. *Faith without knowledge; is that the problem?*

She shelved the question, loaded the pickup, returned one last time to the shed. For minutes she lay full-length on the bunk, sharing her warmth with the rigid form of Paul Evans. Then she was in the pickup, driving in a fury toward the cave. She knew Shigeo had not become lost, even in the dark. A week's water, still more food and air: time enough if she did not waste energy. She could remain near the cave, promising whatever was necessary, and could return to the module in her metaphorical eleventh hour. She knew nothing of optimum launch timing because Paul had not thought to tell her. Lacking contact with Grissom, neither did she worry as Grissom did, for she could not look down on the cloud reefs beyond her horizon, reefs that gradually spun into the shape of a spiral nebula.

She picked her way to the cave loaded down with air bottles. For a moment she did not understand the new shrine that sat before the cave. It was both Shinto and Christian, and below it lay a trove of handmade articles. Food, raku ware, carvings, nets, even the small fire wick that Shigeo had taken from the shed. By the ash, she judged it had been there since dawn.

And then she saw his small iron knife and translated Shigeo's message. All his worldly goods sat before the shrine. He had received absolution, even for his desire to die. A Catholic could not suicide, but Shigeo might search for an agent of death.

Shigeo did not intend to return.

The pickup's horn was a mournful hoot, more likely to speed Shigeo on his way than to draw him. Diana feared, too, that he would avoid the soprano-voiced *kami* under any circumstances. Shigeo had spoken warmly of the town where many ships had stopped, of his long watches alone from cliffs overlooking the settlement with its river and its fort. *Agana*, she thought, and received confirmation from her maps. The city sprawled along the western coast midway up the whale's back. The cross-island road was quicker by car, but it would be easier going along the lowlands afoot by the northeast road, avoiding the swordgrass.

With a four-hour start, Shigeo might be halfway to the city by now, unless he met a big dog—or a pack of them. She knew he would not shrink from such a meeting. One death was as good as another when he had waited so long for it.

She searched the road far ahead, expecting every moment to see a small golden man tirelessly jogging toward his destiny. Then, on a hunch, she circled around the most direct approach to Agana and parked atop a hill over the main road. When Shigeo trudged up the highway she would see him from above.

After several hours, Diana tired of fighting eyestrain and drove to meet him. *I keep developing these little faiths*, she reproached. *Hope, then belief, then certainty. And cynicism when the hope proves false.*

After recrossing the island narrows she changed air bottles, rested, and studied her maps. Apra Harbor, with its naval base and imposing breakwater, could have been Shigeo's goal.

She drove back through Agana and along the cliffs to Apra. With approaching darkness she waited for a sign of smoke, an unusual sound borne on the breeze, anything.

Nothing. She drove back to the cliffs over Agana before full dark, lights off, scanning the city and listening again to the croon of a wind that masqueraded innocence from the sea. She ganged her air bottles and slept.

The next day began with a fruitless search. The pickup had less than half a tank of fuel. If she returned to the module she could contact Grissom, but might not fare any better in her search for fuel. *And why run to Mama when I have nothing Mama wants to hear?*

She elected to seek solutions where she was, yet a two-hour search for Shigeo and fuel proved a waste. A scrap of

billboard writhed past a downtown intersection, harbinger of
a rising sea wind, and direct audio hinted at a moaning in the
trees. The weather front approached too slowly for a local
shower, she knew. Diana continued searching for fuel; cans,
gravity-fed tank, whatever. She dared not risk an unlabeled
fuel and her suit prevented identification by odor.

It never occurred to Diana that she might simply puncture
fuel tanks of automobiles and collect the effluent. When at
last she thought of hand-pumped siphons, the sunlight was
diffuse in a burnished gray-brown gaze. The wind was no
longer playful.

She had driven some distance from the parts shops, uncon-
sciously fleeing from the sea. Reversing her direction, she
stared into the featureless wall of sky that already pummeled
the vehicle with wallowing gusts. Winds on Guam had been
known to exceed 280 klicks. She respected Shigeo's fear of
the typhoon now.

The pickup was pelted by horizontal raindrops like metal
pellets. She found that the wipers did not work, peered
through the glass, and slammed the brakes as a palm frond
flayed the pickup's hood. As she released the brakes, the
pickup began to coast backward. Up an incline.

She ran the pickup past sloping lawn into the lee of the first
big structure she saw, snatched up spare bottles, was hurled
up concrete steps toward a doorway. Through the glass she
saw front desk, files, viewers. It seemed a final insult that
some dying hand had locked the public library.

Diana would have run to the pickup but literally could not
move against the awesome wind. She hunkered down, squatting atop her air supply, wondering if she could have punched
through the glass with a sledge. The wind rose insensibly to a
gutteral howl, spattering her with foliage and, once, a bird.
And eventually brought the sledge.

When the great palm fell three blocks from Diana, it
sideswiped a bank, freeing a molded cornice which fled
before the spendthrift wind. One great fragment bent like a
three-meter boomerang, spun on the gale, hurtled invisibly
through the storm.

Tempered two-centimeter glass has its limits. The cornice struck the steps in front of Diana, ricocheted into the glass at shoulder height. Face averted, Diana felt a staggering impact against the bottle on her side. She bounced against door facing, glass disintegrating above her, and was pinned by debris. The largest piece, a triangle of glass the size of a coffee table, dropped like a guillotine, missing her arm but not the suit. She saw the curled edge of nulon past the rain-swept visor, knew the tough plastic was shaved away. She suffered a hallucination of herself, trapped there, passing through the torments of plague while the typhoon still raged. She would die of anoxia before that.

No, I will die when I'm damned good and ready. She flailed at the glass with her free arm, the wind her assistant. Wooden framing shifted and she was free, half-flung through the shattered doorway, bottles clanging after. She scrambled for the bottles, stumbled into the main card-file area. The pocket illuminator revealed what she had not dared hope: the glistening nulon, though shaven, was not penetrated. With luck she might outlive the typhoon.

The eye of the storm passed after dark, giving Diana time to search the place. She wondered how Shigeo had managed so well without modern trappings, and the question followed naturally: *what was Guam like before this century?*

The wind began to pound the building's backside now, as Diana pursued her new suspicion. The main files told her of site studies by archaeologists Reinman and Calkins. These led her to the special collections below, away from the triphammer wind. She scanned curled photographs, maps, manuscripts which resolutely spelled *Agaña* the old way. Her gaze fell on an old photo, badly tinted, of a picture postcard setting.

The village of Umatac lay before her, stark white houses lining the southwest shore. Dominating the harbor was the inevitable church. To the east lay low peaks which, from their other flanks, fed the stream that fed Shigeo.

Magalhães, Magellan, had landed there in 1521, she read; only traces were left of the ancient fort. Her charts revealed a stream that, in heavy rains, Shigeo might call a river. Her fingers shook with excitement yet Diana refused to attach all her hopes to this surmise until she had checked other locales. Umatac was too near Shigeo's haunts, too pat an answer. She had taken enough of those.

Hours later, her illuminator failed. Somehow she slept through the hum and slam of the furies outside and in the morning she found the city quiet, lacking even the birdcalls she had taken for granted. She found the pickup, its windows smashed, cowering in shrubs against the library foundation. Eventually it started.

Imperceptibly the storm damage decreased as she drove down the coast. To the south the road climbed along green ridges, and then she came upon Umatac. The town had been spared the typhoon's full rage. She wondered if the return module had fared as well.

Diana eased the pickup along, let it glide to a stop when she spied the whitewashed steeple cocked over ragged palms. Then she walked. There was no reason to feel such certainty, such faith. He was here, or he wasn't. *Then why are you so sure?* She studiously rejected expectation—and walked up the church steps expectantly.

He squatted, head almost between his knees, below the Virgin. Diana stepped between the sprung main doors, her eyes adjusting to the gloom, the sunlight streaming in behind her. Certainly he had heard her footfalls but had not stirred; might have been of plaster. His ability to keep still, she knew, was astonishing.

"Shigeo." She began imperiously, then let the name trail off. After a moment he arose, turned, bowed. He made no other move, gave her no expression to interpret. "Why do I find you here?" *Asinine question. You know why.*

"The *kami* said God might let me die," he said. "I am waiting."

"Nothing is certain. He may only punish you for risking death."

He though on this awhile. "This is true?"

Enough! "I do not know, Shigeo. In this place and time, I

must be beyond lies. There are things I do not know, or cannot tell. But I honor this place—no, I honor you—by telling no lies."

"The priest. Did he die?"

The briefest of hesitations. "The man died."

"But in the service of God."

She shrugged. "That may be. He did it in the service of people. It was a risk he took deliberately, Shigeo. There was another man as well."

A quick glance around him. "He is here?"

"He is—is dead also. He did not deliberate the risk he took but, when it came, took it quickly."

"*Seppuk'*, suicide," he murmured, impressed.

"*Iye'*, not exactly. But sacrifices."

"For what?" Shigeo asked.

She swallowed hard. "For all people now living, or who will live. There are only a few left, Shigeo. Anywhere," she waved her arms wide. "They may all soon die, as you will, if you do not return to your home. Truly, for them to live, you must live."

"*Shigata ga nai*, can't be helped." Yet he was troubled.

"*You* can help; I have tried. My *hombun*, duty. If you really believe we return after death in new bodies, it is your duty too."

The tranquil mask slipped to show the tortured man beneath. "There is no *wa*, harmony, in my days. It is an endless dying," he whispered.

"I have known this in my *hara*, soul, as well." A flash of something crossed his face, his body muscles stiffening. "Are you well, Shigeo?"

He slowly squatted, put hands to his flat belly. "Yesterday I thought the *kami* lied about dying. Then I thought the *taifun* was blind and walked over me without seeing." Another muscle spasm, and he rubbed his abdomen. "Today I believe the *kami*. Yet this is smaller sacrifice than living," he said.

"That is true," she nodded. "Dying is easier than living in—some ways."

"Then we agree," Shigeo said placidly. "*Iye'*, I will not

return. There is no advantage in the greater sacrifice."

"We do *not* agree," she cried. "There is the advantage of
the very greatest honor, if the act benefits all people."

"*Iye*." He defied the *kami* without malice, fear, or hope.

She searched for some lever to move him from his resolve,
grasped the one that had grown unexamined within her. He
might lay death aside, if—. *Complementary opposite sacrifice,* she thought. *Well, how much do I believe the things I
say?*

Diana knelt, facing him directly. "Would you choose to
return to life in your home—if you had a woman? Even a
clumsy *maiko*," she added in false gaiety, using the word for
a novice geisha. The rumble of her heart filled her with terror;
fear that he would accept.

At last he consummated her fear. "*Hai*, if I took her to
wife."

With fingers that balked, thoughts that raced foolishly
from squalor to striptease, Diana undid the seals. Her helmet
off, she pulled her blue-black hair from its knot and shook it.
Shook it again, this time proudly, as she met and conquered
an odor she had known from childhood. *I won't smell like
frangipani when I'm on his diet, either,* she thought. It
steadied her past,—*if I live*.

Few things, she guessed, had ever strained Shigeo more
than the effort to maintain calm as she removed the suit.
There was nothing graceful about her one-piece undergar-
ment or the body attachments she removed, but like most
underwear it followed her body faithfully.

A slow admiring smile from Shigeo. "More *kami*
magic?"

"You will find that I am only a woman. These clothes
protected me. Now you will protect me." It seemed more
true as she thought about it.

He dropped his hands to hang between his knees and Diana
saw evidence of his desire. And of his essential humility.
"This is wrong in this place," was his only comment.

"It is only a final honesty, Shigeo. I do not think it wrong.
But truly I tell you that we must go in the growl machine to

your—to our home, or I will surely die soon. I may die in any case.''

''As the priest did?''

Her resolve to be truthful met its test, failed and passed it in the same equivocation. ''If he was not a priest,'' she said, ''perhaps a saint.'' A silence fell between them.

''You will come with me,'' he said then, and stood. She sensed his effort to be the forceful husband, feared he would be gauche in his new role, knew she would be in hers. For which he would beat her. Carrying the suit, padding behind her primeval master, Diana Moi strode into sunlight.

After three days, she knew that Shigeo would survive the plague symptoms that racked him.

After ten days, she wondered if her own bouts of illness had been plague, or merely the result of the damnedest diet she had ever seen. She had quickly recovered on the same diet. Diana could not know which factors defeated plague, but that was secondary. *Some*thing did. This was primary.

After fifteen days, her nostrils became accustomed to their new stimuli. And she was beaten, lightly but firmly, for tearing a shrimp trap.

There was a purpose to the motions in Shigeo's daily life that Diana had not seen while watching the sensor displays. Soon, she knew, it would be necessary to get his approval for a quick trip—if the growl machine would start—to the return module. The typhoon had destroyed or displaced the FM relays in the nearby hills, she judged; twice she had received line-of-sight transmissions from Grissom in her headset, though they obviously could not hear her replies. Grissom was cautiously optimistic at seeing the lander still upright after the great storm, and very patient with the silence from below. They would have more optimism and less caution after she talked to them.

The next lander might contain a hundred experts, one-way volunteers, convinced that if Diana Moi could make it, anybody could. She would insist that they not invest Shigeo's life with a plague of people.

Or, in a less tasteful scenario, they might remain at a distance to study every detail of her days for the benefit of all. Their rationale would be impeccable. And sooner or later, she was sure, she could end her forced atavism.

She sighed, spread the palolo worms for a fresh drying after the autumn rain. It would be no pleasure to know they watched her most private moments, but it couldn't last forever.

Could it? She glanced at Shigeo. *Banzai* . . .

The sacrifice of self, as we've just read, often involves hellishly complicated motives. But the sacrifice of others can be as simple and swift and sure as the pounce of a leopard.

"On the other hand," as Mr. Dooley said, "Not so fast!" Maybe the motive is the only simple part. And maybe I should get out of your way before my introduction grows longer than the story.

One thing, though: this little piece owes a lot to editor Jim Baen, who suggested a bit of deft surgery to improve the ending. It's a better ending now, but I like it Jim's way for its irony, too: author/editor symbiosis in a piece about predation!

Fleas

The quarry swam more for show than for efficiency because he knew that Maels was quietly watching. Down the "Y" pool, then back, seeming to ignore the bearded older man as Maels, in turn, seemed to ignore the young swimmer.

Maels reviewed each datum: brachycephalic; under thirty years old; body mass well over the forty kilo minimum; skin tone excellent; plenty of hair. And unless Maels was deceived—he rarely was—the quarry offered subtle homosexual nuances which might simplify his isolation.

Maels smiled to himself and delivered an enormous body-stretching yawn that advertised his formidable biceps, triceps, laterals. The quarry approached swimming; symbolically, thought Maels, a breast stroke. Great.

Maels made a pedal gesture. A joke, really, since the gay world had developed the language of the foot for venues more crowded than this. The quarry bared small even teeth in his innocent approval. Better.

"I could watch you all evening," Maels rumbled, and added the necessary lie: "You swim exquisitely."

"But I can't go on forever," the youth replied in tones that were, as Maels had expected, distinctly unbutchy. "I feel like relaxing." Treading water, he smiled a plea for precise communication. Perfect.

"You can with me," Maels said, and swept himself up with an ageless grace. He towered, masculine and commanding, above the suppliant swimmer. A strong grin split his beard as Maels turned toward the dressing room. He left the building quickly, then waited.

Invisible in a shop alcove, Maels enjoyed the quarry's anxious glances from the elevated platform of the "Y" steps.

Maels strolled out then into the pale light of the streetlamp and the quarry, seeing him, danced down the steps toward his small destiny.

Later, kneeling beneath tree shadows as his fingers probed the dying throat-pulse, Maels thought: *All according to formula, to the old books.* Really no problem when you have the physical strength of a mature anaconda. Hell, it wasn't even much fun for an adult predator. At this introspection Maels chuckled. Adult for several normal lifespans, once he had discovered he was a feeder. With such long practice, self-assurance in the hunt took spice from the kill. Still probing the carotid artery, Maels thought: *Uncertainty is the oregano of pursuit.* He might work that into a scholarly paper one day.

Then Maels fed.

It was a simple matter for Maels to feed in a context that police could classify as psychosexual. Inaccurate, but— perhaps not wholly. Survival and sexuality: his gloved hands guiding scalpel and bone saw almost by rote, Maels composed the sort of trivia his sophomores would love.

> Research confirms the grimoires'
> Ancient sanity;
> Predation brings unending lust—
> An old causality

The hypothalamus, behind armoring bone, was crucial. Maels took it all. Adrenal medulla, a strip of mucous membrane, smear of marrow. Chewing reflectively, Maels thought: *Eye of newt, toe of frog. A long way from the real guts of immortality.*

He had known a feeder, an academic like himself, who read so much Huxley he tried to substitute carp viscera for the only true prescription. Silly bastard had nearly died before Maels, soft-hearted Karl Maels, brought him the bloody requisites in a baggie. At some personal sacrifice, too: the girl had been Maels' best graduate student in a century.

Sacrifice, he reflected, was one criterion largely ignored by the Darwinists. They prattled so easily of a species as though the single individual mattered little. But if you are one of a rare subspecies, feeders whose members were few and camouflaged? A back-burner question, he decided. He could let it simmer. With admirable economy of motion Maels further vandalized the kill to disguise his motive. Minutes later he was in his rented sedan, en route back to his small college town. Maels felt virile, coruscating, efficient. The seasonal special feeding, in its way, had been a thing of beauty.

Ninety-three days later, Maels drove his own coupe to another city and left it, before dusk, in a parking lot. He was overdue to feed but thought it prudent to avoid patterns. The city, the time of day, even the moon phase should be different. If the feeding itself no longer gave joy, at least he might savor its planning.

He adjusted his turtleneck and inspected the result in a storefront reflection. Maybe he would shave the beard soon. It was a damned nuisance anyhow when he fed.

Maels recalled a student's sly criticism the day before: when was a beard a symbiote, and when parasitic? Maels had turned the question to good classroom use, sparking a lively debate on the definitions of parasite and predator. Maels cited the German Brown trout, predator on its own kind yet not a parasite. The flea was judged parasitic; for the hundredth time Maels was forced to smile through his irritation at misquotation of elegant Dean Swift:

> So, naturalists observe, a flea
> Hath smaller fleas that on him prey.
> And these have smaller fleas to bite 'em,
> And so proceed, *ad infinitum*.

Which only prompted the class to define parasites in terms of size. Maels accepted their judgement; trout and feeder preyed on smaller fry, predators by spurious definition.

Comfortably chewing on the trout analogy, Maels cruised the singles bars through their happy hour. He nurtured his image carefully, a massive gentle bear of a man with graceful hands and self-deprecating wit. At the third spa he maneuvered, on his right, a pliable file clerk with adenoids and lovely skin. She pronounced herself simply thrilled to meet a real, self-admitted traveling salesman. Maels found her rather too plump for ideal quarry, but no matter: she would do. He felt pale stirrings of excitement and honed them, titillated them. Perhaps he would grant her a sexual encounter before he fed. Perhaps.

Then Karl Maels glanced into the mirror behind the bar, and the pliant clerk was instantly and brutally forgotten. He sipped bourbon and his mouth was drier than before as he focused on the girl who had captured the seat to his left.

It was not merely that she was lovely. By all criteria she was also flawless quarry. Maels fought down his excitement and smiled his best smile. "I kept your place," he said with just enough pretended gruffness.

"Am I all that predictable?" Her voice seemed to vibrate in his belly. He estimated her age at twenty-two but, sharing her frank gaze, elevated that estimate a bit.

Maels wisely denied her predictability, asked where she found earrings of beaten gold aspen leaves, and learned that she was from Pueblo, Colorado. To obtain a small commitment he presently said, "The body is a duty, and duty calls. Will you keep my place?"

The long natural lashes barely flickered, the chin rose and dropped a minute fraction. Maels made his needless round-trip to the men's room, but hesitated on his return. He saw the girl speak a bit crossly to a tall young man who would otherwise have taken Maels' seat. Maels assessed her fine strong calves, the fashionable wedge heels cupping voluptuous high insteps. His palms were sweating.

Maels waited until the younger man had turned away, then reclaimed his seat. After two more drinks he had her name, Barbara, and her weakness, seafood; and knew that he could claim his quarry as well.

He did not need to feign his easy laugh in saying, "Well, now you've made me ravenous. I believe there's a legendary crab cocktail at a restaurant near the wharf. Feel like exploring?"

She did. It was only a short walk, he explained, silently adding that a taxi was risky. Barbara happily took his arm. The subtle elbow pressures, her matching of his stride, the

increasing frequency of hip contact were clear messages of
desire. When Maels drew her toward the fortuitous
schoolyard, Barbara purred in pleasure. Moments later, their
coats an improvised couch, they knelt in mutual explora-
tion, then lay together in the silent mottled shadows.

He entered her cautiously, then profoundly, gazing down
at his quarry with commingled lust and hunger. Smiling, she
undid her blouse to reveal perfect breasts. She moved against
him gently and, with great deliberation, thrust his sweater up
from the broad striated ribcage. Then she pressed erect nipples against his body. Maels cried out once.

When European gentlemen still wore rapiers, Maels had
taken a blade in the shoulder. The memory flickered past him
as her nipples, hypodermic-sharp, incredibly elongated,
pierced him on lances of agony.

Skewered above her, Maels could not move. Indeed, he
did not lose his functional virility, as the creature completed
her own pleasure and then, grasping his arms, rolled him over
without uncoupling. He felt tendons snap in his forearms but
oddly the pain was distant. He could think clearly at first.
Maels thought: *How easily she rends me.* She manipulated
him as one might handle a brittle doll.

Maels felt a warm softening in his guts with a growing
anaesthesia. Maels thought: *The creature is consuming me as
I watch.*

Maels thought: *A new subspecies?* He wondered how often
her kind must feed. *A very old subspecies?* He saw her smile.

Maels thought: *Is it possible that she feeds only on feeders?
Does she read my thoughts?*

"Of course," she whispered, almost lovingly.

Some yards away, a tiny animal scrabbled in the leaves.

He thought at her: ". . . *and so on,* ad infinitum. *I wonder
what feeds on you. . . .*"

FRED SABERHAGEN

FAFHRD AND THE
GRAY MOUSER
SAGA

☐ 79176	SWORDS AND DEVILTRY	$2.25
☐ 79156	SWORDS AGAINST DEATH	$2.25
☐ 79185	SWORDS IN THE MIST	$2.25
☐ 79165	SWORDS AGAINST WIZARDRY	$2.25
☐ 79223	THE SWORDS OF LANKHMAR	$1.95
☐ 79169	SWORDS AND ICE MAGIC	$2.25

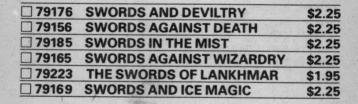